PENGUIN CLASSICS

ARSÈNE LUPIN, GENTLEMAN-THIEF

MAURICE LEBLANC was born in Rouen, France in 1864. He began his writing career with realistic works in the manner of his heroes Flaubert and Maupassant, producing such novels as *La Femme* in 1887. He is remembered today, however, for his dozens of inventive and amusing stories and novels about the masterful thief Arsène Lupin, a burglar and confidence man who eventually also becomes a detective. Leblanc created Lupin in 1905 for a series requested by a magazine editor. There were five collections of Lupin stories: *Arsène Lupin, Gentleman-Burglar* (1906), *Arsène Lupin versus Herlock Sholmes* (1908), *The Confessions of Arsène Lupin* (1912), *The Eight Strokes of the Clock* (1922), and *Arsène Lupin Intervenes* (1928). Leblanc wrote several Lupin novels; the best are *The Hollow Needle* (1908) and *813* (1910). Leblanc's sister was Georgette Leblanc, the popular actress who was mistress and later wife of the playwright Maurice Maeterlinck. Leblanc was also a playwright, co-authoring the first stage version of Lupin adventures, which launched a century of theatrical and cinematic adaptations. Leblanc was awarded the ribbon of the French Legion of Honor. He died in Perpignan in 1941.

MICHAEL SIMS is the author of *Adam's Navel: A Natural and Cultural History of the Human Form*, which was a *New York Times* Notable Book and a *Library Journal* Best Science Book, and *Darwin's Orchestra: An Almanac of Nature in History and the Arts*. He has written for many publications, including the *Los Angeles Times Book Review*, *New Statesman*, and *American Archaeology*. For Penguin Classics he also edited *The Annotated Archy and Mehitabel*. His Web site is www.michaelsimsbooks.com.

MAURICE LEBLANC

Arsène Lupin, Gentleman-Thief

Introduction and Notes by
MICHAEL SIMS

PENGUIN BOOKS

PENGUIN BOOKS

Published by the Penguin Group
Penguin Group (USA) Inc., 375 Hudson Street, New York, New York 10014, U.S.A.
Penguin Group (Canada), 90 Eglinton Avenue East, Suite 700, Toronto, Ontario, Canada M4P 2Y3
(a division of Pearson Penguin Canada Inc.)
Penguin Books Ltd, 80 Strand, London WC2R 0RL, England
Penguin Ireland, 25 St Stephen's Green, Dublin 2, Ireland (a division of Penguin Books Ltd)
Penguin Group (Australia), 250 Camberwell Road, Camberwell, Victoria 3124, Australia
(a division of Pearson Australia Group Pty Ltd)
Penguin Books India Pvt Ltd, 11 Community Centre, Panchsheel Park, New Delhi - 110 017, India
Penguin Group (NZ), 67 Apollo Drive, Mairangi Bay, Auckland 1310, New Zealand
(a division of Pearson New Zealand Ltd.)
Penguin Books (South Africa) (Pty) Ltd, 24 Sturdee Avenue, Rosebank, Johannesburg 2196, South Africa

Penguin Books Ltd, Registered Offices:
80 Strand, London WC2R 0RL, England

First published in Penguin Books 2007

LIBRARY OF CONGRESS CATALOGING IN PUBLICATION DATA
Leblanc, Maurice, 1864–1941.
[Arsène Lupin, gentleman-cambrioleur. English]
Arsène Lupin, gentleman-thief / Maurice Leblanc ; introduction and notes by Michael Sims.
p. cm.—(Penguin classics)
ISBN 978-0-14-310486-5
I. Sims, Michael, 1958– II. Title. III. Series.
PQ2623.E24A77213 2007
843'.912—dc22   2006047479

Printed in the United States of America
Set in Adobe Sabon

Contents

Contents

Introduction

The Musical Sound of Breaking the Law

"The criminal is the creative artist, the detective only the critic."

This observation by a character in one of G. K. Chesterton's Father Brown stories sums up the attitude of the most entertaining felon in literature—Arsène Lupin. Created by Maurice Leblanc during the first decade of the twentieth century, uniting the traditions of gentleman rogue and heroic adventurer, this witty confidence man and burglar is the Sherlock Holmes of criminals. In several stories (the first of which is included in this collection), Leblanc borrowed Holmes for a few clashes with Lupin, who outwits the great detective at every turn—and even steals his watch.

Lupin is a rogue, not a villain. The poor and the innocent have nothing to fear from him; often they profit from his spontaneous generosity. Parvenu and predator, however, tremble as they double-check their safe deposit boxes at the Crédit Lyonnais. The gendarmerie flounder behind like baying hounds, with one Inspector Ganimard serving as Lupin's particular foil. Poor Ganimard finds himself the butt of newspaper stories extolling Lupin's intelligence over his own—and then, in "The Red Silk Scarf," finds Lupin teasingly lobbing him clues toward solving a crime. The reader can rest assured that Lupin hasn't suddenly developed a sense of civic duty; he will profit from the solution.

This hybrid adventure marks Lupin's turn toward detective work, which would occupy the bulk of the last two of the five collections that Leblanc wrote about him. The present volume includes several stories from this later period, but emphasizes the early adventures, during which Lupin remains the prince of thieves. Although almost every one of the short

Lupin adventures deserves republication, the present volume admits only the crème de la crème from each collection, resulting in the first "best of" overview of Lupin in English. Although each adventure stands alone, some refer to each other and develop themes, so the best way to read them is in order of publication, as reprinted here.

THE CYRANO OF THE UNDERWORLD

Maurice Marie Emile Leblanc was born December 11, 1864 in Rouen to an Italian father and a French mother who died young. He was educated in Berlin and Manchester. Although Leblanc earned a law degree and performed the requisite stint in the family shipping business, he was restless for more. He wrote several realistic novels in the vein of Flaubert and Maupassant, beginning in 1893 with *A Woman*, attracting modest critical praise but little financial success. In time he drifted into journalism and began to be known for his magazine stories and articles.

The Lupin stories first appeared in a new periodical called *Je Sais Tout*. It was patterned somewhat on the hugely successful *Strand* magazine in London, a forerunner of twentieth-century periodicals that promised the revolutionary lure of a picture on every page. The *Strand* was the venue for the astonishingly popular Sherlock Holmes. Arthur Conan Doyle had published two longer Holmes adventures that attracted little more than warehouse dust and curt dismissal ("shilling dreadful") until he published the first Holmes story, "A Scandal in Bohemia," in the newly launched *Strand* in 1891. Fourteen years later Pierre Lafitte, the editor of *Je Sais Tout*, asked Maurice Leblanc to contribute a story of adventure along the same lines. Leblanc later claimed that he sat down without an idea in his head and found Arsène Lupin on the page. The first story, "The Arrest of Arsène Lupin," proved instantly popular.

"Keep it up," urged Lafitte. "Give us more tales about Arsène Lupin and you may have as much success as Conan Doyle has had with those Sherlock Holmes stories."

"But I can't keep it up," protested Leblanc. "Lupin has been arrested!"

"Bah! Think it over." And Lafitte uttered an important sentence in the history of crime fiction: "Lupin is worth saving."

Leblanc agreed to save him. But how? He had begun the series with his audacious hero's *arrest*. Should he ignore this development and write about events that occurred earlier? No, if Lupin were so brilliant, surely he could find a way out of this situation. In his second Lupin story, "Arsène Lupin in Prison," Leblanc wrote a funny and ingenious classic of crime fiction and further defined his hero's character and personality. Readers could see that it would take more than mere incarceration to halt Lupin's career. Then, establishing his habit of writing a series of interconnected stories that read like chapters in a novel, Leblanc topped this performance with a third story, in which Lupin escapes. "I grew to like the fellow," remembered the author fondly. He gathered the first nine stories into a collection, *Arsène-Lupin, Gentleman-Cambrioleur* (Burglar), in 1906. Lupin was a burglar one day and a con man the next, so the present volume gathers his adventures under the more inclusive term *thief*.

Maurice Leblanc was not the only accomplished member of his family. His sister Georgette grew up to become a popular actress and singer, companion (at first while married to someone else), wife, and widow of the Symbolist playwright Maurice Maeterlinck, and the woman for whom he wrote numerous plays. The familial relationship with Maeterlinck may have contributed to Leblanc's polished and successful plays, and it unquestionably led to an important collaboration. Leblanc's best translator, Alexander Teixeira de Mattos, who translated all of the stories in the present volume, is primarily known as Maeterlinck's usual translator. Teixeira de Mattos was a versatile man who translated from Danish, German, Dutch, and other languages, but most of his translations are of French writers such as Maeterlinck and the pioneer naturalist J.-Henri Fabre. He was also the unofficial head of a London organization called the Lutetian Society, which included among its members the influential translator Ernest Dowson. Like Sir Richard Burton's

Kama Shastra Society, the Lutetian was a small, private non-profit organization that published unexpurgated editions—often new translations—of banned books, including Zola's.

In their native French and in other languages, including English as translated by Teixeira de Mattos and others, the Lupin tales were wildly popular. They sold prodigiously and inspired plays and eventually movies, beginning with a silent one in 1917 and including the latest installment as recently as 2004. Leblanc wound up with the ribbon of the Légion d'Honneur. The Lupin saga has never been out of print in France, where he is as well known as Sherlock Holmes. Lupin remains popular enough to have been resurrected for a late twentieth-century series written by Pierre Boileau and Thomas Narcejac, authors of the novels behind the films *Les Diaboliques* and Hitchcock's *Vertigo*. There is a Japanese anime series called "Lupin III," starring a decidedly illegitimate grandson of the man you will meet in this volume. Although there have been occasional reprints of a single collection, today in the United States Lupin is known mostly by die-hard fans willing to seek out used editions, and a critic's complaint from 1945 is still true: "Leblanc's contribution to the literature of crime is still sadly underestimated."

This American neglect is inexplicable, because Lupin certainly shows up everywhere else. While planning her first detective novel during World War I, Agatha Christie considered and rejected the possibility of basing a detective upon Lupin, and Hercule Poirot may owe to the French thief some of his egotism and perhaps even his devotion to intuition over physical evidence. Christie also famously employed a very tricky narrator in one of her novels, and Leblanc is the king of tricky narrators. Georges Simenon, in his apprentice years of 1920–21—when he still thought of himself as a budding humorist in the Mark Twain mode—co-wrote with a friend a parody of Leblanc and Gaston Leroux, whose novels were being serialized in the Paris *Gazette* at the time. Jean Cocteau wrote in his diaries about reading the Lupin stories. Jean-Paul Sartre declared his affection for Lupin and called him "the Cyrano of the underworld." Late in life T. S. Eliot remarked of Lupin, "I used to read him, but I have now graduated to Inspector Maigret," which not all of us would consider a promotion.

Leblanc died in Perpignan, in southern France near the Spanish border. It was November 6, 1941 and he was a month shy of seventy-six. The same year, mystery writer and critic Ellery Queen proclaimed Lupin "the greatest thief in the whole world." Arsène Lupin is the only character who appears twice in Queen's pioneer anthology 101 Years' Entertainment: The Great Detective Stories 1841–1941. He shows up among both the criminals and the detectives.

THE COMFORTABLE PROFESSION
OF BURGLAR

We tend to imagine the period of the early Lupin stories as a simpler time—before the Russian Revolution, before the assassination of Archduke Ferdinand, before airborne bombing and poison gas ravaged Europe. After all, the French themselves coined the term le belle epoque for the relatively prosperous and serene time between the end of the Franco-Prussian War in 1871 and the outbreak of World War I. When Leblanc began writing, no war had yet earned the adjective World.

Arsène Lupin's era seems inescapably quaint to us—brave madmen piloting aeroplanes wobbly with extra wings, bewhiskered tycoons shouting into primitive telephones. Grand convertible automobiles still bore the evolutionary traces of their horse-drawn ancestors, and women moored their hats with scarves before recklessly climbing aboard. Sophisticates saw themselves as living in an age of speed. Telephones had surpassed the already miraculous telegraph, and transportation seemed to be catching up; reality had quickly outrun Jules Verne's imaginary eighty days of circumnavigation. Wireless telegraphy plays a key role in the very first Lupin story, in which the narrator remarks, "The imagination no longer has the resource of picturing wires along which the invisible message glides; the mystery is even more insoluble, more poetic; and we

must have recourse to the winds to explain the new miracle."
This lyrical aside demonstrates Leblanc's unique tone of voice;
like his hero, he notices the world around him.

Maurice Leblanc's style reflects his dizzy epoch. Not for him
the leisurely accounts of Wilkie ("make 'em wait") Collins or
the exhaustively detailed investigations of his popular country-
man Emile Gaboriau, whose Inspector Lecoq had helped in-
spire Arthur Conan Doyle. Leblanc was a playwright. His
stories open *in media res* and race forward without time for in-
trospection. Seldom will you overhear his characters holding
forth about society and anarchy, as they do in Chesterton's *The
Man Who Was Thursday*, which appeared at about the same
time. (Chesterton's novel does include, however, a remark about
crime that could have been uttered by Lupin: "Thieves respect
property. They merely wish the property to become their property that they may the more perfectly respect it.") Not that
Lupin lacks a philosophy of life. In fact he seems to feel that,
like those ideal citizens described by Thoreau, he personally im-
proves, revitalizes, and takes the measure of society.

The first Lupin adventures appeared in a popular periodical,
surrounded by news stories, and are sometimes couched in the
tone of a follow-up feature on some widely reported occurrence.
"If you were a French newspaper-reader of pre–1914 Paris,"
wrote the British critic William Vivian Butler, "you took your
Lupin between sips of Pernod at cafe-tables on the boulevardes:
you allowed him to entice your idle eye away from neighbouring
columns about Bleriot's channel-crossing or the assassination of
the Archduke Charles."

But a pretense of journalistic verisimilitude never demotes
Leblanc's writing to merely reportorial. His style is graceful,
well-dressed, light on its feet. One of its most entertaining features is a reckless unpredictability. "There hangs over many of
the Lupin stories," wrote Butler, "a feeling that some kind of
joke is being played on somebody, but so amazing is the author's ingenuity, so incredible his sleight-of-hand, that you
don't really mind if that somebody should turn out to be you."
It's true that the Lupin saga demands considerable suspension
of disbelief as our hero dashes from one opaque masquerade to

another, for Lupin is that versatile staple of early crime fiction, a master of disguise. But why should readers always recognize him? We aren't watching a familiar actor on a television series. (Actually a series might solve the problem of viewer recognition by having a different actor play Lupin in each episode.) At least Lupin doesn't have the superhero peculiarity of Hamilton Cleek, "the Man with Forty Faces," who appeared in 1910 and who suffers from a fortunately rare skin condition that renders his facial features pliable.

Leblanc employs a variety of narrators. The story may be recounted by Lupin's nameless chronicler, a Watsonian admirer roughly conterminous with the author, and to whom Lupin remarks in Sherlockian mode, "My dear friend, you may have a certain skill at recounting my exploits, but sometimes you are a bit dense"; by some other person who witnessed key events; by a third-person narrator who holds his cards close to his vest and delights in trumping our expectations; by what seems to be the collective voice of the newspaper-reading public; or by Lupin himself. One story is told by Lupin's friend until suddenly Lupin goes off without him—at which point the story abandons the narrator and follows the thief, who allegedly supplied details later.

In some stories he isn't identified as Lupin at all. Because the scoundrel's name is a household word, when attempting to rescue someone or perform some other noble deed he must not disclose his identity. It would be counterproductive for those in need to worry that their benefactor is actually scheming to profit from their misfortune. In one story you will learn that Arsène Lupin is not even his real name, but to say more now would be cheating. Often Lupin calls himself Horace Velmont. Some of his aliases are anagrams—Paul Sernine, for example. All of the stories in the third collection, 1921's *The Eight Strokes of the Clock*, star one Prince Serge Rénine, although Leblanc makes clear in a preface that Renine is Lupin. "But there comes a time when you cease to know yourself amid all these changes," murmurs Lupin with a straight face, "and that is very sad."

In the 1929 fifth collection, *Arsène Lupin Intervenes*, he appears as Jim Barnett, a private detective who admits that he is

funded by none other than the notorious Lupin. But as his behavior indicates, and as Leblanc makes clear in another prefa-
tory note, Barnett is merely a new persona for Lupin. Readers
had clamored for the thief to turn his talents to detective work
and Leblanc was trying to oblige. These later adventures are excellent detective stories, but the present edition concentrates on
Lupin's unlawful phase, as exhibited in the earlier collections,
especially the first and second.

A consummate publicist, Lupin assures that his painstakingly
cultivated reputation precedes him. When necessary he can
score a psychological triumph merely by identifying himself at
the perfect moment. A greed-driven thief might assume that
anonymity would best serve his professional needs, but Lupin
sees himself as an artist. He needs an audience. His saving grace
as a character is that, like Rex Stout's detective Nero Wolfe, he
is self-aware enough to admit his vanity and ambition. "You
know what a fool Lupin can be," admits Lupin to his friend;
"the idea of appearing suddenly as a good genie and dazzling
others would make him commit any number of offenses."

A major stockholder in the Parisian newspaper *Echo de
France*, for which his creator wrote, Lupin doesn't hesitate to use
his influence to run articles written about (or even by) himself.
This particular Leblanc joke inverted an already established routine. From the genre's inception, detectives employed the popular
press to help them achieve their aims. It is a standard ploy for
Sherlock Holmes to place an advertisement in a newspaper to
entice a suspect—a trait, like so many others, that Conan Doyle
pilfered from Edgar Allan Poe. In "The Murders in the Rue
Morgue," C. Auguste Dupin employs a *Le Monde* advertisement
to lure the sailor who has misplaced a homicidal orangutan. Usually, when Lupin's latest caper receives its inevitable behind-the-
scenes newspaper treatment, the public sympathizes with him.
Leblanc's devious method places the reader in the point-of-view
of the other characters. It adds to our entertainment that they are
not privy to one key fact in our own possession—that if Lupin
isn't visible onstage for awhile, he must be directing the action
from the wings.

A theatrical metaphor seems apt. Lupin quickly made the

metamorphosis from the page to the boards—and thence, of course, to the screen. Leblanc co-wrote the first dramatization, *Arsène Lupin*, with the popular playwright Francis de Croisset. In the summer of 1909 the many theatergoers who enjoyed it included Marcel Proust, who was diverting himself with baccarat in Cabourg and saw a production of the play in the theater of the Grand-Hôtel. How odd to imagine the profound and verbose Proust sitting in the audience of a play written by the blithe and concise Leblanc, but one trait they have in common is an omnipresent irony. Moreover, an aspect of crime fiction—besides its plethora of unreliable narrators—that would later make it a pet form of the *nouvelle roman* is its emphasis on structure, always one of Proust's chief concerns.

THE BELLE EPOQUE OF CRIME

Lupin's own humor is omnipresent. The stories are outrageous, melodramatic, and literate, and they sparkle with amusing banter. When he explains that he is posing as an ex-cabinet minister, Lupin adds, "I had to select a rather overstocked profession, so as not to attract attention." Often he speaks of himself in the third-person: "Lupin juggles deductions like a detective in a flashy novel." On one occasion he thinks, "I sometimes ask myself why everybody doesn't choose the comfortable profession of a burglar. Given a little skill and reflective power, there's nothing more charming."

The thief taunts his intended victims as well as the police. In one story he writes letters from prison inviting a wealthy banker to ship his art collection to him rather than cause Lupin the trouble of stealing it—and he adds that the larger Watteau in the dining room is a forgery. His frequent laugh is the triumphant guffaw of Robin Hood once more outwitting the Sheriff of Nottingham. An outrageous sense of play underlies every caper. Lupin strategizes with the zest of a novelist, foreseeing alternatives and accommodating them in advance. He flouts rules because rules constrict. "By Jove, I wouldn't sell this moment for a fortune!" he exclaims when anyone else might simply abandon the (illicit) task at hand. "Who dares pretend that life is monotonous?"

Such irreverent glee shows up in other great outlaws, although not quite to Lupin's manic extent. Edwardian criminals had little patience with Victorian standards of good behavior, and during the first decades of the new century brash rogues were rampant. Guy Boothby created the aristocratic thief Simon Carne in 1897. The same year, Grant Allen published his superb interconnected stories about confidence man Colonel Clay and united them in *An African Millionaire*. In 1899 E. W. Hornung published the first half-dozen Raffles stories in *Cassell's* magazine. Although he is the best known of all this crew, largely because Hornung was such a fine writer, Raffles was actually a small-time thief, repeatedly demonstrating that he deserved the adjective in the first collection's title, *The Amateur Cracksman*.

In 1902, writing under the pseudonym Clifford Ashdown, R. Austin Freeman—creator of the first great scientific detective, Dr. Thorndyke—and John James Pitcairn launched a series about a gentleman thief named Romney Pringle. Soon after the debut of Father Brown in 1911, G. K. Chesterton supplied the death-attracting curate with a recurring adversary, master thief Flambeau, about whose artistic talent for crime both author and detective wax poetic. The only American of this period who compares with British and continental thieves, Frederick Irving Anderson's Godahl (nicknamed "the Infallible," probably by himself), enjoys nothing in life more than outwitting someone who is trying to outwit him. Jeff Peters, the con man in O. Henry's 1908 collection *The Gentle Grafter*—although penny-ante compared even with Raffles—particularly enjoys gulling a bumpkin who is out to take advantage of the stranger in town.

"He is not to be dreaded by widows and orphans," says O. Henry of Peters; "he is a reducer of surplusage. His favorite disguise is that of the target-bird at which the spendthrift or the reckless investor may shy a few inconsequential dollars." Scoundrels real and fictional found such a guise useful, in an era when Pittsburgh moguls were building castles out of the lives of coal miners, when the latest millionaire in London might have been cracking the whip a month before over diamond sifters in Kimberly. Readers gradually discover that Grant Allen's sly "colonel" is waging a war against Gilded Age hubris as much as replenishing his own coffers, and Allen's stroke of genius was to have his thief repeatedly target *the same victim*. Piratical capitalists were becoming a popular mark. Jeff Peters maintains that his partner is so dishonest he couldn't trace his family tree any farther back than a corporation. By the 1920s another deft disguise artist, Edgar Wallace's Four Square Jane, was robbing "people with bloated bank balances" and donating "very large sums to all kinds of charities." Lupin laments the greediness of the middle class and sometimes claims to be performing a public service.

"Take him for all in all," said Leblanc of his character, "there is more good in him than in some rich lords and barons." In one of these stories—it would be unfair to name it, because the discovery arrives toward the end—we glimpse the formative youth of our hero. Naturally he began his career with a spectacular burglary at a precocious age, and naturally we sympathize with his motive.

On the slippery slope of morality, just downhill from disrespect for bourgeois values lies disdain for authority. Wallace's clever Jane doesn't hesitate to taunt the police with telegrams à la Lupin: "Please take all precautions. Don't let me escape this time." Clearly men were not the only ones having unlawful fun. Frederick Irving Anderson's protagonists include the jewel thief Sophie Lang, who was incarnated in three 1930s movies before the Hays Office declared that no criminals would profit from their crimes on wholesome American screens. Roy Vickers, now remembered mostly for his Department of Dead Ends stories, wrote of his thief character Fidelity Dove, "There was a spirit of sportsmanship, of fun, even in Fidelity's most hazardous exploits."

Perhaps the best statement of felonious bravado was made in the 1930s, by Leslie Charteris, creator of Simon Templar, alias the Saint—the only fictional character worthy of inheriting the mantle of Lupin. Charteris's remark could have been about his French ancestor: "The Law, in the Saint's opinion, was a stodgy and elephantine institution which was chiefly justified in its existence by the pleasantly musical explosive noises it made when he broke it."

It is worth noting, however, that such outlaw notions were not exclusive to criminals. Their opponents could be equally autonomous. In the first Sherlock Holmes story, Holmes asks Watson, "You don't mind breaking the law?"

And his sidekick casually replies, "Not in the least."

ALMOST LITERATURE

By the second decade of the century, the already famous Leblanc was spending most of his year in Passy, an exclusive Right Bank neighborhood in the affluent Sixteenth Arrondisement. He wrote in a shed in his garden. It held a work table and chairs, an inkwell and pens, and had only three walls, leaving the fourth side open to the elements. Even in cold weather, gloved, muffled to the ears, Leblanc could be found in the shed writing. But no one was supposed to go looking for him there; he was not to be disturbed.

Summers Leblanc spent near Honfleur on the Normandy coast, across the narrow mouth of the Seine estuary from the larger and more bustling Le Havre. A medieval port, Honfleur had become over the last half-century a favorite haunt of Courbet, Renoir, and other painters. Just upriver was Tancarville, where Leblanc stayed at the chateau with his wife and son. The area boasted Norman towers and a Roman amphitheater, and not far away were the Bayeux tapestry and Rouen Cathedral—and the site, three decades later, of the D-Day invasions. Leblanc loved this history-drenched region of apple orchards and half-timbered houses. "I have some Italian blood in my veins," he sighed, "but here at Tancarville I am Norman—only Norman." He set many Lupin adventures in Normandy.

At the chateau Leblanc kept his muse obedient by following the routine he had established in Paris. He went so far as to have a shed built like the one he used in his city garden, and of course he surrounded it with the same strict privacy. In Normandy, however, his view extended across the fields and marsh to the slowly meandering river. When not working he still avoided most of the chateau life. His bedroom was in an isolated building, the Tour de l'Aigle, the "Eagle's Tower," which had been constructed a century before out of stones from the castle. About five every afternoon he went into his bedroom and closed the curtains and—in total darkness, he claimed—thought through his next day's work.

But the popular author was no recluse. In August 1912 the English critic and dramatist Charles Henry Meltzer journeyed across the channel to meet with Leblanc at his summer home, and the following spring he described this encounter in the British magazine *Cosmopolitan*. Meltzer is careful to establish from his opening sentence that an interest in fictional roguery is not unworthy of a cultured gentleman. "Crime," he intones, "has at all times charmed the loftiest minds." As evidence he invokes *Macbeth* and *Crime and Punishment* and even Shelley's *Cenci*, although each involves homicide rather than larceny. He could have cited even Daniel's astute cross-examination of the elders who slander Susannah. We have always written about crime; the Code of Hammurabi is older than the *Odyssey*.

By the time that Meltzer visited him, Leblanc had already published two collections—*Arsène Lupin, Gentleman-Burglar* in 1907 and *Arsène Lupin Contre Herlock Sholmes* in 1908. The second was an entire volume of feeble parodies in which Lupin bests a straw man who little resembles Conan Doyle's detective. For some reason, Alexander Teixeira de Mattos twisted the name further, into Holmlock Shears, but the present edition presumes to restore Sherlock Holmes's real name, which Leblanc was going to use until Conan Doyle's attorneys squawked loudly enough to be heard across the channel.

Leblanc had also already published his two best novels, *The Hollow Needle* in 1909 and *813* in 1910, although he would go on to write several more. The Lupin of these longer outings rises to an even more outrageous, almost mythic, level. *The Hollow Needle*, a roller-coaster of deception on several levels, reads like a hybrid of the last Captain Nemo adventure and the first James Bond, and *813* blends the Knights Templar and international intrigue a century ahead of *The Da Vinci Code*. A new novel, *The Crystal Stopper*, was in press, and 1912 would also see publication of the third collection, *The Confessions of Arsène Lupin*.

"His novels and short tales are more than clever," says Meltzer of Leblanc, and bestows the maladroit tribute, "They have the merit of being almost literature." It was Meltzer who penned *the* quotable blurb about Arsène Lupin: ". . . a scoundrel who, to the skill of Sherlock Holmes and the resourcefulness of Raffles, adds the refinement of a casuist, the epigrammatical nimbleness of a La Rouchefoucauld, and the gallantry of a Du Guesclin." The latter (less well known off his native soil) was a fourteenth-century adventurer with a wildly varied and risky life.

The Chateau de Tancarville dates back to the tenth century. Founded by a favorite of William the Conqueror—whose mother's grave is nearby—it has been destroyed and rebuilt several times over the centuries. Now its crumbled ramparts arched over grass and were clothed with ivy. Meltzer arrived in heavy rain. Ahead, at the end of a shaded avenue, Leblanc was waiting for him against the ruins. Expecting a crime-savvy cynic, Meltzer found instead a sedate and gracious host with "kindly eyes." A frequent smile peeked out from under a valance of unruly mustache darker than his sparse gray hair.

When asked how he knew so much about criminology, Leblanc laughed and exclaimed, "But I am blankly ignorant! I never met or talked with thieves and rogues. They do not interest me. I never had the faintest wish to know them. My stories are pure romance—the fictions of my brain—the merest fancies."

Meltzer asked if he had ever studied criminology at all, and Leblanc replied that he had read Edgar Allan Poe and studied Balzac. "All the romance of crime was suggested in Poe's works. I don't remember anything besides Poe and Balzac that could have helped me work out my plots—unless my fondness for the game of chess was useful. Chess helps one to make plays. And why not novels?"

Leblanc neglected to mention France's pioneer detective story writer Emile Gaboriau, who in 1868 had based his insightful Monsieur Lecoq on the real life of thief-turned-policeman François Eugène Vidocq, who rose from guttersnipe to founder of the Sûreté. But Gaboriau's painstaking detective work and restoration of order were not for Leblanc—and much of Gaboriau's style was also inspired by Poe and Balzac. In his famous survey of the crime genre, *Murder for Pleasure*, the mystery critic Howard Haycraft described a crucial distinction: "Leblanc is perhaps not quite the equal of Gaboriau . . . in the realm of pure ratiocination, but he is an infinitely more resourceful and convincing storyteller, a finer master of plot and situation. . . ." Some critics suggest that another inspiration was Rocambole, the cavalier rogue in Ponson de Terrail's series of novels *The Dramas of Paris*.

After a genial discussion of the character and the series, "I have to charge you with a grave offense," said Meltzer. "Do you not think you have done some harm by making a hero of a man like Arsène Lupin?"

"No, I think my conscience is at least as nice as most." Leblanc did Meltzer the courtesy of not smiling. "And if I thought that I had harmed my fellows— But I do not." Leblanc admitted that at one time he worried about this issue himself, that for awhile he didn't want his son Claude to read his books. "Since then, however," said the creator of the thief who picked the pocket of Sherlock Holmes, "I have changed my mind."

Suggestions for Further Reading

SELECTED BOOKS BY MAURICE LEBLANC

Publication dates given are for first French editions, although titles have been translated into English. English and American editions usually appeared the next year.

A Woman (1887)

Arsène Lupin, Gentleman-Burglar (1907), published in English variously as *The Exploits of Arsène Lupin, The Seven of Hearts*, and other titles

Arsène Lupin versus Herlock Sholmes (1908)

The Hollow Needle (1908)

813 (1910)

The Frontier (1912)

The Confessions of Arsène Lupin (1912)

The Crystal Stopper (1913)

The Teeth of the Tiger (1915)

The Woman of Mystery (1916)

The Eight Strokes of the Clock (1922)

The Secret Tomb (1923)

The Tremendous Event (1924)

Arsène Lupin Intervenes (1928)

Wanton Venus (1934)

OTHER WORKS
(Including Those Referred to
or Useful in the Introduction)

William Vivian Butler, *The Durable Desperadoes: A Critical Study of Some Enduring Heroes* (London: Macmillan, 1973).

Frank Wadleigh Chandler, *The Literature of Roguery* (New York: Houghton, Mifflin, 1907).

Howard Haycraft, *Murder for Pleasure: The Life and Times of the Detective Story* (revised edition, New York: Carroll & Graf, 1984).

Charles Henry Meltzer, "Arsène Lupin at Home," *Cosmopolitan*, v. 54 n. 6 (May, 1913), reprinted in *Twentieth-Century Literary Criticism*, v. 49. Most of the Leblanc quotations are taken from Meltzer's article.

Ellery Queen, *101 Years Entertainment: The Great Detective Stories 1841–1941* (New York: Modern Library, 1941).

Agnes Reppelier, "A Short Defense of Villains," in *Essays in Miniature* (New York: Houghton, Mifflin, 1895).

Edward Thorpe, *The Seine from Havre to Paris* (London: Macmillan, 1913).

Arsène Lupin,
Gentleman-Thief

THE ARREST OF
ARSÈNE LUPIN

The strangest of journeys! And yet it had begun so well! I, for
my part, had never made a voyage that started under better aus-
pices. The *Provence* is a swift and comfortable transatlantic liner,
commanded by the most genial of men. The company gathered
on board was of a very select character. Acquaintances were
formed and amusements organized. We had the delightful feeling of being separated from the rest of the world, reduced to our
own devices, as though upon an unknown island, and obliged,
therefore, to make friends with one another. And we grew more
and more intimate. . . .

Have you ever reflected on the element of originality and surprise contained in this grouping of a number of people who,
but a day earlier, had never seen one another, and who are now,
for a few days, destined to live together in the closest contact,
between the infinite sky and the boundless sea, defying the fury
of the ocean, the alarming onslaught of the waves, the malice
of the winds, and the distressing calmness of the slumbering
waters?

Life itself, in fact, with its storms and its greatnesses, its mo-
notony and its variety, becomes a sort of tragic epitome; and
that, perhaps, is why we enjoy with a fevered haste and an in-
tensified delight this short voyage of which we see the end at
the very moment when we embark upon it.

But, of late years, a thing has happened that adds curiously to
the excitement of the passage. The little floating island is no
longer entirely separated from the world from which we believed
ourselves cut adrift. One link remains, and is at intervals tied and
at intervals untied in mid-ocean. The wireless telegraph![1] As

who should say a summons from another world, whence we receive news in the most mysterious fashion! The imagination no longer has the resource of picturing wires along which the invisible message glides: the mystery is even more insoluble, more poetic; and we must have recourse to the winds to explain the new miracle.

And so, from the start, we felt that we were being followed, escorted, even preceded by that distant voice which, from time to time, whispered to one of us a few words from the continent which we had quitted. Two of my friends spoke to me. Ten others, twenty others sent to all of us, through space, their sad or cheery greetings.

Now, on the stormy afternoon of the second day, when we were five hundred miles from the French coast, the wireless telegraph sent us a message of the following tenor:

> "Arsène Lupin on board your ship, first class, fair hair, wound on right forearm, travelling alone under alias R—"

At that exact moment, a violent thunderclap burst in the dark sky. The electric waves were interrupted. The rest of the message failed to reach us. We knew only the initial of the name under which Arsène Lupin was concealing his identity.

Had the news been any other, I have no doubt but that the secret would have been scrupulously kept by the telegraph-clerks and the captain and his officers. But there are certain events that appear to overcome the strictest discretion. Before the day was past, though no one could have told how the rumor had got about, we all knew that the famous Arsène Lupin was hidden in our midst.

Arsène Lupin in our midst! The mysterious housebreaker whose exploits had been related in all the newspapers for months! The baffling individual with whom old Ganimard, our greatest detective, had entered upon that duel to the death of which the details were being unfolded in so picturesque a fashion! Arsène Lupin, the fastidious gentleman who confines his operations to country-houses and fashionable drawing-rooms, and who one night, after breaking in at Baron Schormann's, had gone away empty-handed, leaving his visiting-card:

> ### ARSÈNE LUPIN
>
> *Gentleman-Burglar*

with these words added in pencil:

> "Will return when your things are genuine."

Arsène Lupin, the man with a thousand disguises, by turns chauffeur, opera-singer, book-maker, gilded youth, young man, old man, Marseillese bagman, Russian doctor, Spanish bull-fighter![2]

Picture the situation: Arsène Lupin moving about within the comparatively restricted compass of a transatlantic liner, nay—more, within the small space reserved to the first-class passengers—where one might come across him at any moment, in the saloon, the drawing-room, the smoking-room! Why, Arsène Lupin might be that gentleman over there . . . or this one close by . . . or my neighbor at table . . . or the passenger sharing my stateroom. . . .

"And just think, this is going to last for five days!" cried Miss Nellie Underdown, on the following day. "Why, it's awful! I do hope they'll catch him!" And, turning to me, "Do say, Monsieur d'Andrézy, you're such friends with the captain, haven't you heard anything?"

I wished that I had, if only to please Nellie Underdown. She was one of those magnificent creatures that become the cynosure of all eyes wherever they may be. Their beauty is as dazzling as their fortune. A court of fervent enthusiasts follow in their train.

She had been brought up in Paris by her French mother, and was now on her way to Chicago to join her father, Underdown, the American millionaire. A friend, Lady Gerland, was chaperoning her on the voyage.

I had paid her some slight attentions from the first. But, almost immediately, in the rapid intimacy of ocean travel, her charms had gained upon me, and my emotions now exceeded those of a mere flirtation whenever her great dark eyes met mine. She, on her side, received my devotion with a certain favor. She condescended to laugh at my jokes and to be interested in my stories. A vague sympathy seemed to respond to the assiduity which I displayed.

One rival alone, perhaps, could have given me cause for anxiety: a rather good-looking fellow, well-dressed and reserved in manner, whose silent humor seemed at times to attract her more than did my somewhat "butterfly" Parisian ways.

He happened to form one of the group of admirers surrounding Miss Underdown at the moment when she spoke to me. We were on deck, comfortably installed in our chairs. The storm of the day before had cleared the sky. It was a delightful afternoon.

"I have heard nothing very definite," I replied. "But why should we not be able to conduct our own inquiry just as well as old Ganimard,[3] Lupin's personal enemy, might do?"

"I say, you're going very fast!"

"Why? Is the problem so complicated?"

"Most complicated."

"You only say that because you forget the clews which we possess towards its solution."

"Which clews?"

"First, Lupin is travelling under the name of Monsieur R—."

"That's rather vague."

"Secondly, he's travelling alone."

"If you consider that a sufficient detail!"

"Thirdly, he is fair."

"Well, then?"

"Then we need only consult the list of first-class passengers and proceed by elimination."

I had the list in my pocket. I took it out and glanced through it:

"To begin with, I see that there are only thirteen persons whose names begin with an R."

"Only thirteen?"

"In the first class, yes. Of these thirteen R's, as you can ascertain for yourself, nine are accompanied by their wives, children, or servants. That leaves four solitary passengers: the Marquis de Raverdan . . ."

"Secretary of legation," interrupted Miss Underdown. "I know him."

"Major Rawson . . ."

"That's my uncle," said some one.

"Signor Rivolta . . ."

"Here!" cried one of us, an Italian, whose face disappeared from view behind a huge black beard.

Miss Underdown had a fit of laughing:

"That gentleman is not exactly fair!"

"Then," I continued, "we are bound to conclude that the criminal is the last on the list."

"Who is that?"

"Monsieur Rozaine. Does any one know Monsieur Rozaine?"

No one answered. But Miss Underdown, turning to the silent young man whose assiduous presence by her side vexed me, said:

"Well, Monsieur Rozaine, have you nothing to say?"

All eyes were turned upon him. He was fair-haired!

I must admit I felt a little shock pass through me. And the constrained silence that weighed down upon us showed me that the other passengers present also experienced that sort of choking feeling. The thing was absurd, however, for, after all, there was nothing in his manner to warrant our suspecting him.

"Have I nothing to say?" he replied. "Well, you see, realizing what my name was and the color of my hair and the fact that I am travelling by myself, I have already made a similar inquiry and arrived at the same conclusion. My opinion, therefore, is that I ought to be arrested."

He wore a queer expression as he uttered these words. His thin, pale lips grew thinner and paler still. His eyes were bloodshot.

There was no doubt but that he was jesting. And yet his appearance and attitude impressed us. Miss Underdown asked, innocently:

"But have you a wound?"

"That's true," he said. "The wound is missing."

With a nervous movement, he pulled up his cuff and uncovered his arm. But a sudden idea struck me. My eyes met Miss Underdown's: he had shown his left arm.

And, upon my word, I was on the point of remarking upon this, when an incident occurred to divert our attention. Lady Gerland, Miss Underdown's friend, came running up.

She was in a state of great agitation. Her fellow-passengers crowded round her; and it was only after many efforts that she succeeded in stammering out:

"My jewels! . . . My pearls! . . . They've all been stolen!"

No, they had not all been stolen, as we subsequently discovered; a much more curious thing had happened: the thief had made a selection!

From the diamond star, the pendant of uncut rubies, the broken necklaces and bracelets, he had removed not the largest, but the finest, the most precious stones—those, in fact, which had the greatest value and at the same time occupied the smallest space. The settings were left lying on the table. I saw them, we all saw them, stripped of their gems like flowers from which the fair, bright-colored petals had been torn.

And to carry out this work, he had had, in broad daylight, while Lady Gerland was taking tea, to break in the door of the state-room in a frequented passage, to discover a little jewel-case purposely hidden at the bottom of a bandbox, to open it and make his choice!

We all uttered the same cry. There was but one opinion among the passengers when the theft became known: it was Arsène Lupin. And, indeed, the theft had been committed in his own complicated, mysterious, inscrutable . . . and yet logical manner, for we realized that, though it would have been difficult to conceal the cumbersome mass which the ornaments as a whole would have formed, he would have much less trouble with such small independent objects as single pearls, emeralds, and sapphires.

At dinner this happened: the two seats to the right and left of

Rozaine remained unoccupied. And, in the evening, we knew that he had been sent for by the captain.

His arrest, of which no one entertained a doubt, caused a genuine relief. We felt at last that we could breathe. We played charades in the saloon. We danced. Miss Underdown, in particular, displayed an obstreperous gayety which made it clear to me that, though Rozaine's attentions might have pleased her at first, she no longer gave them a thought. Her charm conquered me entirely. At midnight, under the still rays of the moon, I declared myself her devoted lover in emotional terms which she did not appear to resent.

But, the next day, to the general stupefaction, it became known that the charges brought against him were insufficient. Rozaine was free.

It seemed that he was the son of a wealthy Bordeaux merchant. He had produced papers which were in perfect order. Moreover, his arms showed not the slightest trace of a wound.

"Papers, indeed!" exclaimed Rozaine's enemies. "Birth-certificates! Tush! Why, Arsène Lupin can supply them by the dozen! As for the wound, it only shows that he never had a wound . . . or that he has removed its traces!"

Somebody suggested that, at the time when the theft was committed, Rozaine—this had been proved—was walking on deck. In reply to this it was urged that, with a man of Rozaine's stamp, it was not really necessary for the thief to be present at his own crime. And, lastly, apart from all other considerations, there was one point upon which the most sceptical had nothing to say: who but Rozaine was travelling alone, had fair hair, and was called by a name beginning with the letter R? Who but Rozaine answered to the description in the wireless telegram?

And when Rozaine, a few minutes before lunch, boldly made for our group, Lady Gerland and Miss Underdown rose and walked away.

It was a question of pure fright.

An hour later a manuscript circular was passed from hand to hand among the staff of the vessel, the crew, and the passengers of all classes. M. Louis Rozaine had promised a reward of ten thousand francs to whosoever should unmask Arsène Lupin or discover the possessor of the stolen jewels.

"And if no one helps me against the ruffian," said Rozaine to the captain, "I'll settle his business myself."

The contest between Rozaine and Arsène Lupin, or rather, in the phrase that soon became current, between Arsène Lupin himself and Arsène Lupin, was not lacking in interest.[4]

It lasted two days. Rozaine was observed wandering to right and left, mixing with the crew, questioning and ferreting on every hand. His shadow was seen prowling about at night.

The captain, on his side, displayed the most active energy. The *Provence* was searched from stem to stern, in every nook and corner. Every state-room was turned out, without exception, under the very proper pretext that the stolen objects must be hidden somewhere—anywhere rather than in the thief's own cabin.

"Surely they will end by finding something?" asked Miss Underdown. "Wizard though he may be, he can't make pearls and diamonds invisible."

"Of course they will," I replied, "or else they will have to search the linings of our hats and clothes and anything that we carry about with us." And, showing her my five-by-four Kodak,[5] with which I never wearied of photographing her in all manner of attitudes, I added, "Why, even in a camera no larger than this there would be room to stow away all Lady Gerland's jewels. You pretend to take snapshots and the thing is done."

"Still, I have heard say that every burglar always leaves a clew of some kind behind him."

"There is one who never does: Arsène Lupin."

"Why?"

"Why? Because he thinks not only of the crime which he is committing, but of all the circumstances that might tell against him."

"You were more confident at first."

"Ah, but I had not seen him at work then!"

"And so you think . . ."

"I think that we are wasting our time."

As a matter of fact, the investigations produced no result

whatever, or, at least, that which was produced did not corre-
spond with the general effort: the captain lost his watch.

He was furious, redoubled his zeal, and kept an even closer
eye than before on Rozaine, with whom he had several interviews. The next day, with a delightful irony, the watch was found
among the second officer's collars.

All this was very wonderful, and pointed clearly to the humorous handiwork of a burglar, if you like, but an artist besides. He worked at his profession for a living, but also for his
amusement. He gave the impression of a dramatist who thoroughly enjoys his own plays and who stands in the wings laughing heartily at the comic dialogue and diverting situations which
he himself has invented.

He was decidedly an artist in his way; and, when I observed
Rozaine, so gloomy and stubborn, and reflected on the two-faced
part which this curious individual was doubtless playing, I was
unable to speak of him without a certain feeling of admiration.

Well, on the night but one before our arrival in America, the
officer of the watch heard groans on the darkest portion of the
deck. He drew nearer, went up, and saw a man stretched at full
length, with his head wrapped in a thick, gray muffler, and his
hands tied together with a thin cord.

They unfastened his bonds, lifted him, and gave him a
restorative.

The man was Rozaine.

Yes, it was Rozaine, who had been attacked in the course of
one of his expeditions, knocked down, and robbed. A visiting-
card pinned to his clothes bore these words:

"Arsène Lupin accepts M. Rozaine's ten thousand francs, with
thanks."

As a matter of fact, the stolen pocket-book contained twenty
thousand-franc notes.

Of course, the unfortunate man was accused of counterfeiting
this attack upon his own person. But, apart from the fact that it
would have been impossible for him to bind himself in this way,
it was proved that the writing on the card differed absolutely

from Rozaine's handwriting, whereas it was exactly like that of Arsène Lupin, as reproduced in an old newspaper which had been found on board.

So Rozaine was not Arsène Lupin! Rozaine was Rozaine, the son of a Bordeaux merchant! And Arsène Lupin's presence had been asserted once again and by means of what a formidable act!

Sheer terror ensued. The passengers no longer dared stay alone in their cabins nor wander unaccompanied to the remoter parts of the ship. Those who felt sure of one another kept prudently together. And even here an instinctive mistrust divided those who knew one another best. The danger no longer threatened from a solitary individual kept under observation and therefore less dangerous. Arsène Lupin now seemed to be . . . to be everybody. Our over-excited imaginations ascribed to him the possession of a miraculous and boundless power. We supposed him capable of assuming the most unexpected disguises, of being by turns the most respectable Major Rawson, or the most noble Marquis de Raverdan, or even—for we no longer stopped at the accusing initial—this or that person known to all, and travelling with wife, children, and servants.

The wireless telegrams brought us no news; at least, the captain did not communicate them to us. And this silence was not calculated to reassure us.

It was small wonder, therefore, that the last day appeared interminable. The passengers lived in the anxious expectation of a tragedy. This time it would not be a theft; it would not be a mere assault; it would be crime—murder. No one was willing to admit that Arsène Lupin would rest content with those two insignificant acts of larceny. He was absolute master of the ship; he reduced the officers to impotence; he had but to wreak his will upon us. He could do as he pleased; he held our lives and property in his hands.

These were delightful hours to me, I confess, for they won for me the confidence of Nellie Underdown. Naturally timid and impressed by all these events, she spontaneously sought at my side the protection which I was happy to offer her.

In my heart, I blessed Arsène Lupin. Was it not he who had brought us together? Was it not to him that I owed the right to abandon myself to my fondest dreams? Dreams of love and dreams more practical: why not confess it? The d'Andrézys are of good Poitevin stock, but the gilt of their blazon is a little worn; and it did not seem to me unworthy of a man of family to think of restoring the lost lustre of his name.

Nor, I was convinced, did these dreams offend Nellie. Her smiling eyes gave me leave to indulge them. Her soft voice bade me hope.

And we remained side by side until the last moment, with our elbows resting on the bulwark rail, while the outline of the American coast grew more and more distinct.

The search had been abandoned. All seemed expectation. From the first-class saloon to the steerage, with its swarm of emigrants, every one was waiting for the supreme moment when the insoluble riddle would be explained. Who was Arsène Lupin? Under what name, under what disguise was the famous Arsène Lupin lurking?

The supreme moment came. If I live to be a hundred, never shall I forget its smallest detail.

"How pale you look, Nellie!" I said, as she leaned, almost fainting, on my arm.

"And you, too. Oh, how you have changed!" she replied.

"Think what an exciting minute this is and how happy I am to pass it at your side. I wonder, Nellie, if your memory will sometimes linger . . ."

All breathless and fevered, she was not listening. The gang-plank was lowered. But, before we were allowed to cross it, men came on board: custom-house officers, men in uniform, postmen.

Nellie murmured:

"I shouldn't be surprised even if we heard that Arsène Lupin had escaped during the crossing!"

"He may have preferred death to dishonor, and plunged into the Atlantic rather than submit to arrest!"

"Don't jest about it," said she, in a tone of vexation.

Suddenly I gave a start and, in answer to her question, I replied:

"Do you see that little old man standing by the gang-plank?"

"The one in a green frock-coat with an umbrella?"

"That's Ganimard."

"Ganimard?"

"Yes, the famous detective who swore that he would arrest Arsène Lupin with his own hand. Ah, now I understand why we received no news from this side of the ocean. Ganimard was here, and he does not care to have any one interfering in his little affairs."

"So Arsène Lupin is sure of being caught?"

"Who can tell? Ganimard has never seen him, I believe, except made-up and disguised. Unless he knows the name under which he is travelling . . ."

"Ah," she said, with a woman's cruel curiosity, "I should love to see the arrest!"

"Have patience," I replied. "No doubt Arsène Lupin has already observed his enemy's presence. He will prefer to leave among the last, when the old man's eyes are tired."

The passengers began to cross the gang-plank. Leaning on his umbrella with an indifferent air, Ganimard seemed to pay no attention to the throng that crowded past between the two hand-rails. I noticed that one of the ship's officers, standing behind him, whispered in his ear from time to time.

The Marquis de Raverdan, Major Rawson, Rivolta, the Italian, went past, and others and many more. Then I saw Rozaine approaching.

Poor Rozaine! He did not seem to have recovered from his misadventures!

"It may be he, all the same," said Nellie. "What do you think?"

"I think it would be very interesting to have Ganimard and Rozaine in one photograph. Would you take the camera? My hands are so full."

I gave it to her, but too late for her to use it. Rozaine crossed. The officer bent over to Ganimard's ear; Ganimard gave a shrug of the shoulders; and Rozaine passed on.

But then who, in Heaven's name, was Arsène Lupin?

"Yes," she said, aloud, "who is it?"

There were only a score of people left. Nellie looked at them, one after the other, with the bewildered dread that *he* was not one of the twenty.

I said to her:

"We cannot wait any longer."

She moved on. I followed her. But we had not taken ten steps when Ganimard barred our passage.

"What does this mean?" I exclaimed.

"One moment, sir. What's your hurry?"

"I am escorting this young lady."

"One moment," he repeated, in a more mysterious voice.

He stared hard at me, and then, looking me straight in the eyes, said:

"Arsène Lupin, I believe."

I gave a laugh.

"No, Bernard d'Andrézy, simply."

"Bernard d'Andrézy died in Macedonia, three years ago."

"If Bernard d'Andrézy were dead I could not be here. And it's not so. Here are my papers."

"They are his papers. And I shall be pleased to tell you how you became possessed of them."

"But you are mad! Arsène Lupin took his passage under a name beginning with R."

"Yes, another of your tricks—a false scent upon which you put the people on the other side. Oh, you have no lack of brains, my lad! But, this time, your luck has turned. Come, Lupin, show that you're a good loser."

I hesitated for a second. He struck me a smart blow on the right forearm. I gave a cry of pain. He had hit the unhealed wound mentioned in the telegram.

There was nothing for it but to submit. I turned to Miss Underdown. She was listening, with a white face, staggering where she stood.

Her glance met mine, and then fell upon the Kodak which I had handed her. She made a sudden movement, and I received the impression, the certainty, that she had understood. Yes, it was there—between the narrow boards covered with black morocco, inside the little camera which I had taken the precaution to place in her hands before Ganimard arrested me—it was there that Rozaine's twenty thousand francs and Lady Gerland's pearls and diamonds lay concealed.

Now I swear that, at this solemn moment, with Ganimard and two of his minions around me, everything was indifferent to me—my arrest, the hostility of my fellow-men, everything, save only this: the resolve which Nellie Underdown would take in regard to the object I had given into her charge.

Whether they had this material and decisive piece of evidence against me, what cared I? The only question that obsessed my mind was, would Nelly furnish it or not?

Would she betray me? Would she ruin me? Would she act as an irreconcilable foe, or as a woman who remembers, and whose contempt is softened by a touch of indulgence—a shade of sympathy?

She passed before me. I bowed very low, without a word. Mingling with the other passengers, she moved towards the gang-board, carrying my Kodak in her hand.

"Of course," I thought, "she will not dare to, in public. She will hand it over presently—in an hour."

But, on reaching the middle of the plank, with a pretended movement of awkwardness, she dropped the Kodak in the water, between the landing-stage and the ship's side.

Then I watched her walk away.

Her charming profile was lost in the crowd, came into view again, and disappeared. It was over—over for good and all.

For a moment I stood rooted to the deck, sad and, at the same time, pervaded with a sweet and tender emotion. Then, to Ganimard's great astonishment, I sighed:

"Pity, after all, that I'm a rogue!"

It was in these words that Arsène Lupin, one winter's evening, told me the story of his arrest.[6] Chance and a series of incidents which I will some day describe had established between us bonds of . . . shall I say friendship? Yes, I venture to think that Arsène Lupin honors me with a certain friendship; and it is owing to this friendship that he occasionally drops in upon me unexpectedly, bringing into the silence of my study his youthful gayety, the radiance of his eager life, his high spirits—the spirits of a man for whom fate has little but smiles and favors in store.

His likeness? How can I trace it? I have seen Arsène Lupin a score of times, and each time a different being has stood before me . . . or rather the same being under twenty distorted images reflected by as many mirrors, each image having its special eyes, its particular facial outline, its own gestures, profile, and character.

"I myself," he once said to me, "have forgotten what I am really like. I no longer recognize myself in a glass."

A paradoxical whim of the imagination, no doubt; and yet true enough as regards those who come into contact with him, and who are unaware of his infinite resources, his patience, his unparalleled skill in make-up, and his prodigious faculty for changing even the proportions of his face and altering the relations of his features one to the other.

"Why," he asked, "should I have a definite, fixed appearance? Why not avoid the dangers attendant upon a personality that is always the same? My actions constitute my identity sufficiently."

And he added, with a touch of pride:

"It is all the better if people are never able to say with certainty: 'There goes Arsène Lupin.' The great thing is that they should say without fear of being mistaken: 'That action was performed by Arsène Lupin.'"

It is some of those actions of his, some of those exploits, that I will endeavor to narrate, thanks to the confidences with which he has had the kindness to favor me on certain winter evenings in the silence of my study. . . .

ARSÈNE LUPIN IN PRISON

Every tripper by the banks of the Seine must have noticed, between the ruins of Jumièges and those of Saint-Wandrille,[1] the curious little feudal castle of the Malaquis, proudly seated on its rock in mid-stream. A bridge connects it with the road. The base of its turrets seem to make one with the granite that bears it—a huge block detached from a mountain-top, and flung where it stands by some formidable convulsion of nature. All around the calm water of the broad river ripples among the reeds, while water-wagtails perch trembling on the top of the moist pebbles.

The history of the Malaquis is as rough as its name, as harsh as its outlines, and consists of endless fights, sieges, assaults, sacks, and massacres. Stories are told in the Caux district,[2] late at night, with a shiver, of the crimes committed there. Mysterious legends are conjured up. There is talk of a famous underground passage that led to the Abbey of Jumièges and to the manor-house of Agnés Sorel, once the favorite of Charles VII.

This erstwhile haunt of heroes and robbers is now occupied by Baron Nathan Cahorn—or Baron Satan, as he used to be called on the Bourse, where he made his fortune a little too suddenly. The ruined owners of the Malaquis had to sell the abode of their ancestors to him for a song. Here he installed his wonderful collections of pictures and furniture, of pottery and carved wood. He lives here alone, with three old servants. No one ever enters the doors. No one has ever beheld, in the setting of these ancient halls, his three Rubens, his two Watteaus, his pulpit carved by Jean Goujon, and all the other marvels snatched by force of money from before the eyes of the wealthiest frequenters of the public salesrooms.

Baron Satan leads a life of fear. He is afraid, not for himself, but for the treasures which he has accumulated with so tenacious a passion and with the perspicacity of a collector whom not the most cunning of dealers can boast of having ever taken in. He loves his curiosities with all the greed of a miser, with all the jealousy of a lover.

Daily, at sunset, the four iron-barred doors that command both ends of the bridge and the entrance to the principal court are locked and bolted. At the least touch electric bells would ring through the surrounding silence. There is nothing to be feared on the side of the Seine, where the rock rises sheer from the water.

One Friday in September the postman appeared as usual at the bridge-head, and, in accordance with his daily rule, the baron himself opened the heavy door.

He examined the man as closely as if he had not for years known that good jolly face and those crafty peasant's eyes. And the man said, with a laugh:

"It's me all right, monsieur le baron. It's not another chap in my cap and blouse."

"One never knows," muttered Cahorn.

The postman handed him a pile of newspapers. Then he added:

"And now, monsieur le baron, I have something special for you."

"Something special! What do you mean?"

"A letter . . . and a registered letter at that!"

Living cut off from everybody, with no friends nor any one that took an interest in him, the baron never received letters; and this suddenly struck him as an ill-omened event which gave him good cause for nervousness. Who was the mysterious correspondent that came to worry him in his retreat?

"I shall want your signature, monsieur le baron."

He signed the receipt, cursing as he did so. Then he took the letter, waited until the postman had disappeared round the turn of the road, and, after taking a few steps to and fro, leaned against the parapet of the bridge and opened the envelope. It contained a sheet of ruled paper, headed, in writing:

"Prison de la Santé, Paris."[3]

He looked at the signature:

"ARSÈNE LUPIN."

Utterly dumbfounded, he read:

"MONSIEUR LE BARON,—In the gallery that connects your two drawing-rooms there is a picture by Philippe de Champaigne, an excellent piece of work, which I admire greatly. I also like your Rubens pictures and the smaller of your two Watteaus. In the drawing-room on the right I note the Louis XIII. credence-table, the Beauvais tapestries, the Empire stand, signed by Jacob, and the Renaissance chest. In the room on the left the whole of the case of trinkets and miniatures.

"This time I will be satisfied with these objects, which, I think, can be easily turned into cash. I will therefore ask you to have them properly packed, and to send them to my name, carriage paid, to the Gare de Batignolles, on or before this day week, failing which I will myself see to their removal on the night of Wednesday, the 27th instant. In the latter case, as is only fair, I shall not be content with the above-mentioned objects.

"Pray excuse the trouble which I am giving you, and believe me to be

Yours very truly,
"ARSÈNE LUPIN."

"P.S.—Be sure not to send me the larger of the two Watteaus. Although you paid thirty thousand francs for it at the salesrooms, it is only a copy, the original having been burned under the Directory, by Barras, in one of his orgies. See Garat's unpublished Memoirs.

"I do not care either to have the Louis XV. chatelaine, which appears to me to be of doubtful authenticity."

This letter thoroughly upset Baron Cahorn. It would have alarmed him considerably had it been signed by any other hand. But signed by Arsène Lupin! . . .

He was a regular reader of the newspapers, knew of everything that went on in the way of theft and crime, and had heard all about the exploits of the infernal housebreaker. He was quite aware that Lupin had been arrested in America by his enemy, Ganimard; that he was safely under lock and key; and that the preliminaries to his trial were now being conducted . . . with great difficulty, no doubt! But he also knew that one could always expect anything of Arsène Lupin. Besides, this precise knowledge of the castle, of the arrangement of the pictures and furniture was a very formidable sign. Who had informed Lupin of things which nobody had ever seen?

The baron raised his eyes and gazed at the frowning outline of the Malaquis, its abrupt pedestal, the deep water that surrounds it. He shrugged his shoulders. No, there was no possible danger. No one in the world could penetrate to the inviolable sanctuary that contained his collections.

No one in the world, perhaps; but Arsène Lupin? Did doors, draw-bridges, walls, so much as exist for Arsène Lupin? Of what use were the most ingeniously contrived obstacles, the most skilful precautions, once that Arsène Lupin had decided to attain a given object? . . .

That same evening he wrote to the public prosecutor at Rouen. He enclosed the threatening letter, and demanded police protection.

The reply came without delay: the said Arsène Lupin was at that moment a prisoner at the Santé, where he was kept under strict surveillance and not allowed to write. The letter, therefore, could only be the work of a hoaxer. Everything went to prove this: logic, common sense, and the actual facts. However, so as to make quite sure, the letter had been submitted to a handwriting expert, who declared that, notwithstanding certain points of resemblance, it was not in the prisoner's writing.

"Notwithstanding certain points of resemblance." The baron saw only these five bewildering words, which he regarded as the confession of a doubt which alone should have been enough to justify the intervention of the police. His fears increased. He read the letter over and over again. "I will myself see to their removal." And that fixed date, the night of Wednesday the 27th of September!

Of a naturally suspicious and silent disposition, he dared not unburden himself to his servants, whose devotion he did not consider proof against all tests. And yet, for the first time for many years, he felt a need to speak, to take advice. Abandoned by the law of his country, he had no hope of protecting himself by his own resources, and was nearly going to Paris to beg for the assistance of some retired detective or other.

Two days elapsed. On the third day, as he sat reading his newspapers, he gave a start of delight. The *Réveil de Caudebec* contained the following paragraph:

"We have had the pleasure of numbering among our visitors, for nearly three weeks, Chief-Inspector Ganimard, one of the veterans of the detective service. M. Ganimard, for whom his last feat, the arrest of Arsène Lupin, has won an European reputation, is enjoying a rest from his arduous labors and spending a short holiday fishing for bleak and gudgeon in the Seine."

Ganimard! The very man that Baron Cahorn wanted! Who could baffle Lupin's plans better than the cunning and patient Ganimard?

The baron lost no time. It is a four-mile walk from the castle to the little town of Caudebec. He did the distance with a quick and joyous step, stimulated by the hope of safety.

After many fruitless endeavors to discover the chief-inspector's address, he went to the office of the *Réveil*, which is on the quay. He found the writer of the paragraph, who, going to the window, said:

"Ganimard! Why, you're sure to meet him, rod in hand, on the quay. That's where I picked up with him, and read his name, by accident, on his fishing-rod. Look, there he is, the little old man in the frock-coat and a straw hat, under the trees!"

"A frock-coat and a straw hat?"

"Yes. He's a queer specimen—close-tongued, and a trifle testy."

Five minutes later the baron accosted the famous Ganimard,

introduced himself, and made an attempt to enter into conversation. Failing in this, he broached the question frankly, and laid his case before him.

The other listened without moving a muscle or taking his eyes from the water. Then he turned his head to the baron, eyed him from head to foot with a look of profound pity, and said:

"Sir, it is not usual for criminals to warn the people whom they mean to rob. Arsène Lupin, in particular, never indulges in that sort of bounce."

"Still . . ."

"Sir, if I had the smallest doubt, believe me, the pleasure of once more locking up that dear Lupin would outweigh every other consideration. Unfortunately, the youth is already in prison."

"Suppose he escapes? . . ."

"People don't escape from the Santé."

"But Lupin . . ."

"Lupin no more than another."

"Still . . ."

"Very well, if he does escape, so much the better; I'll nab him again. Meanwhile you can sleep soundly and cease frightening my fish."

The conversation was ended. The baron returned home feeling more or less reassured by Ganimard's unconcern. He saw to his bolts, kept a watch upon his servants, and another forty-eight hours passed, during which he almost succeeded in persuading himself that, after all, his fears were groundless. There was no doubt about it: as Ganimard had said, criminals don't warn the people whom they mean to rob.

The date was drawing near. On the morning of Tuesday the twenty-sixth nothing particular happened. But at three o'clock in the afternoon a boy rang and handed in this telegram:

"No goods Batignolles. Get everything ready for to-morrow night.
                                                        ARSÈNE."

Once again Cahorn lost his head—so much so that he asked himself whether he would not do better to yield to Arsène Lupin's demands.

He hurried off to Caudebec. Ganimard was seated on a camp-stool fishing on the same spot as before. The baron handed him the telegram without a word.

"Well?" said the detective.

"Well what? It's for to-morrow!"

"What is?"

"The burglary! The theft of my collections!"

Ganimard turned to him, and, folding his arms across his chest, cried in a tone of impatience:

"Why, you don't really mean to say that you think I'm going to trouble myself about this stupid business?"

"What fee will you take to spend Wednesday night at the castle?"

"Not a penny. Don't bother me!"

"Name your own price. I am a rich man—a very rich man."

The brutality of the offer took Ganimard aback. He replied, more calmly:

"I am here on leave and I have no right to . . ."

"No one shall know. I undertake to be silent, whatever happens."

"Oh, nothing will happen."

"Well, look here, is three thousand francs enough?"

The inspector took a pinch of snuff, reflected, and said:

"Very well. But it's only fair to tell you that you are throwing your money away."

"I don't mind."

"In that case . . . And besides, after all, one can never tell with that devil of a Lupin! He must have a whole gang at his orders. . . . Are you sure of your servants?"

"Well, I . . ."

"Then we must not rely upon them. I'll wire to two of my own men; then we shall feel safer. . . . And now leave me; we must not be seen together. To-morrow evening at nine o'clock."

On the morning of the next day, the date fixed by Arsène Lupin, Baron Cahorn took down his trophy of arms, polished up his pistols, and made a thorough inspection of the Malaquis without discovering anything suspicious.

At half-past eight in the evening he dismissed his servants for the night. They slept in a wing facing the road, but set a little way back, and right at the end of the castle. As soon as he was alone he softly opened the four doors. In a little while he heard footsteps approaching.

Ganimard introduced his assistants—two powerfully built fellows, with bull necks, and huge, strong hands—and asked for certain explanations. After ascertaining the disposition of the place he carefully closed and barricaded every issue by which the threatened rooms could be entered. He examined the walls, raised the tapestries, and finally installed his detectives in the central gallery.

"No nonsense, do you understand? You're not here to sleep. At the least sound open the windows on the court and call me. Keep a look-out also on the water-side. Thirty feet of steep cliff doesn't frighten blackguards of that stamp."

He locked them in, took away the keys, and said to the baron: "And now to our post."

He had selected as the best place in which to spend the night a small room contrived in the thickness of the outer walls, between the two main doors. It had at one time been the watchman's lodge. A spy-hole opened upon the bridge, another upon the court. In one corner was what looked like the mouth of a well.

"You told me, did you not, monsieur le baron, that this well is the only entrance to the underground passage, and that it has been stopped up since the memory of man?"

"Yes."

"Therefore, unless there should happen to be another outlet, unknown to any but Arsène Lupin, which seems pretty unlikely, we can be easy in our minds."

He placed three chairs in a row, settled himself comfortably at full length, lit his pipe and sighed.

"Upon my word, monsieur le baron, I must be very eager to build an additional story to the little house in which I mean to end my days to accept so elementary a job as this. I shall tell the story to our friend Lupin; he'll split his sides with laughter."

The baron did not laugh. With ears pricked up he questioned the silence with ever-growing restlessness. From time to time he

leaned over the well and plunged an anxious eye into the yawning cavity.

The clock struck eleven; midnight; one o'clock.

Suddenly he seized the arm of Ganimard, who woke with a
start.

"Do you hear that?"

"Yes."

"What is it?"

"It's myself, snoring!"

"No, no, listen. . . ."

"Oh yes, it's a motor-horn."

"Well?"

"Well, it's as unlikely that Lupin should come by motor-car
as that he should use a battering-ram to demolish your castle.
So I should go to sleep if I were you, monsieur le baron . . . as I
shall have the honor of doing once more. Good-night!"

This was the only alarm. Ganimard resumed his interrupted
slumbers, and the baron heard nothing save his loud and regular snoring.

At break of day they left their cell. A great calm peace—the
peace of the morning by the cool water-side—reigned over the
castle. Cahorn, beaming with joy, and Ganimard, placid as
ever, climbed the staircase. Not a sound. Nothing suspicious.

"What did I tell you, monsieur le baron? I really ought not to
have accepted . . . I feel ashamed of myself . . ."

He took the keys and entered the gallery.

On two chairs, with bent bodies and hanging arms, sat the
two detectives, fast asleep.

"What, in the name of all the . . ." growled the inspector.

At the same moment the baron uttered a cry:

"The pictures! . . . The credence-table! . . ."

He stammered and spluttered, with his hand outstretched towards the dismantled walls, with their bare nails and slack cords.
The Watteau and the three Rubens had disappeared! The tapestries had been removed, the glass-cases emptied of their trinkets!

"And my Louis XVI sconces! . . . And the Regency chande-
lier! . . . And my twelfth-century Virgin! . . ."

He ran from place to place, maddened, in despair. Distraught with rage and grief, he quoted the purchase-prices, added up his losses, piled up figures, all promiscuously, in indistinct words and incompleted phrases. He stamped with his feet, flung himself about, and, in short, behaved like a ruined man who had nothing before him but suicide.

If anything could have consoled him it would have been the sight of Ganimard's stupefaction. Contrary to the baron, the inspector did not move. He seemed petrified, and, with a dazed eye, examined things. The windows? They were fastened. The locks of the doors? Untouched. There was not a crack in the ceiling, not a hole in the floor. Everything was in perfect order. The whole thing must have been carried out methodically, after an inexorable and logical plan.

"Arsène Lupin! . . . Arsène Lupin!" he muttered, giving way. . . .

Suddenly he leaped upon the two detectives, as though at last overcome with rage, and shook them and swore at them furiously. They did not wake up.

"The deuce!" he said. "Can they have been . . . ?"

He leaned over and closely scrutinized them, one after the other; they were both asleep, but their sleep was not natural. He said to the baron:

"They have been put to sleep."

"But by whom?"

"By him, of course . . . or by his gang, acting under his instructions. It's a trick in his own manner. I recognize his touch."

"In that case, I am undone; the thing is hopeless."

"Hopeless."

"But this is abominable!—it's monstrous!"

"Lodge an information."

"What's the good?"

"Well, you may as well try . . . the law has its resources. . . ."

"The law! But you can see for yourself. . . . Why, at this very moment, when you might be looking for a clew, discovering something, you're not even stirring!"

"Discover something, with Arsène Lupin! But, my dear sir,

Arsène Lupin never leaves anything behind him! There's no chance with Arsène Lupin! I am beginning to wonder whether he got himself arrested by me of his own free will in America!"

"Then I must give up the hope of recovering my pictures or anything! But he has stolen the pearls of my collection. I would give a fortune to get them back. If there's nothing to be done against him, let him name his price."

Ganimard looked at him steadily.

"That's a sound notion. Do you stick to it?"

"Yes, yes, yes! But why do you ask?"

"I have an idea."

"What idea?"

"We'll talk of it if nothing comes of the inquiry. . . . Only, not a word about me to a soul if you wish me to succeed."

And he added, between his teeth:

"Besides, I have nothing to be proud of."

The two men gradually recovered consciousness, with the stupefied look of men awakening from an hypnotic sleep. They opened astounded eyes, tried to make out what had happened. Ganimard questioned them. They remembered nothing.

"Still, you must have seen somebody."

"No."

"Try and think."

"No."

"Did you have a drink?"

They reflected, and one of them replied:

"Yes, I had some water."

"Out of that bottle there?"

"Yes."

"I had some too," said the other.

Ganimard smelled the water, tasted it. It had no particular scent or flavor.

"Come," he said, "we are wasting our time. Problems set by Arsène Lupin can't be solved in five minutes. But, by jingo, I swear I'll catch him! He's won the second bout. The rubber game to me!"

That day a charge of aggravated larceny was laid by Baron Cahorn against Arsène Lupin, a prisoner awaiting trial at the Santé.

The baron often regretted having laid his information when he saw the Malaquis made over to the gendarmes, the public prosecutor, the examining magistrate, the newspaper reporters, and all the idle, curious people who worm themselves in wherever they have no business to be.

Already the case was filling the public mind. It had taken place under such peculiar conditions, and the name of Arsène Lupin excited men's imaginations to such a pitch, that the most fantastic stories crowded the columns of the press and found acceptance with the public.

But the original letter of Arsène Lupin which was published by the *Echo de France*[4]—and no one ever knew who had supplied the text: the letter in which Baron Cahorn was insolently warned of what threatened him—caused the greatest excitement. Fabulous explanations were offered forthwith. The old legends were revived. The newspapers reminded their readers of the existence of the famous subterranean passages. And the public prosecutor, influenced by these statements, pursued his search in this direction.

The castle was ransacked from top to bottom. Every stone was examined; the wainscotings and chimneys, the frames of the mirrors and the rafters of the ceilings were carefully inspected. By the light of torches the searchers investigated the immense cellars, in which the lords of the Malaquis had been used to pile up their provisions and munitions of war. They sounded the very bowels of the rock. All to no purpose. They discovered not the slightest trace of a tunnel. No secret passage existed.

Very well, was the answer on every side, but pictures and furniture don't vanish like ghosts. They go out through doors and windows, and the people that take them also go in and out through doors and windows. Who are these people? How did they get in? And how did they get out?

The public prosecutor of Rouen, persuaded of his own incompetence, asked for the assistance of the Paris police. M. Dudouis, the chief of the detective service, sent the most efficient blood-hounds in his employ. He himself paid a forty-eight hours' visit to the Malaquis, but met with no better success.

It was after his return that he sent for Chief-Inspector Ganimard, whose services he had so often had occasion to value.

Ganimard listened in silence to the instructions of his superior, and then, tossing his head, said:

"I think we shall be on a false scent while we continue to search the castle. The solution lies elsewhere."

"With Arsène Lupin! If you think that, then you believe that he took part in the burglary."

"I do think so. I go further: I consider it certain."

"Come, Ganimard, this is ridiculous. Arsène Lupin is in prison."

"Arsène Lupin is in prison, I agree. He is being watched, I grant you. But if he had his legs in irons, his hands bound, and his mouth gagged I should still be of the same opinion."

"But why this persistency?"

"Because no one else is capable of contriving a plan on so large a scale, and of contriving it in such a way that it succeeds . . . as this has succeeded."

"Words, Ganimard!"

"They are true words, for all that. Only, it's no use looking for underground passages, for stones that turn on a pivot, and stuff and nonsense of that kind. Our friend does not employ any of those antiquated measures. He is a man of to-day, or, rather, of to-morrow."

"And what do you conclude?"

"I conclude by asking you straight to let me spend an hour with Lupin."

"In his cell?"

"Yes. We were on excellent terms during the crossing from America, and I venture to think that he is not without a friendly feeling for the man who arrested him. If he can tell me what I want to know, without compromising himself, he will be quite willing to spare me an unnecessary journey."

It was just after mid-day when Ganimard was shown into Arsène Lupin's cell. Lupin, who was lying on his bed, raised his head, and uttered an exclamation of delight.

"Well, this is a surprise! Dear old Ganimard here!"

"Himself."

"I have hoped for many things in this retreat of my own choosing, but for none more eagerly than the pleasure of welcoming you here."

"You are too good."

"Not at all, not at all. I have the liveliest feelings of esteem for you."

"I am proud to hear it."

"I have said so a thousand times: Ganimard is our greatest detective. He's *almost*—see how frank I am—*almost* as good as Sherlock Holmes. But, really, I'm awfully sorry to have nothing better than this stool to offer you. And not a drink of any kind! Not so much as a glass of beer! Do forgive me: I am only passing through!"

Ganimard smiled and sat down, and the prisoner, glad of the opportunity of speaking, continued:

"By Jove, what a treat to see a decent man's face! I am sick of the looks of all those spies who go through my cell and my pockets ten times a day, to make sure that I am not planning an escape. Gad, how fond the government must be of me!"

"They show their taste."

"No, no! I should be so happy if they would let me lead my quiet little life."

"On other people's money."

"Just so. It would be so simple. But I'm letting my tongue run on. I'm talking nonsense, and I dare say you're in a hurry. Come, Ganimard, tell me to what I owe the honor of this visit?"

"The Cahorn case," said Ganimard, straight out.

"Stop! Wait a bit. . . . You see, I have so many on hand! First, let me search my brain for the Cahorn pigeon-hole. . . . Ah, I have it! Cahorn case, Château du Malaquis, Seine-Inférieure. . . . Two Rubens, a Watteau, and a few minor trifles."

"Trifles!"

"Oh yes; all this is of small importance. I have bigger things on hand. However, you're interested in the case, and that's enough for me. . . . Go ahead, Ganimard."

"I need not tell you, need I, how far we have got with the investigation?"

"No, not at all. I have seen the morning papers. And I will even take the liberty of saying that you are not making much progress."

"That's just why I have come to throw myself upon your kindness."

"I am entirely at your service."

"First of all, the thing was done by you, was it not?"

"From start to finish."

"The registered letter? The telegram?"

"Were sent by yours truly; in fact, I ought to have the receipts somewhere."

Arsène opened the drawer of a little deal table which, with the bed and the stool, composed all the furniture of his cell, took out two scraps of paper, and handed them to Ganimard.

"Hullo!" cried the latter. "Why, I thought you were being kept under constant observation and searched on the slightest pretext. And it appears that you read the papers and collect post-office receipts. . . ."

"Bah! Those men are such fools! They rip up the lining of my waistcoat, explore the soles of my boots, listen at the walls of my cell; but not one of them ever thought that Arsène Lupin would be silly enough to choose so obvious a hiding-place. That's just what I reckoned on."

Ganimard exclaimed, in amusement:

"What a funny chap you are! You're beyond me! Come, tell me the story."

"Oh, I say! Not so fast! Initiate you into all my secrets . . . reveal my little tricks to you? That's a serious matter."

"Was I wrong in thinking that I could rely on you to oblige me?"

"No, Ganimard, and, as you insist upon it . . ."

Arsène Lupin took two or three strides across his cell. Then, stopping:

"What do you think of my letter to the baron?" he asked.

"I think you wanted to have some fun, to tickle the gallery a bit."

"Ah, there you go! Tickle the gallery, indeed! Upon my

word, Ganimard, I gave you credit for more sense! Do you really imagine that I, Arsène Lupin, waste my time with such childish pranks as that? Is it likely that I should have written the letter if I could have rifled the baron without it? Do try and understand that the letter was the indispensable starting-point— the main-spring that set the whole machine in motion. Look here, let us proceed in order, and, if you like, prepare the Malaquis burglary together."

"Very well."

"Now follow me. I have to do with an impregnable and closely guarded castle. Am I to throw up the game and give up the treasures which I covet because the castle that contains them happens to be inaccessible?"

"Clearly not."

"Am I to try to carry it by assault, as in the old days, at the head of a band of adventurers?"

"That would be childish."

"Am I to enter it by stealth?"

"Impossible."

"There remains only one way, which is to get myself invited by the owner of the aforesaid castle."

"It's an original idea."

"And so easy! Suppose that one day the said owner receives a letter, warning him of a plot hatched against him by one Arsène Lupin, a notorious housebreaker. What is he sure to do?"

"Send the letter to the public prosecutor."

"Who will laugh at him, *because the said Lupin is actually locked up!* The natural consequence is the utter bewilderment of the worthy man, who is ready and anxious to ask the assistance of the first-comer. Am I right?"

"Quite so."

"And if he happens to read in the local news-sheet that a famous detective is staying in the neighborhood . . ."

"He will go and apply to that detective."

"Exactly. But, on the other hand, let us assume that, foreseeing this inevitable step, Arsène Lupin has asked one of his ablest friends to take up his quarters at Caudebec, to pick up acquaintance with a contributor to the *Réveil*, a paper to which the baron, mark you, subscribes, and to drop a hint that he is so-and-so, the famous detective. What will happen next?"

"The contributor will send a paragraph to the *Réveil*, stating that the detective is staying at Caudebec."

"Exactly; and one of two things follows: either the fish (I mean Cahorn) does not rise to the bait, in which case nothing happens, or else (and this is the more likely presumption) he nibbles, in which case you have our dear Cahorn imploring the assistance of one of my own friends against me!"

"This is becoming more and more original."

"Of course the sham detective begins by refusing. Thereupon a telegram from Arsène Lupin. Dismay of the baron, who renews his entreaties with my friend, and offers him so much to watch over his safety. The friend aforesaid accepts, and brings with him two chaps of our gang, who, during the night, while Cahorn is kept in sight by his protector, remove a certain number of things through the window, and lower them with ropes into a barge freighted for the purpose. It's as simple as . . . Lupin."

"And it's just wonderful," cried Ganimard, "and I have no words in which to praise the boldness of the idea and the ingenuity of the details! But I can hardly imagine a detective so illustrious that his name should have attracted and impressed the baron to that extent."

"There is one and one only."

"Who?"

"The most illustrious of them all, the archenemy of Arsène Lupin—in short, Inspector Ganimard."

"What! myself?"

"Yourself, Ganimard. And that's the delightful part of it: if you go down and persuade the baron to talk you will end by discovering that it is your duty to arrest yourself, just as you arrested me in America. A humorous revenge, what? I shall have Ganimard arrested by Ganimard!"

Arsène Lupin laughed long and loud, while the inspector bit his lips with vexation. The joke did not appear to him worthy of so much merriment.

The entrance of a warder gave him time to recover. The man

brought the meal which Arsène Lupin, by special favor, was allowed to have sent in from the neighboring restaurant. After placing the tray on the table he went away. Arsène sat down, broke his bread, ate a mouthful or two, and continued:

"But be easy, my dear Ganimard, you will not have to go down there. I am going to reveal a thing to you that will strike you dumb: the Cahorn case is about to be withdrawn."

"What?"

"About to be withdrawn, I said."

"Nonsense! I have just left the chief."

"And then? Does Monsieur Dudouis know more than I do about what concerns me? You must learn that Ganimard—excuse me—that the sham Ganimard has remained on very good terms with Baron Cahorn. The baron—and this is the main reason why he has kept the thing quiet—has charged him with the very delicate mission of negotiating a deal with me; and the chances are that, by this time, on payment of a certain sum, the baron is once more in possession of his pet knicknacks, in return for which he will withdraw the charge. Wherefore, there is no question of theft. Wherefore, the public prosecutor will have to abandon . . ."

Ganimard gazed at the prisoner with an air of stupefaction.

"But how do you know all this?"

"I have just received the telegram I was expecting."

"You have just received a telegram?"

"This very moment, my friend. I was too polite to read it in your presence. But if you will allow me . . ."

"You're poking fun at me, Lupin."

"Be so good, my dear friend, as to cut off the top of that egg gently. You will see for yourself that I am not poking fun at you."

Ganimard obeyed mechanically, and broke the egg with the blade of a knife. A cry of surprise escaped him. The shell was empty but for a sheet of blue paper. At Arsène's request, he unfolded it. It was a telegram, or, rather, a portion of a telegram, from which the postal indications had been removed. He read:

"Arrangement settled. Hundred thousand spondulics[5] delivered. All well."

"Hundred thousand spondulics?" he uttered.

"Yes, a hundred thousand francs. It's not much, but these are hard times. . . . And my general expenses are so heavy! If you knew the amount of my budget . . . it's like the budget of a big town!"

Ganimard rose to go. His ill-humor had left him. He thought for a few moments, and cast a mental glance over the whole business, to try to discover a weak point. Then, in a voice that frankly revealed his admiration as an expert, he said:

"It's a good thing that there are not dozens like you, or there would be nothing for us but to shut up shop."

Arsène Lupin assumed a modest simper, and replied:

"Oh, I had to do something to amuse myself, to occupy my spare time . . . especially as this stroke could only succeed while I was in prison."

"What do you mean?" exclaimed Ganimard. "Your trial, your defence, your examination: isn't that enough for you to amuse yourself with?"

"No, because I have decided not to attend my trial."

"Oh, I say!"

Arsène Lupin repeated, deliberately:

"I shall not attend my trial."

"Really!"

"Why, my dear fellow, you surely don't think that I mean to rot in gaol? The mere suggestion is an insult. Let me tell you that Arsène Lupin remains in prison as long as he thinks fit, and not a moment longer."

"It might have been more prudent to begin by not entering it," said the inspector, ironically.

"Ah, so you're chaffing me, sirrah? Do you remember that you had the honor to effect my arrest? Well, learn from me, my respectable friend, that no one, neither you nor another, could have laid a hand upon me if a much more important interest had not occupied my attention at that critical moment."

"You surprise me."

"A woman had cast her eyes upon me, Ganimard, and I loved her. Do you realize all that the fact implies when a woman whom one loves casts her eyes upon one? I cared about little else, I assure you. And that is why I'm here."

"Since some considerable time, allow me to observe."

"I was anxious to forget. Don't laugh; it was a charming adventure, and I still have a touching recollection of it . . . And then I am suffering a little from nervous prostration. We lead such a feverish existence nowadays! It's a good thing to take a rest-cure from time to time. And there's no place for it like this. They carry out the cure in all its strictness at the Santé."

"Arsène Lupin," said Ganimard, "you're pulling my leg."

"Ganimard," replied Lupin, "this is Friday. On Wednesday next I'll come and smoke a cigar with you in the Rue Pergolèse at four o'clock in the afternoon."

"Arsène Lupin, I shall expect you."

They shook hands like two friends who have a proper sense of each other's value, and the old detective turned towards the door.

"Ganimard!"

Ganimard looked round.

"What is it?"

"Ganimard, you've forgotten your watch."

"My watch?"

"Yes, I've just found it in my pocket."

He returned it, with apologies.

"Forgive me. They've taken mine, but that's no reason why I should rob you of yours—especially as I have a chronometer here which keeps perfect time and satisfies all my requirements."

He took out of the drawer a large, thick, comfortable-looking gold watch, hanging to a heavy chain.

"And out of whose pocket does this come?" asked Ganimard.

Arsène Lupin carelessly inspected the initials:

" 'J. B.' . . . Oh yes, I remember: Jules Bouvier, my examining magistrate, a charming fellow. . . ."

THE ESCAPE OF
ARSÈNE LUPIN

Arsène Lupin finished his mid-day meal, took a good cigar from his pocket, and complacently studied the gold-lettered inscription on its band. At that moment the door of his cell opened. He had just a second in which to throw the cigar into the drawer of the table and to move away. The warden came in to tell him that it was time to take his exercise.

"I was waiting for you, old chap!" cried Lupin, with his unfailing good-humor.

They went out together. Hardly had they turned the corner of the passage when two men entered the cell and began to make a minute examination. One of these was Inspector Dieuzy, the other Inspector Folenfant.

They wanted to have the matter settled once and for all. There was no doubt about it: Arsène Lupin was keeping up a correspondence with the outside world and communicating with his confidants. Only the day before the *Grand Journal* had published the following lines, addressed to its legal contributor:

"SIR,—In an article published a few days ago you ventured to express yourself concerning me in utterly unwarrantable terms. I shall come and call you to account a day or two before my trial commences.

"Yours faithfully,
"ARSÈNE LUPIN."

The handwriting was Arsène Lupin's. Therefore, he was sending letters. Therefore, he was receiving letters. Therefore, it was certain that he was preparing the escape which he had so arrogantly announced.

The position was becoming intolerable. By arrangement with the examining magistrate, M. Dudouis himself, the head of the detective service, went to the Santé to explain to the prison governor the measures which it was thought advisable to take, and on his arrival he sent two of his men to the prisoner's cell.

The men raised every one of the flag-stones, took the bed to pieces, did all that is usually done in such cases, and ended by discovering nothing. They were about to abandon their search when the warden came running in, and said:

"The drawer . . . look in the drawer of the table! I thought I saw him shut it when I came in just now."

They looked, and Dieuzy exclaimed:

"Gad, we've caught our customer this time!"

Folenfant stopped him.

"Don't do anything, my lad; let the chief take the inventory."

"Still, this Havana . . ."

"Leave it alone, and let us tell the chief."

Two minutes later M. Dudouis was exploring the contents of the drawer. He found, first, a collection of press-cuttings concerning Arsène Lupin; next, a tobacco-pouch, a pipe, and some foreign post-paper; and, lastly, two books.

He looked at the titles: Carlyle's *Heroes and Hero-worship*,[1] in English, and a charming Elzevir,[2] in the contemporary binding: a German translation of the *Manual of Epictetus*,[3] published at Leyden in 1634. He glanced through them, and observed that every page was scored, underlined, and annotated. Were these conventional signs, or were they marks denoting the reader's devotion to a particular book?

"We'll go into this in detail," said M. Dudouis.

He investigated the tobacco-pouch, the pipe. Then, taking up the magnificent cigar in its gold band:

"By Jove!" he cried, "our friend does himself well! A Henry Clay!"[4]

With the mechanical movement of a smoker he put it to his ear and crackled it. An exclamation escaped him. The cigar had given way under the pressure of his fingers! He examined it more attentively, and soon perceived something that showed white between the leaves of the tobacco. And carefully, with the aid of a pin, he drew out a scroll of very thin paper, no thicker than a toothpick. It was a note. He unrolled it, and read the following words, in a small, female hand:

"Maria has taken the other's place. Eight out of ten are prepared. On pressing outside foot, metal panel moves upward. H. P. will wait from 12 to 16 daily. But where? Reply at once. Have no fear: your friend is looking after you."

M. Dudouis reflected for a moment and said:

"That's clear enough. . . . Maria, the prison-van . . . the eight compartments. . . . Twelve to sixteen; that is, from twelve to four o'clock. . . ."

"But who is H. P.? Who is to wait for him?"

"H. P. stands for horse-power, of course—a motor-car."

He rose and asked:

"Had the prisoner finished his lunch?"

"Yes."

"And, as he has not yet read this message, as the condition of the cigar shows, the chances are that he had only just received it."

"By what means?"

"How can I tell? In his food; inside a roll or a potato."

"That's impossible. He was only permitted to have his meals from the outside so that we might trap him and we have found nothing."

"We will look for Lupin's reply this evening. Meantime keep him out of his cell. I will take this to Monsieur Bouvier,[5] the examining magistrate. If he agrees, we will have the letter photographed at once, and in an hour's time you can put these other things back in the drawer, together with an exactly similar cigar containing the original message. The prisoner must not be allowed to suspect anything."

It was not without a certain curiosity that M. Dudouis, accompanied by Inspector Dieuzy, returned to the office of the Santé in the evening. In a corner, on the stove, were three plates.

"Has he had his dinner?"

"Yes," replied the governor.

"Dieuzy, cut those pieces of macaroni into very thin shreds and open that bit of bread. . . . Is there nothing there?"

"No, sir."

M. Dudouis examined the plates, the fork, the spoon, and, lastly, the knife—a regulation knife with a rounded blade. He twisted the handle to the left and then to the right. When turned to the right the handle gave way and became unscrewed. The knife was hollow, and served as a sheath for a slip of paper.

"Pooh!" he said, "that's not very artful for a man like Arsène. But let us waste no time. Do you go to the restaurant, Dieuzy, and make your inquiries."

Then he read:

"I leave it to you. Let H. P. follow every day at a distance. I shall go in front. I shall see you soon, my dear and adorable friend."

"At last!" cried M. Dudouis, rubbing his hands. "Things are going better, I think. With a little assistance from our side the escape will succeed . . . just enough to enable us to bag the accomplices."

"And suppose Arsène Lupin slips through your fingers?" said the governor.

"We shall employ as many men as are necessary. If, however, he shows himself too clever . . . well, then, so much the worse for him! As for the rest of the gang, since the leader refuses to talk the others must be made to."

The fact was that Arsène Lupin did not talk much. For some months M. Jules Bouvier, the examining magistrate, had been exerting himself to no purpose. The interrogatories were reduced to uninteresting colloquies between the magistrate and Maître Danval, one of the leaders of the bar, who, for that matter, knew as much and as little about the defendant as the man in the street.

From time to time, out of politeness, Arsène Lupin would let fall a remark:

"Quite so, sir; we are agreed. The robbery at the Crédit Lyonnais, the robbery in the Rue de Babylone, the uttering of the forged notes, the affair of the insurance policies, the burglaries at the Châteaux d'Armesnil, de Gouret, d'Imblevain, des Groseillers, du Malaquis: that's all my work."[6]

"Then perhaps you will explain . . ."

"There's no need of it. I confess to everything in the lump—everything, and ten times as much."

Tired out, the magistrate had suspended these wearisome interrogatories. He resumed them, after being shown the two intercepted missives. And regularly at twelve o'clock every day Arsène Lupin was taken from the Santé to the police-station in a van, with a number of other prisoners. They left again at three or four in the day.

One afternoon the return journey took place under exceptional conditions. As the other criminals from the Santé had not yet been examined, it was decided to take Arsène Lupin back first. He therefore stepped into the van alone.

These prison-vans, vulgarly known as *paniers à salade*, or salad-baskets, in France, and as "Black Marias" in England, are divided lengthwise by a central passage, giving admittance to ten compartments or boxes, five on each side. Each of these boxes is so arranged that its occupant has to adopt a sitting posture, and the five prisoners are consequently seated one beside the other, and are separated by parallel partitions. A municipal guard sits at the end and watches the central passage.

Arsène was placed in the third box on the right, and the heavy vehicle started. He perceived that they had left the Quai de l'Horloge, and were passing before the Palais de Justice. When they reached the middle of the Pont Saint-Michel he pressed his outer foot—that is to say, his right foot, as he had always done—against the sheet-iron panel that closed his cell. Suddenly something was thrown out of gear, and the panel opened outward imperceptibly. He saw that he was just between the two wheels.

He waited, with a watchful eye. The van went along the Boulevard Saint-Michel at a foot's pace. At the Carrefour Saint-Germain it pulled up. A dray-horse had fallen. The traffic was stopped, and soon there was a block of cabs and omnibuses.

Arsène Lupin put out his head. Another prison-van was standing beside the one in which he was sitting. He raised the panel farther, put his foot on one of the spokes of the hind wheel, and jumped to the ground.

A cab-driver saw him, choked with laughing, and then tried to call out. But his voice was lost in the din of the traffic, which had started afresh. Besides, Arsène Lupin was already some distance away.

He had taken a few steps at a run; but, crossing to the left-hand pavement, he turned back, cast a glance around him, and seemed to be taking his breath, like a man who is not quite sure which direction he means to follow. Then, making up his mind, he thrust his hands into his pockets, and, with the careless air of a person taking a stroll, continued to walk along the boulevard.

The weather was mild: it was a bright, warm autumn day. The cafés were full of people. He sat down outside one of them.

He called for a *bock* and a packet of cigarettes. He emptied his glass with little sips, calmly smoked a cigarette and lit a second. Lastly, he stood up and asked the waiter to fetch the manager.

The manager came, and Arsène said, in a voice loud enough to be heard by all around:

"I am very sorry, but I have come out without my purse. Possibly you know my name and will not mind trusting me for a day or two: I am Arsène Lupin."

The manager looked at him, thinking he was joking. But Arsène repeated:

"Lupin, a prisoner at the Santé, just escaped. I venture to hope that my name inspires you with every confidence."

And he walked away amid the general laughter before the other dreamed of raising a protest.

He slanted across the Rue Soufflot, and turned down the Rue Saint-Jacques. He proceeded along this street quietly, looking at the shop-windows, and smoking one cigarette after the other. On reaching the Boulevard de Port-Royal he took his bearings, asked the way, and walked straight towards the Rue de la Santé. Soon the frowning walls of the prison came into view. He skirted them, and, going up to the municipal guard who was standing sentry at the gate, raised his hat, and said:

"Is this the Santé Prison?"

"Yes."

"I want to go back to my cell, please. The van dropped me on the way, and I should not like to abuse . . ."

The guard grunted.

"Look here, my man, you just go your road, and look sharp about it!"

"I beg your pardon, but my road lies through this gate. And, if you keep Arsène Lupin out, it may cost you dear, my friend."

"Arsène Lupin! What's all this?"

"I am sorry I haven't a card on me," said Arsène, pretending to feel in his pockets.

The guard, utterly nonplussed, eyed him from head to foot. Then, without a word and as though in spite of himself, he rang a bell. The iron door opened.

A few minutes later the governor hurried into the office, gesticulating and pretending to be in a violent rage. Arsène smiled.

"Come, sir, don't play a game with me! What! You take the precaution to bring me back alone in the van, you prepare a nice little block in the traffic, and you think that I am going to take to my heels and rejoin my friends! And what about the twenty detectives escorting us on foot, on bicycles, and in cabs? They'd have made short work of me: I should never have got off alive! Perhaps that was what they were reckoning on?" Shrugging his shoulders, he added: "I beg you, sir, don't let them trouble about me. When I decide to escape I shall want nobody's assistance."

Two days later the *Écho de France*, which was undoubtedly becoming the official gazette of the exploits of Arsène Lupin—he was said to be one of the principal shareholders—published the fullest details of his attempted escape. The exact text of the letters exchanged between the prisoner and his mysterious woman friend, the means employed for this correspondence, the part played by the police, the drive along the Boulevard Saint-Michel, the incident at the Café Soufflot—everything was told in print. It was known that the inquiries of Inspector Dieuzy among the waiters of the restaurant had led to no result. And, in addition, the public were made aware of this bewildering fact, which showed the infinite variety of the resources which the man had at his disposal: the prison-van in which he had been carried was "faked" from end to end, and had been substituted by his accomplices for one of the six regular vans that compose the prison service.

No one entertained any further doubt as to Arsène Lupin's coming escape. He himself proclaimed it in categorical terms, as was shown by his reply to M. Bouvier on the day after the incident. The magistrate having bantered him on the check which he had encountered, he looked at him and said, coldly:

"Listen to me, sir, and take my word for it: this attempted escape formed part of my plan of escape."

"I don't understand," grinned the magistrate.

"There is no need that you should."

And when, in the course of this private interrogatory, which appeared at full length in the columns of the *Écho de France*, the magistrate resumed his cross-examination, Lupin exclaimed, with a weary air:

"Oh dear, oh dear, oh dear! What *is* the use of going on? All these questions have no importance whatever."

"How do you mean, no importance?"

"Of course not, seeing that I shall not attend my trial."

"You will not attend? . . ."

"No, it's a fixed idea of mine, an irrevocable decision. Nothing will induce me to depart from it."

This assurance, combined with the inexplicable indiscretions committed day after day, ended by enervating and disconcerting the officers of the law. Secrets were revealed, known to Arsène Lupin alone, the divulging of which could, therefore, come from none but him. But with what object did he divulge them? And by what means?

They changed Arsène Lupin's cell, moved him to a lower floor. The magistrate, on his side, closed the examination, and delivered the materials for the indictment.

A two months' silence ensued. These two months Arsène Lupin passed stretched on his bed, with his face almost constantly turned to the wall. The change of cell seemed to have crushed his spirits. He refused to see his counsel. He exchanged hardly a word with his wardens.

In the fortnight immediately preceding his trial he seemed to revive. He complained of lack of air. He was sent into the yard for exercise very early in the morning with a man on either side of him.

Meanwhile public curiosity had not abated. The news of his escape was expected daily; it was almost hoped for, so greatly had he caught the fancy of the crowd with his pluck, his gayety, his variety, his inventive genius, and the mystery of his life. Arsène Lupin was bound to escape. It was inevitable. People were even astonished that he put it off so long. Every morning the prefect of police asked his secretary:

"Well, isn't he gone yet?"

"No, sir."

"Then it will be to-morrow."

And on the day before the trial a gentleman called at the office of the *Grand Journal*, asked to see the legal contributor, flung his card at his head, and made a rapid exit. The card bore the words:

"Arsène Lupin always keeps his promises."

It was in these conditions that the trial opened.

The crowd was enormous. Everybody wanted to see the famous Arsène Lupin, and was enjoying in advance the way in which he was sure to baffle the presiding judge. The court was thronged with barristers, magistrates, reporters, artists, society men and women—with all, in fact, that go to make up a first-night audience in Paris.

It was raining; the light was bad outside; it was difficult to see Arsène Lupin when his wardens ushered him into the dock. However, his torpid attitude, the manner in which he let himself fall into his chair, his indifferent and passive lack of movement, did not tell in his favor. His counsel—one of Maître Danval's "devils," the great man himself having regarded the part to which he was reduced as beneath him—spoke to him several times. He jerked his head and made no reply.

The clerk of the court read the indictment. Then the presiding judge said:

"Prisoner at the bar, stand up. Give your name, your age, and your occupation."

Receiving no answer, he repeated:

"Your name—what is your name?"

A thick and tired voice articulated the words:

"Désiré Baudru."

There was a murmur in court. But the judge retorted:

"Désiré Baudru? Is this a new incarnation? As it is about the eighth name to which you lay claim, and no doubt as imaginary as the rest, we will keep, if you don't mind, to that of Arsène Lupin, under which you are more favorably known."

The judge consulted his notes, and continued:

"For, notwithstanding all inquiries, it has been impossible to reconstruct your identity. You present the case, almost unparalleled in our modern society, of a man without a past. We do not know who you are, whence you come, where your childhood was spent—in short, we know nothing about you. You sprang up suddenly, three years ago, from an uncertain source, to reveal yourself as Arsène Lupin—that is to say, as a curious compound of intelligence and perversity, of criminality and generosity. The data which we have concerning you before that time are of the nature of suppositions. It seems probable that the so-called Rostat, who, eight years ago, was acting as assistant to Dickson, the conjurer, was none other than Arsène Lupin. It seems probable that the Russian student who, six years ago, used to attend Dr. Altier's laboratory at St. Louis' Hospital, and who often astonished the master by the ingenious character of his hypotheses on bacteriology and by the boldness of his experiments in the diseases of the skin—it seems probable that he too was none other than Arsène Lupin. So was the professor of Japanese wrestling, who established himself in Paris long before *jiu-jitsu* had been heard of. So, we believe, was the racing cyclist who won the great prize at the Exhibition, took his ten thousand francs, and has never been seen since. So, perhaps, was the man who saved so many people from burning at the Charity Bazaar, helping them through the little dormer window . . . and robbing them of their belongings."[7]

The judge paused for a moment, and concluded:

"Such was that period which seems to have been devoted entirely to a careful preparation for the struggle upon which you had embarked against society, a methodical apprenticeship in which you improved your force, your energy, and your skill to the highest pitch of perfection. Do you admit the accuracy of these facts?"

During this speech the defendant had shifted from foot to foot, with rounded back, and arms hanging slackly before him. As the light increased the spectators were able to distinguish his extreme emaciation, his sunken jaws, his curiously prominent cheek-bones, his earthen countenance, mottled with little red stains, and framed in a sparse and straggling beard. Prison had greatly aged and withered him. The clean-cut profile, the attractive, youthful features which had so often been reproduced in the papers, had passed away beyond all recognition.

He seemed not to have heard the question. It was twice repeated to him. At last he raised his eyes, appeared to think, and then, making a violent effort, muttered:

"Désiré Baudru."

The judge laughed.

"I fail to follow exactly the system of defence which you have adopted, Arsène Lupin. If it be to play the irresponsible imbecile, you must please yourself. As far as I am concerned, I shall go straight to the point without troubling about your fancies."

And he enumerated in detail the robberies, swindles, and forgeries ascribed to Arsène Lupin. Occasionally he put a question to the prisoner. The latter gave a grunt or made no reply. Witness after witness entered the box. The evidence of several of them was insignificant; others delivered more important testimony; but all of them had one characteristic in common, which was that each contradicted the other. The trial was shrouded in a puzzling obscurity until Chief-Inspector Ganimard was called, when the general interest woke up.

Nevertheless, the old detective caused a certain disappointment from the first. He seemed not so much shy—he was too old a hand for that—as restless and ill at ease. He kept turning his eyes with visible embarrassment towards the prisoner. However, with his two hands resting on the ledge of the box, he described the incidents in which he had taken part, his pursuit of Lupin across Europe, his arrival in America. And the crowded court listened to him greedily, as it would have listened to the story of the most exciting adventures. But towards the close of his evidence, twice over, after alluding to his interviews with Arsène Lupin, he stopped with an absent and undecided air.

It was obvious that he was under the influence of some obsession. The judge said:

"If you are not feeling well, you can stand down and continue your evidence later."

"No, no, only . . ."

He stopped, took a long and penetrating look at the prisoner, and said:

"Might I be allowed to see the prisoner more closely? There is a mystery which I want to clear up."

He stepped across to the dock, gazed at the prisoner longer still, concentrating all his attention upon him, and returned to the witness-box. Then, in a solemn voice, he said:

"May it please the court, I swear that the man before me is not Arsène Lupin."

A great silence greeted these words. The judge, at first taken aback, exclaimed:

"What do you mean? What are you saying? You are mad!"

The inspector declared, deliberately:

"At first sight one might be deceived by a likeness which, I admit, exists; but it needs only a momentary examination. The nose, the mouth, the hair, the color of the skin: why, it's not Arsène Lupin at all. And look at the eyes: did he ever have those drunkard's eyes?"

"Come, come, explain yourself, witness. What do you mean?"

"I don't know. He must have substituted in his place and stead some poor wretch who would have been found guilty in his place and stead . . . unless this man is an accomplice."

This unexpected *dénouement* caused the greatest sensation in court. Cries of laughter and astonishment rose from every side. The judge gave instructions for the attendance of the examining magistrate, the governor of the Santé, and the warders—and suspended the sitting.

After the adjournment M. Bouvier and the governor, on being confronted with the prisoner, declared that there was only a very slight resemblance in features between the man and Arsène Lupin.

"But, in that case," cried the judge, "who is this man? Where does he come from? How does he come to be in the dock?"

The two warders from the Santé were called. To the general astonishment, they recognized the prisoner, whom it had been their business to watch by turns. The judge drew a breath.

But one of the warders went on to say:

"Yes, yes, I think it's the man."

"What do you mean by saying you think?"

"Well, I hardly ever saw him. He was handed over to me at night, and for two months he was always lying on his bed with his face to the wall."

"But before those two months?"

"Oh, before that, he was not in Cell 24."

The governor of the prison explained:

"We changed his cell after his attempted escape."

"But you, as governor, must have seen him since the last two months."

"No, I had no occasion to see him . . . he kept quiet."

"And this man is not the prisoner who was given into your keeping?"

"No."

"Then who is he?"

"I don't know."

"We have, therefore, to do with a substitution of personalities effected two months ago. How do you explain it?"

"I can't explain it."

"Then. . . ."

In despair the judge turned to the prisoner, and, in a coaxing voice, said:

"Prisoner, cannot you explain to me how and since when you come to be in the hands of the law?"

It seemed as though this benevolent tone disarmed the mistrust or stimulated the understanding of the man. He strove to reply.

At last, skilfully and kindly questioned, he succeeded in putting together a few sentences which revealed that, two months before, he had been taken to the police-station and charged with vagrancy. He spent a night and a morning in the cells. Being found to possess a sum of seventy-five centimes, he was dismissed. But as he was crossing the yard two officers had caught him by the arm and taken him to the prison-van. Since that time he had been living in Cell 24. . . . He had been comfortable. . . . Had had plenty to eat. . . . Had slept pretty well. . . . So he had not protested. . . .

All this seemed probable. Amid laughter and a great effervescence of spirits the judge adjourned the case to another sitting for further inquiries.

The inquiries forthwith revealed the existence of an entry in the gaol-book to the effect that, eight weeks previously, a man of the name of Désiré Baudru had spent the night at the police-station. He was released the next day, and left the station at two o'clock in the afternoon. Well, at two o'clock on that day, Arsène Lupin, after undergoing his final examination, had left the police-station in the prison-van for the Santé.

Had the warders made a mistake? Had they themselves, in an inattentive moment, deceived by the superficial likeness, substituted this man for their prisoner? This seemed hardly possible in view of the length of their service.

Had the substitution been planned in advance? Apart from the fact that the disposition of the localities made this almost unrealizable, it would have been necessary, in that case, that Baudru should be an accomplice, and cause himself to be arrested with the precise object of taking Arsène Lupin's place. But, then, by what miracle could a plan of this sort have succeeded, based, as it was, entirely on a series of improbable chances, of fortuitous meetings and fabulous mistakes?

Désiré Baudru was subjected to the anthropometrical test:[8] there was not a single record corresponding with his description. Besides, traces of him were easily discovered. He was known at Courbevoie, at Asnières, at Levallois. He lived by begging, and slept in one of those rag-pickers' huts of which there are so many near the Barrière des Ternes. He had disappeared from sight for about a year.

Had he been suborned by Arsène Lupin? There were no grounds for thinking so. And even if this were so, it threw no light upon the prisoner's escape. The marvel remained as extraordinary as before. Of a score of suppositions put forward in explanation, not one was satisfactory. Of the escape alone there was no doubt: an incomprehensible, sensational escape, in which the public as well as the authorities felt the effect of a long preparation, a combination of wonderfully dove-tailed actions. And the upshot of it all was to justify Arsène Lupin's boastful prophecy:

"I shall not be present at my trial."

After a month of careful investigations the puzzle continued to present the same inscrutable character. Still, it was impossible to keep that poor wretch of a Baudru indefinitely locked up. To try him would have been absurd—what charge was there against him? The magistrate signed the order for his release. But the head of the detective service resolved to keep an active super-vision upon his movements.

The idea was suggested by Ganimard. In his opinion, there was complicity and no accident in the matter. Baudru was an instrument that Arsène Lupin had employed with his amazing skill. With Baudru at large, they might hope, through him, to come upon Arsène Lupin, or, at least, upon one of his gang.

Inspectors Folenfant and Dieuzy were told off as assistants to Ganimard, and one foggy morning in January the prison gates were thrown open to Désiré Baudru.

At first he seemed rather embarrassed, and walked like a man who has no very precise idea as to how to employ his time. He went down the Rue de la Santé and the Rue Saint-Jacques. Stopping outside an old-clothes shop, he took off his jacket and waistcoat, sold his waistcoat for a few sous, put on his jacket again, and went on.

He crossed the Seine. At the Châtelet an omnibus passed him. He tried to get into it. It was full. The ticket-collector advised him to take a number. He entered the waiting-room.

Ganimard beckoned to his two men, and, keeping his eyes on the office, said, quickly:

"Stop a cab . . . no, two cabs, that's better. I'll take one of you with me. We'll follow him."

The men did as they were told. Baudru, however, did not appear. Ganimard went into the waiting-room: there was no one there.

"What a fool I am!" he muttered. "I forgot the other door."

The office, as a matter of fact, is connected with the other office in the Rue Saint-Martin. Ganimard rushed through the communicating passage. He was just in time to catch sight of Baudru on the top of the omnibus from Batignolles to the Jardin des Plantes, which was turning the corner of the Rue de Rivoli. He ran after the omnibus and caught it up. But he had lost his two assistants, and was continuing the pursuit alone.

In his rage he felt like taking Baudru by the collar without further form or ceremony. Was it not by premeditation and thanks to an ingenious trick that the so-called idiot had separated him from his two auxiliaries? He looked at Baudru. The man was dozing where he sat, and his head shook from right to left. His mouth was half open, his face wore an incredible expression of stupidity. No, this was not an adversary capable of taking old Ganimard in; chance had favored him, that was all.

At the Carrefour des Galeries-Lafayette, Baudru changed from the omnibus to the La Muette tram-car. Ganimard followed his example. They went along the Boulevard Haussmann and the Avenue Victor-Hugo. Baudru alighted at the stopping-place at La Muette, and, with a lounging step, entered the Bois de Boulogne.

He passed from one alley to another, retraced his steps, and went on again. What was he looking for? Had he an object in view?

After an hour of these manœuvres he seemed tired and worn out. Catching sight of a bench, he sat down upon it. The spot was not far from Auteuil, on the brink of a little lake hidden among the trees, and was absolutely deserted. Half an hour elapsed. At last, losing patience, Ganimard resolved to enter into conversation.

He therefore went up and took a seat by Baudru's side. He lit a cigarette, drew a pattern in the sand with the end of his walking-stick, and said:

"A cold day."

Silence. And suddenly in this silence a peal of laughter rang out—a peal of glad and happy laughter, the laughter of a child seized with a fit of laughter, and utterly unable to keep from laughing, laughing, laughing. Ganimard felt his hair literally and positively stand on end on his head. That laugh, that infernal laugh, which he knew so well! . . .

With an abrupt movement he caught the man by the lapels of his jacket, and gave him a violent and penetrating look—looked at him even more closely than he had done at the criminal court; and, in truth, it was no longer the man he had seen. It *was* the man, but, at the same time, it was the other, the real man.

Aided by the wish which is father to the thought, he rediscovered the glowing light in the eyes, he filled in the sunken features, he saw the real flesh under the wizened skin, the real mouth through the grimace which deformed it. And it was the other's eyes, it was the other's mouth, it was—it was, above all—his keen, lively, mocking, witty expression, so bright and so young!

"Arsène Lupin! Arsène Lupin!" he stammered.

And in a sudden access of rage he caught him by the throat and tried to throw him down. Notwithstanding his fifty years, he was still a man of uncommon vigor, whereas his adversary seemed quite out of condition. And what a master-stroke it would be if he succeeded in bringing him back!

The struggle was short. Arsène Lupin hardly made a movement in defence and Ganimard let go as promptly as he had attacked. His right arm hung numbed and lifeless by his side.

"If they taught you *jiu-jitsu*[9] at the Quai des Orfèvres," said Lupin, "you would know that they call this movement *udi-shi-ghi* in Japanese." And he added, coldly: "Another second and I should have broken your arm, and you would have had no more than you deserve. What! You, an old friend, whom I esteem, before whom I reveal my *incognito* of my own accord, would you abuse my confidence? It's very wrong of you! . . . Hullo, what's the matter now?"

Ganimard was silent. This escape, for which he held himself responsible—was it not he who, by his sensational evidence, had diverted the ends of justice?—this escape seemed to him to mark the disgrace of his career. A tear trickled slowly down his cheek towards his gray mustache.

"Why, goodness me, Ganimard, don't take on like that! If you hadn't spoken I should have arranged for some one else to speak. Come, come, how could I have allowed them to find a verdict against Désiré Baudru?"

"So it was you that were there?" muttered Ganimard. "And it is you that are here?"

"Yes, I, I, no one but me."

"Is it possible?"

"Oh, one needn't be a wizard for that. It is enough, as that worthy judge said, to prepare one's self for a dozen years or so in order to be ready for every eventuality."

"But your face? Your eyes?"

"You can understand that when I worked for eighteen months at St. Louis' with Dr. Altier it was not for love of art. I felt that the man who would one day have the honor of calling himself Arsène Lupin ought to be exempt from the ordinary laws of personal appearance and identity. You can modify your appearance as you please. A hypodermic injection of paraffin puffs up your skin to just the extent desired. Pyrogallic acid turns you into a Cherokee Indian. Celandine juice adorns you with blotches and pimples of the most pleasing kind. A certain chemical process affects the growth of your hair and beard, another the sound of your voice. Add to that, two months of dieting in Cell 24, incessant practice, at opening my mouth with this particular grimace and carrying my head at this angle and my back at this stoop. Lastly, five drops of atrophine in the eyes to make them haggard and dilated, and the trick is done!"

"I can't see how the warders . . . ."

"The change was slow and progressive. They could never have noticed its daily evolution."

"But Désiré Baudru . . . ?"

"Baudru is a real person. He is a poor, harmless beggar whom I met last year, and whose features are really not quite unlike my own. Foreseeing an always possible arrest, I placed him in safe-keeping, and applied myself from the first to picking out the points of dissimilarity between us, so as to diminish these in myself as far as I could. My friends made him pass a night at the police-station in such a way that he left it at about the same time as I did and the coincidence could be easily established. For, observe, it was necessary that his passage should be traceable, else the lawyers would have wanted to know who I was; whereas, by offering them that excellent Baudru I made it inevitable—do you follow me?—inevitable that they should jump at him, in spite of the insurmountable difficulties of a substitution—prefer to believe in that substitution rather than admit their ignorance."

"Yes, yes, that's true," muttered Ganimard.

"And then," cried Arsène Lupin, "I held a formidable trump in my hand, a card which I had prepared from the start: the universal expectation of my escape! And there you see the clumsy mistake into which you and all of you fell in this exciting game which the law and I were playing, with my liberty for the stakes: you again thought that I was bragging, that I was intoxicated with my successes, like the veriest greenhorn! Fancy me, Arsène Lupin, guilty of such weakness! And, just as in the Cahorn case, you failed to say to yourselves: 'As soon as Arsène Lupin proclaims from the house-tops that he means to escape he must have some reason that obliges him to proclaim it.' But, hang it all, don't you see that, in order to escape . . . without escaping, it was essential that people should believe beforehand in my escape, that it should be an article of faith, an absolute conviction, a truth clear as daylight? And that is what it became, in accordance with my will. Arsène Lupin intended to escape, Arsène Lupin did not intend to be present at his trial. And when you stood up and said, 'That man is not Arsène Lupin,' it would have been beyond human nature for all those present not at once to believe that I was not Arsène Lupin. Had only one person expressed a doubt, had only one person uttered this simple reservation, 'But suppose it *is* Arsène Lupin?' . . . that very moment I should have been lost. They had only to bend over and look at me, not with the idea that I was not Arsène Lupin, as you and the rest did, but with the idea that I might be Arsène Lupin, and, in spite of all my precautions, I should have been recognized. But I was quite easy in my mind. It was logically and psychologically impossible for anybody to have that simple little idea."

He suddenly seized Ganimard's hand.

"Look here, Ganimard, confess that, a week after our interview at the Santé prison, you stayed in for me, at four o'clock, as I asked you to?"

"And your prison-van?" said Ganimard, evading the question.

"Bluff, mere bluff. My friends had faked up that old discarded van and substituted it for the other, and they wanted to try the experiment. But I knew that it was impracticable without the co-operation of exceptional circumstances. Only I thought it useful to complete this attempted escape and to give it the proper publicity. A first escape, boldly planned, gave to the second the full value of an escape realized in advance."

"So the cigar . . ."

"Was scooped out by myself; and the knife, too."

"And the notes?"

"Written by me."

"And the mysterious correspondent?"

"She and I were one. I can write any hand I please."

Ganimard thought for a moment, and said:

"How was it that, when they took Baudru's measurements in the anthropometrical room, these were not found to coincide with the record of Arsène Lupin?"

"Arsène Lupin's record does not exist."

"Nonsense!"

"Or, at least, it is not correct. This is a question to which I have devoted a good deal of study. The Bertillon system allows for, first, a visual description—and you have seen that this is not infallible—and, next, a description by measurements: measurements of the head, the fingers, the ears, and so on. There is nothing to be done against that."

"So? . . ."

"So I had to pay. Before my return from America one of the clerks of the staff accepted a definite bribe to enter one false

measurement at the start. This is enough to throw the whole
system out of gear, and to cause a record to stray into a compartment diametrically opposite to the compartment in which it
ought to go. The Baudru record could not, therefore, possibly
agree with the Arsène Lupin record."

There was another silence, and then Ganimard asked:

"And what are you going to do now?"

"Now!" exclaimed Lupin. "I am going to take a rest, feed myself up, and gradually become myself again. It's all very well to be
Baudru or another, to change your personality as you would your
boots, and to select your appearance, your voice, your expression, your handwriting. But there comes a time when you cease to
know yourself amid all these changes, and that is very sad. I feel
at present as the man must have felt who lost his shadow. I am
going to look for myself . . . and to find myself."

He walked up and down. The daylight was waning. He
stopped in front of Ganimard.

"We've said all that we had to say to each other, I suppose?"

"No," replied the inspector. "I should like to know if you intend to publish the truth about your escape . . . and the mistake
I made . . ."

"Oh, no one will ever know that it was Arsène Lupin that
was released. I have too great an interest to serve in heaping up
the most mysterious darkness around me, and I should not
dream of depriving my flight of its almost miraculous character. So have no fear, my dear friend; and good-bye. I am dining
out to-night, and have only just time to dress."

"I thought you were so anxious for a rest."

"Alas, there are social engagements from which it is impossible to escape. My rest must begin to-morrow."

"And where are you dining, may I ask?"

"At the British Embassy."

THE MYSTERIOUS
RAILWAY PASSENGER

I had sent my motor-car to Rouen by road on the previous day. I was to meet it by train, and go on to some friends, who have a house on the Seine.[1]

A few minutes before we left Paris my compartment was invaded by seven gentlemen, five of whom were smoking. Short though the journey by the fast train be, I did not relish the prospect of taking it in such company, the more so as the old-fashioned carriage had no corridor. I therefore collected my overcoat, my newspapers, and my railway guide, and sought refuge in one of the neighboring compartments.

It was occupied by a lady. At the sight of me, she made a movement of vexation which did not escape my notice, and leaned towards a gentleman standing on the foot-board—her husband, no doubt, who had come to see her off. The gentleman took stock of me, and the examination seemed to conclude to my advantage; for he whispered to his wife and smiled, giving her the look with which we reassure a frightened child. She smiled in her turn, and cast a friendly glance in my direction, as though she suddenly realized that I was one of those well-bred men with whom a woman can remain locked up for an hour or two in a little box six feet square without having anything to fear.

Her husband said to her:

"You must not mind, darling; but I have an important appointment, and I must not wait."

He kissed her affectionately, and went away. His wife blew him some discreet little kisses through the window, and waved her handkerchief.

Then the guard's whistle sounded, and the train started.

At that moment, and in spite of the warning shouts of the railway officials, the door opened, and a man burst into our carriage. My travelling companion, who was standing up and arranging her things in the rack, uttered a cry of terror, and dropped down upon the seat.

I am no coward—far from it; but I confess that these sudden incursions at the last minute are always annoying. They seem so ambiguous, so unnatural. There must be something behind them, else. . . .

The appearance of the new-comer, however, and his bearing were such as to correct the bad impression produced by the manner of his entrance. He was neatly, almost smartly, dressed; his tie was in good taste, his gloves clean; he had a powerful face. . . . But, speaking of his face, where on earth had I seen it before? For I had seen it: of that there was no possible doubt; or at least, to be accurate, I found within myself that sort of recollection which is left by the sight of an oft-seen portrait of which one has never beheld the original. And at the same time I felt the uselessness of any effort of memory that I might exert, so inconsistent and vague was that recollection.

But when my eyes reverted to the lady I sat astounded at the pallor and disorder of her features. She was staring at her neighbor—he was seated on the same side of the carriage—with an expression of genuine affright, and I saw one of her hands steal trembling towards a little travelling-bag that lay on the cushion a few inches from her lap. She ended by taking hold of it, and nervously drew it to her.

Our eyes met, and I read in hers so great an amount of uneasiness and anxiety that I could not help saying:

"I hope you are not unwell, madame. . . . Would you like me to open the window?"

She made no reply, but, with a timid gesture, called my attention to the individual beside her. I smiled as her husband had done, shrugged my shoulders, and explained to her by signs that she had nothing to fear, that I was there, and that, besides, the gentleman in question seemed quite harmless.

Just then he turned towards us, contemplated us, one after

the other, from head to foot, and then huddled himself into his corner, and made no further movement.

A silence ensued; but the lady, as though she had summoned up all her energies to perform an act of despair, said to me, in a hardly audible voice:

"You know he is in our train."

"Who?"

"Why, he . . . he himself . . . I assure you."

"Whom do you mean?"

"Arsène Lupin!"

She had not removed her eyes from the passenger, and it was at him rather than at me that she flung the syllables of that alarming name.

He pulled his hat down upon his nose. Was this to conceal his agitation, or was he merely preparing to go to sleep?

I objected.

"Arsène Lupin was sentenced yesterday, in his absence, to twenty years' penal servitude. It is not likely that he would commit the imprudence of showing himself in public to-day. Besides, the newspapers have discovered that he has been spending the winter in Turkey ever since his famous escape from the Santé."

"He is in this train," repeated the lady, with the ever more marked intention of being overheard by our companion. "My husband is a deputy prison-governor, and the station-inspector himself told us that they were looking for Arsène Lupin."

"That is no reason why . . ."

"He was seen at the booking-office. He took a ticket for Rouen."

"It would have been easy to lay hands upon him."

"He disappeared. The ticket-collector at the door of the waiting-room did not see him; but they thought that he must have gone round by the suburban platforms and stepped into the express that leaves ten minutes after us."

"In that case, they will have caught him there."

"And supposing that, at the last moment, he jumped out of that express and entered this, our own train . . . as he probably . . . as he most certainly did?"

"In that case they will catch him here; for the porters and the police cannot have failed to see him going from one train to the other, and, when we reach Rouen, they will net him finely."

"Him? Never! He will find some means of escaping again."

"In that case I wish him a good journey."

"But think of all that he may do in the mean time!"

"What?"

"How can I tell? One must be prepared for anything."

She was greatly agitated; and, in point of fact, the situation, to a certain degree, warranted her nervous state of excitement. Almost in spite of myself, I said:

"There are such things as curious coincidences, it is true. . . . But calm yourself. Admitting that Arsène Lupin is in one of these carriages, he is sure to keep quiet, and, rather than bring fresh trouble upon himself, he will have no other idea than that of avoiding the danger that threatens him."

My words failed to reassure her. However, she said no more, fearing, no doubt, lest I should think her troublesome.

As for myself, I opened my newspapers and read the reports of Arsène Lupin's trial. They contained nothing that was not already known, and they interested me but slightly. Moreover, I was tired, I had had a poor night, I felt my eyelids growing heavy, and my head began to nod.

"But surely, sir, you are not going to sleep?"

The lady snatched my paper from my hands, and looked at me with indignation.

"Certainly not," I replied. "I have no wish to."

"It would be most imprudent," she said.

"Most," I repeated.

And I struggled hard, fixing my eyes on the landscape, on the clouds that streaked the sky. And soon all this became confused in space, the image of the excited lady and the drowsy man was obliterated in my mind, and I was filled with the great, deep silence of sleep.

It was soon made agreeable by light and incoherent dreams, in which a being who played the part and bore the name of Arsène Lupin occupied a certain place. He turned and shifted on the horizon, his back laden with valuables, clambering over walls and stripping country-houses of their contents.

But the outline of this being, who had ceased to be Arsène Lupin, grew more distinct. He came towards me, grew bigger and bigger, leaped into the carriage with incredible agility, and fell full upon my chest.

A sharp pain . . . a piercing scream . . . I awoke. The man, my fellow-traveller, with one knee on my chest, was clutching my throat.

I saw this very dimly, for my eyes were shot with blood. I also saw the lady in a corner writhing in a violent fit of hysterics. I did not even attempt to resist. I should not have had the strength for it had I wished to: my temples were throbbing, I choked . . . my throat rattled. . . . Another minute . . . and I should have been suffocated.

The man must have felt this. He loosened his grip. Without leaving hold of me, with his right hand he stretched a rope, in which he had prepared a slipknot, and, with a quick turn, tied my wrists together. In a moment I was bound, gagged—rendered motionless and helpless.

And he performed this task in the most natural manner in the world, with an ease that revealed the knowledge of a master, of an expert in theft and crime. Not a word, not a fevered movement. Sheer coolness and audacity. And there lay I on the seat, roped up like a mummy—I, Arsène Lupin!

It was really ridiculous. And notwithstanding the seriousness of the circumstances I could not but appreciate and almost enjoy the irony of the situation. Arsène Lupin "done" like a novice, stripped like the first-comer! For of course the scoundrel relieved me of my pocket-book and purse! Arsène Lupin victimized in his turn—duped and beaten! What an adventure!

There remained the lady. He took no notice of her at all. He contented himself with picking up the wrist-bag that lay on the floor, and extracting the jewels, the purse, the gold and silver knicknacks which it contained. The lady opened her eyes, shuddered with fright, took off her rings and handed them to the man as though she wished to spare him any superfluous exertion. He took the rings, and looked at her: she fainted away.

Then, calm and silent as before, without troubling about us further, he resumed his seat, lit a cigarette, and abandoned

himself to a careful scrutiny of the treasures which he had cap-
tured, the inspection of which seemed to satisfy him completely.

I was much less satisfied. I am not speaking of the twelve thousand francs of which I had been unduly plundered: this was
a loss which I accepted only for the time; I had no doubt that
those twelve thousand francs would return to my possession
after a short interval, together with the exceedingly important
papers which my pocket-book contained: plans, estimates, spec-
ifications, addresses, lists of correspondents, letters of a compromising character. But, for the moment, a more immediate and
serious care was worrying me: what was to happen next?

As may be readily imagined, the excitement caused by my
passing through the Gare Saint-Lazare[2] had not escaped me.
As I was going to stay with friends who knew me by the name
of Guillaume Berlat, and to whom my resemblance to Arsène
Lupin was the occasion of many a friendly jest, I had not been
able to disguise myself after my wont, and my presence had
been discovered. Moreover, a man, doubtless Arsène Lupin,
had been seen to rush from the express into the fast train.
Hence it was inevitable and fated that the commissary of police
at Rouen, warned by telegram, would await the arrival of the
train, assisted by a respectable number of constables, question
any suspicious passengers, and proceed to make a minute inspection of the carriages.

All this I had foreseen, and had not felt greatly excited about
it; for I was certain that the Rouen police would display no
greater perspicacity than the Paris police, and that I should have
been able to pass unperceived: was it not sufficient for me, at
the wicket, carelessly to show my deputy's card, thanks to
which I had already inspired the ticket-collector at Saint-Lazare
with every confidence? But how things had changed since then!
I was no longer free. It was impossible to attempt one of my
usual moves. In one of the carriages the commissary would discover the Sieur Arsène Lupin, whom a propitious fate was sending to him bound hand and foot, gentle as a lamb, packed up
complete. He had only to accept delivery, just as you receive a
parcel addressed to you at a railway station, a hamper of game,
or a basket of vegetables and fruit.

And to avoid this annoying catastrophe, what could I do, entangled as I was in my bonds?

And the train was speeding towards Rouen, the next and the only stopping-place; it rushed through Vernon, through Saint-Pierre. . . .

I was puzzled also by another problem in which I was not so directly interested, but the solution of which aroused my professional curiosity: What were my fellow-traveller's intentions?

If I had been alone he would have had ample time to alight quite calmly at Rouen. But the lady? As soon as the carriage door was opened the lady, meek and quiet as she sat at present, would scream, and throw herself about, and cry for help!

Hence my astonishment. Why did he not reduce her to the same state of powerlessness as myself, which would have given him time to disappear before his twofold misdeed was discovered?

He was still smoking, his eyes fixed on the view outside, which a hesitating rain was beginning to streak with long, slanting lines. Once, however, he turned round, took up my railway guide, and consulted it.

As for the lady, she made every effort to continue fainting, so as to quiet her enemy. But a fit of coughing, produced by the smoke, gave the lie to her pretended swoon.

Myself, I was very uncomfortable, and had pains all over my body. And I thought . . . I planned . . .

Pont-de-l'Arche . . . Oissel. . . . The train was hurrying on, glad, drunk with speed. . . . Saint-Etienne. . . .

At that moment the man rose and took two steps towards us, to which the lady hastened to reply with a new scream and a genuine fainting fit.

But what could his object be? He lowered the window on our side. The rain was now falling in torrents, and he made a movement of annoyance at having neither umbrella nor overcoat. He looked up at the rack: the lady's *en-tout-cas*[3] was there; he took it. He also took my overcoat and put it on.

We were crossing the Seine. He turned up his trousers, and then, leaning out of the window, raised the outer latch.

Did he mean to fling himself on the permanent way? At the rate at which we were going it would have been certain death. We plunged into the tunnel pierced under the Côte Sainte-Catherine. The man opened the door, and, with one foot, felt for the step. What madness! The darkness, the smoke, the din—all combined to give a fantastic appearance to any such attempt. But suddenly the train slowed up, the Westinghouse brakes counteracted the movement of the wheels. In a minute the pace from fast became normal, and decreased still more. Without a doubt there was a gang at work repairing this part of the tunnel; this would necessitate a slower passage of the trains for some days perhaps, and the man knew it.

He had only, therefore, to put his other foot on the step, climb down to the foot-board, and walk away quietly, not without first closing the door, and throwing back the latch.

He had scarcely disappeared when the smoke showed whiter in the daylight. We emerged into a valley. One more tunnel, and we should be at Rouen.

The lady at once recovered her wits, and her first care was to bewail the loss of her jewels. I gave her a beseeching glance. She understood, and relieved me of the gag which was stifling me. She wanted also to unfasten my bonds, but I stopped her.

"No, no; the police must see everything as it was. I want them to be fully informed as regards that blackguard's actions."

"Shall I pull the alarm-signal?"

"Too late. You should have thought of that while he was attacking me."

"But he would have killed me! Ah, sir, didn't I tell you that he was travelling by this train? I knew him at once, by his portrait. And now he's taken my jewels!"

"They'll catch him, have no fear."

"Catch Arsène Lupin! Never."

"It all depends on you, madam. Listen. When we arrive be at the window, call out, make a noise. The police and porters will come up. Tell them what you have seen in a few words: the assault of which I was the victim, and the flight of Arsène Lupin. Give his description: a soft hat, an umbrella—yours—a gray frock-overcoat . . ."

"Yours," she said.

"Mine? No, his own. I didn't have one."

"I thought that he had none either when he got in."

"He must have had . . . unless it was a coat which some one left behind in the rack. In any case, he had it when he got out, and that is the essential thing. . . . A gray frock-overcoat, remember. . . . Oh, I was forgetting . . . tell them your name to start with. Your husband's functions will stimulate the zeal of all those men."

We were arriving. She was already leaning out of the window. I resumed, in a louder, almost imperious voice, so that my words should sink into her brain:

"Give my name also, Guillaume Berlat. If necessary, say you know me . . . That will save time . . . we must hurry on the preliminary inquiries . . . the important thing is to catch Arsène Lupin . . . with your jewels. . . . You quite understand, don't you? Guillaume Berlat, a friend of your husband's."

"Quite . . . Guillaume Berlat."

She was already calling out and gesticulating. Before the train had come to a standstill a gentleman climbed in, followed by a number of other men. The critical hour was at hand.

Breathlessly the lady exclaimed:

"Arsène Lupin . . . he attacked us . . . he has stolen my jewels. . . . I am Madame Renaud . . . my husband is a deputy prison-governor. . . . Ah, here's my brother, Georges Andelle, manager of the Crédit Rouennais. . . . What I want to say is . . ."

She kissed a young man who had just come up, and who exchanged greetings with the commissary. She continued, weeping:

"Yes, Arsène Lupin. . . . He flew at this gentleman's throat in his sleep. . . . Monsieur Berlat, a friend of my husband's."

"But where is Arsène Lupin?"

"He jumped out of the train in the tunnel, after we had crossed the Seine."

"Are you sure it was he?"

"Certain. I recognized him at once. Besides, he was seen at the Gare Saint-Lazare. He was wearing a soft hat . . ."

"No; a hard felt hat, like this," said the commissary, pointing to my hat.

"A soft hat, I assure you," repeated Madame Renaud, "and a gray frock-overcoat."

"Yes," muttered the commissary; "the telegram mentions a gray frock-overcoat with a black velvet collar."

"A black velvet collar, that's it!" exclaimed Madame Renaud, triumphantly.

I breathed again. What a good, excellent friend I had found in her!

Meanwhile the policemen had released me from my bonds. I bit my lips violently till the blood flowed. Bent in two, with my handkerchief to my mouth, as seems proper to a man who has long been sitting in a constrained position, and who bears on his face the blood-stained marks of the gag, I said to the commissary, in a feeble voice:

"Sir, it was Arsène Lupin, there is no doubt of it. . . . You can catch him if you hurry. . . . I think I may be of some use to you. . . ."

The coach, which was needed for the inspection by the police, was slipped. The remainder of the train went on towards Le Havre. We were taken to the station-master's office through a crowd of on-lookers who filled the platform.

Just then I felt a hesitation. I must make some excuse to absent myself, find my motor-car, and be off. It was dangerous to wait. If anything happened, if a telegram came from Paris, I was lost.

Yes; but what about my robber? Left to my own resources, in a district with which I was not very well acquainted, I could never hope to come up with him.

"Bah!" I said to myself. "Let us risk it, and stay. It's a difficult hand to win, but a very amusing one to play. And the stakes are worth the trouble."

And as we were being asked provisionally to repeat our depositions, I exclaimed:

"Mr. Commissary, Arsène Lupin is getting a start of us. My motor is waiting for me in the yard. If you will do me the pleasure to accept a seat in it, we will try . . ."

The commissary gave a knowing smile.

"It's not a bad idea . . . such a good idea, in fact, that it's already being carried out."

"Oh!"

"Yes; two of my officers started on bicycles . . . some time ago."

"But where to?"

"To the entrance to the tunnel. There they will pick up the clews and the evidence, and follow the track of Arsène Lupin."

I could not help shrugging my shoulders.

"Your two officers will pick up no clews and no evidence."

"Really!"

"Arsène Lupin will have arranged that no one should see him leave the tunnel. He will have taken the nearest road, and from there . . ."

"From there make for Rouen, where we shall catch him."

"He will not go to Rouen."

"In that case, he will remain in the neighborhood, where we shall be even more certain . . ."

"He will not remain in the neighborhood."

"Oh! Then where will he hide himself?"

I took out my watch.

"At this moment Arsène Lupin is hanging about the station at Darnétal. At ten-fifty—that is to say, in twenty-two minutes from now—he will take the train which leaves Rouen from the Gare du Nord for Amiens."

"Do you think so? And how do you know?"

"Oh, it's very simple. In the carriage Arsène Lupin consulted my railway guide. What for? To see if there was another line near the place where he disappeared, a station on that line, and a train which stopped at that station. I have just looked at the guide myself, and learned what I wanted to know."

"Upon my word, sir," said the commissary, "you possess marvellous powers of deduction. What an expert you must be!"

Dragged on by my certainty, I had blundered by displaying too much cleverness. He looked at me in astonishment, and I saw that a suspicion flickered through his mind. Only just, it is true; for the photographs despatched in every direction were so unlike, represented an Arsène Lupin so different from the one that stood before him, that he could not possibly recognize the original in me. Nevertheless, he was troubled, restless, perplexed.

There was a moment of silence. A certain ambiguity and

doubt seemed to interrupt our words. A shudder of anxiety passed through me. Was luck about to turn against me? Mastering myself, I began to laugh.

"Ah well, there's nothing to sharpen one's wits like the loss of a pocket-book and the desire to find it again. And it seems to me that, if you will give me two of your men, the three of us might, perhaps. . . ."

"Oh, please, Mr. Commissary," exclaimed Madame Renaud, "do what Monsieur Berlat suggests."

My kind friend's intervention turned the scale. Uttered by her, the wife of an influential person, the name of Berlat became mine in reality, and conferred upon me an identity which no suspicion could touch. The commissary rose.

"Believe me, Monsieur Berlat, I shall be only too pleased to see you succeed. I am as anxious as yourself to have Arsène Lupin arrested."

He accompanied me to my car. He introduced two of his men to me: Honoré Massol and Gaston Delivet. They took their seats. I placed myself at the wheel. My chauffeur started the engine. A few seconds later we had left the station. I was saved.

I confess that as we dashed in my powerful 35-h.p. Moreau-Lepton[4] along the boulevards that skirt the old Norman city I was not without a certain sense of pride. The engine hummed harmoniously. The trees sped behind us to right and left. And now, free and out of danger, I had nothing to do but to settle my own little private affairs with the co-operation of two worthy representatives of the law. Arsène Lupin was going in search of Arsène Lupin!

Ye humble mainstays of the social order of things, Gaston Delivet and Honoré Massol, how precious was your assistance to me! Where should I have been without you? But for you, at how many cross-roads should I have taken the wrong turning! But for you, Arsène Lupin would have gone astray and the other escaped!

But all was not over yet. Far from it. I had first to capture the fellow and next to take possession, myself, of the papers of which he had robbed me. At no cost must my two satellites be allowed to catch a sight of those documents, much less lay hands upon them. To make use of them and yet act independently of them was what I wanted to do; and it was no easy matter.

We reached Darnétal three minutes after the train had left. I had the consolation of learning that a man in a gray frock-overcoat with a black velvet collar had got into a second-class carriage with a ticket for Amiens. There was no doubt about it: my first appearance as a detective was a promising one.

Delivet said:

"The train is an express, and does not stop before Montérolier-Buchy, in nineteen minutes from now. If we are not there before Arsène Lupin, he can go on towards Amiens, branch off to Clères, and, from there, make for Dieppe or Paris."

"How far is Montérolier?"

"Fourteen miles and a half."

"Fourteen miles and a half in nineteen minutes . . . We shall be there before he is."

It was a stirring race. Never had my trusty Moreau-Lepton responded to my impatience with greater ardor and regularity. It seemed to me as though I communicated my wishes to her directly, without the intermediary of levers or handles. She shared my desires. She approved of my determination. She understood my animosity against that blackguard Arsène Lupin. The scoundrel! The sneak! Should I get the best of him? Or would he once more baffle authority, that authority of which I was the incarnation?

"Right!" cried Delivet. . . . "Left! . . . Straight ahead! . . ."

We skimmed the ground. The mile-stones looked like little timid animals that fled at our approach.

And suddenly at the turn of a road a cloud of smoke—the north express!

For half a mile it was a struggle side by side—an unequal struggle, of which the issue was certain—we beat the train by twenty lengths.

In three seconds we were on the platform in front of the second class. The doors were flung open. A few people stepped out. My thief was not among them. We examined the carriages. No Arsène Lupin.

"By Jove!" I exclaimed, "he must have recognized me in

the motor while we were going alongside of him, and jumped!"

The guard of the train confirmed my supposition. He had seen a man scrambling down the embankment at two hundred yards from the station.

"There he is! . . . Look! . . . At the level crossing!"

I darted in pursuit, followed by my two satellites, or, rather, by one of them; for the other, Massol, turned out to be an uncommonly fast sprinter, gifted with both speed and staying power. In a few seconds the distance between him and the fugitive was greatly diminished. The man saw him, jumped a hedge, and scampered off towards a slope, which he climbed. We saw him, farther still, entering a little wood.

When we reached the wood we found Massol waiting for us. He had thought it no use to go on, lest he should lose us.

"You were quite right, my dear fellow," I said. "After a run like this our friend must be exhausted. We've got him."

I examined the skirts of the wood while thinking how I could best proceed alone to arrest the fugitive, in order myself to effect certain recoveries which the law, no doubt, would only have allowed after a number of disagreeable inquiries. Then I returned to my companions.

"Look here, it's very easy. You, Massol, take up your position on the left. You, Delivet, on the right. From there you can watch the whole rear of the wood, and he can't leave it unseen by you except by this hollow, where I shall stand. If he does not come out, I'll go in and force him back towards one or the other of you. You have nothing to do, therefore, but wait. Oh, I was forgetting: in case of alarm, I'll fire a shot."

Massol and Delivet moved off, each to his own side. As soon as they were out of sight I made my way into the wood with infinite precautions, so as to be neither seen nor heard. It consisted of close thickets, contrived for the shooting, and intersected by very narrow paths, in which it was only possible to walk by stooping, as though in a leafy tunnel.

One of these ended in a glade, where the damp grass showed the marks of footsteps. I followed them, taking care to steal through the underwood. They led me to the bottom of a little mound, crowned by a tumble-down lath-and-plaster hovel.

"He must be there," I thought. "He has selected a good post of observation."

I crawled close up to the building. A slight sound warned me of his presence, and, in fact, I caught sight of him through an opening with his back turned towards me.

Two bounds brought me upon him. He tried to point the revolver which he held in his hand. I did not give him time, but pulled him to the ground in such a way that his two arms were twisted and caught under him, while I held him pinned down with my knee upon his chest.

"Listen to me, old chap," I whispered in his ear. "I am Arsène Lupin. You've got to give me back, this minute and without any fuss, my pocket-book and the lady's wrist-bag . . . in return for which I'll save you from the clutches of the police and enroll you among my friends. Which is it to be: yes or no?"

"Yes," he muttered.

"That's right. Your plan of this morning was cleverly thought out. We shall be good friends."

I got up. He fumbled in his pocket, fetched out a great knife, and tried to strike me with it.

"You ass!" I cried.

With one hand I parried the attack. With the other I caught him a violent blow on the carotid artery, the blow which is known as "the carotid hook." He fell back stunned.

In my pocket-book I found my papers and bank-notes. I took his own out of curiosity. On an envelope addressed to him I read his name: Pierre Onfrey.

I gave a start. Pierre Onfrey, the perpetrator of the murder in the Rue Lafontaine at Auteuil! Pierre Onfrey, the man who had cut the throats of Madame Delbois and her two daughters. I bent over him. Yes, that was the face which, in the railway-carriage, had aroused in me the memory of features which I had seen before.

But time was passing. I placed two hundred-franc notes in an envelope, with a visiting-card bearing these words:

"Arsène Lupin to his worthy assistants, Honoré Massol and Gaston Delivet, with his best thanks."

I laid this where it could be seen, in the middle of the room. Beside it I placed Madame Renaud's wrist-bag. Why should it not be restored to the kind friend who had rescued me? I confess, however, that I took from it everything that seemed in any way interesting, leaving only a tortoise-shell comb, a stick of lip-salve, and an empty purse. Business is business, when all is said and done! And, besides, her husband followed such a disreputable occupation! . . .

There remained the man. He was beginning to move. What was I to do? I was not qualified either to save or to condemn him.

I took away his weapons, and fired my revolver in the air.

"That will bring the two others," I thought. "He must find a way out of his own difficulties. Let fate take its course."

And I went down the hollow road at a run.

Twenty minutes later a cross-road which I had noticed during our pursuit brought me back to my car.

At four o'clock I telegraphed to my friends from Rouen that an unexpected incident compelled me to put off my visit. Between ourselves, I greatly fear that, in view of what they must now have learned, I shall be obliged to postpone it indefinitely. It will be a cruel disappointment for them!

At six o'clock I returned to Paris by L'Isle-Adam, Enghien, and the Porte Bineau.

I gathered from the evening papers that the police had at last succeeded in capturing Pierre Onfrey.

The next morning—why should we despise the advantages of intelligent advertisement?—the *Écho de France* contained the following sensational paragraph:

"Yesterday, near Buchy, after a number of incidents, Arsène Lupin effected the arrest of Pierre Onfrey. The Auteuil murderer had robbed a lady of the name of Renaud, the wife of the deputy prison-governor, in the train between Paris and Le Havre. Arsène Lupin has restored to Madame Renaud the wrist-bag which contained her jewels, and has generously rewarded the two detectives who assisted him in the matter of this dramatic arrest."

THE QUEEN'S NECKLACE

Two or three times a year, on the occasion of important functions, such as the balls at the Austrian Embassy or Lady Billingstone's receptions, the Comtesse de Dreux-Soubise would wear the Queen's Necklace.

This was really the famous necklace, the historic necklace, which Böhmer and Bassenge, the crown jewellers, had designed for the Du Barry, which the Cardinal de Rohan-Soubise believed himself to be presenting to Queen Marie-Antoinette, and which Jeanne de Valois, Comtesse de La Motte, the adventuress, took to pieces, one evening in February, 1785, with the assistance of her husband and their accomplice, Rétaux de Villette.

As a matter of fact, the setting alone was genuine. Rétaux de Villette had preserved it, while Sieur de La Motte and his wife dispersed to the four winds of heaven the stones so brutally unmounted, the admirable stones once so carefully chosen by Böhmer. Later, Rétaux sold it, in Italy, to Gaston de Dreux-Soubise, the cardinal's nephew and heir, who had been saved by his uncle at the time of the notorious bankruptcy of the Rohan-Guéménée family, and who, in grateful memory of this kindness, bought up the few diamonds that remained in the possession of Jeffreys, the English jeweller, completed them with others of much smaller value, but of identical dimensions, and thus succeeded in reconstructing the wonderful necklace in the form in which it had left Böhmer and Bassenge's hands.[1]

The Dreux-Soubises had plumed themselves upon the possession of this ornament for nearly a century. Although their fortune had been considerably diminished by various circumstances, they preferred to reduce their establishment rather than part with the precious royal relic. The reigning count in particular clung to it as a man clings to the home of his fathers. For prudence' sake, he hired a safe at the Crédit Lyonnais in which to keep it. He always fetched it there himself on the afternoon of any day on which his wife proposed to wear it; and he as regularly took it back the next morning.

That evening, at the Palais de Castille, then occupied by Isabella II. of Spain, the Countess had a great success, and King Christian of Denmark, in whose honor the reception was given, remarked upon her magnificent beauty. The gems streamed round her slender neck. The thousand facets of the diamonds shone and sparkled like flames in the light of the brilliantly illuminated rooms. None but she could have carried with such ease and dignity the burden of that marvellous jewel.

It was a twofold triumph which the Comte de Dreux enjoyed most thoroughly, and upon which he congratulated himself when they returned to their bedroom in the old house in the Faubourg Saint-Germain. He was proud of his wife, and quite as proud, perhaps, of the ornament which had shed its lustre upon his family for four generations. And the countess, too, derived from it a vanity which was a little childish, and yet quite in keeping with her haughty nature.

She took the necklace from her shoulders, not without regret, and handed it to her husband, who examined it with admiring eyes, as though he had never seen it before. Then, after replacing it in its red morocco case, stamped with the cardinal's arms, he went into an adjoining linen-closet, originally a sort of alcove, which had been cut off from the room, and which had only one entrance—a door at the foot of the bed. He hid it, according to his custom, among the bandboxes and stacks of linen on one of the upper shelves. He returned, closed the door behind him, and undressed himself.

In the morning he rose at nine o'clock, with the intention of going to the Crédit Lyonnais before lunch. He dressed, drank his coffee, and went down to the stables, where he gave his orders for the day. One of the horses seemed out of condition. He made the groom walk and trot it up and down before him in the yard. Then he went back to his wife.

She had not left the room, and was having her hair dressed by her maid. She said:

"Are you going out?"

"Yes, to take it back . . ."

"Oh, of course, yes, that will be safest . . ."

He entered the linen-closet. But in a few seconds he asked, without, however, displaying the least astonishment:

"Have you taken it out, dear?"

She replied:

"What do you mean? No, I've taken nothing."

"But you've moved it?"

"Not at all. . . . I haven't even opened the door."

He appeared in the doorway with a bewildered air, and stammered, in hardly intelligible accents:

"You haven't . . . you didn't . . . but then . . ."

She ran to join him, and they made a feverish search, throwing the bandboxes to the floor, and demolishing the stacks of linen. And the count kept on saying:

"It's useless. . . . All that we are doing is quite useless. . . . I put it up here, on this shelf."

"You may have forgotten."

"No, no; it was here, on this shelf, and nowhere else."

They lit a candle, for the light in the little room was bad, and removed all the linen and all the different things with which it was crowded. And when the closet was quite empty they were compelled to admit, in despair, that the famous necklace, the Queen's Necklace, was gone.

The countess, who was noted for her determined character, wasted no time in vain lamentations, but sent for the commissary of police, M. Valorbe, whose sagacity and insight they had already had occasion to appreciate. He was put in possession of the details, and his first question was:

"Are you sure, monsieur le comte, that no one can have passed through your room at night?"

"Quite sure. I am a very light sleeper, and, besides, the bedroom door was bolted. I had to unfasten it this morning when my wife rang for the maid."

"Is there no other inlet through which it is possible to enter the closet?"

"None."

"No window?"

"Yes, but it is blocked up."

"I should like to see it."

Candles were lit, and M. Valorbe at once remarked that the window was only blocked halfway by a chest, which, besides, did not absolutely touch the casements.

"It is close enough up to prevent its being moved without making a great deal of noise."

"What does the window look out on?"

"On a small inner yard."

"And you have another floor above this?"

"Two; but at the level of the servants' floor the yard is protected by a close-railed grating. That is what makes the light so bad."

Moreover, when they moved the chest they found that the window was latched, which would have been impossible if any one had entered from the outside.

"Unless," said the count, "he went out through our room."

"In which case you would not have found the door bolted in the morning."

The commissary reflected for a moment, and then, turning to the countess, asked:

"Did your people know, madame, that you were going to wear the necklace last night?"

"Certainly; I made no mystery about it. But nobody knew that we put it away in the linen-closet."

"Nobody?"

"No . . . unless . . ."

"I must beg you, madame, to be exact. It is a most important point."

She said to her husband:

"I was thinking of Henriette."

"Henriette? She knew no more about it than the others."

"Who is this lady?" asked M. Valorbe.

"One of my convent friends who quarrelled with her family, and married a sort of artisan. When her husband died I took her in here with her son, and furnished a couple of rooms for them in the house." And she added, with a certain confusion: "She does me a few little services. She is a very handy person."

"What floor does she live on?"

"On our own floor, not far off . . . at the end of the passage. . . . And, now that I think of it, her kitchen window . . ."

"Looks out on this yard?"

"Yes, it is just opposite."

A short silence followed upon this statement.

Then M. Valorbe asked to be taken to Henriette's rooms.

They found her busy sewing, while her son Raoul, a little fellow of six or seven, sat reading beside her. Somewhat surprised at the sight of the poor apartment which had been furnished for her, and which consisted in all of one room without a fireplace, and of a sort of recess or box-room that did duty for a kitchen, the commissary questioned her. She seemed upset at hearing of the robbery. The night before she had herself dressed the countess, and fastened the necklace round her throat.

"Good gracious!" she exclaimed, "who would ever have thought it?"

"And you have no idea, not the smallest inkling? You know it is possible that the thief may have passed through your room."

She laughed whole-heartedly, as though not imagining for a moment that the least suspicion could rest upon her.

"Why, I never left my room! I never go out, you know. And, besides, look!" She opened the window of the kitchen. "There, it's quite three yards to the ledge opposite."

"Who told you that we were considering the likelihood of a theft committed by this way?"

"Why, wasn't the necklace in the closet?"

"How do you know?"

"Goodness me, I always knew that they put it there at night! . . . They used to talk of it before me. . . ."

Her face, which was still young, but scored by care and sorrow,

showed great gentleness and resignation. Nevertheless, in the silence that ensued, it suddenly assumed an expression of anguish, as though a danger had threatened its owner. Henriette
drew her son to her. The child took her hand, and impressed a
tender kiss upon it.

"I presume," said M. de Dreux to the commissary, when they
were alone again—"I presume that you do not suspect her? I
will answer for her. She is honesty itself."

"Oh, I am quite of your opinion," declared M. Valorbe. "At
most, the thought of an unconscious complicity passed through
my mind. But I can see that we must abandon this explanation . . . it does not in the least help to solve the problem that
faces us."

The commissary did not arrive any further with the inquiry,
which was taken up by the examining magistrate, and completed in the course of the days that followed. He questioned the
servants, experimented on the way in which the window of the
linen-closet opened and shut, explored the little inner yard from
top to bottom. . . . It was all fruitless. The latch was untouched.
The window could not be opened or closed from the outside.

The inquiries were aimed more particularly at Henriette, for,
in spite of everything, the question always reverted in her direction. Her life was carefully investigated. It was ascertained
that in three years she had only four times left the house, and it
was possible to trace her movements on each of these occasions. As a matter of fact, she served Madame de Dreux in the
capacity of lady's maid and dressmaker, and her mistress treated
her with a strictness to which all the servants, in confidence,
bore witness.

"Besides," said the magistrate, who, by the end of the first
week, had come to the same conclusions as the commissary,
"admitting that we know the culprit—and we do not—we are
no wiser as to the manner in which the theft was committed. We
are hemmed in on either side by two obstacles—a locked window and a locked door. There are two mysteries: How could the
thief get in? and, more difficult still, How could he get out, and
leave a bolted door and a latched window behind him?"

After four months' investigation the magistrate's private impression was that M. and Mme. de Dreux, driven by their monetary needs, which were known to be considerable and pressing, had sold the Queen's Necklace. He filed the case, and dismissed it from his mind.

The theft of the priceless jewel struck the Dreux-Soubises a blow from which it took them long to recover. Now that their credit was no longer sustained by the sort of reserve-fund which the possession of that treasure constituted, they found themselves confronted with less reasonable creditors and less willing money-lenders. They were compelled to resort to energetic measures, to sell and mortgage their property; in short, it would have meant absolute ruin if two fat legacies from distant relatives had not come in the nick of time to save them.

They also suffered in their pride, as though they had lost one of the quarterings of their coat. And, strange to say, the countess wreaked her resentment upon her old school friend. She bore her a real grudge, and accused her openly. Henriette was first banished to the servants' floor, and afterwards given a day's notice to quit.

The life of M. and Mme. de Dreux passed without any event of note. They travelled a great deal.

One fact alone must be recorded as belonging to this period. A few months after Henriette's departure the countess received a letter from her that filled her with amazement:

"MADAME,—I do not know how to thank you. For it was you, was it not, who sent me that? It must have been you. No one else knows of my retreat in this little village. Forgive me if I am mistaken, and, in any case, accept the expression of my gratitude for your past kindnesses."

What did she mean? The countess' past and present kindnesses to Henriette amounted to a number of acts of injustice. What was the meaning of these thanks?

Henriette was called upon to explain, and replied that she had received by post, in an unregistered envelope, two notes of a thousand francs each. She enclosed the envelope in her letter.

It was stamped with the Paris post-mark, and bore only her address, written in an obviously disguised hand.

Where did that two thousand francs come from? Who had sent it? And why had it been sent? The police made inquiries. But what possible clew could they follow up in that darkness?

The same incident was repeated twelve months later; and a third time; and a fourth time; and every year for six years, with this difference: that in the fifth and sixth year the amount sent was doubled, which enabled Henriette, who had suddenly fallen ill, to provide for proper nursing. There was another difference: the postal authorities having seized one of the letters, on the pretext that it was not registered, the two last letters were handed in for registration—one at Saint-Germain, the other at Suresnes. The sender had signed his name first as Anquetry, next as Péchard. The addresses which he gave were false.

At the end of six years Henriette died. The riddle remained unsolved.

All these particulars are matters of public knowledge. The case was one of those which stir men's minds, and it was strange that this necklace, after setting all France by the ears at the end of the eighteenth century, should succeed in causing so much renewed excitement more than a hundred years later. But what I am now about to relate is known to none, except the principals interested and a few persons upon whom the count imposed absolute secrecy. As it is probable that they will break their promises sooner or later, I have no scruple in tearing aside the veil; and thus my readers will receive, together with the key to the riddle, the explanation of the paragraph that appeared in the newspapers two mornings ago—an extraordinary paragraph, which added, if possible, a fresh modicum of darkness and mystery to the obscurity in which this drama was already shrouded.

We must go five days back. Among M. de Dreux-Soubise's guests at lunch were his two nieces and a cousin; the men were the Président d'Essaville; M. Bachas, the deputy; the Cavaliere Floriani, whom the count had met in Sicily; and General the Marquis de Rouzières, an old club acquaintance.

After lunch the ladies served coffee in the drawing-room, and the gentlemen were given leave to smoke, on condition that they stayed where they were and talked. One of the girls amused them by telling their fortunes on the cards. The conversation afterwards turned on the subject of celebrated crimes. And thereupon M. de Rouzières, who never neglected an opportunity of teasing the count, brought up the affair of the necklace—a subject which M. de Dreux detested.

Every one proceeded to give his opinion. Every one summed up the evidence in his own way. And, of course, all the conclusions were contradictory, and all equally inadmissible.

"And what is your opinion, monsieur?" asked the countess of the Cavaliere Floriani.

"Oh, I have no opinion, madame."

There was a general outcry of protest, inasmuch as the chevalier had only just been most brilliantly describing a series of adventures in which he had taken part with his father, a magistrate at Palermo, and in which he had given evidence of his taste for these matters and of his sound judgment.

"I confess," he said, "that I have sometimes managed to succeed where the experts had abandoned all their attempts. But I am far from considering myself a Sherlock Holmes. . . . And, besides, I hardly know the facts. . . ."

All faces were turned to the master of the house, who was reluctantly compelled to recapitulate the details. The chevalier listened, reflected, put a few questions, and murmured:

"It's odd . . . at first sight the thing does not seem to me so difficult to guess at."

The count shrugged his shoulders. But the others flocked round the chevalier, who resumed, in a rather dogmatic tone:

"As a general rule, in order to discover the author of a theft or other crime, we have first to determine how this theft or crime has been committed, or at least how it might have been committed. In the present case nothing could be simpler, in my view, for we find ourselves face to face not with a number of different suppositions, but with one hard certainty, which is that the individual was able to enter only by the door of the bedroom or the window of the linen-closet. Now, a bolted door cannot be opened from the outside. Therefore, he must have entered by the window."

"It was closed, and it was found closed," said M. de Dreux, flatly.

Floriani took no notice of the interruption, and continued:

"In order to do so he had only to fix a bridge of some sort— say, a plank or a ladder—between the balcony outside the kitchen and the ledge of the window; and, as soon as the jewel-case . . ."

"But I tell you the window was closed!" cried the count, impatiently.

This time Floriani was obliged to reply. He did so with the greatest calmness, like a man who refuses to be put out by so insignificant an objection.

"I have no doubt that it was. But was there no hinged pane?"

"What makes you think so?"

"To begin with, it is almost a rule in the casement windows of that period. And, next, there must have been one, because otherwise the theft would be inexplicable."

"As a matter of fact, there was one, but it was closed, like the window. We did not even pay attention to it."

"That was a mistake; for if you had paid attention to it, you would obviously have seen that it had been opened."

"And how?"

"I presume that, like all of them, it opens by means of a twisted iron wire, furnished with a ring at its lower end?"

"Yes."

"And did this ring hang down between the casement and the chest?"

"Yes, but I do not understand . . ."

"It is like this. Through some cleft or cranny in the pane they must have contrived, with the aid of an instrument of some sort—say, an iron rod ending in a hook—to grip the ring, press down upon it, and open the pane."

The count sneered.

"That's perfect! Perfect! You settle it all so easily! Only you have forgotten one thing, my dear sir, which is that there was no cleft or cranny in the pane."

"Oh, but there was!"

"How can you say that? We should have seen it."

"To see a thing one must look, and you did not look. The cleft exists, it is materially impossible that it should not exist, down the side of the pane, along the putty . . . vertically, of course . . ."

The count rose. He seemed greatly excited, took two or three nervous strides across the room, and, going up to Floriani, said:

"Nothing has been changed up there since that day . . . no one has set foot in that closet."

"In that case, monsieur, it is open to you to assure yourself that my explanation is in accordance with reality."

"It is in accordance with none of the facts which the police ascertained. You have seen nothing, you know nothing, and you go counter to all that we have seen and to all that we know."

Floriani did not seem to remark the count's irritation, and said, with a smile:

"Well, monsieur, I am trying to see plainly, that is all. If I am wrong you have only to prove me so. . . ."

"So I will, this very minute. . . . I confess that, in the long run, your assurance . . ."

M. de Dreux mumbled a few words more, and then suddenly turned to the door and went out.

No one spoke a word. All waited anxiously, as though convinced that a particle of the truth was about to appear. And the silence was marked by an extreme gravity.

At last the count was seen standing in the doorway. He was pale, and singularly agitated. He addressed his friends in a voice trembling with emotion:

"I beg your pardon. . . . Monsieur Floriani's revelations have taken me so greatly by surprise. . . . I should never have thought . . ."

His wife asked him, eagerly:

"What is it? . . . Tell us! . . . Speak! . . ."

He stammered out:

"The cleft is there . . . at the very place mentioned . . . down the side of the pane . . ."

Abruptly seizing the chevalier's arm, he said, in an imperious tone:

"And now, monsieur, continue. . . . I admit that you have been right so far, but now . . . That is not all. . . . Tell me . . . what happened, according to you?"

Floriani gently released his arm, and, after a moment's interval, said:

"Well, according to me, this is what happened: The individual, whoever he was, knowing that Madame de Dreux was going to wear the necklace at the reception, put his foot-bridge in position during your absence. He watched you through the window, and saw you hide the diamonds. As soon as you were gone he passed some implement down the pane and pulled the ring."

"Very well; but the distance was too great to allow of his reaching the latch of the window through the hinged pane."

"If he was unable to open the window he must have got in through the hinged pane itself."

"Impossible; there is not a man so slight in figure as to obtain admission that way."

"Then it was not a man."

"What do you mean?"

"What I say. If the passage was too narrow to admit a man, then it must have been a child."

"A child?"

"Did you not tell me that your friend had a son?"

"I did; a son called Raoul."

"It is extremely likely that Raoul committed the theft."

"What evidence have you?"

"What evidence? . . . There is no lack of evidence. . . . For instance . . ." He was silent, and reflected for a few seconds. Then he continued: "For instance, it is incredible that the child could have brought a foot-bridge from the outside and taken it away again unperceived. He must have employed what lay ready to hand. In the little room where Henriette did her cooking, were there not some shelves against the wall on which she kept her pots and pans?"

"There were two shelves, as far as I remember."

"We must find out if these shelves were really fixed to the wooden brackets that supported them. If so, we are entitled to believe that the child unscrewed them and then fastened them to-gether. Perhaps, also, if there was a range, we shall discover a stove-hook or plate-lifter which he would have employed to open the hinged pane."

The count went out without a word, and this time the others did not even feel that little touch of anxiety attendant upon the unknown which they had experienced on the first occasion. They knew, they knew absolutely, that Floriani's views were correct. There emanated from that man an impression of such strict certainty that they listened to him not as though he were deducting facts one from the other, but as though he were de-scribing events the accuracy of which it was easy to verify as he proceeded. And no one felt surprised when the count returned and said:

"Yes, it's the child . . . there's no doubt about it . . . every-thing proves it . . ."

"Did you see the shelves . . . the plate-lifter?"

But Madame de Dreux-Soubise exclaimed:

"The child! . . . You mean his mother. Henriette is the only guilty person. She must have compelled her son to . . ."

"No," said the chevalier, "the mother had nothing to do with it."

"Come, come! They lived in the same room; the child cannot have acted unknown to Henriette."

"They occupied the same room; but everything happened in the adjoining recess, at night, while the mother was asleep."

"And what about the necklace?" said the count. "It would have been found among the child's things."

"I beg your pardon. *He* used to go out. The very morning when you found him with his book he had come back from school, and perhaps the police, instead of exhausting their resources against the innocent mother, would have been better advised to make a search there, in his desk, among his lesson-books."

"Very well. But the two thousand francs which Henriette re-ceived every year: is not that the best sign of her complicity?"

"Would she have written to thank you for the money if she had been an accomplice? Besides, was she not kept under su-pervision? Whereas the child was free, and had every facility for going to the nearest town, seeing a dealer, and selling him a diamond cheaply, or two diamonds, as the case demanded . . . the only condition being that the money should be sent from Paris, in consideration of which the transaction would be repeated next year."

The Dreux-Soubises and their guests were oppressed by an undefinable sense of uneasiness. There was really in Floriani's tone and attitude something more than that certainty which had so greatly irritated the count from the beginning. There was something resembling irony—an irony, moreover, that seemed hostile rather than sympathetic and friendly, as it ought to have been. The count affected to laugh.

"All this is delightfully ingenious. Accept my compliments. What a brilliant imagination you possess!"

"No, no, no!" cried Floriani, with more seriousness. "I am not imagining anything; I am recalling circumstances which were inevitably such as I have described them to you."

"What do you know of them?"

"What you yourself have told me. I picture the life of the mother and the child down there in the country: the mother falling ill, the tricks and inventions of the little fellow to sell the stones and save his mother, or at least to ease her last moments. Her illness carries her off. She dies. Years pass. The child grows up, becomes a man. And then—this time, I am willing to admit that I am giving scope to my imagination—suppose that this man should feel a longing to return to the places where his childhood was spent, that he sees them once again, that he finds the people who have suspected and accused his mother: think of the poignant interest of such an interview in the old house under whose roof the different stages of the drama were enacted!"

His words echoed for a moment or two in the restless silence, and the faces of M. and Mme. de Dreux revealed a desperate endeavor to understand, combined with an agonizing dread of understanding. The count asked, between his teeth:

"Tell me, sir! Who are you?"

"I? Why, the Cavaliere Floriani, whom you met at Palermo, and whom you have had the kindness to invite to your house time after time."

"Then what is the meaning of this story?"

"Oh, nothing at all! It is a mere joke on my part. I am trying to picture to myself the delight which Henriette's son, if he were still alive, would take in telling you that he is the only culprit, and that he became so because his mother was on the point of losing her place as a . . . as a domestic servant, which was her only means of livelihood, and because the child suffered at the sight of his mother's unhappiness."

He had half risen from his seat, and, bending towards the countess, was expressing himself in terms of suppressed emotion. There was no doubt possible. The Cavaliere Floriani was none other than Henriette's son. Everything in his attitude, in his words, proclaimed the fact. Besides, was it not his evident intention, his wish, to be recognized as such?

The count hesitated. What line of conduct was he to adopt towards this daring individual? To ring the bell? Provoke a scandal? Unmask the villain who had robbed him? But it was so long ago! And who would believe this story of a guilty child? No, it was better to accept the position and pretend not to grasp its real meaning. And the count, going up to Floriani, said, playfully:

"Your little romance is very interesting and very entertaining. It has quite taken hold of me, I assure you. But, according to you, what became of that exemplary young man, that model son? I trust that he did not stop on his prosperous road to fortune."

"Certainly not!"

"Why, of course not! After so fine a start, too! At the age of six to capture the Queen's Necklace, the celebrated necklace coveted by Marie-Antoinette!"

"And to capture it, mind you," said Floriani, entering into the count's mood, "to capture it without its costing him the smallest unpleasantness, the police never taking it into their heads to examine the condition of the panes, or noticing that the window-ledge was too clean after he had wiped it so as to obliterate the traces of his feet on the thick dust. . . . You must admit that this was enough to turn the head of a scapegrace of his years. It was all too easy. He had only to wish and to put out his hand. . . . Well, he wished . . ."

"And put out his hand?"

"Both hands!" replied the chevalier, with a smile.

A shudder passed through his hearers. What mystery concealed the life of this self-styled Floriani? How extraordinary must be the existence of this adventurer, a gifted thief at the age of six, who to-day, with the refined taste of a dilettante in search of an emotion, or, at most, to satisfy a sense of revenge, had come to brave his victim in that victim's own house, audaciously, madly, and yet with all the good-breeding of a man of the world on a visit!

He rose, and went up to the countess to take his leave. She suppressed a movement of recoil. He smiled.

"Ah, madame, you are frightened! Have I carried my little comedy of drawing-room magic too far?"

"Not at all, monsieur. On the contrary, the legend of that good son has interested me greatly, and I am happy to think that my necklace should have been the occasion of so brilliant a career. But does it not seem to you that the son of that . . . of that woman, of Henriette, was, above all things, obeying his natural vocation?"

He started, felt the point of her remark, and replied:

"I am sure he was; and, in fact, his vocation must have been quite serious, or the child would have been discouraged."

"Why?"

"Well, you know, most of the stones were false. The only real ones were the few diamonds bought of the English jeweller. The others had been sold, one by one, in obedience to the stern necessities of life."

"It was the Queen's Necklace, monsieur, for all that," said the countess, haughtily, "and that, it seems to me, is what Henriette's son was unable to understand."

"He must have understood, madame, that, false or genuine, the necklace was, before all, a show thing, a sign-board."

M. de Dreux made a movement. His wife stopped him at once.

"Monsieur," she said, "if the man to whom you allude has the least vestige of shame . . ."

She hesitated, shrinking before Floriani's calm gaze. He repeated after her:

"If he has the least feeling of shame . . ."

She felt that she would gain nothing by speaking to him in this way; and, despite her anger and indignation, quivering with humiliated pride, she said, almost politely:

"Monsieur, tradition says that Rétaux de Villette, when the Queen's Necklace was in his hands, forced out all the diamonds with Jeanne de Valois, but he dared not touch the setting. He understood that the diamonds were but the ornaments, the accessories, whereas the setting was the essential work, the creation of the artist; and he respected it. Do you think that this man understood as much?"

"I have no doubt but that the setting exists. The child respected it."

"Well, monsieur, if ever you happen to meet him, tell him that he is acting unjustly in keeping one of those relics which are the property and the glory of certain families, and that though he may have removed the stones, the Queen's Necklace continues to belong to the house of Dreux-Soubise. It is ours as much as our name or our honor."

The chevalier replied, simply:

"I will tell him so, madame."

He bowed low before her, bowed to the count, bowed to all the visitors, one after the other, and went out.

Four days later Madame de Dreux found a red morocco case, stamped with the arms of the Cardinal de Rohan, on her bedroom table. She opened it. It contained the necklace of Marie-Antoinette.

But as in the life of any logical and single-minded man all things must needs concur towards the same object—and a little advertisement never does any harm—the *Écho de France* of the next day contained the following sensational paragraph:

"The Queen's Necklace, the famous historic jewel stolen many years since from the Dreux-Soubise family, has been recovered by Arsène Lupin. Arsène Lupin has hastened to restore it to its lawful owners. This delicate and chivalrous attention is sure to meet with universal commendation."[2]

SHERLOCK HOLMES
ARRIVES TOO LATE

"It's really curious, your likeness to Arsène Lupin, my dear Velmont."

"Do you know him?"

"Oh, just as everybody does—by his photographs, not one of which in the least resembles the others; but they all leave the impression of the same face . . . which is undoubtedly yours."

Horace Velmont seemed rather annoyed.

"I suppose you're right, Devanne. You're not the first to tell me of it, I assure you."

"Upon my word," persisted Devanne, "if you had not been introduced to me by my cousin d'Estavan, and if you were not the well-known painter whose charming sea-pieces I admire so much, I'm not sure but that I should have informed the police of your presence at Dieppe."

The sally was received with general laughter. There were gathered, in the great dining-room of Thibermesnil Castle, in addition to Velmont, the Abbé Gélis, rector of the village, and a dozen officers whose regiments were taking part in the manœuvres in the neighborhood, and who had accepted the invitation of Georges Devanne, the banker, and his mother. One of them exclaimed:

"But, I say, wasn't Arsène Lupin seen on the coast after his famous performance in the train between Paris and Le Havre?"

"Just so, three months ago; and the week after that I made the acquaintance, at the Casino, of our friend Velmont here, who has since honored me with a few visits: an agreeable preliminary to a more serious call which I presume he means to pay me one of these days . . . or, rather, one of these nights!"

The company laughed once more, and moved into the old guard-room—a huge, lofty hall which occupies the whole of the lower portion of the Tour Guillaume, and in which Georges Devanne has arranged all the incomparable treasures accumulated through the centuries by the lords of Thibermesnil. It is filled and adorned with old chests and credence-tables, fire-dogs and candelabra. Splendid tapestries hang on the stone-walls. The deep embrasures of the four windows are furnished with seats and end in pointed casements with leaded panes. Between the door and the window on the left stands a monumental Renaissance book-case, on the pediment of which is inscribed, in gold letters, the word "THIBERMESNIL" and underneath it the proud motto of the family: *"Fais ce que veulx."*[1]

And as they were lighting their cigars, Devanne added:

"But you will have to hurry, Velmont, for this is the last night on which you will have a chance."

"And why the last night?" said the painter, who certainly took the jest in very good part.

Devanne was about to reply when his mother made signs to him. But the excitement of the dinner and the wish to interest his guests were too much for him:

"Pooh!" he muttered. "Why shouldn't I tell them? There's no indiscretion to be feared now."

They sat round him, filled with a lively curiosity, and he declared, with the self-satisfied air of a man announcing a great piece of news:

"To-morrow, at four o'clock in the afternoon, I shall have here, as my guest, Sherlock Holmes, the great English detective, for whom no mystery exists, the most extraordinary solver of riddles that has ever been known, the wonderful individual who might have been the creation of a novelist's brain."

There was a general exclamation. Sherlock Holmes at Thibermesnil! The thing was serious, then? Was Arsène Lupin really in the district?

"Arsène Lupin and his gang are not very far away. Without counting Baron Cahorn's mishap, to whom are we to ascribe the daring burglaries at Montigny and Gruchet and Crasville if not to our national thief? To-day it's my turn."

"And have you had a warning, like Baron Cahorn?"

"The same trick does not succeed twice."

"Then? . . ."

"Look here."

He rose, and, pointing to a little empty space between two tall folios on one of the shelves of the bookcase, said:

"There was a book here—a sixteenth-century book, entitled *The Chronicles of Thibermesnil*—which was the history of the castle since the time of its construction by Duke Rollo, on the site of a feudal fortress. It contained three engraved plates. One of them presented a general view of the domain as a whole; the second a plan of the building; and the third—I call your special attention to this—the sketch of an underground passage, one of whose outlets opens outside the first line of the ramparts, while the other ends here—yes, in this very hall where we are sitting. Now this book disappeared last month."

"By Jove!" said Velmont, "that's a bad sign. Only it's not enough to justify the intervention of Sherlock Holmes."

"Certainly it would not have been enough if another fact had not come to give its full significance to that which I have just told you. There was a second copy of the chronicle in the Bibliothèque Nationale, and the two copies differed in certain details concerning the underground passage, such as the addition of a sectional drawing, and a scale and a number of notes, not printed, but written in ink and more or less obliterated. I knew of these particulars, and I knew that the definite sketch could not be reconstructed except by carefully collating the two plans. Well, on the day after that on which my copy disappeared the one in the Bibliothèque Nationale was applied for by a reader who carried it off without leaving any clew as to the manner in which the theft had been effected."

These words were greeted with many exclamations.

"This time the affair grows serious."

"Yes; and this time," said Devanne, "the police were roused, and there was a double inquiry which, however, led to no result."

"Like all those aimed at Arsène Lupin."

"Exactly. It then occurred to me to write and ask for the help of Sherlock Holmes, who replied that he had the keenest wish to come into contact with Arsène Lupin."

"What an honor for Arsène Lupin!" said Velmont. "But if our national thief, as you call him, should not be contemplating a project upon Thibermesnil, then there will be nothing for Sherlock Holmes to do but twiddle his thumbs."

"There is another matter which is sure to interest him: the discovery of the underground passage."

"Why, you told us that one end opened in the fields and the other here, in the guard-room!"

"Yes, but in what part of it? The line that represents the tunnel on the plans finishes, at one end, at a little circle accompanied by the initials T. G., which, of course, stand for Tour Guillaume. But it's a round tower, and who can decide at which point in the circle the line in the drawing touches?"

Devanne lit a second cigar, and poured himself out a glass of Benedictine.[2] The others pressed him with questions. He smiled with pleasure at the interest which he had aroused. At last, he said:

"The secret is lost. Not a person in the world knows it. The story says that the high and mighty lords handed it down to one another, on their death-beds, from father to son, until the day when Geoffrey, the last of the name, lost his head on the scaffold, on the seventh of Thermidor, Year Second, in the nineteenth year of his age."

"Yes, but more than a century has passed since then; and it must have been looked for."

"It has been looked for, but in vain. I myself, after I bought the castle from the great-grand-nephew of Leribourg of the National Convention, had excavations made. What was the good? Remember that this tower is surrounded by water on every side, and only joined to the castle by a bridge, and that, consequently, the tunnel must pass under the old moats. The plan in the Bibliothèque Nationale shows a series of four staircases, comprising forty-eight steps, which allows for a depth of over ten yards, and the scale annexed to the other plan fixes the length at two hundred yards. As a matter of fact, the whole problem lies here, between this floor, that ceiling, and these walls; and, upon my word, I do not feel inclined to have them pulled down."

"And is there no clew?"

"Not one."

The Abbé Gélis objected.

"Monsieur Devanne, we have to reckon with two quotations . . ."

"Oh," cried Devanne, laughing, "the rector is a great rummager of family papers, a great reader of memoirs, and he fondly loves everything that has to do with Thibermesnil. But the explanation to which he refers only serves to confuse matters."

"But tell us what it is."

"Do you really care to hear?"

"Immensely."

"Well, you must know that, as the result of his reading, he has discovered that two kings of France held the key to the riddle."

"Two kings of France?"

"Henry IV. and Louis XVI."

"Two famous men. And how did the rector find out?"

"Oh, it's very simple," continued Devanne. "Two days before the battle of Arques, King Henry IV. came to sup and sleep in the castle, and on this occasion Duke Edgar confided the family secret to him. This secret Henry IV. revealed later to Sully, his minister, who tells the story in his *Royales Œconomies d'État*, without adding any comment besides this incomprehensible phrase: '*La hache tournoie dans l'air qui frémit, mais l'aile s'ouvre et l'on va jusqu' à Dieu.*' "[3]

A silence followed, and Velmont sneered:

"It's not as clear as daylight, is it?"

"That's what I say. The rector maintains that Sully set down the key to the puzzle by means of those words, without betraying the secret to the scribes to whom he dictated his memoirs."

"It's an ingenious supposition."

"True. But what is the axe that turns? What bird is it whose wing opens?"

"And who goes to God?"

"Goodness knows!"

"And what about our good King Louis XVI.?" asked Velmont.

"Louis XVI. stayed at Thibermesnil in 1784, and the famous Iron Cupboard discovered at the Louvre on the information of Gamain, the locksmith, contained a paper with these words written in the king's hand: 'Thibermesnil, 2-6-12.'"

Horace Velmont laughed aloud.

"Victory! The darkness is dispelled. Twice six are twelve!"

"Laugh as you please, sir," said the rector. "Those two quotations contain the solution for all that, and one of these days some one will come along who knows how to interpret them."

"Sherlock Holmes, first of all," said Devanne, "unless Arsène Lupin forestalls him. What do you think, Velmont?"

Velmont rose, laid his hand on Devanne's shoulder, and declared:

"I think that the data supplied by your book and the copy in the Bibliothèque Nationale lacked just one link of the highest importance, and that you have been kind enough to supply it. I am much obliged to you."

"Well? . . ."

"Well, now that the axe has turned and the bird flown, and that twice six are twelve, all I have to do is to set to work."

"Without losing a minute?"

"Without losing a second! You see, I must rob your castle to-night, that is to say, before Sherlock Holmes arrives."

"You're quite right; you have only just got time. Would you like me to drive you?"

"To Dieppe?"

"Yes, I may as well fetch Monsieur and Madame d'Androl and a girl friend of theirs, who are arriving by the midnight train."

Then, turning to the officers:

"We shall all meet here at lunch to-morrow, sha'n't we, gentlemen? I rely upon you, for the castle is to be invested by your regiments and taken by assault at eleven in the morning."

The invitation was accepted, the officers took their leave, and a minute later a powerful motor-car was carrying Devanne and Velmont along the Dieppe road. Devanne dropped the painter at the Casino, and went on to the station.

His friends arrived at midnight, and at half-past twelve the motor passed through the gates of Thibermesnil. At one o'clock, after a light supper served in the drawing-room, every one went to bed. The lights were extinguished one by one. The deep silence of the night enshrouded the castle.

But the moon pierced the clouds that veiled it, and, through two of the windows, filled the hall with the light of its white beams. This lasted for but a moment. Soon the moon was hidden behind the curtain of the hills, and all was darkness. The silence increased as the shadows thickened. At most it was disturbed, from time to time, by the creaking of the furniture or the rustling of the reeds in the pond which bathes the old walls with its green waters.

The clock told the endless beads of its seconds. It struck two. Then once more the seconds fell hastily and monotonously in the heavy stillness of the night. Then three struck.

And suddenly something gave a clash, like the arm of a railway-signal that drops as a train passes, and a thin streak of light crossed the hall from one end to the other, like an arrow, leaving a glittering track behind it. It issued from the central groove of a pilaster against which the pediment of the bookcase rests upon the right. It first lingered upon the opposite panel in a dazzling circle, next wandered on every side like a restless glance searching the darkness, and then faded away, only to appear once more, while the whole of one section of the bookcase turned upon its axis, and revealed a wide opening shaped like a vault.

A man entered, holding an electric lantern in his hand. Another man and a third emerged, carrying a coil of rope and different implements. The first man looked round the room, listened, and said:

"Call the pals."

Eight of these pals came out of the underground passage—eight strapping fellows, with determined faces. And the removal began.

It did not take long. Arsène Lupin passed from one piece of furniture to another, examined it, and, according to its size or its artistic value, spared it or gave an order:

"Take it away."

And the piece in question was removed, swallowed by the yawning mouth of the tunnel, and sent down into the bowels of the earth.

And thus were juggled away six Louis XV. armchairs and as many occasional chairs, a number of Aubusson tapestries, some candelabra signed by Gouthière, two Fragonards and a Nattier, a bust by Houdon, and some statuettes. At times Arsène Lupin would stop before a magnificent oak chest or a splendid picture and sigh:

"That's too heavy . . . Too big . . . What a pity!"

And he would continue his expert survey.

In forty minutes the hall was "cleared," to use Arsène's expression. And all this was accomplished in an admirably orderly manner, without the least noise, as though all the objects which the men were handling had been wrapped in thick wadding.

To the last man who was leaving, carrying a clock signed by Boule, he said:

"You need not come back. You understand, don't you, that as soon as the motor-van is loaded you're to make for the barn at Roquefort?"

"What about yourself, governor?"

"Leave me the motor-cycle."

When the man had gone he pushed the movable section of the bookcase back into its place, and, after clearing away the traces of the removal and the footmarks, he raised a curtain and entered a gallery which served as a communication between the tower and the castle. Half-way down the gallery stood a glass case, and it was because of this case that Arsène Lupin had continued his investigations.

It contained marvels: an unique collection of watches, snuff-boxes, rings, chatelaines, miniatures of the most exquisite workmanship. He forced the lock with a jimmy, and it was an unspeakable pleasure to him to finger those gems of gold and silver, those precious and dainty little works of art.

Hanging round his neck was a large canvas bag specially contrived to hold these windfalls. He filled it. He also filled the pockets of his jacket, waistcoat, and trousers. And he was stuffing under his left arm a heap of those pearl reticules beloved of our ancestors and so eagerly sought after by our present fashion . . . when a slight sound fell upon his ear.

He listened; he was not mistaken; the noise became clearer.

And suddenly he remembered. At the end of the gallery an inner staircase led to a room which had been hitherto unoccupied, but which had been allotted that evening to the young girl whom Devanne had gone to meet at Dieppe with his friends the d'Androls.

With a quick movement he pressed the spring of his lantern and extinguished it. He had just time to hide in the recess of a window when the door at the top of the staircase opened and the gallery was lit by a faint gleam.

He had a feeling—for, half-hidden behind a curtain, he could not see—that a figure was cautiously descending the top stairs. He hoped that it would come no farther. It continued, however, and took several steps into the gallery. But it gave a cry. It must have caught sight of the broken case, three-quarters emptied of its contents.

By the scent he recognized the presence of a woman. Her dress almost touched the curtain that concealed him, and he seemed to hear her heart beating, while she must needs herself perceive the presence of another person behind her in the dark, within reach of her hand. He said to himself:

"She's frightened . . . she'll go back . . . she is bound to go back."

She did not go back. The candle shaking in her hand became steadier. She turned round, hesitated for a moment, appeared to be listening to the alarming silence, and then, with a sudden movement, pulled back the curtain.

Their eyes met.

Arsène murmured, in confusion:

"You . . . you . . . Miss Underdown!"

It was Nellie Underdown, the passenger on the *Provence,* the girl who had mingled her dreams with his during that never-to-be-forgotten crossing, who had witnessed his arrest, and who, rather than betray him, had generously flung into the sea the kodak in which he had hidden the stolen jewels and banknotes! . . . It was Nellie Underdown, the dear, sweet girl whose image had so often saddened or gladdened his long hours spent in prison!

So extraordinary was their chance meeting in this castle and at that hour of the night that they did not stir, did not utter a word, dumfounded and, as it were, hypnotized by the fantastic apparition which each of them presented to the other's eyes.

Nellie, shattered with emotion, staggered to a seat.

He remained standing in front of her. And gradually, as the interminable seconds passed, he became aware of the impression which he must be making at that moment, with his arms loaded with curiosities, his pockets stuffed, his bag filled to bursting. A great sense of confusion mastered him, and he blushed to find himself there in the mean plight of a robber caught in the act. To her henceforth, come what might, he was the thief, the man who puts his hand into other men's pockets, the man who picks locks and enters doors by stealth.

One of the watches rolled upon the carpet, followed by another. And more things came slipping from under his arms, which were unable to retain them. Then, quickly making up his mind, he dropped a part of his booty into a chair, emptied his pockets, and took off his bag.

He now felt easier in Nellie's presence, and took a step towards her, with the intention of speaking to her. But she made a movement of recoil and rose quickly, as though seized with fright, and ran to the guard-room. The curtain fell behind her. He followed her. She stood there, trembling and speechless, and her eyes gazed in terror upon the great devastated hall.

Without a moment's hesitation, he said:

"At three o'clock to-morrow everything shall be restored to its place. . . . The things shall be brought back."

She did not reply; and he repeated:

"At three o'clock to-morrow, I give you my solemn pledge. . . . No power on earth shall prevent me from keeping my promise. . . . At three o'clock to-morrow."

A long silence weighed upon them both. He dared not break it, and the girl's emotion made him suffer in every nerve. Softly, without a word, he moved away.

And he thought to himself:

"She must go! . . . She must feel that she is free to go! . . . She must not be afraid of me! . . ."

But suddenly she started, and stammered:

"Hark! . . . Footsteps! . . . I hear some one coming . . ."

He looked at her with surprise. She appeared distraught, as though at the approach of danger.

"I hear nothing," he said, "and, even so . . ."

"Why, you must fly! . . . Quick, fly! . . ."

"Fly . . . why?"

"You must! . . . you must! . . . Ah, don't stay!"

She rushed to the entrance to the gallery and listened. No, there was no one there. Perhaps the sound had come from the outside. . . . She waited a second, and then, reassured, turned round.

Arsène Lupin had disappeared.

Devanne's first thought, on ascertaining that his castle had been pillaged, found expression in the words which he spoke to himself:

"This is Velmont's work, and Velmont is none other than Arsène Lupin."

All was explained by this means, and nothing could be explained by any other. And yet the idea only just passed through his mind, for it seemed almost impossible that Velmont should not be Velmont—that is to say, the well-known painter, the club friend of his cousin d'Estavan. And when the sergeant of gendarmes had been sent for and arrived, Devanne did not even think of telling him of this absurd conjecture.

The whole of that morning was spent, at Thibermesnil, in an indescribable hubbub. The gendarmes, the rural police, the commissary of police from Dieppe, the inhabitants of the village thronged the passages, the park, the approaches to the castle. The arrival of the troops taking part in the manœuvres and the crack of the rifles added to the picturesqueness of the scene.

The early investigations furnished no clew. The windows had not been broken nor the doors smashed in. There was no doubt but that the removal had been effected through the secret outlet. And yet there was no trace of footsteps on the carpet, no unusual mark upon the walls.

There was one unexpected thing, however, which clearly pointed to the fanciful methods of Arsène Lupin: the famous sixteenth-century chronicle had been restored to its old place in the bookcase, and beside it stood a similar volume, which was none other than the copy stolen from the Bibliothèque Nationale.

The officers arrived at eleven. Devanne received them gayly; however annoyed he might feel at the loss of his artistic treasures, his fortune was large enough to enable him to bear it without showing ill-humor. His friends the d'Androls and Nellie came down from their rooms, and the officers were introduced.

One of the guests was missing: Horace Velmont. Was he not coming? He walked in upon the stroke of twelve, and Devanne exclaimed:

"Good! There you are at last!"

"Am I late?"

"No, but you might have been . . . after such an exciting night! You have heard the news, I suppose?"

"What news?"

"You robbed the castle last night."

"Nonsense!"

"I tell you, you did. But give your arm to Miss Underdown, and let us go in to lunch . . . Miss Underdown, let me introduce . . ."

He stopped, struck by the confusion on the girl's features. Then, seized with a sudden recollection, he said:

"By the way, of course, you once travelled on the same ship with Arsène Lupin . . . before his arrest . . . You are surprised by the likeness, are you not?"

She did not reply. Velmont stood before her, smiling. He bowed; she took his arm. He led her to her place, and sat down opposite to her. . . .

During lunch they talked of nothing but Arsène Lupin, the stolen furniture, the underground passage, and Sherlock Holmes. Not until the end of the meal, when other subjects were broached, did Velmont join in the conversation. He was amusing and serious, eloquent and witty, by turns. And whatever he said he appeared to say with the sole object of interesting Nellie. She, wholly engrossed in her own thoughts, seemed not to hear him.

Coffee was served on the terrace overlooking the court-yard and the French garden in front of the castle. The regimental band played on the lawn, and a crowd of peasants and soldiers strolled about the walks in the park.

Nellie was thinking of Arsène Lupin's promise:

"At three o'clock everything will be there. I give you my solemn pledge."

At three o'clock! And the hands of the great clock in the right wing pointed to twenty to three. In spite of herself, she kept on looking at it. And she also looked at Velmont, who was swinging peacefully in a comfortable rocking-chair.

Ten minutes to three . . . five minutes to three . . . A sort of impatience, mingled with a sense of exquisite pain, racked the young girl's mind. Was it possible for the miracle to be accomplished and to be accomplished at the fixed time, when the castle, the court-yard, and the country around were filled with people, and when, at that very moment, the public prosecutor and the examining magistrate were pursuing their investigations?

And still . . . still, Arsène Lupin had given such a solemn promise!

"It will happen just as he said," she thought, impressed by all the man's energy, authority, and certainty.

And it seemed to her no longer a miracle, but a natural event that was bound to take place in the ordinary course of things.

For a second their eyes met. She blushed, and turned away her head.

Three o'clock. . . . the first stroke rang out, the second, the third. . . . Horace Velmont took out his watch, glanced up at the clock, and put his watch back in his pocket. A few seconds elapsed. And then the crowd opened out around the lawn to make way for two carriages that had just passed through the park gates, each drawn by two horses. They were two of those regimental wagons which carry the cooking-utensils of the officers' mess and the soldiers' kits. They stopped in front of the steps. A quarter-master sergeant jumped down from the box of the first wagon and asked for M. Devanne.

Devanne ran down the steps. Under the awnings, carefully

packed and wrapped up, were his pictures, his furniture, his works of art of all kinds.

The sergeant replied to the questions put to him by producing the order which the adjutant on duty had given him, and which the adjutant himself had received that morning in the orderly room. The order stated that No. 2 company of the fourth battalion was to see that the goods and chattels deposited at the Halleux cross-roads, in the Forest of Arques, were delivered at three o'clock to M. Georges Devanne, the owner of Thibermensil Castle. It bore the signature of Colonel Beauvel.

"I found everything ready for us at the cross-roads," added the sergeant, "laid out on the grass, under the charge of . . . any one passing. That struck me as queer, but . . . well, sir, the order was plain enough!"

One of the officers examined the signature: it was a perfect copy, but forged.

The band had stopped. The wagons were emptied, and the furniture carried in-doors.

In the midst of this excitement Nellie Underdown was left standing alone at one end of the terrace. She was grave and anxious, full of vague thoughts, which she did not seek to formulate. Suddenly she saw Velmont coming up to her. She wished to avoid him, but the corner of the balustrade that borders the terrace hemmed her in on two sides, and a row of great tubs of shrubs—orange-trees, laurels, and bamboos—left her no other way of escape than that by which Velmont was approaching. She did not move. A ray of sunlight quivered on her golden hair, shaken by the frail leaves of a bamboo-plant. She heard a soft voice say:

"I have kept the promise I made you last night."

Arsène Lupin stood by her side, and there was no one else near them.

He repeated, in a hesitating attitude and a timid voice:

"I have kept the promise I made you last night."

He expected a word of thanks, a gesture at least, to prove the interest which she took in his action. She was silent.

Her scorn irritated Arsène Lupin, and at the same time he received a profound sense of all that separated him from Nellie, now that she knew the truth. He would have liked to exonerate himself, to seek excuses, to show his life in its bolder and greater aspects. But the words jarred upon him before they were uttered, and he felt the absurdity and the impertinence of any explanation. Then, overcome by a flood of recollections, he murmured, sadly:

"How distant the past seems! Do you remember the long hours on the deck of the *Provence?* . . . Ah, stay . . . one day you had a rose in your hand, as you have to-day, a pale rose, like this one. . . . I asked you for it . . . you seemed not to hear. . . . However, when you had gone below, I found the rose . . . you had dropped it, no doubt . . . I have kept it ever since. . . ."

She still made no reply. She seemed very far from him. He continued:

"For the sake of those dear hours, do not think of what you know. Let the past be joined to the present! Let me be not the man whom you saw last night, but your fellow-passenger on that voyage! Oh, turn your eyes and let them look at me, if only for a second, as they looked at me then . . . I implore you. . . . Am I not the same man that I was?"

She raised her eyes, as he asked, and looked at him. Then, without a word, she placed her finger on a ring which he wore on his right hand. Only the circlet was visible, but the bezel, turned inward, was formed of a marvellous ruby.

Arsène Lupin blushed scarlet. The ring belonged to Georges Devanne.

He gave a bitter smile:

"You are right," he said. "What has been will always be. Arsène Lupin is and can be no one but Arsène Lupin; and not even a memory can exist between you and him . . . Forgive me . . . I ought to have understood that my very presence near you must seem an outrage. . . ."

He made way for her, hat in hand, and Nellie passed before him along the balustrade. He felt tempted to hold her back, to beseech her. His courage failed him, and he followed her with his eyes, as he had done on the day long past when she crossed the gang-plank on their arrival at New York. She went up the stairs that lead to the door. For another instant her dainty figure was outlined against the marble of the entrance-hall. Then he saw her no more.

A cloud covered the sun. Arsène Lupin stood motionless, gazing at the marks of the little footprints in the sand. Suddenly he gave a start; on the edge of the bamboo-tub against which Nellie had leaned lay the rose, the pale-pink rose for which he had not dared ask her . . . This one, too, had been dropped, no doubt. But dropped by accident or intention?

He seized it eagerly. Some of the petals fell off. He picked them up, one by one, as though they were relics. . . .

"Come," he said to himself, "I have nothing more to do here. Let us see to our retreat. The more so as, if Sherlock Holmes takes up the matter, it may become too hot for me."

The park was deserted, save for a group of gendarmes standing near the lodge at the entrance. Lupin plunged into the underwood, scaled the wall, and took the nearest way to the station—a path winding through the fields. He had been walking for eight or nine minutes when the road narrowed, boxed in between two slopes; and, as he reached this pass, he saw some one enter it at the opposite end.

It was a man of, perhaps, some fifty summers, pretty powerfully built and clean-shaven, whose dress accentuated his foreign appearance. He carried a heavy walking-stick in his hand and a travelling-bag slung round his neck.

The two men crossed each other. The foreigner asked, in a hardly perceptible English accent:

"Excuse me, sir . . . can you tell me the way to the castle?"

"Straight on and turn to the left when you come to the foot of the wall. They are waiting for you impatiently."

"Ah!"

"Yes, my friend Devanne was announcing your visit to us last night."

"He made a great mistake if he said too much."

"And I am happy to be the first to pay you my compliments. Sherlock Holmes has no greater admirer than myself."

There was the slightest shade of irony in his voice, which he regretted forthwith, for Sherlock Holmes took a view of him from head to foot with an eye at once so all-embracing and so piercing that Arsène Lupin felt himself seized, caught, and registered by that glance more exactly and more essentially than he had ever been by any photographic apparatus.

"The snapshot's taken," he thought. "It will never be worth my while to disguise myself when this joker is about. Only . . . did he recognize me or not?"

They exchanged bows. But a noise of hoofs rang out, the clinking sound of horses trotting along the road. It was the gendarmes. The two men had to fall back against the slope, in the tall grass, to save themselves from being knocked over. The gendarmes passed, and as they were riding in single file, at quite a distance each from the other, this took some time. Lupin thought:

"It all depends upon whether he recognized me. If so, does he intend to take his advantage? . . ."

When the last horseman had passed, Sherlock Holmes drew himself up and, without saying a word, brushed the dust from his clothes. The strap of his bag had caught in a branch of thorns. Arsène Lupin hastened to release him. They looked at each other for another second. And if any one could have surprised them at that moment he would have beheld a stimulating sight in the first meeting of these two men, both so out of the common, so powerfully armed, both really superior characters, and inevitably destined by their special aptitudes to come into collision, like two equal forces which the order of things drives one against the other in space.

Then the Englishman said:

"I am much obliged to you."

"At your service," replied Lupin.

They went their respective ways—Lupin to the station, Sherlock Holmes to the castle.

The examining magistrate and the public prosecutor had left, after a long but fruitless investigation, and the others were awaiting Sherlock Holmes with an amount of curiosity fully justified by his reputation. They were a little disappointed by his very ordinary appearance, which was so different from the pictures which they had formed of him. There was nothing of the novel-hero about him, nothing of the enigmatic and diabolical personality which the idea of Sherlock Holmes evokes in us. However, Devanne exclaimed, with exuberant delight:

"So you have come at last! This is indeed a joy! I have so long been hoping . . . I am almost glad of what has happened, since it gives me the pleasure of seeing you. But, by the way, how did you come?"

"By train."

"What a pity! I sent my motor to the landing-stage to meet you!"

"An official arrival, I suppose," growled the Englishman, "with a brass-band marching ahead! An excellent way of helping me in my business."

This uninviting tone disconcerted Devanne, who, making an effort to jest, retorted:

"The business, fortunately, is easier than I wrote to you."

"Why so?"

"Because the burglary took place last night."

"If you had not announced my visit beforehand, the burglary would probably have not taken place last night."

"When would it?"

"To-morrow, or some other day."

"And then?"

"Arsène Lupin would have been caught in a trap."

"And my things . . . ?"

"Would not have been carried off."

"My things are here."

"Here?"

"They were brought back at three o'clock."

"By Lupin?"

"By a quarter-master sergeant, in two military wagons!"

Sherlock Holmes violently thrust his cap down upon his head and adjusted his bag; but Devanne, in a fever of excitement, exclaimed:

"What are you doing?"

"I am going."

"Why should you?"

"Your things are here. Arsène Lupin is gone. There is nothing left for me to do."

"Why, my dear sir, I simply can't get on without you. What happened last night may be repeated to-morrow, seeing that we know nothing of the most important part: how Arsène Lupin effected his entrance, how he left, and why, a few hours later, he proceeded to restore what he had stolen."

"Oh, I see; you don't know . . ."

The idea of a secret to be discovered mollified Sherlock Holmes.

"Very well, let's look into it. But at once, please, and, as far as possible, alone."

The phrase clearly referred to the bystanders. Devanne took the hint, and showed the Englishman into the guard-room. Holmes put a number of questions to him touching the previous evening, the guests who were present, and the inmates and frequenters of the castle. He next examined the two volumes of the Chronicle, compared the plans of the underground passage, made Devanne repeat the two sentences noted by the Abbé Gélis, and asked:

"You're sure it was yesterday that you first spoke of those two quotations?"

"Yesterday."

"You had never mentioned them to Monsieur Horace Velmont?"

"Never."

"Very well. You might order your car. I shall leave in an hour."

"In an hour?"

"Arsène Lupin took no longer to solve the problem which you put to him."

"I! . . . Which I put to him . . . ?"

"Why, yes, Arsène Lupin or Velmont, it's all the same."

"I thought as much. . . . Oh, the rascal! . . ."

"Well, at ten o'clock last night you supplied Lupin with the facts which he lacked, and which he had been seeking for weeks. And during the course of the night Lupin found time to grasp these facts, to collect his gang, and to rob you of your property. I propose to be no less expeditious."

He walked from one end of the room to the other, thinking as he went, then sat down, crossed his long legs, and closed his eyes.

Devanne waited in some perplexity.

"Is he asleep? Is he thinking?"

In any case, he went out to give his instructions. When he returned he found the Englishman on his knees at the foot of the staircase in the gallery, exploring the carpet.

"What is it?"

"Look at these candle-stains."

"I see . . . they are quite fresh . . ."

"And you will find others at the top of the stairs, and more still around this glass case which Arsène Lupin broke open, and from which he removed the curiosities and placed them on this chair."

"And what do you conclude?"

"Nothing. All these facts would no doubt explain the restitution which he effected. But that is a side of the question which I have no time to go into. The essential thing is the map of the underground passage."

"You still hope? . . ."

"I don't hope; I know. There's a chapel at two or three hundred yards from the castle, is there not?"

"Yes, a ruined chapel, with the tomb of Duke Rollo."

"Tell your chauffeur to wait near the chapel."

"My chauffeur is not back yet. . . . They are to let me know. . . . So, I see, you consider that the underground passage ends at the chapel. What indication . . . ?"

Sherlock Holmes interrupted him:

"May I ask you to get me a ladder and a lantern?"

"Oh, do you want a ladder and a lantern?"

"I suppose so, or I wouldn't ask you for them."

Devanne, a little taken aback by this cold logic, rang the bell. The ladder and the lantern were brought.

Orders succeeded one another with the strictness and precision of military commands:

"Put the ladder against the bookcase, to the left of the word Thibermesnil . . ."

Devanne did as he was asked, and the Englishman continued:

"More to the left . . . to the right. . . . Stop! . . . Go up. . . . Good. . . . The letters are all in relief, are they not?"

"Yes."

"Catch hold of the letter H, and tell me whether it turns in either direction?"

Devanne grasped the letter H, and exclaimed:

"Yes, it turns! A quarter of a circle to the right! How did you discover that? . . ."

Holmes, without replying, continued:

"Can you reach the letter R from where you stand? Yes. . . . Move it about, as you would a bolt which you were pushing or drawing."

Devanne moved the letter R. To his great astonishment, something became unlatched inside.

"Just so," said Sherlock Holmes. All that you now have to do is to push your ladder to the other end; that is to say, to the end of the word Thibermesnil. . . . Good. . . . Now, if I am not mistaken, if things go as they should, the letter L will open like a shutter."

With a certain solemnity, Devanne took hold of the letter L. The letter L opened, but Devanne tumbled off his ladder, for the whole section of the bookcase comprised between the first and last letters of the word swung round upon a pivot and disclosed the opening of the tunnel.

Sherlock Holmes asked, phlegmatically:

"Have you hurt yourself?"

"No, no," said Devanne, scrambling to his feet. "I'm not hurt, but flurried, I admit. . . . Those moving letters . . . that yawning tunnel . . ."

"And what then? Doesn't it all fit in exactly with the Sully quotation?"

"How do you mean?"

"Why, *l'H tournoie, l'R fremit, et l'Ls' ouvre* . . ."[4]

"But what about Louis XVI. ?"

"Louis XVI. was a really capable locksmith. I remember reading a *Treatise on Combination-locks* which was ascribed to him. On the part of a Thibermesnil, it would be an act of good courtiership to show his sovereign this masterpiece of mechanics. By the way of a memorandum, the king wrote down '2–6–12'—that is to say, the second, sixth, and twelfth letters of the word: H, R, L."

"Oh, of course. . . . I am beginning to understand. . . . Only, look here. . . . I can see how you get out of this room, but I can't see how Lupin got in; for, remember, he came from the outside."

Sherlock Holmes lit the lantern, and entered the underground passage.

"Look, you can see the whole mechanism here, like the works of a watch, and all the letters are reversed. Lupin, therefore, had only to move them from this side of the wall."

"What proof have you?"

"What proof? Look at this splash of oil. He even foresaw that the wheels would need greasing," said Holmes, not without admiration.

"Then he knew the other outlet?"

"Just as I know it. Follow me."

"Into the underground passage?"

"Are you afraid?"

"No; but are you sure you can find your way?"

"I'll find it with my eyes shut."

They first went down twelve steps, then twelve more, and again twice twelve more. Then they passed through a long tunnel whose brick walls showed traces of successive restorations, and oozed, in places, with moisture. The ground underfoot was damp.

"We are passing under the pond," said Devanne, who felt far from comfortable.

The tunnel ended in a flight of twelve steps, followed by three other flights of twelve steps each, which they climbed with difficulty, and they emerged in a small hollow hewn out of the solid rock. The way did not go any farther.

"Hang it all!" muttered Sherlock Holmes. "Nothing but bare walls. This is troublesome."

"Suppose we go back," suggested Devanne, "for I don't see the use of learning any more. I have seen all I want to."

But on raising his eyes the Englishman gave a sigh of relief: above their heads the same mechanism was repeated as at the entrance. He had only to work the three letters. A block of granite turned on a pivot. On the other side it formed Duke Rollo's tombstone, carved with the twelve letters in relief, "THIBERMES-NIL." And they found themselves in the little ruined chapel of which Sherlock Holmes had spoken.

" 'And you go to God' . . . that is to say, to the chapel," said Holmes, quoting the end of the sentence.

"Is it possible," cried Devanne, amazed at the other's perspicacity and keenness—"is it possible that this simple clew told you all that you wanted to know?"

"Tush!" said the Englishman. "It was even superfluous. In the copy belonging to the Bibliothèque Nationale the drawing of the tunnel ends on the left, as you know, in a circle, and on the right, as you do not know, in a little cross, which is so faintly marked that it can only be seen through a magnifying-glass. This cross obviously points to the chapel."

Poor Devanne could not believe his ears.

"It's wonderful, marvellous, and just as simple as A B C! How is it that the mystery was never seen through?"

"Because nobody ever united the three or four necessary elements; that is to say, the two books and the quotations . . . nobody, except Arsène Lupin and myself."

"But I also," said Devanne, "and the Abbé Gélis . . . we both of us knew as much about it as you, and yet . . ."

Holmes smiled.

"Monsieur Devanne, it is not given to all the world to succeed in solving riddles."

"But I have been hunting for ten years. And you, in ten minutes . . ."

"Pooh! It's a matter of habit."

They walked out of the chapel, and the Englishman exclaimed:

"Hullo, a motor-car waiting!"

"Why, it's mine!"

"Yours? But I thought the chauffeur hadn't returned?"

"No more he had . . . I can't make out . . ."

They went up to the car, and Devanne said to the chauffeur:

"Victor, who told you to come here?"

"Monsieur Velmont, sir," replied the man.

"Monsieur Velmont? Did you meet him?"

"Yes, sir, near the station, and he told me to go to the chapel."

"To go to the chapel! What for?"

"To wait for you, sir . . . and your friend."

Devanne and Sherlock Holmes exchanged glances. Devanne said:

"He saw that the riddle would be child's play to you. He has paid you a delicate compliment."

A smile of satisfaction passed over the detective's thin lips. The compliment pleased him. He jerked his head and said:

"He's a man, that! I took his measure the moment I saw him."

"So you've seen him?"

"We crossed on my way here."

"And you knew that he was Horace Velmont—I mean to say, Arsène Lupin?"

"No, but it did not take me long to guess as much . . . from a certain irony in his talk."

"And you let him escape?"

"I did . . . although I had only to put out my hand . . . five gendarmes rode past us."

"But, bless my soul, you'll never get an opportunity like that again . . ."

"Just so, Monsieur Devanne," said the Englishman, proudly. "When Sherlock Holmes has to do with an adversary like Arsène Lupin, he does not take opportunities . . . he creates them . . ."

But time was pressing, and as Lupin had been so obliging as to send the motor, Devanne and Holmes settled themselves in their seats. Victor started the engine, and they drove off. Fields, clumps of trees sped past. The gentle undulations of the Caux country levelled out before them. Suddenly Devanne's eyes were attracted to a little parcel in one of the carriage pockets.

"Hullo! What's this? A parcel! Whom for? Why, it's for you!"

"For me?"

"Read for yourself: 'Sherlock Holmes, Esq., from Arsène Lupin!' "

The Englishman took the parcel, untied the string, and removed the two sheets of paper in which it was wrapped. It was a watch.

"Oh!" he said, accompanying his exclamation with an angry gesture. . . .

"A watch," said Devanne. "Can he have . . . ?"

The Englishman did not reply.

"What! It's your watch? Is Arsène Lupin returning you your watch? Then he must have taken it! . . . He must have taken your watch! Oh, this is too good! Sherlock Holmes' watch spirited away by Arsène Lupin! Oh, this is too funny for words! No, upon my honor . . . you must excuse me. . . . I can't help laughing!"

He laughed till he cried, utterly unable to restrain himself. When he had done, he declared, in a tone of conviction:

"Yes, he's a man, as you said."

The Englishman did not move a muscle. With his eyes fixed on the fleeting horizon he spoke not a word until they reached Dieppe. His silence was terrible, unfathomable, more violent than the fiercest fury. On the landing-stage he said simply, this time without betraying any anger, but in a tone that revealed all the iron will and energy of his remarkable personality:

"Yes, he's a man, and a man on whose shoulder I shall have great pleasure in laying this hand with which I now grasp yours, Monsieur Devanne. And I have an idea, mark you, that Arsène Lupin and Sherlock Holmes will meet again some day. . . . Yes, the world is too small for them not to meet. . . . And, when they do! . . ."

FLASHES OF SUNLIGHT

"Lupin," I said, "tell me something about yourself."

"Why, what would you have me tell you? Everybody knows my life!" replied Lupin, who lay drowsing on the sofa in my study.

"Nobody knows it!" I protested. "People know from your letters in the newspapers that you were mixed up in this case, that you started that case. But the part which you played in it all, the plain facts of the story, the upshot of the mystery: these are things of which they know nothing."

"Pooh! A heap of uninteresting twaddle!"

"What! Your present of fifty thousand francs to Nicolas Dugrival's wife! Do you call that uninteresting? And what about the way in which you solved the puzzle of the three pictures?"

Lupin laughed:

"Yes, that was a queer puzzle, certainly. I can suggest a title for you if you like: what do you say to *The Sign of the Shadow*?"[1]

"And your successes in society and with the fair sex?" I continued. "The dashing Arsène's love-affairs! . . . And the clue to your good actions? Those chapters in your life to which you have so often alluded under the names of *The Wedding-ring, Shadowed by Death,*[2] and so on! . . . Why delay these confidences and confessions, my dear Lupin? . . . Come, do what I ask you! . . ."

It was at the time when Lupin, though already famous, had not yet fought his biggest battles; the time that preceded the great adventures of *The Hollow Needle* and *813*. He had not yet dreamt of annexing the accumulated treasures of the French Royal House[3] nor of changing the map of Europe under the

Kaiser's nose:[4] he contented himself with milder surprises and humbler profits, making his daily effort, doing evil from day to day and doing a little good as well, naturally and for the love of the thing, like a whimsical and compassionate Don Quixote.

He was silent; and I insisted:

"Lupin, I wish you would!"

To my astonishment, he replied:

"Take a sheet of paper, old fellow, and a pencil."

I obeyed with alacrity, delighted at the thought that he at last meant to dictate to me some of those pages which he knows how to clothe with such vigour and fancy, pages which I, unfortunately, am obliged to spoil with tedious explanations and boring developments.

"Are you ready?" he asked.

"Quite."

"Write down, 20, 1, 11, 5, 14, 15."

"What?"

"Write it down, I tell you."

He was now sitting up, with his eyes turned to the open window and his fingers rolling a Turkish cigarette. He continued:

"Write down, 21, 14, 14, 5. . . ."

He stopped. Then he went on:

"3, 5, 19, 19 . . ."

And, after a pause:

"5, 18, 25 . . ."

Was he mad? I looked at him hard and, presently, I saw that his eyes were no longer listless, as they had been a little before, but keen and attentive and that they seemed to be watching, somewhere, in space, a sight that apparently captivated them.

Meanwhile, he dictated, with intervals between each number:

"18, 9, 19, 11, 19 . . ."

There was hardly anything to be seen through the window but a patch of blue sky on the right and the front of the building opposite, an old private house, whose shutters were closed as usual. There was nothing particular about all this, no detail that struck me as new among those which I had had before my eyes for years. . . .

"1, 2. . . ."

And suddenly I understood . . . or rather I thought I understood, for how could I admit that Lupin, a man so essentially level-headed under his mask of frivolity, could waste his time upon such childish nonsense? What he was counting was the intermittent flashes of a ray of sunlight playing on the dingy front of the opposite house, at the height of the second floor!

"15, 22 . . ." said Lupin.

The flash disappeared for a few seconds and then struck the house again, successively, at regular intervals, and disappeared once more.

I had instinctively counted the flashes and I said, aloud:

"5. . . ."

"Caught the idea? I congratulate you!" he replied, sarcastically.

He went to the window and leant out, as though to discover the exact direction followed by the ray of light. Then he came and lay on the sofa again, saying:

"It's your turn now. Count away!"

The fellow seemed so positive that I did as he told me. Besides, I could not help confessing that there was something rather curious about the ordered frequency of those gleams on the front of the house opposite, those appearances and disappearances, turn and turn about, like so many flash signals.

They obviously came from a house on our side of the street, for the sun was entering my windows slantwise. It was as though some one were alternately opening and shutting a casement, or, more likely, amusing himself by making sunlight flashes with a pocket-mirror.

"It's a child having a game!" I cried, after a moment or two, feeling a little irritated by the trivial occupation that had been thrust upon me.

"Never mind, go on!"

And I counted away. . . . And I put down rows of figures. . . . And the sun continued to play in front of me, with mathematical precision.

"Well?" said Lupin, after a longer pause than usual.

"Why, it seems finished. . . . There has been nothing for some minutes. . . ."

We waited and, as no more light flashed through space, I said, jestingly:

"My idea is that we have been wasting our time. A few figures on paper: a poor result!"

Lupin, without stirring from his sofa, rejoined:

"Oblige me, old chap, by putting in the place of each of those numbers the corresponding letter of the alphabet. Count A as 1, B as 2 and so on. Do you follow me?"

"But it's idiotic!"

"Absolutely idiotic, but we do such a lot of idiotic things in this life. . . . One more or less, you know! . . ."

I sat down to this silly work and wrote out the first letters:

"Take no . . ."

I broke off in surprise:

"Words!" I exclaimed. "Two English words meaning . . ."

"Go on, old chap."

And I went on and the next letters formed two more words, which I separated as they appeared. And, to my great amazement, a complete English sentence lay before my eyes.

"Done?" asked Lupin, after a time.

"Done! . . . By the way, there are mistakes in the spelling. . . ."

"Never mind those and read it out, please. . . . Read slowly."

Thereupon I read out the following unfinished communication, which I will set down as it appeared on the paper in front of me:

"Take no unnecessery risks. Above all, avoid atacks, approach ennemy with great prudance and . . ."

I began to laugh:

"And there you are! *Fiat lux!*⁵ We're simply dazed with light! But, after all, Lupin, confess that this advice, dribbled out by a kitchen-maid, doesn't help you much!"

Lupin rose, without breaking his contemptuous silence, and took the sheet of paper.

I remembered soon after that, at this moment, I happened to look at the clock. It was eighteen minutes past five.

Lupin was standing with the paper in his hand; and I was able at my ease to watch, on his youthful features, that extraordinary mobility of expression which baffles all observers and constitutes his great strength and his chief safeguard. By what signs can one hope to identify a face which changes at pleasure, even without the help of make-up, and whose every transient expression seems to be the final, definite expression? . . . By what signs? There was one which I knew well, an invariable sign: Two little crossed wrinkles that marked his forehead whenever he made a powerful effort of concentration. And I saw it at that moment, saw the tiny tell-tale cross, plainly and deeply scored.

He put down the sheet of paper and muttered:

"Child's play!"

The clock struck half-past five.

"What!" I cried. "Have you succeeded? . . . In twelve minutes? . . ."

He took a few steps up and down the room, lit a cigarette and said:

"You might ring up Baron Repstein, if you don't mind, and tell him I shall be with him at ten o'clock this evening."

"Baron Repstein?" I asked. "The husband of the famous baroness?"

"Yes."

"Are you serious?"

"Quite serious."

Feeling absolutely at a loss, but incapable of resisting him, I opened the telephone-directory and unhooked the receiver. But, at that moment, Lupin stopped me with a peremptory gesture and said, with his eyes on the paper, which he had taken up again:

"No, don't say anything. . . . It's no use letting him know. . . . There's something more urgent . . . a queer thing that puzzles me. . . . Why on earth wasn't the last sentence finished? Why is the sentence . . ."

He snatched up his hat and stick:

"Let's be off. If I'm not mistaken, this is a business that

requires immediate solution; and I don't believe I *am* mistaken."

He put his arm through mine, as we went down the stairs, and said:

"I know what everybody knows. Baron Repstein, the company-promoter and racing-man, whose colt Etna won the Derby and the Grand Prix this year, has been victimized by his wife. The wife, who was well known for her fair hair, her dress and her extravagance, ran away a fortnight ago, taking with her a sum of three million francs, stolen from her husband, and quite a collection of diamonds, pearls and jewellery which the Princesse de Berny had placed in her hands and which she was supposed to buy. For two weeks the police have been pursuing the baroness across France and the continent: an easy job, as she scatters gold and jewels wherever she goes. They think they have her every moment. Two days ago, our champion detective, the egregious Ganimard, arrested a visitor at a big hotel in Belgium, a woman against whom the most positive evidence seemed to be heaped up. On enquiry, the lady turned out to be a notorious chorus-girl called Nelly Darbal. As for the baroness, she has vanished. The baron, on his side, has offered a reward of two hundred thousand francs to whosoever finds his wife. The money is in the hands of a solicitor. Moreover, he has sold his racing-stud, his house on the Boulevard Haussmann and his country-seat of Roquencourt in one lump, so that he may indemnify the Princesse de Berny for her loss."

"And the proceeeds of the sale," I added, "are to be paid over at once. The papers say that the princess will have her money to-morrow. Only, frankly, I fail to see the connection between this story, which you have told very well, and the puzzling sentence . . ."

Lupin did not condescend to reply.

We had been walking down the street in which I live and had passed some four or five houses, when he stepped off the pavement and began to examine a block of flats, not of the latest construction, which looked as if it contained a large number of tenants:

"According to my calculations," he said, "this is where the signals came from, probably from that open window."

"On the third floor?"

"Yes."

He went to the portress and asked her:

"Does one of your tenants happen to be acquainted with Baron Repstein?"

"Why, of course!" replied the woman. "We have M. Lavernoux here, such a nice gentleman; he is the baron's secretary and agent. I look after his flat."

"And can we see him?"

"See him? . . . The poor gentleman is very ill."

"Ill?"

"He's been ill a fortnight . . . ever since the trouble with the baroness. . . . He came home the next day with a temperature and took to his bed."

"But he gets up, surely?"

"Ah, that I can't say!"

"How do you mean, you can't say?"

"No, his doctor won't let any one into his room. He took my key from me."

"Who did?"

"The doctor. He comes and sees to his wants, two or three times a day. He left the house only twenty minutes ago . . . an old gentleman with a grey beard and spectacles. . . . Walks quite bent. . . . But where are you going sir?"

"I'm going up, show me the way," said Lupin, with his foot on the stairs. "It's the third floor, isn't it, on the left?"

"But I mustn't!" moaned the portress, running after him. "Besides, I haven't the key . . . the doctor . . ."

They climbed the three flights, one behind the other. On the landing, Lupin took a tool from his pocket and, disregarding the woman's protests, inserted it in the lock. The door yielded almost immediately. We went in.

At the back of a small dark room we saw a streak of light filtering through a door that had been left ajar. Lupin ran across the room and, on reaching the threshold, gave a cry:

"Too late! Oh, hang it all!"

The portress fell on her knees, as though fainting.

I entered the bedroom, in my turn, and saw a man lying

half-dressed on the carpet, with his legs drawn up under him, his arms contorted and his face quite white, an emaciated, fleshless face, with the eyes still staring in terror and the mouth twisted into a hideous grin.

"He's dead," said Lupin, after a rapid examination.

"But why?" I exclaimed. "There's not a trace of blood!"

"Yes, yes, there is," replied Lupin, pointing to two or three drops that showed on the chest through the open shirt. "Look, they must have taken him by the throat with one hand and pricked him to the heart with the other. I say, 'pricked,' because really the wound can't be seen. It suggests a hole made by a very long needle."

He looked on the floor, all round the corpse. There was nothing to attract his attention, except a little pocket-mirror, the little mirror with which M. Lavernoux had amused himself by making the sunbeams dance through space.

But, suddenly, as the portress was breaking into lamentations and calling for help, Lupin flung himself on her and shook her:

"Stop that! . . . Listen to me . . . you can call out later. . . . Listen to me and answer me. It is most important. M. Lavernoux had a friend living in this street, had he not? On the same side, to the right? An intimate friend?"

"Yes."

"A friend whom he used to meet at the café in the evening and with whom he exchanged the illustrated papers?"

"Yes."

"Was the friend an Englishman?"

"Yes."

"What's his name?"

"Mr. Hargrove."

"Where does he live?"

"At No. 92 in this street."

"One word more: had that old doctor been attending him long?"

"No. I did not know him. He came on the evening when M. Lavernoux was taken ill."

Without another word, Lupin dragged me away once more, ran down the stairs and, once in the street, turned to the right, which took us past my flat again. Four doors further, he stopped at No. 92, a small, low-storied house, of which the ground-floor was occupied by the proprietor of a dram-shop, who stood smoking in his doorway, next to the entrance-passage. Lupin asked if Mr. Hargrove was at home.

"Mr. Hargrove went out about half-an-hour ago," said the publican. "He seemed very much excited and took a taxi-cab, a thing he doesn't often do."

"And you don't know . . ."

"Where he was going? Well, there's no secret about it. He shouted it loud enough! 'Prefecture of Police' is what he said to the driver. . . ."

Lupin was himself just hailing a taxi, when he changed his mind; and I heard him mutter:

"What's the good? He's got too much start of us. . . ."

He asked if any one called after Mr. Hargrove had gone.

"Yes, an old gentleman with a grey beard and spectacles. He went up to Mr. Hargrove's, rang the bell, and went away again."

"I am much obliged," said Lupin, touching his hat.

He walked away slowly without speaking to me, wearing a thoughtful air. There was no doubt that the problem struck him as very difficult, and that he saw none too clearly in the darkness through which he seemed to be moving with such certainty.

He himself, for that matter, confessed to me:

"These are cases that require much more intuition than reflection. But this one, I may tell you, is well worth taking pains about."

We had now reached the boulevards. Lupin entered a public reading-room and spent a long time consulting the last fortnight's newspapers. Now and again, he mumbled:

"Yes . . . yes . . . of course . . . it's only a guess, but it explains everything. . . . Well, a guess that answers every question is not far from being the truth. . . ."[6]

It was now dark. We dined at a little restaurant and I noticed that Lupin's face became gradually more animated. His gestures were more decided. He recovered his spirits, his liveliness. When we left, during the walk which he made me take along the Boulevard Haussmann, towards Baron Repstein's house, he was the real Lupin of the great occasions, the Lupin who had made up his mind to go in and win.

We slackened our pace just short of the Rue de Courcelles. Baron Repstein lived on the left-hand side, between this street and the Faubourg Saint-Honoré, in a three-storied private house of which we could see the front, decorated with columns and caryatides.

"Stop!" said Lupin, suddenly.

"What is it?"

"Another proof to confirm my supposition. . . ."

"What proof? I see nothing."

"I do. . . . That's enough. . . ."

He turned up the collar of his coat, lowered the brim of his soft hat and said:

"By Jove, it'll be a stiff fight! Go to bed, my friend. I'll tell you about my expedition to-morrow . . . if it doesn't cost me my life."

"What are you talking about?"

"Oh, I know what I'm saying! I'm risking a lot. First of all, getting arrested, which isn't much. Next, getting killed, which is worse. But . . ." He gripped my shoulder. "But there's a third thing I'm risking, which is getting hold of two millions. . . . And, once I possess a capital of two millions, I'll show people what I can do! Good-night, old chap, and, if you never see me again. . . ." He spouted Musset's lines:

> "Plant a willow by my grave,
> The weeping willow that I love. . . ."[7]

I walked away. Three minutes later—I am continuing the narrative as he told it to me next day—three minutes later, Lupin rang at the door of the Hôtel Repstein.

"Is monsieur le baron at home?"

"Yes," replied the butler, examining the intruder with an air of surprise, "but monsieur le baron does not see people as late as this."

"Does monsieur le baron know of the murder of M. Lavernoux, his land-agent?"

"Certainly."

"Well, please tell monsieur le baron that I have come about the murder and that there is not a moment to lose."

A voice called from above:

"Show the gentleman up, Antoine."

In obedience to this peremptory order, the butler led the way to the first floor. In an open doorway stood a gentleman whom Lupin recognized from his photograph in the papers as Baron Repstein, husband of the famous baroness and owner of Etna, the horse of the year.

He was an exceedingly tall, square-shouldered man. His clean-shaven face wore a pleasant, almost smiling expression, which was not affected by the sadness of his eyes. He was dressed in a well-cut morning-coat, with a tan waistcoat and a dark tie fastened with a pearl pin, the value of which struck Lupin as considerable.

He took Lupin into his study, a large, three-windowed room, lined with book-cases, sets of pigeonholes, an American desk and a safe. And he at once asked, with ill-concealed eagerness:

"Do you know anything?"

"Yes, monsieur le baron."

"About the murder of that poor Lavernoux?"

"Yes, monsieur le baron, and about madame le baronne also."

"Do you really mean it? Quick, I entreat you. . . ."

He pushed forward a chair. Lupin sat down and began:

"Monsieur le baron, the circumstances are very serious. I will be brief."

"Yes, do, please."

"Well, monsieur le baron, in a few words, it amounts to this: five or six hours ago, Lavernoux, who, for the last fortnight, had been kept in a sort of enforced confinement by his doctor, Lavernoux—how shall I put it?—telegraphed certain revelations by means of signals which were partly taken down by me and which put me on the track of this case. He himself was surprised in the act of making this communication and was murdered."

"But by whom? By whom?"

"By his doctor."

"Who is this doctor?"

"I don't know. But one of M. Lavernoux's friends, an Englishman called Hargrove, the friend, in fact, with whom he was communicating, is bound to know and is also bound to know the exact and complete meaning of the communication, because, without waiting for the end, he jumped into a motor-cab and drove to the Prefecture of Police."

"Why? Why? . . . And what is the result of that step?"

"The result, monsieur le baron, is that your house is surrounded. There are twelve detectives under your windows. The moment the sun rises, they will enter in the name of the law and arrest the criminal."

"Then is Lavernoux's murderer concealed in my house? Who is he? One of the servants? But no, for you were speaking of a doctor! . . ."

"I would remark, monsieur le baron, that when this Mr. Hargrove went to the police to tell them of the revelations made by his friend Lavernoux, he was not aware that his friend Lavernoux was going to be murdered. The step taken by Mr. Hargrove had to do with something else. . . ."

"With what?"

"With the disappearance of madame la baronne, of which he knew the secret, thanks to the communication made by Lavernoux."

"What! They know at last! They have found the baroness! Where is she? And the jewels? And the money she robbed me of?"

Baron Repstein was talking in a great state of excitement. He rose and, almost shouting at Lupin, cried:

"Finish your story, sir! I can't endure this suspense!"

Lupin continued, in a slow and hesitating voice:

"The fact is . . . you see . . . it is rather difficult to explain . . . for you and I are looking at the thing from a totally different point of view."

"I don't understand."

"And yet you ought to understand, monsieur le baron. . . . We begin by saying—I am quoting the newspapers—by saying, do we not, that Baroness Repstein knew all the secrets of your business and that she was able to open not only that safe over there, but also the one at the Crédit Lyonnais in which you kept your securities locked up?"

"Yes."

"Well, one evening, a fortnight ago, while you were at your club, Baroness Repstein, who, unknown to yourself, had converted all those securities into cash, left this house with a travelling-bag, containing your money and all the Princesse de Berny's jewels?"

"Yes."

"And, since then, she has not been seen?"

"No."

"Well, there is an excellent reason why she has not been seen."

"What reason?"

"This, that Baroness Repstein has been murdered. . . ."

"Murdered! . . . The baroness! . . . But you're mad!"

"Murdered . . . and probably that same evening."

"I tell you again, you are mad! How can the baroness have been murdered, when the police are following her tracks, so to speak, step by step?"

"They are following the tracks of another woman."

"What woman?"

"The murderer's accomplice."

"And who is the murderer?"

"The same man who, for the last fortnight, knowing that Lavernoux, through the situation which he occupied in this house, had discovered the truth, kept him imprisoned, forced him to silence, threatened him, terrorized him; the same man who, finding Lavernoux in the act of communicating with a friend, made away with him in cold blood by stabbing him to the heart."

"The doctor, therefore?"

"Yes."

"But who is this doctor? Who is this malevolent genius, this infernal being who appears and disappears, who slays in the dark and whom nobody suspects?"

"Can't you guess?"

"No."

"And do you want to know?"

"Do I want to know? . . . Why, speak, man, speak! . . . You know where he is hiding?"

"Yes."

"In this house?"

"Yes."

"And it is he whom the police are after?"

"Yes."

"And I know him?"

"Yes."

"Who is it?"

"You!"

"I! . . ."

Lupin had not been more than ten minutes with the baron; and the duel was commencing. The accusation was hurled, definitely, violently, implacably.

Lupin repeated:

"You yourself, got up in a false beard and a pair of spectacles, bent in two, like an old man. In short, you, Baron Repstein; and it is you for a very good reason, of which nobody has thought, which is that, if it was not you who contrived the whole plot, the case becomes inexplicable. Whereas, taking you as the criminal, you as murdering the baroness in order to get rid of her and run through those millions with another woman, you as murdering Lavernoux, your agent, in order to suppress an unimpeachable witness, oh, then the whole case is explained! Well, is it pretty clear? And are not you yourself convinced?"

The baron, who, throughout this conversation, had stood bending over his visitor, waiting for each of his words with feverish avidity, now drew himself up and looked at Lupin as though he undoubtedly had to do with a madman. When Lupin had finished speaking, the baron stepped back two or three paces, seemed on the point of uttering words which he ended by not saying, and then, without taking his eyes from his strange visitor, went to the fireplace and rang the bell.

Lupin did not make a movement. He waited smiling:

The butler entered. His master said:

"You can go to bed, Antoine. I will let this gentleman out."

"Shall I put out the lights, sir?"

"Leave a light in the hall."

Antoine left the room and the baron, after taking a revolver from his desk, at once came back to Lupin, put the weapon in his pocket and said, very calmly:

"You must excuse this little precaution, sir. I am obliged to take it in case you should be mad, though that does not seem likely. No, you are not mad. But you have come here with an object which I fail to grasp; and you have sprung upon me an accusation of so astounding a character that I am curious to know the reason. I have experienced so much disappointment and undergone so much suffering that an outrage of this kind leaves me indifferent. Continue, please."

His voice shook with emotion and his sad eyes seemed moist with tears.

Lupin shuddered. Had he made a mistake? Was the surmise which his intuition had suggested to him and which was based upon a frail groundwork of slight facts, was this surmise wrong?

His attention was caught by a detail: through the opening in the baron's waistcoat he saw the point of the pin fixed in the tie and was thus able to realize the unusual length of the pin. Moreover, the gold stem was triangular and formed a sort of miniature dagger, very thin and very delicate, yet formidable in an expert hand.

And Lupin had no doubt but that the pin attached to that magnificent pearl was the weapon which had pierced the heart of the unfortunate M. Lavernoux.

He muttered:

"You're jolly clever, monsieur le baron!"

The other, maintaining a rather scornful gravity, kept silence, as though he did not understand and as though waiting for the explanation to which he felt himself entitled. And, in spite of everything, this impassive attitude worried Arsène Lupin. Nevertheless, his conviction was so profound and, besides, he had staked so much on the adventure that he repeated:

"Yes, jolly clever, for it is evident that the baroness only obeyed your orders in realizing your securities and also in borrowing the princess's jewels on the pretence of buying them.

And it is evident that the person who walked out of your house with a bag was not your wife, but an accomplice, that chorus-girl probably, and that it is your chorus-girl who is deliberately allowing herself to be chased across the continent by our worthy Ganimard. And I look upon the trick as marvellous. What does the woman risk, seeing that it is the baroness who is being looked for? And how could they look for any other woman than the baroness, seeing that you have promised a reward of two hundred thousand francs to the person who finds the baroness? . . . Oh, that two hundred thousand francs lodged with a solicitor: what a stroke of genius! It has dazzled the police! It has thrown dust in the eyes of the most clear-sighted! A gentleman who lodges two hundred thousand francs with a solicitor is a gentleman who speaks the truth. . . . So they go on hunting the baroness! And they leave you quietly to settle your affairs, to sell your stud and your two houses to the highest bidder and to prepare your flight! Heavens, what a joke!"

The baron did not wince. He walked up to Lupin and asked, without abandoning his imperturbable coolness:

"Who are you?"

Lupin burst out laughing.

"What can it matter who I am? Take it that I am an emissary of fate, looming out of the darkness for your destruction!"

He sprang from his chair, seized the baron by the shoulder and jerked out:

"Yes, for your destruction, my bold baron! Listen to me! Your wife's three millions, almost all the princess's jewels, the money you received to-day from the sale of your stud and your real estate: it's all there, in your pocket, or in that safe. Your flight is prepared. Look, I can see the leather of your portmanteau behind that hanging. The papers on your desk are in order. This very night, you would have done a guy. This very night, disguised beyond recognition, after taking all your precautions, you would have joined your chorus-girl, the creature for whose sake you have committed murder, that same Nelly Darbal, no doubt, whom Ganimard arrested in Belgium. But for one sudden, unforeseen obstacle: the police, the twelve detectives who, thanks to Lavernoux's revelations, have been posted under your windows. They've cooked your goose, old chap! . . . Well, I'll save you. A word through the telephone; and, by three or four o'clock in the morning, twenty of my friends will have removed the obstacle, polished off the twelve detectives, and you and I will slip away quietly. My conditions? Almost nothing; a trifle to you: we share the millions and the jewels. Is it a bargain?"

He was leaning over the baron, thundering at him with irresistible energy. The baron whispered:

"I'm beginning to understand. It's blackmail. . . ."

"Blackmail or not, call it what you please, my boy, but you've got to go through with it and do as I say. And don't imagine that I shall give way at the last moment. Don't say to yourself, 'Here's a gentleman whom the fear of the police will cause to think twice. If I run a big risk in refusing, he also will be risking the handcuffs, the cells and the rest of it, seeing that we are both being hunted down like wild beasts.' That would be a mistake, monsieur le baron. I can always get out of it. It's a question of yourself, of yourself alone. . . . Your money or your life, my lord! Share and share alike . . . if not, the scaffold! Is it a bargain?"

A quick movement. The baron released himself, grasped his revolver and fired.

But Lupin was prepared for the attack, the more so as the baron's face had lost its assurance and gradually, under the slow impulse of rage and fear, acquired an expression of almost bestial ferocity that heralded the rebellion so long kept under control.

He fired twice. Lupin first flung himself to one side and then dived at the baron's knees, seized him by both legs and brought him to the ground. The baron freed himself with an effort. The two enemies rolled over in each other's grip; and a stubborn, crafty, brutal, savage struggle followed.

Suddenly, Lupin felt a pain at his chest:

"You villain!" he yelled. "That's your Lavernoux trick; the tie-pin!"

Stiffening his muscles with a desperate effort, he overpowered the baron and clutched him by the throat victorious at last and omnipotent.

"You ass!" he cried. "If you hadn't shown your cards, I might have thrown up the game! You have such a look of the honest

man about you! But what a biceps, my lord! . . . I thought for a
moment. . . . But it's all over, now! . . . Come, my friend, hand
us the pin and look cheerful. . . . No, that's what I call pulling a
face. . . . I'm holding you too tight, perhaps? My lord's at his
last gasp? . . . Come, be good! . . . That's it, just a wee bit of
string round the wrists; do you allow me? . . . Why, you and I
are agreeing like two brothers! It's touching! . . . At heart, you
know, I'm rather fond of you. . . . And now, my bonnie lad,
mind yourself! And a thousand apologies! . . ."

Half raising himself, with all his strength he caught the other
a terrible blow in the pit of the stomach. The baron gave a gur-
gle and lay stunned and unconscious.

"That comes of having a deficient sense of logic, my friend,"
said Lupin. "I offered you half your money. Now I'll give you
none at all . . . provided I know where to find any of it. For
that's the main thing. Where has the beggar hidden his dust? In
the safe? By George, it'll be a tough job! Luckily, I have all the
night before me. . . ."

He began to feel in the baron's pockets, came upon a bunch
of keys, first made sure that the portmanteau behind the curtain
held no papers or jewels, and then went to the safe.

But, at that moment, he stopped short: he heard a noise
somewhere. The servants? Impossible. Their attics were on the
top floor. He listened. The noise came from below. And, suddenly, he understood: the detectives, who had heard the two
shots, were banging at the front door, as was their duty, without
waiting for daybreak. Then an electric bell rang, which Lupin
recognized as that in the hall:

"By Jupiter!" he said. "Pretty work! Here are these jokers
coming . . . and just as we were about to gather the fruits of our
laborious efforts! Tut, tut, Lupin, keep cool! What's expected
of you? To open a safe, of which you don't know the secret, in
thirty seconds. That's a mere trifle to lose your head about!
Come, all you have to do is to discover the secret! How many
letters are there in the word? Four?"

He went on thinking, while talking and listening to the noise
outside. He double-locked the door of the outer room and then
came back to the safe:

"Four ciphers. . . . Four letters . . . four letters. . . . Who can lend me a hand? . . . Who can give me just a tiny hint? . . . Who? Why, Lavernoux, of course! That good Lavernoux, seeing that he took the trouble to indulge in optical telegraphy at the risk of his life. . . . Lord, what a fool I am! . . . Why, of course, why, of course, that's it! . . . By Jove this is too exciting! . . . Lupin, you must count ten and suppress that distracted beating of your heart. If not, it means bad work."

He counted ten and, now quite calm, knelt in front of the safe. He turned the four knobs with careful attention. Next, he examined the bunch of keys, selected one of them, then another, and attempted, in vain, to insert them in the lock:

"There's luck in odd numbers," he mutttered, trying a third key. "Victory! This is the right one! Open Sesame, good old Sesame, open!"

The lock turned. The door moved on its hinges. Lupin pulled it to him, after taking out the bunch of keys:

"The millions are ours," he said. "Baron, I forgive you!"

And then he gave a single bound backward, hiccoughing with fright. His legs staggered beneath him. The keys jingled together in his fevered hand with a sinister sound. And, for twenty, for thirty seconds, despite the din that was being raised and the electric bells that kept ringing through the house, he stood there, wild-eyed, gazing at the most horrible, the most abominable sight: a woman's body, half-dressed, bent in two in the safe, crammed in, like an over-large parcel . . . and fair hair hanging down . . . and blood . . . clots of blood . . . and livid flesh, blue in places, decomposing, flaccid. . . .

"The baroness!" he gasped. "The baroness! . . . Oh, the monster! . . ."

He roused himself from his torpor, suddenly, to spit in the murderer's face and pound him with his heels:

"Take that, you wretch! . . . Take that, you villain! . . . And, with it, the scaffold, the bran-basket! . . ."

Meanwhile, shouts came from the upper floors in reply to the detectives' ringing. Lupin heard footsteps scurrying down the stairs. It was time to think of beating a retreat.

In reality, this did not trouble him greatly. During his

conversation with the baron, the enemy's extraordinary coolness had given him the feeling that there must be a private outlet. Besides, how could the baron have begun the fight, if he were not sure of escaping the police?

Lupin went into the next room. It looked out on the garden. At the moment when the detectives were entering the house, he flung his legs over the balcony and let himself down by a rainpipe. He walked round the building. On the opposite side was a wall lined with shrubs. He slipped in between the shrubs and the wall and at once found a little door which he easily opened with one of the keys on the bunch. All that remained for him to do was to walk across a yard and pass through the empty rooms of a lodge; and in a few moments he found himself in the Rue du Faubourg Saint-Honoré. Of course—and this he had reckoned on—the police had not provided for this secret outlet.

"Well, what do you think of Baron Repstein?" cried Lupin, after giving me all the details of that tragic night. "What a dirty scoundrel! And how it teaches one to distrust appearances! I swear to you, the fellow looked a thoroughly honest man!"

"But what about the millions?" I asked. "The princess's jewels?"

"They were in the safe. I remember seeing the parcel."

"Well?"

"They are there still."

"Impossible!"

"They are, upon my word! I might tell you that I was afraid of the detectives, or else plead a sudden attack of delicacy. But the truth is simpler . . . and more prosaic: the smell was too awful! . . ."

"What?"

"Yes, my dear fellow, the smell that came from that safe . . . from that coffin. . . . No, I couldn't do it . . . my head swam. . . . Another second and I should have been ill. . . . Isn't it silly? . . . Look, this is all I got from my expedition: the tie-pin. . . . The bed-rock value of the pearl is thirty thousand francs. . . . But all the same, I feel jolly well annoyed. What a sell!"

"One more question," I said. "The word that opened the safe!"

"Well?"

"How did you guess it?"

"Oh, quite easily! In fact, I am surprised that I didn't think of it sooner."

"Well, tell me."

"It was contained in the revelations telegraphed by that poor Lavernoux."

"What?"

"Just think, my dear chap, the mistakes in spelling. . . ."

"The mistakes in spelling?"

"Why, of course! They were deliberate. Surely, you don't imagine that the agent, the private secretary of the baron—who was a company-promoter, mind you, and a racing-man—did not know English better than to spell 'necessery' with an 'e,' 'atack' with one 't,' 'ennemy' with two 'n's' and 'prudance' with an 'a'! The thing struck me at once. I put the four letters together and got 'Etna,' the name of the famous horse."

"And was that one word enough?"

"Of course! It was enough to start with, to put me on the scent of the Repstein case, of which all the papers were full, and, next, to make me guess that it was the key-word of the safe, because, on the one hand, Lavernoux knew the gruesome contents of the safe and, on the other, he was denouncing the baron. And it was in the same way that I was led to suppose that Lavernoux had a friend in the street, that they both frequented the same café, that they amused themselves by working out the problems and cryptograms in the illustrated papers and that they had contrived a way of exchanging telegrams from window to window."

"That makes it all quite simple!" I exclaimed.

"Very simple. And the incident once more shows that, in the discovery of crimes, there is something much more valuable than the examination of facts, than observations, deductions, inferences and all that stuff and nonsense. What I mean is, as I said before, intuition . . . intuition and intelligence. . . . And Arsène Lupin, without boasting, is deficient in neither one nor the other! . . ."

THE WEDDING-RING

Yvonne d'Origny kissed her son and told him to be good:

"You know your grandmother d'Origny is not very fond of children. Now that she has sent for you to come and see her, you must show her what a sensible little boy you are." And, turning to the governess, "Don't forget, Fräulein, to bring him home immediately after dinner. . . . Is monsieur still in the house?"

"Yes, madame, monsieur le comte is in his study."

As soon as she was alone, Yvonne d'Origny walked to the window to catch a glimpse of her son as he left the house. He was out in the street in a moment, raised his head and blew her a kiss, as was his custom every day. Then the governess took his hand with, as Yvonne remarked to her surprise, a movement of unusual violence. Yvonne leant further out of the window and, when the boy reached the corner of the boulevard, she suddenly saw a man step out of a motor-car and go up to him. The man, in whom she recognized Bernard, her husband's confidential servant, took the child by the arm, made both him and the governess get into the car, and ordered the chauffeur to drive off.

The whole incident did not take ten seconds.

Yvonne, in her trepidation, ran to her bedroom, seized a wrap and went to the door. The door was locked; and there was no key in the lock.

She hurried back to the boudoir. The door of the boudoir also was locked.

Then, suddenly, the image of her husband appeared before her, that gloomy face which no smile ever lit up, those pitiless eyes in which, for years, she had felt so much hatred and malice.

"It's he . . . it's he!" she said to herself. "He has taken the child. . . . Oh, it's horrible!"

She beat against the door with her fists, with her feet, then flew to the mantelpiece and pressed the bell fiercely.

The shrill sound rang through the house from top to bottom. The servants would be sure to come. Perhaps a crowd would gather in the street. And, impelled by a sort of despairing hope, she kept her finger on the button.

A key turned in the lock. . . . The door was flung wide open. The count appeared on the threshold of the boudoir. And the expression of his face was so terrible that Yvonne began to tremble.

He entered the room. Five or six steps separated him from her. With a supreme effort, she tried to stir, but all movement was impossible; and, when she attempted to speak, she could only flutter her lips and emit incoherent sounds. She felt herself lost. The thought of death unhinged her. Her knees gave way beneath her and she sank into a huddled heap, with a moan.

The count rushed at her and seized her by the throat:

"Hold your tongue . . . don't call out!" he said, in a low voice. "That will be best for you! . . ."

Seeing that she was not attempting to defend herself, he loosened his hold of her and took from his pocket some strips of canvas ready rolled and of different lengths. In a few minutes, Yvonne was lying on a sofa, with her wrists and ankles bound and her arms fastened close to her body.

It was now dark in the boudoir. The count switched on the electric light and went to a little writing-desk where Yvonne was accustomed to keep her letters. Not succeeding in opening it, he picked the lock with a bent wire, emptied the drawers and collected all the contents into a bundle, which he carried off in a cardboard file:

"Waste of time, eh?" he grinned. "Nothing but bills and letters of no importance. . . . No proof against you. . . . Tah! I'll keep my son for all that; and I swear before Heaven that I will not let him go!"

As he was leaving the room, he was joined, near the door, by his man Bernard. The two stopped and talked, in a low voice; but Yvonne heard these words spoken by the servant:

"I have had an answer from the working jeweller. He says he holds himself at my disposal."

And the count replied:

"The thing is put off until twelve o'clock midday, to-morrow. My mother has just telephoned to say that she could not come before."

Then Yvonne heard the key turn in the lock and the sound of steps going down to the ground-floor, where her husband's study was.

She long lay inert, her brain reeling with vague, swift ideas that burnt her in passing, like flames. She remembered her husband's infamous behaviour, his humiliating conduct to her, his threats, his plans for a divorce; and she gradually came to understand that she was the victim of a regular conspiracy, that the servants had been sent away until the following evening by their master's orders, that the governess had carried off her son by the count's instructions and with Bernard's assistance, that her son would not come back and that she would never see him again.

"My son!" she cried. "My son! . . ."

Exasperated by her grief, she stiffened herself with every nerve, with every muscle tense, to make a violent effort. And she was astonished to find that her right hand, which the count had fastened too hurriedly, still retained a certain freedom.

Then a mad hope invaded her; and, slowly, patiently, she began the work of self-deliverance.

It was long in the doing. She needed a deal of time to widen the knot sufficiently and a deal of time afterward, when the hand was released, to undo those other bonds which tied her arms to her body and those which fastened her ankles.

Still, the thought of her son sustained her; and the last shackle fell as the clock struck eight. She was free!

She was no sooner on her feet than she flew to the window and flung back the latch, with the intention of calling the first passer-by. At that moment a policeman came walking along the pavement. She leant out. But the brisk evening air, striking her face, calmed her. She thought of the scandal, of the judicial investigation, of the cross-examination, of her son. O Heaven! What could she do to get him back? How could she escape? The count might appear at the least sound. And who knew but that, in a moment of fury. . . . ?

She shivered from head to foot, seized with a sudden terror. The horror of death mingled, in her poor brain, with the thought of her son; and she stammered, with a choking throat:

"Help! . . . Help! . . ."

She stopped and said to herself, several times over, in a low voice, "Help! . . . Help! . . ." as though the word awakened an idea, a memory within her, and as though the hope of assistance no longer seemed to her impossible. For some minutes she remained absorbed in deep meditation, broken by fears and starts. Then, with an almost mechanical series of movements, she put out her arm to a little set of shelves hanging over the writing-desk, took down four books, one after the other, turned the pages with a distraught air, replaced them and ended by finding, between the pages of the fifth, a visiting-card on which her eyes spelt the name:

HORACE VELMONT,

followed by an address written in pencil:

CERCLE DE LA RUE ROYALE.[1]

And her memory conjured up the strange thing which that man had said to her, a few years before, in that same house, on a day when she was at home to her friends:

"If ever a danger threatens you, if you need help, do not hesitate; post this card, which you see me put into this book; and, whatever the hour, whatever the obstacles, I will come."

With what a curious air he had spoken these words and how well he had conveyed the impression of certainty, of strength, of unlimited power, of indomitable daring!

Abruptly, unconsciously, acting under the impulse of an irresistible determination, the consequences of which she refused to anticipate, Yvonne, with the same automatic gestures, took a pneumatic-delivery envelope, slipped in the card, sealed it, directed it to "Horace Velmont, Cercle de la Rue Royale" and went to the open window. The policeman was walking up and down outside. She flung out the envelope, trusting to fate. Perhaps it would be picked up, treated as a lost letter and posted.

She had hardly completed this act when she realized its absurdity. It was mad to suppose that the message would reach the address and madder still to hope that the man to whom she was sending could come to her assistance, "whatever the hour whatever the obstacles."

A reaction followed which was all the greater inasmuch as the effort had been swift and violent. Yvonne staggered, leant against a chair and, losing all energy, let herself fall.

The hours passed by, the dreary hours of winter evenings when nothing but the sound of carriages interrupts the silence of the street. The clock struck, pitilessly. In the half-sleep that numbed her limbs, Yvonne counted the strokes. She also heard certain noises, on different floors of the house, which told her that her husband had dined, that he was going up to his room, that he was going down again to his study. But all this seemed very shadowy to her; and her torpor was such that she did not even think of lying down on the sofa, in case he should come in. . . .

The twelve strokes of midnight. . . . Then half-past twelve . . . then one. . . . Yvonne thought of nothing, awaiting the events which were preparing and against which rebellion was useless. She pictured her son and herself as one pictures those beings who have suffered much and who suffer no more and who take each other in their loving arms. But a nightmare shattered this dream. For now those two beings were to be torn asunder; and she had the awful feeling, in her delirium, that she was crying and choking. . . .

She leapt from her seat. The key had turned in the lock. The count was coming, attracted by her cries. Yvonne glanced round for a weapon with which to defend herself. But the door was pushed back quickly and, astounded, as though the sight that presented itself before her eyes seemed to her the most inexplicable prodigy, she stammered:

"You! . . . You! . . ."

A man was walking up to her, in dress-clothes, with his

opera-hat and cape under his arm, and this man, young, slender
and elegant, she had recognized as Horace Velmont.

"You!" she repeated.

He said, with a bow:

"I beg your pardon, madame, but I did not receive your letter
until very late."

"Is it possible? Is it possible that this is you . . . that you were
able to . . . ?"

He seemed greatly surprised:

"Did I not promise to come in answer to your call?"

"Yes . . . but . . ."

"Well, here I am," he said, with a smile.

He examined the strips of canvas from which Yvonne had
succeeded in freeing herself and nodded his head, while continuing his inspection:

"So those are the means employed? The Comte d'Origny, I
presume? . . . I also saw that he locked you in. . . . But then the
pneumatic letter? . . . Ah, through the window! . . . How careless of you not to close it!"

He pushed both sides to. Yvonne took fright:

"Suppose they hear!"

"There is no one in the house. I have been over it."

"Still . . ."

"Your husband went out ten minutes ago."

"Where is he?"

"With his mother, the Comtesse d'Origny."

"How do you know?"

"Oh, it's very simple! He was rung up by telephone and I
awaited the result at the corner of this street and the boulevard.
As I expected, the count came out hurriedly, followed by his
man. I at once entered, with the aid of special keys."

He told this in the most natural way, just as one tells a mean-
ingless anecdote in a drawing-room. But Yvonne, suddenly seized
with fresh alarm, asked:

"Then it's not true? . . . His mother is not ill? . . . In that
case, my husband will be coming back. . . ."

"Certainly, the count will see that a trick has been played on
him and in three quarters of an hour at the latest. . . ."

"Let us go. . . . I don't want him to find me here. . . . I must go to my son. . . ."

"One moment. . . ."

"One moment! . . . But don't you know that they have taken him from me? . . . That they are hurting him, perhaps? . . ."

With set face and feverish gestures, she tried to push Velmont back. He, with great gentleness, compelled her to sit down and, leaning over her in a respectful attitude, said, in a serious voice:

"Listen, madame, and let us not waste time, when every minute is valuable. First of all, remember this: we met four times, six years ago. . . . And, on the fourth occasion, when I was speaking to you, in the drawing-room of this house, with too much—what shall I say?—with too much feeling, you gave me to understand that my visits were no longer welcome. Since that day I have not seen you. And, nevertheless, in spite of all, your faith in me was such that you kept the card which I put between the pages of that book and, six years later, you send for me and none other. That faith in me I ask you to continue. You must obey me blindly. Just as I surmounted every obstacle to come to you, so I will save you, whatever the position may be."

Horace Velmont's calmness, his masterful voice, with the friendly intonation, gradually quieted the countess. Though still very weak, she gained a fresh sense of ease and security in that man's presence.

"Have no fear," he went on. "The Comtesse d'Origny lives at the other end of the Bois de Vincennes. Allowing that your husband finds a motor-cab, it is impossible for him to be back before a quarter-past three. Well, it is twenty-five to three now. I swear to take you away at three o'clock exactly and to take you to your son. But I will not go before I know everything."

"What am I to do?" she asked.

"Answer me and very plainly. We have twenty minutes. It is enough. But it is not too much."

"Ask me what you want to know."

"Do you think that the count had any . . . any murderous intentions?"

"No."

"Then it concerns your son?"

"Yes."

"He is taking him away, I suppose, because he wants to divorce you and marry another woman, a former friend of yours, whom you have turned out of your house. Is that it? Oh, I entreat you, answer me frankly! These are facts of public notoriety; and your hesitation, your scruples, must all cease, now that the matter concerns your son. So your husband wished to marry another woman?"

"Yes."

"The woman has no money. Your husband, on his side, has gambled away all his property and has no means beyond the allowance which he receives from his mother, the Comtesse d'Origny, and the income of a large fortune which your son inherited from two of your uncles. It is this fortune which your husband covets and which he would appropriate more easily if the child were placed in his hands. There is only one way: divorce. Am I right?"

"Yes."

"And what has prevented him until now is your refusal?"

"Yes, mine and that of my mother-in-law, whose religious feelings are opposed to divorce. The Comtesse d'Origny would only yield in case . . ."

"In case . . . ?"

"In case they could prove me guilty of shameful conduct."

Velmont shrugged his shoulders:

"Therefore he is powerless to do anything against you or against your son. Both from the legal point of view and from that of his own interests, he stumbles against an obstacle which is the most insurmountable of all: the virtue of an honest woman. And yet, in spite of everything, he suddenly shows fight."

"What do you mean?"

"I mean that, if a man like the count, after so many hesitations and in the face of so many difficulties, risks so doubtful an adventure, it must be because he thinks he has command of weapons . . ."

"What weapons?"

"I don't know. But they exist . . . or else he would not have begun by taking away your son."

Yvonne gave way to her despair:

"Oh, this is horrible! . . . How do I know what he may have done, what he may have invented?"

"Try and think. . . . Recall your memories. . . . Tell me, in this desk which he has broken open, was there any sort of letter which he could possibly turn against you?"

"No . . . only bills and addresses. . . ."

"And, in the words he used to you, in his threats, is there nothing that allows you to guess?"

"Nothing."

"Still . . . still," Velmont insisted, "there must be something." And he continued, "Has the count a particularly intimate friend . . . in whom he confides?"

"No."

"Did anybody come to see him yesterday?"

"No, nobody."

"Was he alone when he bound you and locked you in?"

"At that moment, yes."

"But afterward?"

"His man, Bernard, joined him near the door and I heard them talking about a working jeweller. . . ."

"Is that all?"

"And about something that was to happen the next day, that is, to-day, at twelve o'clock, because the Comtesse d'Origny could not come earlier."

Velmont reflected:

"Has that conversation any meaning that throws a light upon your husband's plans?"

"I don't see any."

"Where are your jewels?"

"My husband has sold them all."

"You have nothing at all left?"

"No."

"Not even a ring?"

"No," she said, showing her hands, "none except this."

"Which is your wedding-ring?"

"Which is my . . . wedding- . . ."

She stopped, nonplussed. Velmont saw her flush as she stammered:

"Could it be possible? . . . But no . . . no . . . he doesn't know. . . ."

Velmont at once pressed her with questions and Yvonne stood silent, motionless, anxious-faced. At last, she replied, in a low voice:

"This is not my wedding-ring. One day, long ago, it dropped from the mantelpiece in my bedroom, where I had put it a minute before and, hunt for it as I might, I could not find it again. So I ordered another, without saying anything about it . . . and this is the one, on my hand. . . ."

"Did the real ring bear the date of your wedding?"

"Yes . . . the 23rd of October."

"And the second?"

"This one has no date."

He perceived a slight hesitation in her and a confusion which, in point of fact, she did not try to conceal.

"I implore you," he exclaimed, "don't hide anything from me. . . . You see how far we have gone in a few minutes, with a little logic and calmness. . . . Let us go on, I ask you as a favour."

"Are you sure," she said, "that it is necessary?"

"I am sure that the least detail is of importance and that we are nearly attaining our object. But we must hurry. This is a crucial moment."

"I have nothing to conceal," she said, proudly raising her head. "It was the most wretched and the most dangerous period of my life. While suffering humiliation at home, outside I was surrounded with attentions, with temptations, with pitfalls, like any woman who is seen to be neglected by her husband. Then I remembered: before my marriage, a man had been in love with me. I had guessed his unspoken love; and he has died since. I had the name of that man engraved inside the ring; and I wore it as a talisman. There was no love in me, because I was the wife of another. But, in my secret heart, there was a memory, a sad dream, something sweet and gentle that protected me. . . ."

She had spoken slowly, without embarrassment, and Velmont

did not doubt for a second that she was telling the absolute truth. He kept silent; and she, becoming anxious again, asked:

"Do you suppose . . . that my husband . . . ?"

He took her hand and, while examining the plain gold ring, said:

"The puzzle lies here. Your husband, I don't know how, knows of the substitution of one ring for the other. His mother will be here at twelve o'clock. In the presence of witnesses, he will compel you to take off your ring; and, in this way, he will obtain the approval of his mother and, at the same time, will be able to obtain his divorce, because he will have the proof for which he was seeking."

"I am lost!" she moaned. "I am lost!"

"On the contrary, you are saved! Give me that ring . . . and presently he will find another there, another which I will send you, to reach you before twelve, and which will bear the date of the 23rd of October. So . . ."

He suddenly broke off. While he was speaking, Yvonne's hand had turned ice-cold in his; and, raising his eyes, he saw that the young woman was pale, terribly pale:

"What's the matter? I beseech you . . ."

She yielded to a fit of mad despair:

"This is the matter, that I am lost! . . . This is the matter, that I can't get the ring off! It has grown too small for me! . . . Do you understand? . . . It made no difference and I did not give it a thought. . . . But to-day . . . this proof . . . this accusation. . . . Oh, what torture! . . . Look . . . it forms part of my finger . . . it has grown into my flesh . . . and I can't . . . I can't. . . ."

She pulled at the ring, vainly, with all her might, at the risk of injuring herself. But the flesh swelled up around the ring; and the ring did not budge.

"Oh!" she cried, seized with an idea that terrified her. "I remember . . . the other night . . . a nightmare I had. . . . It seemed to me that some one entered my room and caught hold of my hand. . . . And I could not wake up. . . . It was he! It was he! He had put me to sleep, I was sure of it . . . and he was looking at the ring. . . . And presently he will pull it off before his mother's eyes. . . . Ah, I understand everything: that working jeweller! . . .

He will cut it from my hand to-morrow. . . . You see, you see. . . .
I am lost! . . ."

She hid her face in her hands and began to weep. But, amid
the silence, the clock struck once . . . and twice . . . and yet
once more. And Yvonne drew herself up with a jerk:

"There he is!" she cried. "He is coming! . . . It is three
o'clock! . . . Let us go! . . ."

She grabbed at her cloak and ran to the door. . . . Velmont
barred the way and, in a masterful tone:

"You shall not go!"

"My son. . . . I want to see him, to take him back. . . ."

"You don't even know where he is!"

"I want to go."

"You shall not go! . . . It would be madness. . . ."

He took her by the wrists. She tried to release herself; and
Velmont had to employ a little force to overcome her resistance.
In the end, he succeeded in getting her back to the sofa, then in
laying her at full length and, at once, without heeding her lamentations, he took the canvas strips and fastened her wrists and
ankles:

"Yes," he said. "It would be madness! Who would have set
you free? Who would have opened that door for you? An accomplice? What an argument against you and what a pretty use your
husband would make of it with his mother! . . . And, besides,
what's the good? To run away means accepting divorce . . . and
what might that not lead to? . . . You must stay here. . . ."

She sobbed:

"I'm frightened. . . . I'm frightened . . . this ring burns
me. . . . Break it. . . . Take it away. . . . Don't let him find it!"

"And if it is not found on your finger, who will have broken
it? Again an accomplice. . . . No, you must face the music . . .
and face it bodly, for I answer for everything. . . . Believe me . . .
I answer for everything. . . . If I have to tackle the Comtesse
d'Origny bodily and thus delay the interview. . . . If I had to
come myself before noon . . . it is the real wedding-ring that
shall be taken from your finger—that I swear!—and your son
shall be restored to you."

Swayed and subdued, Yvonne instinctively held out her hands

to the bonds. When he stood up, she was bound as she had been before.

He looked round the room to make sure that no trace of his visit remained. Then he stooped over the countess again and whispered:

"Think of your son and, whatever happens, fear nothing. . . . I am watching over you."

She heard him open and shut the door of the boudoir and, a few minutes later, the hall-door.

At half-past three, a motor-cab drew up. The door downstairs was slammed again; and, almost immediately after, Yvonne saw her husband hurry in, with a furious look in his eyes. He ran up to her, felt to see if she was still fastened and, snatching her hand, examined the ring. Yvonne fainted. . . .

She could not tell, when she woke, how long she had slept. But the broad light of day was filling the boudoir; and she perceived, at the first movement which she made, that her bonds were cut. Then she turned her head and saw her husband standing beside her, looking at her:

"My son . . . my son . . ." she moaned. "I want my son. . . ."

He replied, in a voice of which she felt the jeering insolence:

"Our son is in a safe place. And, for the moment, it's a question not of him, but of you. We are face to face with each other, probably for the last time, and the explanation between us will be a very serious one. I must warn you that it will take place before my mother. Have you any objection?"

Yvonne tried to hide her agitation and answered:

"None at all."

"Can I send for her?"

"Yes. Leave me, in the meantime. I shall be ready when she comes."

"My mother is here."

"Your mother is here?" cried Yvonne, in dismay, remembering Horace Velmont's promise.

"What is there to astonish you in that?"

"And is it now . . . is it at once that you want to . . . ?"

"Yes."

"Why? . . . Why not this evening? . . . Why not to-morrow?"

"To-day and now," declared the count. "A rather curious incident happened in the course of last night, an incident which I cannot account for and which decided me to hasten the explanation. Don't you want something to eat first?"

"No . . . no. . . ."

"Then I will go and fetch my mother."

He turned to Yvonne's bedroom. Yvonne glanced at the clock. It marked twenty-five minutes to eleven!

"Ah!" she said, with a shiver of fright.

Twenty-five minutes to eleven! Horace Velmont would not save her and nobody in the world and nothing in the world would save her, for there was no miracle that could place the wedding-ring upon her finger.

The count, returning with the Comtesse d'Origny, asked her to sit down. She was a tall, lank, angular woman, who had always displayed a hostile feeling to Yvonne. She did not even bid her daughter-in-law good-morning, showing that her mind was made up as regards the accusation:

"I don't think," she said, "that we need speak at length. In two words, my son maintains. . . ."

"I don't maintain, mother," said the count, "I declare. I declare on my oath that, three months ago, during the holidays, the upholsterer, when laying the carpet in this room and the boudoir, found the wedding-ring which I gave my wife lying in a crack in the floor. Here is the ring. The date of the 23rd of October is engraved inside."

"Then," said the countess, "the ring which your wife carries. . . ."

"That is another ring, which she ordered in exchange for the real one. Acting on my instructions, Bernard, my man, after long searching, ended by discovering in the outskirts of Paris, where he now lives, the little jeweller to whom she went. This man remembers perfectly and is willing to bear witness that his customer did not tell him to engrave a date, but a name. He has forgotten the name, but the man who used to work with him in his shop may be able to remember it. This working jeweller has been informed by letter that I required his services and he replied yesterday, placing himself at my disposal. Bernard went to fetch him at nine o'clock this morning. They are both waiting in my study."

He turned to his wife:

"Will you give me that ring of your own free will?"

"You know," she said, "from the other night, that it won't come off my finger."

"In that case, can I have the man up? He has the necessary implements with him."

"Yes," she said, in a voice faint as a whisper.

She was resigned. She conjured up the future as in a vision: the scandal, the decree of divorce pronounced against herself, the custody of the child awarded to the father; and she accepted this, thinking that she would carry off her son, that she would go with him to the ends of the earth and that the two of them would live alone together and happy. . . .

Her mother-in-law said:

"You have been very thoughtless, Yvonne."

Yvonne was on the point of confessing to her and asking for her protection. But what was the good? How could the Comtesse d'Origny possibly believe her innocent? She made no reply.

Besides, the count at once returned, followed by his servant and by a man carrying a bag of tools under his arm.

And the count said to the man:

"You know what you have to do?"

"Yes," said the workman. "It's to cut a ring that's grown too small. . . . That's easily done. . . . A touch of the nippers. . . ."

"And then you will see," said the count, "if the inscription inside the ring was the one you engraved."

Yvonne looked at the clock. It was ten minutes to eleven. She seemed to hear, somewhere in the house, a sound of voices raised in argument; and, in spite of herself, she felt a thrill of hope. Perhaps Velmont has succeeded. . . . But the sound was renewed; and she perceived that it was produced by some costermongers passing under her window and moving farther on.

It was all over. Horace Velmont had been unable to assist her. And she understood that, to recover her child, she must rely upon her own strength, for the promises of others are vain.

She made a movement of recoil. She had felt the workman's heavy hand on her hand; and that hateful touch revolted her.

The man apologized, awkwardly. The count said to his wife: "You must make up your mind, you know."

Then she put out her slim and trembling hand to the workman, who took it, turned it over and rested it on the table, with the palm upward. Yvonne felt the cold steel. She longed to die, then and there; and, at once attracted by that idea of death, she thought of the poisons which she would buy and which would send her to sleep almost without her knowing it.

The operation did not take long. Inserted on the slant, the little steel pliers pushed back the flesh, made room for themselves and bit the ring. A strong effort . . . and the ring broke. The two ends had only to be separated to remove the ring from the finger. The workman did so.

The count exclaimed, in triumph:

"At last! Now we shall see! . . . The proof is there! And we are all witnesses. . . ."

He snatched up the ring and looked at the inscription. A cry of amazement escaped him. The ring bore the date of his marriage to Yvonne: "23rd of October"! . . .

We were sitting on the terrace at Monte Carlo. Lupin finished his story, lit a cigarette and calmly puffed the smoke into the blue air.

I said:

"Well?"

"Well what?"

"Why, the end of the story. . . ."

"The end of the story? But what other end could there be?"

"Come . . . you're joking . . ."

"Not at all. Isn't that enough for you? The countess is saved. The count, not possessing the least proof against her, is compelled by his mother to forego the divorce and to give up the child. That is all. Since then, he has left his wife, who is living happily with her son, a fine lad of sixteen."

"Yes . . . yes . . . but the way in which the countess was saved?"

Lupin burst out laughing:

"My dear old chap"—Lupin sometimes condescends to address me in this affectionate manner—"my dear old chap, you may be rather smart at relating my exploits, but, by Jove, you do want to have the i's dotted for you! I assure you, the countess did not ask for explanations!"

"Very likely. But there's no pride about me," I added, laughing. "Dot those i's for me, will you?"

He took out a five-franc piece and closed his hand over it.

"What's in my hand?"

"A five-franc piece."

He opened his hand. The five-franc piece was gone.

"You see how easy it is! A working jeweller, with his nippers, cuts a ring with a date engraved upon it: 23rd of October. It's a simple little trick of sleight-of-hand, one of many which I have in my bag. By Jove, I didn't spend six months with Dickson, the conjurer,[2] for nothing!"

"But then . . . ?"

"Out with it!"

"The working jeweller?"

"Was Horace Velmont! Was good old Lupin! Leaving the countess at three o'clock in the morning, I employed the few remaining minutes before the husband's return to have a look round his study. On the table I found the letter from the working jeweller. The letter gave me the address. A bribe of a few louis enabled me to take the workman's place; and I arrived with a wedding-ring ready cut and engraved. Hocus-pocus! Pass! . . . The count couldn't make head or tail of it."

"Splendid!" I cried. And I added, a little chaffingly, in my turn, "But don't you think that you were humbugged a bit yourself, on this occasion?"

"Oh! And by whom, pray?"

"By the countess?"

"In what way?"

"Hang it all, that name engraved as a talisman! . . . The mysterious Adonis who loved her and suffered for her sake! . . . All that story seems very unlikely; and I wonder whether, Lupin though you be, you did not just drop upon a pretty love-story, absolutely genuine and . . . none too innocent."

Lupin looked at me out of the corner of his eye:

"No," he said.

"How do you know?"

"If the countess made a misstatement in telling me that she knew that man before her marriage—and that he was dead—and if she really did love him in her secret heart, I, at least, have a positive proof that it was an ideal love and that he did not suspect it."

"And where is the proof?"

"It is inscribed inside the ring which I myself broke on the countess's finger . . . and which I carry on me. Here it is. You can read the name she had engraved on it."

He handed me the ring. I read:

"Horace Velmont."

There was a moment of silence between Lupin and myself; and, noticing it, I also observed on his face a certain emotion, a tinge of melancholy.

I resumed:

"What made you tell me this story . . . to which you have often alluded in my presence?"

"What made me . . . ?"

He drew my attention to a woman, still exceedingly handsome, who was passing on a young man's arm. She saw Lupin and bowed.

"It's she," he whispered. "She and her son."

"Then she recognized you?"

"She always recognizes me, whatever my disguise."

"But since the burglary at the Château de Thibermesnil,[3] the police have identified the two names of Arsène Lupin and Horace Velmont."

"Yes."

"Therefore she knows who you are."

"Yes."

"And she bows to you?" I exclaimed, in spite of myself.

He caught me by the arm and, fiercely:

"Do you think that I am Lupin to her? Do you think that I am a burglar in her eyes, a rogue, a cheat? . . . Why, I might be the lowest of miscreants, I might be a murderer even . . . and still she would bow to me!"

"Why? Because she loved you once?"

"Rot! That would be an additional reason, on the contrary, why she should now despise me."

"What then?"

"I am the man who gave her back her son!"

THE RED SILK SCARF

On leaving his house one morning, at his usual early hour for going to the Law Courts, Chief-Inspector Ganimard noticed the curious behaviour of an individual who was walking along the Rue Pergolèse in front of him. Shabbily dressed and wearing a straw hat, though the day was the first of December, the man stooped at every thirty or forty yards to fasten his boot-lace, or pick up his stick, or for some other reason. And, each time, he took a little piece of orange-peel from his pocket and laid it stealthily on the curb of the pavement. It was probably a mere display of eccentricity, a childish amusement to which no one else would have paid attention; but Ganimard was one of those shrewd observers who are indifferent to nothing that strikes their eyes and who are never satisfied until they know the secret cause of things. He therefore began to follow the man.

Now, at the moment when the fellow was turning to the right, into the Avenue de la Grande-Armée, the inspector caught him exchanging signals with a boy of twelve or thirteen, who was walking along the houses on the left-hand side. Twenty yards farther, the man stooped and turned up the bottom of his trousers legs. A bit of orange-peel marked the place. At the same moment, the boy stopped and, with a piece of chalk, drew a white cross, surrounded by a circle, on the wall of the house next to him.

The two continued on their way. A minute later, a fresh halt. The strange individual picked up a pin and dropped a piece of orange-peel; and the boy at once made a second cross on the wall and again drew a white circle round it.

"By Jove!" thought the chief-inspector, with a grunt of satisfaction. "This is rather promising. . . . What on earth can those
two merchants be plotting?"

The two "merchants" went down the Avenue Friedland and
the Rue du Faubourg-Saint-Honoré, but nothing occurred that
was worthy of special mention. The double performance was
repeated at almost regular intervals and, so to speak, mechanically. Nevertheless, it was obvious, on the one hand, that the
man with the orange-peel did not do his part of the business until after he had picked out with a glance the house that was to
be marked and, on the other hand, that the boy did not mark
that particular house until after he had observed his companion's signal. It was certain, therefore, that there was an agreement between the two; and the proceedings presented no small
interest in the chief-inspector's eyes.

At the Place Beauveau the man hesitated. Then, apparently
making up his mind, he twice turned up and twice turned
down the bottom of his trousers legs. Hereupon, the boy sat
down on the curb, opposite the sentry who was mounting
guard outside the Ministry of the Interior, and marked the flag-
stone with two little crosses contained within two circles. The
same ceremony was gone through a little further on, when they
reached the Elysée. Only, on the pavement where the Presi-
dent's sentry was marching up and down, there were three signs
instead of two.

"Hang it all!" muttered Ganimard, pale with excitement and
thinking, in spite of himself, of his inveterate enemy, Lupin,
whose name came to his mind whenever a mysterious circum-
stance presented itself. "Hang it all, what does it mean?"

He was nearly collaring and questioning the two "merchants."
But he was too clever to commit so gross a blunder. The man
with the orange-peel had now lit a cigarette; and the boy, also
placing a cigarette-end between his lips, had gone up to him, apparently with the object of asking for a light.

They exchanged a few words. Quick as thought, the boy
handed his companion an object which looked—at least, so the
inspector believed—like a revolver. They both bent over this object; and the man, standing with his face to the wall, put his

hand six times in his pocket and made a movement as though he were loading a weapon.

As soon as this was done, they walked briskly to the Rue de Suréne; and the inspector, who followed them as closely as he was able to do without attracting their attention, saw them enter the gateway of an old house of which all the shutters were closed, with the exception of those on the third or top floor.

He hurried in after them. At the end of the carriage-entrance he saw a large courtyard, with a house-painter's sign at the back and a staircase on the left.

He went up the stairs and, as soon as he reached the first floor, ran still faster, because he heard, right up at the top, a din as of a free-fight.

When he came to the last landing he found the door open. He entered, listened for a second, caught the sound of a struggle, rushed to the room from which the sound appeared to proceed and remained standing on the threshold, very much out of breath and greatly surprised to see the man of the orange-peel and the boy banging the floor with chairs.

At that moment a third person walked out of an adjoining room. It was a young man of twenty-eight or thirty, wearing a pair of short whiskers in addition to his moustache, spectacles, and a smoking-jacket with an astrakhan collar and looking like a foreigner, a Russian.

"Good morning, Ganimard," he said. And turning to the two companions, "Thank you, my friends, and all my congratulations on the successful result. Here's the reward I promised you."

He gave them a hundred-franc note, pushed them outside and shut both doors.

"I am sorry, old chap," he said to Ganimard. "I wanted to talk to you . . . wanted to talk to you badly."

He offered him his hand and, seeing that the inspector remained flabbergasted and that his face was still distorted with anger, he exclaimed:

"Why, you don't seem to understand! . . . And yet it's clear enough. . . . I wanted to see you particularly. . . . So what could I do?" And, pretending to reply to an objection, "No, no, old chap," he continued. "You're quite wrong. If I had written or telephoned, you would not have come . . . or else you would have come with a regiment. Now I wanted to see you all alone; and I thought the best thing was to send those two decent fellows to meet you, with orders to scatter bits of orange-peel and draw crosses and circles, in short, to mark out your road to this place. . . . Why, you look quite bewildered! What is it? Perhaps you don't recognize me? Lupin. . . . Arsène Lupin. . . . Ransack your memory. . . . Doesn't the name remind you of anything?"

"You dirty scoundrel!" Ganimard snarled between his teeth.

Lupin seemed greatly distressed and, in an affectionate voice:

"Are you vexed? Yes, I can see it in your eyes. . . . The Dugrival business, I suppose?[1] I ought to have waited for you to come and take me in charge? . . . There now, the thought never occurred to me! I promise you, next time. . . ."

"You scum of the earth!" growled Ganimard.

"And I thinking I was giving you a treat! Upon my word, I did. I said to myself, 'That dear old Ganimard! We haven't met for an age. He'll simply rush at me when he sees me!' "

Ganimard, who had not yet stirred a limb, seemed to be waking from his stupor. He looked around him, looked at Lupin, visibly asked himself whether he would not do well to rush at him in reality and then, controlling himself, took hold of a chair and settled himself in it, as though he had suddenly made up his mind to listen to his enemy:

"Speak," he said. "And don't waste my time with any nonsense. I'm in a hurry."

"That's it," said Lupin, "let's talk. You can't imagine a quieter place than this. It's an old manor-house, which once stood in the open country, and it belongs to the Duc de Rochelaure. The duke, who has never lived in it, lets this floor to me and the outhouses to a painter and decorator. I always keep up a few establishments of this kind: it's a sound, practical plan. Here, in spite of my looking like a Russian nobleman, I am M. Daubreuil, an ex-cabinet-minister. . . . You understand, I had to select a rather overstocked profession, so as not to attract attention. . . ."

"Do you think I care a hang about all this?" said Ganimard, interrupting him.

"Quite right, I'm wasting words and you're in a hurry. Forgive me. I shan't be long now. . . . Five minutes, that's all . . . I'll start at once . . . Have a cigar? No? Very well, no more will I."

He sat down also, drummed his fingers on the table, while thinking, and began in this fashion:

"On the 17th of October, 1599, on a warm and sunny autumn day . . . Do you follow me? . . . But, now that I come to think of it, is it really necessary to go back to the reign of Henry IV, and tell you all about the building of the Pont-Neuf? No, I don't suppose you are very well up in French history; and I should only end by muddling you.² Suffice it, then, for you to know that, last night, at one o'clock in the morning, a boatman passing under the last arch of the Pont-Neuf aforesaid, along the left bank of the river, heard something drop into the front part of his barge. The thing had been flung from the bridge and its evident destination was the bottom of the Seine. The bargee's dog rushed forward, barking, and, when the man reached the end of his craft, he saw the animal worrying a piece of newspaper that had served to wrap up a number of objects. He took from the dog such of the contents as had not fallen into the water, went to his cabin and examined them carefully. The result struck him as interesting; and, as the man is connected with one of my friends, he sent to let me know. This morning I was woke up and placed in possession of the facts and of the objects which the man had collected. Here they are."

He pointed to them, spread out on a table. There were, first of all, the torn pieces of a newspaper. Next came a large cut-glass inkstand, with a long piece of string fastened to the lid. There was a bit of broken glass and a sort of flexible cardboard, reduced to shreds. Lastly, there was a piece of bright scarlet silk, ending in a tassel of the same material and colour.

"You see our exhibits, friend of my youth," said Lupin. "No doubt, the problem would be more easily solved if we had the other objects which went overboard owing to the stupidity of the dog. But it seems to me, all the same, that we ought to be able to manage, with a little reflection and intelligence. And those are just your great qualities. How does the business strike you?"

Ganimard did not move a muscle. He was willing to stand Lupin's chaff, but his dignity commanded him not to speak a single word in answer nor even to give a nod or shake of the head that might have been taken to express approval or criticism.

"I see that we are entirely of one mind," continued Lupin, without appearing to remark the chief-inspector's silence. "And I can sum up the matter briefly, as told us by these exhibits. Yesterday evening, between nine and twelve o'clock, a showily dressed young woman was wounded with a knife and then caught round the throat and choked to death by a well-dressed gentleman, wearing a single eyeglass and interested in racing, with whom the aforesaid showily dressed young lady had been eating three meringues and a coffee éclair."

Lupin lit a cigarette and, taking Ganimard by the sleeve:

"Aha, that's up against you, chief-inspector! You thought that, in the domain of police deductions, such feats as those were prohibited to outsiders! Wrong, sir! Lupin juggles with inferences and deductions for all the world like a detective in a novel. My proofs are dazzling and absolutely simple."

And, pointing to the objects one by one, as he demonstrated his statement, he resumed:

"I said, after nine o'clock yesterday evening. This scrap of newspaper bears yesterday's date, with the words, 'Evening edition.' Also, you will see here, pasted to the paper, a bit of one of those yellow wrappers in which the subscribers' copies are sent out. These copies are always delivered by the nine o'clock post. Therefore, it was after nine o'clock. I said, a well-dressed man. Please observe that this tiny piece of glass has the round hole of a single eyeglass at one of the edges and that the single eyeglass is an essentially aristocratic article of wear. This well-dressed man walked into a pastry-cook's shop. Here is the very thin cardboard, shaped like a box, and still showing a little of the cream of the meringues and éclairs which were packed in it in the usual way. Having got his parcel, the gentleman with the eyeglass joined a young person whose eccentricity in the matter of dress is pretty clearly indicated by this bright-red silk scarf. Having joined her, for some reason as yet unknown he first stabbed her with a knife and then strangled her with the help of this same scarf. Take your magnifying glass, chief-inspector, and you will see, on the silk, stains of a darker red which are, here, the marks of a knife wiped on the scarf and, there, the marks of a hand, covered with blood, clutching the material. Having committed the murder, his next business is to leave no trace behind him. So he takes from his pocket, first, the newspaper to which he subscribes—a racing-paper, as you will see by glancing at the contents of this scrap; and you will have no difficulty in discovering the title—and, secondly, a cord, which, on inspection, turns out to be a length of whip-cord. These two details prove—do they not?—that our man is interested in racing and that he himself rides. Next, he picks up the fragments of his eyeglass, the cord of which has been broken in the struggle. He takes a pair of scissors—observe the hacking of the scissors—and cuts off the stained part of the scarf, leaving the other end, no doubt, in his victim's clenched hands. He makes a ball of the confectioner's cardboard box. He also puts in certain things that would have betrayed him, such as the knife, which must have slipped into the Seine. He wraps everything in the newspaper, ties it with the cord and fastens this cut-glass ink-stand to it, as a make-weight. Then he makes himself scarce. A little later, the parcel falls into the waterman's barge. And there you are. Oof, it's hot work! . . . What do you say to the story?"[3]

He looked at Ganimard to see what impression his speech had produced on the inspector. Ganimard did not depart from his attitude of silence.

Lupin began to laugh:

"As a matter of fact, you're annoyed and surprised. But you're suspicious as well: 'Why should that confounded Lupin hand the business over to me,' say you, 'instead of keeping it for himself, hunting down the murderer and rifling his pockets, if there was a robbery?' The question is quite logical, of course. But—there is a 'but'—I have no time, you see. I am full up with work at the present moment: a burglary in London, another at Lausanne, an exchange of children at Marseilles, to say nothing of having to save a young girl who is at this moment shadowed by death. That's always the way: it never rains but it pours. So I said to myself, 'Suppose I handed the business over to my dear old Ganimard? Now that it is half-solved for him, he is quite capable of succeeding. And what a service I shall be doing him! How magnificently he will be able to distinguish himself!' No sooner said than done. At eight o'clock in the morning, I sent the joker with the orange-peel to meet you. You swallowed the bait; and you were here by nine, all on edge and eager for the fray."

Lupin rose from his chair. He went over to the inspector and, with his eyes in Ganimard's, said:

"That's all. You now know the whole story. Presently, you will know the victim: some ballet-dancer, probably, some singer at a music-hall. On the other hand, the chances are that the criminal lives near the Pont-Neuf, most likely on the left bank. Lastly, here are all the exhibits. I make you a present of them. Set to work. I shall only keep this end of the scarf. If ever you want to piece the scarf together, bring me the other end, the one which the police will find round the victim's neck. Bring it me in four weeks from now to the day, that is to say, on the 29th of December, at ten o'clock in the morning. You can he sure of finding me here. And don't be afraid: this is all perfectly serious, friend of my youth; I swear it is. No humbug, honour bright. You can go straight ahead. Oh, by the way, when you arrest the fellow with the eyeglass, be a bit careful: he is left-handed! Good-bye, old dear, and good luck to you!"

Lupin spun round on his heel, went to the door, opened it and disappeared before Ganimard had even thought of taking a decision. The inspector rushed after him, but at once found that the handle of the door, by some trick of mechanism which he did not know, refused to turn. It took him ten minutes to un-screw the lock and ten minutes more to unscrew the lock of the hall-door. By the time that he had scrambled down the three flights of stairs, Ganimard had given up all hope of catching Arsène Lupin.

Besides, he was not thinking of it. Lupin inspired him with a queer, complex feeling, made up of fear, hatred, involuntary admiration, and also the vague instinct that he, Ganimard, in

spite of all his efforts, in spite of the persistency of his endeav-
ours, would never get the better of this particular adversary. He
pursued him from a sense of duty and pride, but with the con-
tinual dread of being taken in by that formidable hoaxer and
scouted and fooled in the face of a public that was always only
too willing to laugh at the chief-inspector's mishaps.

This business of the red scarf, in particular, struck him as most
suspicious. It was interesting, certainly, in more ways than one,
but so very improbable! And Lupin's explanation, apparently so
logical, would never stand the test of a severe examination!

"No," said Ganimard, "this is all swank: a parcel of suppositions and guesswork based upon nothing at all. I'm not to be
caught with chaff."

When he reached the headquarters of police, at 36 Quai des
Orfèvres,[4] he had quite made up his mind to treat the incident
as though it had never happened.

He went up to the Criminal Investigation Department. Here,
one of his fellow-inspectors said:

"Seen the chief?"

"No."

"He was asking for you just now."

"Oh, was he?"

"Yes, you had better go after him."

"Where?"

"To the Rue de Berne . . . there was a murder there last
night."

"Oh! Who's the victim?"

"I don't know exactly . . . a music-hall singer, I believe."

Ganimard simply muttered:

"By Jove!"

Twenty minutes later he stepped out of the underground
railway-station and made for the Rue de Berne.

The victim, who was known in the theatrical world by her
stage-name of Jenny Saphir, occupied a small flat on the second
floor of one of the houses. A policeman took the chief-inspector
upstairs and showed him the way, through two sitting-rooms,
to a bedroom, where he found the magistrates in charge of the

inquiry, together with the divisional surgeon and M. Dudouis, the head of the detective-service.

Ganimard started at the first glance which he gave into the room. He saw, lying on a sofa, the corpse of a young woman whose hands clutched a strip of red silk! One of the shoulders, which appeared above the low-cut bodice, bore the marks of two wounds surrounded with clotted blood. The distorted and almost blackened features still bore an expression of frenzied terror.

The divisional surgeon, who had just finished his examination, said:

"My first conclusions are very clear. The victim was twice stabbed with a dagger and afterward strangled. The immediate cause of death was asphyxia."

"By Jove!" thought Ganimard again, remembering Lupin's words and the picture which he had drawn of the crime.

The examining-magistrate objected:

"But the neck shows no discoloration."

"She may have been strangled with a napkin or a handkerchief," said the doctor.

"Most probably," said the chief detective, "with this silk scarf, which the victim was wearing and a piece of which remains, as though she had clung to it with her two hands to protect herself."

"But why does only that piece remain?" asked the magistrate. "What has become of the other?"

"The other may have been stained with blood and carried off by the murderer. You can plainly distinguish the hurried slashing of the scissors."

"By Jove!" said Ganimard, between his teeth, for the third time. "That brute of a Lupin saw everything without seeing a thing!"

"And what about the motive of the murder?" asked the magistrate. "The locks have been forced, the cupboards turned upside down. Have you anything to tell me, M. Dudouis?"

The chief of the detective-service replied:

"I can at least suggest a supposition, derived from the statements made by the servant. The victim, who enjoyed a greater reputation on account of her looks than through her talent as a singer, went to Russia, two years ago, and brought back with her a magnificent sapphire, which she appears to have received from some person of importance at the court. Since then, she went by the name of Jenny Saphir and seems generally to have been very proud of that present, although, for prudence sake, she never wore it. I daresay that we shall not be far out if we presume the theft of the sapphire to have been the cause of the crime."

"But did the maid know where the stone was?"

"No, nobody did. And the disorder of the room would tend to prove that the murderer did not know either."

"We will question the maid," said the examining-magistrate.

M. Dudouis took the chief-inspector aside and said:

"You're looking very old-fashioned, Ganimard. What's the matter? Do you suspect anything?"

"Nothing at all, chief."

"That's a pity. We could do with a bit of showy work in the department. This is one of a number of crimes, all of the same class, of which we have failed to discover the perpetrator. This time we want the criminal . . . and quickly!"

"A difficult job, chief."

"It's got to be done. Listen to me, Ganimard. According to what the maid says, Jenny Saphir led a very regular life. For a month past she was in the habit of frequently receiving visits, on her return from the music-hall, that is to say, at about half-past ten, from a man who would stay until midnight or so. 'He's a society man,' Jenny Saphir used to say, 'and he wants to marry me.' This society man took every precaution to avoid being seen, such as turning up his coat-collar and lowering the brim of his hat when he passed the porter's box. And Jenny Saphir always made a point of sending away her maid, even before he came. This is the man whom we have to find."

"Has he left no traces?"

"None at all. It is obvious that we have to deal with a very clever scoundrel, who prepared his crime beforehand and committed it with every possible chance of escaping unpunished. His arrest would be a great feather in our cap. I rely on you, Ganimard."

"Ah, you rely on me, chief?" replied the inspector. "Well, we shall see . . . we shall see. . . . I don't say no. . . . Only . . ."

He seemed in a very nervous condition, and his agitation struck M. Dudouis.

"Only," continued Ganimard, "only I swear . . . do you hear, chief? I swear. . . ."

"What do you swear?"

"Nothing. . . . We shall see, chief . . . we shall see. . . ."

Ganimard did not finish his sentence until he was outside, alone. And he finished it aloud, stamping his foot, in a tone of the most violent anger:

"Only, I swear to Heaven that the arrest shall be effected by my own means, without my employing a single one of the clues with which that villain has supplied me. Ah, no! Ah, no! . . ."

Railing against Lupin, furious at being mixed up in this business and resolved, nevertheless, to get to the bottom of it, he wandered aimlessly about the streets. His brain was seething with irritation; and he tried to adjust his ideas a little and to discover, among the chaotic facts, some trifling detail, unperceived by all, unsuspected by Lupin himself, that might lead him to success.

He lunched hurriedly at a bar, resumed his stroll and suddenly stopped, petrified, astounded and confused. He was walking under the gateway of the very house in the Rue de Surène to which Lupin had enticed him a few hours earlier! A force stronger than his own will was drawing him there once more. The solution of the problem lay there. There and there alone were all the elements of the truth. Do and say what he would, Lupin's assertions were so precise, his calculations so accurate, that, worried to the innermost recesses of his being by so prodigious a display of perspicacity, he could not do other than take up the work at the point where his enemy had left it.

Abandoning all further resistance, he climbed the three flights of stairs. The door of the flat was open. No one had touched the exhibits. He put them in his pocket and walked away.

From that moment, he reasoned and acted, so to speak, mechanically, under the influence of the master whom he could not choose but obey.

Admitting that the unknown person whom he was seeking

lived in the neighbourhood of the Pont-Neuf, it became necessary to discover, somewhere between that bridge and the Rue
de Berne, the first-class confectioner's shop, open in the evenings, at which the cakes were bought. This did not take long
to find. A pastry-cook near the Gare Saint-Lazare showed him
some little cardboard boxes, identical in material and shape
with the one in Ganimard's possession. Moreover, one of the
shop-girls remembered having served, on the previous evening,
a gentleman whose face was almost concealed in the collar of
his fur coat, but whose eyeglass she had happened to notice.

"That's one clue checked," thought the inspector. "Our man
wears an eyeglass."

He next collected the pieces of the racing-paper and showed
them to a newsvendor, who easily recognized the *Turf Illustré*.
Ganimard at once went to the offices of the *Turf* and asked to
see the list of subscribers. Going through the list, he jotted
down the names and addresses of all those who lived anywhere
near the Pont-Neuf and principally—because Lupin had said
so—those on the left bank of the river.

He then went back to the Criminal Investigation Department, took half a dozen men and packed them off with the necessary instructions.

At seven o'clock in the evening, the last of these men returned
and brought good news with him. A certain M. Prévailles, a
subscriber to the *Turf*, occupied an entresol flat on the Quai des
Augustins. On the previous evening, he left his place, wearing a
fur coat, took his letters and his paper, the *Turf Illustré*, from
the porter's wife, walked away and returned home at midnight.
This M. Prévailles wore a single eyeglass. He was a regular
race-goer and himself owned several hacks which he either rode
himself or jobbed out.

The inquiry had taken so short a time and the results obtained
were so exactly in accordance with Lupin's predictions that
Ganimard felt quite overcome on hearing the detective's report.
Once more he was measuring the prodigious extent of the resources at Lupin's disposal. Never in the course of his life—and
Ganimard was already well-advanced in years—had he come
across such perspicacity, such a quick and far-seeing mind.

He went in search of M. Dudouis.

"Everything's ready, chief. Have you a warrant?"

"Eh?"

"I said, everything is ready for the arrest, chief."

"You know the name of Jenny Saphir's murderer?"

"Yes."

"But how? Explain yourself."

Ganimard had a sort of scruple of conscience, blushed a little and nevertheless replied:

"An accident, chief. The murderer threw everything that was likely to compromise him into the Seine. Part of the parcel was picked up and handed to me."

"By whom?"

"A boatman who refused to give his name, for fear of getting into trouble. But I had all the clues I wanted. It was not so difficult as I expected."

And the inspector described how he had gone to work.

"And you call that an accident!" cried M. Dudouis. "And you say that it was not difficult! Why, it's one of your finest performances! Finish it yourself, Ganimard, and be prudent."

Ganimard was eager to get the business done. He went to the Quai des Augustins with his men and distributed them around the house. He questioned the portress, who said that her tenant took his meals out of doors, but made a point of looking in after dinner.

A little before nine o'clock, in fact, leaning out of her window, she warned Ganimard, who at once gave a low whistle. A gentleman in a tall hat and a fur coat was coming along the pavement beside the Seine. He crossed the road and walked up to the house.

Ganimard stepped forward:

"M. Prévailles, I believe?"

"Yes, but who are you?"

"I have a commission to . . ."

He had not time to finish his sentence. At the sight of the men appearing out of the shadow, Prévailles quickly retreated to the wall and faced his adversaries, with his back to the door of a shop on the ground-floor, the shutters of which were closed.

"Stand back!" he cried. "I don't know you!"

His right hand brandished a heavy stick, while his left was slipped behind him and seemed to be trying to open the door.

Ganimard had an impression that the man might escape through this way and through some secret outlet:

"None of this nonsense," he said, moving closer to him. "You're caught. . . . You had better come quietly."

But, just as he was laying hold of Prévailles' stick, Ganimard remembered the warning which Lupin gave him: Prévailles was left-handed; and it was his revolver for which he was feeling behind his back.

The inspector ducked his head. He had noticed the man's sudden movement. Two reports rang out. No one was hit.

A second later, Prévailles received a blow under the chin from the butt-end of a revolver, which brought him down where he stood. He was entered at the Dépôt soon after nine o'clock.

Ganimard enjoyed a great reputation even at that time. But this capture, so quickly effected, by such very simple means, and at once made public by the police, won him a sudden celebrity. Prévailles was forthwith saddled with all the murders that had remained unpunished; and the newspapers vied with one another in extolling Ganimard's prowess.

The case was conducted briskly at the start. It was first of all ascertained that Prévailles, whose real name was Thomas Derocq, had already been in trouble. Moreover, the search instituted in his rooms, while not supplying any fresh proofs, at least led to the discovery of a ball of whip-cord similar to the cord used for doing up the parcel and also to the discovery of daggers which would have produced a wound similar to the wounds on the victim.

But, on the eighth day, everything was changed. Until then Prévailles had refused to reply to the questions put to him; but now, assisted by his counsel, he pleaded a circumstantial alibi and maintained that he was at the Folies-Bergère on the night of the murder.

As a matter of fact, the pockets of his dinner-jacket contained the counterfoil of a stall-ticket and a programme of the performance, both bearing the date of that evening.

"An alibi prepared in advance," objected the examining-magistrate.

"Prove it," said Prévailles.

The prisoner was confronted with the witnesses for the prosecution. The young lady from the confectioner's "thought she knew" the gentleman with the eyeglass. The hall-porter in the Rue de Berne "thought he knew" the gentleman who used to come to see Jenny Saphir. But nobody dared to make a more definite statement.

The examination, therefore, led to nothing of a precise character, provided no solid basis whereon to found a serious accusation.

The judge sent for Ganimard and told him of his difficulty.

"I can't possibly persist, at this rate. There is no evidence to support the charge."

"But surely you are convinced in your own mind, monsieur le juge d'instruction! Prévailles would never have resisted his arrest unless he was guilty."

"He says that he thought he was being assaulted. He also says that he never set eyes on Jenny Saphir; and, as a matter of fact, we can find no one to contradict his assertion. Then again, admitting that the sapphire has been stolen, we have not been able to find it at his flat."

"Nor anywhere else," suggested Ganimard.

"Quite true, but that is no evidence against him. I'll tell you what we shall want, M. Ganimard, and that very soon: the other end of this red scarf."

"The other end?"

"Yes, for it is obvious that, if the murderer took it away with him, the reason was that the stuff is stained with the marks of the blood on his fingers."

Ganimard made no reply. For several days he had felt that the whole business was tending to this conclusion. There was no other proof possible. Given the silk scarf—and in no other circumstances—Prévailles' guilt was certain. Now Ganimard's position required that Prévailles' guilt should be established. He was responsible for the arrest, it had cast a glamour around him, he had been praised to the skies as the most formidable adversary of criminals; and he would look absolutely ridiculous if Prévailles were released.

Unfortunately, the one and only indispensable proof was in Lupin's pocket. How was he to get hold of it?

Ganimard cast about, exhausted himself with fresh investigations, went over the inquiry from start to finish, spent sleepless nights in turning over the mystery of the Rue de Berne, studied the records of Prévailles' life, sent ten men hunting after the invisible sapphire. Everything was useless.

On the 28th of December, the examining-magistrate stopped him in one of the passages of the Law Courts:

"Well, M. Ganimard, any news?"

"No, monsieur le juge d'instruction."

"Then I shall dismiss the case."

"Wait one day longer."

"What's the use? We want the other end of the scarf; have you got it?"

"I shall have it to-morrow."

"To-morrow!"

"Yes, but please lend me the piece in your possession."

"What if I do?"

"If you do, I promise to let you have the whole scarf complete."

"Very well, that's understood."

Ganimard followed the examining-magistrate to his room and came out with the piece of silk:

"Hang it all!" he growled. "Yes, I will go and fetch the proof and I shall have it too . . . always presuming that Master Lupin has the courage to keep the appointment."

In point of fact, he did not doubt for a moment that Master Lupin would have this courage, and that was just what exasperated him. Why had Lupin insisted on this meeting? What was his object, in the circumstances?

Anxious, furious and full of hatred, he resolved to take every precaution necessary not only to prevent his falling into a trap himself, but to make his enemy fall into one, now that the opportunity offered. And, on the next day, which was the 29th of December, the date fixed by Lupin, after spending the night in studying the old manor-house in the Rue de Surène and convincing himself that there was no other outlet than the front door, he warned his men that he was going on a dangerous expedition and arrived with them on the field of battle.

He posted them in a café and gave them formal instructions: if he showed himself at one of the third-floor windows, or if he failed to return within an hour, the detectives were to enter the house and arrest any one who tried to leave it.

The chief-inspector made sure that his revolver was in working order and that he could take it from his pocket easily. Then he went upstairs.

He was surprised to find things as he had left them, the doors open and the locks broken. After ascertaining that the windows of the principal room looked out on the street, he visited the three other rooms that made up the flat. There was no one there.

"Master Lupin was afraid," he muttered, not without a certain satisfaction.

"Don't be silly," said a voice behind him.

Turning round, he saw an old workman, wearing a house-painter's long smock, standing in the doorway.

"You needn't bother your head," said the man. "It's I, Lupin. I have been working in the painter's shop since early morning. This is when we knock off for breakfast. So I came upstairs."

He looked at Ganimard with a quizzing smile and cried:

"'Pon my word, this is a gorgeous moment I owe you, old chap! I wouldn't sell it for ten years of your life; and yet you know how I love you! What do you think of it, artist? Wasn't it well thought out and well foreseen? Foreseen from alpha to omega? Did I understand the business? Did I penetrate the mystery of the scarf? I'm not saying that there were no holes in my argument, no links missing in the chain . . . But what a masterpiece of intelligence! Ganimard, what a reconstruction of events! What an intuition of everything that had taken place and of everything that was going to take place, from the discovery of the crime to your arrival here in search of a proof! What really marvellous divination! Have you the scarf?"

"Yes, half of it. Have you the other?"

"Here it is. Let's compare."

They spread the two pieces of silk on the table. The cuts made by the scissors corresponded exactly. Moreover, the colours were identical.

"But I presume," said Lupin, "that this was not the only thing you came for. What you are interested in seeing is the marks of the blood. Come with me, Ganimard: it's rather dark in here."

They moved into the next room, which, though it overlooked the courtyard, was lighter; and Lupin held his piece of silk against the windowpane:

"Look," he said, making room for Ganimard.

The inspector gave a start of delight. The marks of the five fingers and the print of the palm were distinctly visible. The evidence was undeniable. The murderer had seized the stuff in his blood-stained hand, in the same hand that had stabbed Jenny Saphir, and tied the scarf round her neck.

"And it is the print of a left hand," observed Lupin. "Hence my warning, which had nothing miraculous about it, you see. For, though I admit, friend of my youth, that you may look upon me as a superior intelligence, I won't have you treat me as a wizard."

Ganimard had quickly pocketed the piece of silk. Lupin nodded his head in approval:

"Quite right, old boy, it's for you. I'm so glad you're glad! And, you see, there was no trap about all this . . . only the wish to oblige . . . a service between friends, between pals. . . . And also, I confess, a little curiosity. . . . Yes, I wanted to examine this other piece of silk, the one the police had. . . . Don't be afraid: I'll give it back to you. . . . Just a second. . . ."

Lupin, with a careless movement, played with the tassel at the end of this half of the scarf, while Ganimard listened to him in spite of himself:

"How ingenious these little bits of women's work are! Did you notice one detail in the maid's evidence? Jenny Saphir was very handy with her needle and used to make all her own hats and frocks. It is obvious that she made this scarf herself. . . . Besides,

I noticed that from the first. I am naturally curious, as I have already told you, and I made a thorough examination of the piece of silk which you have just put in your pocket. Inside the tassel, I found a little sacred medal, which the poor girl had stitched into it to bring her luck. Touching, isn't it, Ganimard? A little medal of Our Lady of Good Succour."

The inspector felt greatly puzzled and did not take his eyes off the other. And Lupin continued:

"Then I said to myself, 'How interesting it would be to explore the other half of the scarf, the one which the police will find round the victim's neck!' For this other half, which I hold in my hands at last, is finished off in the same way . . . so I shall be able to see if it has a hiding-place too and what's inside it. . . . But look, my friend, isn't it cleverly made? And so simple! All you have to do is to take a skein of red cord and braid it round a wooden cup, leaving a little recess, a little empty space in the middle, very small, of course, but large enough to hold a medal of a saint . . . or anything. . . . A precious stone, for instance. . . . Such as a sapphire. . . ."

At that moment he finished pushing back the silk cord and, from the hollow of a cup he took between his thumb and forefinger a wonderful blue stone, perfect in respect of size and purity.

"Ha! What did I tell you, friend of my youth?"

He raised his head. The inspector had turned livid and was staring wild-eyed, as though fascinated by the stone that sparkled before him. He at last realized the whole plot:

"You dirty scoundrel!" he muttered, repeating the insults which he had used at the first interview. "You scum of the earth!"

The two men were standing one against the other.

"Give me back that," said the inspector.

Lupin held out the piece of silk.

"And the sapphire," said Ganimard, in a peremptory tone.

"Don't be silly."

"Give it back, or . . ."

"Or what, you idiot!" cried Lupin. "Look here, do you think I put you on to this soft thing for nothing?"

"Give it back!"

THE RED SILK SCARF

"You haven't noticed what I've been about, that's plain! What! For four weeks I've kept you on the move like a deer; and you want to . . . ! Come, Ganimard, old chap, pull yourself together! . . . Don't you see that you've been playing the good dog for four weeks on end? . . . Fetch it, Rover! . . . There's a nice blue pebble over there, which master can't get at. Hunt it, Ganimard, fetch it . . . bring it to master. . . . Ah, he's his master's own good little dog! . . . Sit up! Beg! . . . Does'ms want a bit of sugar, then? . . ."

Ganimard, containing the anger that seethed within him, thought only of one thing, summoning his detectives. And, as the room in which he now was looked out on the courtyard, he tried gradually to work his way round to the communicating door. He would then run to the window and break one of the panes.

"All the same," continued Lupin, "what a pack of dunderheads you and the rest must be! You've had the silk all this time and not one of you ever thought of feeling it, not one of you ever asked himself the reason why the poor girl hung on to her scarf. Not one of you! You just acted at haphazard, without reflecting, without foreseeing anything. . . ."

The inspector had attained his object. Taking advantage of a second when Lupin had turned away from him, he suddenly wheeled round and grasped the door-handle. But an oath escaped him: the handle did not budge.

Lupin burst into a fit of laughing:

"Not even that! You did not even foresee that! You lay a trap for me and you won't admit that I may perhaps smell the thing out beforehand. . . . And you allow yourself to be brought into this room without asking whether I am not bringing you here for a particular reason and without remembering that the locks are fitted with a special mechanism. Come now, speaking frankly, what do you think of it yourself?"

"What do I think of it?" roared Ganimard, beside himself with rage.

He had drawn his revolver and was pointing it straight at Lupin's face.

"Hands up!" he cried. "That's what I think of it!"

Lupin placed himself in front of him and shrugged his shoulders:

"Sold again!" he said.

"Hands up, I say, once more!"

"And sold again, say I. Your deadly weapon won't go off."

"What?"

"Old Catherine, your housekeeper, is in my service. She damped the charges this morning while you were having your breakfast coffee."

Ganimard made a furious gesture, pocketed the revolver and rushed at Lupin.

"Well?" said Lupin, stopping him short with a well-aimed kick on the shin.

Their clothes were almost touching. They exchanged defiant glances, the glances of two adversaries who mean to come to blows. Nevertheless, there was no fight. The recollection of the earlier struggles made any present struggle useless. And Ganimard, who remembered all his past failures, his vain attacks, Lupin's crushing reprisals, did not lift a limb. There was nothing to be done. He felt it. Lupin had forces at his command against which any individual force simply broke to pieces. So what was the good?

"I agree," said Lupin, in a friendly voice, as though answering Ganimard's unspoken thought, "you would do better to let things be as they are. Besides, friend of my youth, think of all that this incident has brought you: fame, the certainty of quick promotion and, thanks to that, the prospect of a happy and comfortable old age! Surely, you don't want the discovery of the sapphire and the head of poor Arsène Lupin in addition! It wouldn't be fair. To say nothing of the fact that poor Arsène Lupin saved your life. . . . Yes, sir! Who warned you, at this very spot, that Prévailles was left-handed? . . . And is this the way you thank me? It's not pretty of you, Ganimard. Upon my word, you make me blush for you!"

While chattering, Lupin had gone through the same preformance as Ganimard and was now near the door. Ganimard saw that his foe was about to escape him. Forgetting all prudence, he tried to block his way and received a tremendous butt in the stomach, which sent him rolling to the opposite wall.

Lupin dexterously touched a spring, turned the handle, opened the door and slipped away, roaring with laughter as he went.

Twenty minutes later, when Ganimard at last succeeded in joining his men, one of them said to him:

"A house-painter left the house, as his mates were coming back from breakfast, and put a letter in my hand. 'Give that to your governor,' he said. 'Which governor?' I asked; but he was gone. I suppose it's meant for you."

"Let's have it."

Ganimard opened the letter. It was hurriedly scribbled in pencil and contained these words:

"This is to warn you, friend of my youth, against excessive credulity. When a fellow tells you that the cartridges in your revolver are damp, however great your confidence in that fellow may be, even though his name be Arsène Lupin, never allow yourself to be taken in. Fire first; and, if the fellow hops the twig, you will have acquired the proof (1) that the cartridges are not damp; and (2) that old Catherine is the most honest and respectable of housekeepers.

"One of these days, I hope to have the pleasure of making her acquaintance.

"Meanwhile, friend of my youth, believe me always affectionately and sincerely yours,

"ARSÈNE LUPIN."

EDITH SWAN-NECK

"Arsène Lupin, what's your real opinion of Inspector Ganimard?"

"A very high one, my dear fellow."

"A very high one? Then why do you never miss a chance of turning him into ridicule?"

"It's a bad habit; and I'm sorry for it. But what can I say? It's the way of the world. Here's a decent detective-chap, here's a whole pack of decent men, who stand for law and order, who protect us against the apaches, who risk their lives, for honest people like you and me; and we have nothing to give them in return but flouts and gibes. It's preposterous!"

"Bravo, Lupin! you're talking like a respectable ratepayer!"

"What else am I? I may have peculiar views about other people's property; but I assure you that it's very different when my own's at stake. By Jove, it doesn't do to lay hands on what belongs to me! Then I'm out for blood! Aha! It's *my* pocket, *my* money, *my* watch . . . hands off! I have the soul of a conservative, my dear fellow, the instincts of a retired tradesman and a due respect for every sort of tradition and authority. And that is why Ganimard inspires me with no little gratitude and esteem."

"But not much admiration?"

"Plenty of admiration too. Over and above the dauntless courage which comes natural to all those gentry at the Criminal Investigation Department, Ganimard possesses very sterling qualities: decision, insight and judgment. I have watched him at work. He's somebody, when all's said. Do you know the Edith Swan-neck story, as it was called?"

"I know as much as everybody knows."

"That means that you don't know it at all. Well, that job was, I daresay, the one which I thought out most cleverly, with the utmost care and the utmost precaution, the one which I shrouded in the greatest darkness and mystery, the one which it took the biggest generalship to carry through. It was a regular game of chess, played according to strict scientific and mathematical rules. And yet Ganimard ended by unravelling the knot. Thanks to him, they know the truth to-day on the Quai des Orfèvres. And it is a truth quite out of the common, I assure you."

"May I hope to hear it?"

"Certainly . . . one of these days . . . when I have time . . . But the Brunelli is dancing at the Opera to-night; and, if she were not to see me in my stall . . . !"

I do not meet Lupin often. He confesses with difficulty, when it suits him. It was only gradually, by snatches, by odds and ends of confidences, that I was able to obtain the different incidents and to piece the story together in all its details.

The main features are well known and I will merely mention the facts.

Three years ago, when the train from Brest arrived at Rennes, the door of one of the luggage vans was found smashed in. This van had been booked by Colonel Sparmiento, a rich Brazilian, who was travelling with his wife in the same train. It contained a complete set of tapestry-hangings. The case in which one of these was packed had been broken open and the tapestry had disappeared.

Colonel Sparmiento started proceedings against the railway-company, claiming heavy damages, not only for the stolen tapestry, but also for the loss in value which the whole collection suffered in consequence of the theft.

The police instituted inquiries. The company offered a large reward. A fortnight later, a letter which had come undone in the post was opened by the authorities and revealed the fact that the theft had been carried out under the direction of Arsène Lupin and that a package was to leave next day for the United States. That same evening, the tapestry was discovered in a trunk deposited in the cloak-room at the Gare Saint-Lazare.

The scheme, therefore, had miscarried. Lupin felt the disappointment so much that he vented his ill-humour in a communication to Colonel Sparmiento, ending with the following words, which were clear enough for anybody:

"It was very considerate of me to take only one. Next time, I shall take the twelve. *Verbum sap.*[1]

"A. L."

Colonel Sparmiento had been living for some months in a house standing at the end of a small garden at the corner of the Rue de la Faisanderie and the Rue Dufresnoy. He was a rather thick-set, broad-shouldered man, with black hair and a swarthy skin, always well and quietly dressed. He was married to an extremely pretty but delicate Englishwoman, who was much upset by the business of the tapestries. From the first she implored her husband to sell them for what they would fetch. The Colonel had much too forcible and dogged a nature to yield to what he had every right to describe as a woman's fancies. He sold nothing, but he redoubled his precautions and adopted every measure that was likely to make an attempt at burglary impossible.

To begin with, so that he might confine his watch to the garden-front, he walled up all the windows on the ground-floor and the first floor overlooking the Rue Dufresnoy. Next, he enlisted the services of a firm which made a speciality of protecting private houses against robberies. Every window of the gallery in which the tapestries were hung was fitted with invisible burglar alarms, the position of which was known to none but himself. These, at the least touch, switched on all the electric lights and set a whole system of bells and gongs ringing.

In addition to this, the insurance companies to which he applied refused to grant policies to any considerable amount unless he consented to let three men, supplied by the companies and paid by himself, occupy the ground-floor of his house every night. They selected for the purpose three ex-detectives, tried and trustworthy men, all of whom hated Lupin like poison. As for the servants, the colonel had known them for years and was ready to vouch for them.

After taking these steps and organizing the defence of the house as though it were a fortress, the colonel gave a great house-warming, a sort of private view, to which he invited the members of both his clubs, as well as a certain number of ladies, journalists, art-patrons and critics.

They felt, as they passed through the garden-gate, much as if they were walking into a prison. The three private detectives, posted at the foot of the stairs, asked for each visitor's invitation card and eyed him up and down suspiciously, making him feel as though they were going to search his pockets or take his finger-prints.

The colonel, who received his guests on the first floor, made laughing apologies and seemed delighted at the opportunity of explaining the arrangements which he had invented to secure the safety of his hangings. His wife stood by him, looking charmingly young and pretty, fair-haired, pale and sinuous, with a sad and gentle expression, the expression of resignation often worn by those who are threatened by fate.

When all the guests had come, the garden-gates and the hall-doors were closed. Then everybody filed into the middle gallery, which was reached through two steel doors, while its windows, with their huge shutters, were protected by iron bars. This was where the twelve tapestries were kept.

They were matchless works of art and, taking their inspiration from the famous Bayeux Tapestry, attributed to Queen Matilda, they represented the story of the Norman Conquest. They had been ordered in the fourteenth century by the descendant of a man-at-arms in William the Conqueror's train; were executed by Jehan Gosset, a famous Arras weaver; and were discovered, five hundred years later, in an old Breton manor-house. On hearing of this, the colonel had struck a bargain for fifty thousand francs. They were worth ten times the money.

But the finest of the twelve hangings composing the set, the most uncommon because the subject had not been treated by Queen Matilda, was the one which Arsène Lupin had stolen and which had been so fortunately recovered. It portrayed Edith Swan-neck on the battlefield of Hastings, seeking among the dead for the body of her sweetheart Harold, last of the Saxon kings.[2]

The guests were lost in enthusiasm over this tapestry, over the unsophisticated beauty of the design, over the faded colours, over the life-like grouping of the figures and the pitiful sadness of the scene. Poor Edith Swan-neck stood drooping like an over-weighted lily. Her white gown revealed the lines of her languid figure. Her long, tapering hands were outstretched in a gesture of terror and entreaty. And nothing could be more mournful than her profile, over which flickered the most dejected and de-spairing of smiles.

"A harrowing smile," remarked one of the critics, to whom the others listened with deference. "A very charming smile, besides; and it reminds me, Colonel, of the smile of Mme. Sparmiento."

And seeing that the observation seemed to meet with ap-proval, he enlarged upon his idea:

"There are other points of resemblance that struck me at once, such as the very graceful curve of the neck and the deli-cacy of the hands . . . and also something about the figure, about the general attitude. . . ."

"What you say is so true," said the colonel, "that I confess that it was this likeness that decided me to buy the hangings. And there was another reason, which was that, by a really curi-ous chance, my wife's name happens to be Edith. I have called her Edith Swan-neck ever since." And the colonel added, with a laugh, "I hope that the coincidence will stop at this and that my dear Edith will never have to go in search of her true-love's body, like her prototype."

He laughed as he uttered these words, but his laugh met with no echo; and we find the same impression of awkward silence in all the accounts of the evening that appeared during the next few days. The people standing near him did not know what to say. One of them tried to jest:

"Your name isn't Harold, Colonel?"

"No, thank you," he declared, with continued merriment. "No, that's not my name; nor am I in the least like the Saxon king."

All have since agreed in stating that, at that moment, as the colonel finished speaking, the first alarm rang from the

windows—the right or the middle window: opinions differ on
this point—rang short and shrill on a single note. The peal of
the alarm-bell was followed by an exclamation of terror uttered
by Mme. Sparmiento, who caught hold of her husband's arm.
He cried:

"What's the matter? What does this mean?"

The guests stood motionless, with their eyes staring at the
windows. The colonel repeated:

"What does it mean? I don't understand. No one but myself
knows where that bell is fixed. . . ."

And, at that moment—here again the evidence is unanimous—
at that moment came sudden, absolute darkness, followed immediately by the maddening din of all the bells and all the gongs,
from top to bottom of the house, in every room and at every
window.

For a few seconds, a stupid disorder, an insane terror, reigned.
The women screamed. The men banged with their fists on the
closed doors. They hustled and fought. People fell to the floor and
were trampled under foot. It was like a panic-stricken crowd,
scared by threatening flames or by a bursting shell. And, above
the uproar, rose the colonel's voice, shouting:

"Silence! . . . Don't move! . . . It's all right! . . . The switch is
over there, in the corner. . . . Wait a bit. . . . Here!"

He had pushed his way through his guests and reached a corner of the gallery; and, all at once, the electric light blazed up
again, while the pandemonium of bells stopped.

Then, in the sudden light, a strange sight met the eyes. Two
ladies had fainted. Mme. Sparmiento, hanging to her husband's
arm, with her knees dragging on the floor, and livid in the face,
appeared half dead. The men, pale, with their neckties awry,
looked as if they had all been in the wars.

"The tapestries are there!" cried some one.

There was a great surprise, as though the disappearance of
those hangings ought to have been the natural result and the
only plausible explanation of the incident. But nothing had
been moved. A few valuable pictures, hanging on the walls,
were there still. And, though the same din had reverberated all
over the house, though all the rooms had been thrown into

darkness, the detectives had seen no one entering or trying to enter.

"Besides," said the colonel, "it's only the windows of the gallery that have alarms. Nobody but myself understands how they work; and I had not set them yet."

People laughed loudly at the way in which they had been frightened, but they laughed without conviction and in a more or less shamefaced fashion, for each of them was keenly alive to the absurdity of his conduct. And they had but one thought—to get out of that house where, say what you would, the atmosphere was one of agonizing anxiety.

Two journalists stayed behind, however; and the colonel joined them, after attending to Edith and handing her over to her maids. The three of them, together with the detectives, made a search that did not lead to the discovery of anything of the least interest. Then the colonel sent for some champagne; and the result was that it was not until a late hour—to be exact, a quarter to three in the morning—that the journalists took their leave, the colonel retired to his quarters, and the detectives withdrew to the room which had been set aside for them on the ground-floor.

They took the watch by turns, a watch consisting, in the first place, in keeping awake and, next, in looking round the garden and visiting the gallery at intervals.

These orders were scrupulously carried out, except between five and seven in the morning, when sleep gained the mastery and the men ceased to go their rounds. But it was broad daylight out of doors. Besides, if there had been the least sound of bells, would they not have woke up?

Nevertheless, when one of them, at twenty minutes past seven, opened the door of the gallery and flung back the shutters, he saw that the twelve tapestries were gone.

This man and the others were blamed afterward for not giving the alarm at once and for starting their own investigations before informing the colonel and telephoning to the local commissary. Yet this very excusable delay can hardly be said to have hampered the action of the police. In any case, the colonel was not told until half-past eight. He was dressed and ready to go out. The news did not seem to upset him beyond measure, or, at least, he managed to control his emotion. But the effort must have been too much for him, for he suddenly dropped into a chair and, for some moments, gave way to a regular fit of despair and anguish, most painful to behold in a man of his resolute appearance.

Recovering and mastering himself, he went to the gallery, stared at the bare walls and then sat down at a table and hastily scribbled a letter, which he put into an envelope and sealed:

"There," he said. "I'm in a hurry. . . . I have an important engagement. . . . Here is a letter for the commissary of police." And, seeing the detectives' eyes upon him, he added, "I am giving the commissary my views . . . telling him of a suspicion that occurs to me. . . . He must follow it up. . . . I will do what I can. . . ."

He left the house at a run, with excited gestures which the detectives were subsequently to remember.

A few minutes later, the commissary of police arrived. He was handed the letter, which contained the following words:

"I am at the end of my tether. The theft of those tapestries completes the crash which I have been trying to conceal for the past year. I bought them as a speculation and was hoping to get a million francs for them, thanks to the fuss that was made about them. As it was, an American offered me six hundred thousand. It meant my salvation. This means utter destruction.

"I hope that my dear wife will forgive the sorrow which I am bringing upon her. Her name will be on my lips at the last moment."

Mme. Sparmiento was informed. She remained aghast with horror, while inquiries were instituted and attempts made to trace the colonel's movements.

Late in the afternoon, a telephone-message came from Ville d'Avray. A gang of railway-men had found a man's body lying at the entrance to a tunnel after a train had passed. The body was hideously mutilated; the face had lost all resemblance to anything human. There were no papers in the pockets. But the description answered to that of the colonel.

Mme. Sparmiento arrived at Ville d'Avray, by motor-car, at seven o'clock in the evening. She was taken to a room at the railway-station. When the sheet that covered it was removed, Edith, Edith Swan-neck, recognized her husband's body.

In these circumstances, Lupin did not receive his usual good notices in the press:

"Let him look to himself," jeered one leader-writer, summing up the general opinion. "It would not take many exploits of this kind for him to forfeit the popularity which has not been grudged him hitherto. We have no use for Lupin, except when his rogueries are perpetrated at the expense of shady company-promoters, foreign adventurers, German barons, banks and financial companies. And, above all, no murders! A burglar we can put up with; but a murderer, no! If he is not directly guilty, he is at least responsible for this death. There is blood upon his hands; the arms on his escutcheon are stained gules. . . ."

The public anger and disgust were increased by the pity which Edith's pale face aroused. The guests of the night before gave their version of what had happened, omitting none of the impressive details; and a legend formed straightway around the fair-haired Englishwoman, a legend that assumed a really tragic character, owing to the popular story of the swan-necked heroine.

And yet the public could not withold its admiration of the extraordinary skill with which the theft had been effected. The police explained it, after a fashion. The detectives had noticed from the first and subsequently stated that one of the three windows of the gallery was wide open. There could be no doubt that Lupin and his confederates had entered through this window. It seemed a very plausible suggestion. Still, in that case, how were they able, first, to climb the garden railings, in coming and going, without being seen; secondly, to cross the garden and put up a ladder on the flower-border, without leaving the least trace behind; thirdly, to open the shutters and the window, without starting the bells and switching on the lights in the house?

The police accused the three detectives of complicity. The magistrate in charge of the case examined them at length, made minute inquiries into their private lives and stated formally that they were above all suspicion. As for the tapestries, there seemed to be no hope that they would be recovered.

It was at this moment that Chief-Inspector Ganimard returned from India, where he had been hunting for Lupin on the strength of a number of most convincing proofs supplied by former confederates of Lupin himself. Feeling that he had once more been tricked by his everlasting adversary, fully believing that Lupin had dispatched him on this wild-goose chase so as to be rid of him during the business of the tapestries, he asked for a fortnight's leave of absence, called on Mme. Sparmiento and promised to avenge her husband.

Edith had reached the point at which not even the thought of vengeance relieves the sufferer's pain. She had dismissed the three detectives on the day of the funeral and engaged just one man and an old cook-housekeeper to take the place of the large staff of servants the sight of whom reminded her too cruelly of the past. Not caring what happened, she kept her room and left Ganimard free to act as he pleased.

He took up his quarters on the ground-floor and at once instituted a series of the most minute investigations. He started the inquiry afresh, questioned the people in the neighbourhood, studied the distribution of the rooms and set each of the burglar-alarms going thirty and forty times over.

At the end of the fortnight, he asked for an extension of leave. The chief of the detective-service, who was at that time M. Dudouis, came to see him and found him perched on the top of a ladder, in the gallery. That day, the chief-inspector admitted that all his searches had proved useless.

Two days later, however, M. Dudouis called again and discovered Ganimard in a very thoughtful frame of mind. A bundle of newspapers lay spread in front of him. At last, in reply to his superior's urgent questions, the chief-inspector muttered:

"I know nothing, chief, absolutely nothing; but there's a confounded notion worrying me. . . . Only it seems so absurd. . . .

And then it doesn't explain things. . . . On the contrary, it con-
fuses them rather. . . ."

"Then. . . . ?"

"Then I implore you, chief, to have a little patience . . . to let
me go my own way. But if I telephone to you, some day or
other, suddenly, you must jump into a taxi, without losing a
minute. It will mean that I have discovered the secret."

Forty-eight hours passed. Then, one morning, M. Dudouis received a telegram:

> "Going to Lille."
>
> "GANIMARD."

"What the dickens can he want to go to Lille for?" wondered
the chief-detective.

The day passed without news, followed by another day. But
M. Dudouis had every confidence in Ganimard. He knew his
man, knew that the old detective was not one of those people
who excite themselves for nothing. When Ganimard "got a
move on him," it meant that he had sound reasons for doing so.

As a matter of fact, on the evening of that second day, M.
Dudouis was called to the telephone.

"Is that you, chief?"

"Is it Ganimard speaking?"

Cautious men both, they began by making sure of each
other's identity. As soon as his mind was eased on this point,
Ganimard continued, hurriedly:

"Ten men, chief, at once. And please come yourself."

"Where are you?"

"In the house, on the ground-floor. But I will wait for you
just inside the garden-gate."

"I'll come at once. In a taxi, of course?"

"Yes, chief. Stop the taxi fifty yards from the house. I'll let
you in when you whistle."

Things took place as Ganimard had arranged. Shortly after
midnight, when all the lights were out on the upper floors, he
slipped into the street and went to meet M. Dudouis. There was
a hurried consultation. The officers distributed themselves as

Ganimard ordered. Then the chief and the chief-inspector walked back together, noiselessly crossed the garden and closeted themselves with every precaution:

"Well, what's it all about?" asked M. Dudouis. "What does all this mean? Upon my word, we look like a pair of conspirators!"

But Ganimard was not laughing. His chief had never seen him in such a state of perturbation, nor heard him speak in a voice denoting such excitement:

"Any news, Ganimard?"

"Yes, chief, and . . . this time . . . ! But I can hardly believe it myself. . . . And yet I'm not mistaken: I know the real truth. . . . It may be as unlikely as you please, but it is the truth, the whole truth and nothing but the truth."

He wiped away the drops of perspiration that trickled down his forehead and, after a further question from M. Dudouis, pulled himself together, swallowed a glass of water and began:

"Lupin has often got the better of me. . . ."

"Look here, Ganimard," said M. Dudouis, interrupting him. "Why can't you come straight to the point? Tell me, in two words, what's happened."

"No, chief," retorted the chief-inspector, "it is essential that you should know the different stages which I have passed through. Excuse me, but I consider it indispensable." And he repeated: "I was saying, chief, that Lupin has often got the better of me and led me many a dance. But, in this contest in which I have always come out worst . . . so far . . . I have at least gained experience of his manner of play and learnt to know his tactics. Now, in the matter of the tapestries, it occurred to me almost from the start to set myself two problems. In the first place, Lupin, who never makes a move without knowing what he is after, was obviously aware that Colonel Sparmiento had come to the end of his money and that the loss of the tapestries might drive him to suicide. Nevertheless, Lupin, who hates the very thought of bloodshed, stole the tapestries."

"There was the inducement," said M. Dudouis, "of the five or six hundred thousand francs which they are worth."

"No, chief, I tell you once more, whatever the occasion might be, Lupin would not take life, nor be the cause of another person's death, for anything in this world, for millions and millions. That's the first point. In the second place, what was the object of all that disturbance, in the evening, during the house-warming party? Obviously, don't you think, to surround the business with an atmosphere of anxiety and terror, in the shortest possible time, and also to divert suspicion from the truth, which, otherwise, might easily have been suspected? . . . You seem not to understand, chief?"

"Upon my word, I do not!"

"As a matter of fact," said Ganimard, "as a matter of fact, it is not particularly plain. And I myself, when I put the problem before my mind in those same words, did not understand it very clearly . . . And yet I felt that I was on the right track . . . Yes, there was no doubt about it that Lupin wanted to divert suspicions . . . to divert them to himself, Lupin, mark you . . . so that the real person who was working the business might remain unknown. . . ."

"A confederate," suggested M. Dudouis. "A confederate, moving among the visitors, who set the alarms going . . . and who managed to hide in the house after the party had broken up."

"You're getting warm, chief, you're getting warm! It is certain that the tapestries, as they cannot have been stolen by any one making his way surreptitiously into the house, were stolen by somebody who remained in the house; and it is equally certain that, by taking the list of the people invited and inquiring into the antecedents of each of them, one might . . ."

"Well?"

"Well, chief, there's a 'but,' namely, that the three detectives had this list in their hands when the guests arrived and that they still had it when the guests left. Now sixty-three came in and sixty-three went away. So you see . . ."

"Then do you suppose a servant? . . ."

"No."

"The detectives?"

"No."

"But, still . . . but, still," said the chief, impatiently, "if the robbery was committed from the inside . . ."

"That is beyond dispute," declared the inspector, whose excitement seemed to be nearing fever-point. "There is no question about it. All my investigations led to the same certainty. And my conviction gradually became so positive that I ended, one day, by drawing up this startling axiom: in theory and in fact, the robbery can only have been committed with the assistance of an accomplice staying in the house. Whereas there was no accomplice!"

"That's absurd," said Dudouis.

"Quite absurd," said Ganimard. "But, at the very moment when I uttered that absurd sentence, the truth flashed upon me."

"Eh?"

"Oh, a very dim, very incomplete, but still sufficient truth! With that clue to guide me, I was bound to find the way. Do you follow me, chief?"

M. Dudouis sat silent. The same phenomenon that had taken place in Ganimard was evidently taking place in him. He muttered:

"If it's not one of the guests, nor the servants, nor the private detectives, then there's no one left. . . ."

"Yes, chief, there's one left. . . ."

M. Dudouis started as though he had received a shock; and, in a voice that betrayed his excitement:

"But, look here, that's preposterous."

"Why?"

"Come, think for yourself!"

"Go on, chief: say what's in your mind."

"Nonsense! What do you mean?"

"Go on, chief."

"It's impossible! How can Sparmiento have been Lupin's accomplice?"

Ganimard gave a little chuckle.

"Exactly, Arsène Lupin's accomplice! . . . That explains everything. During the night, while the three detectives were downstairs watching, or sleeping rather, for Colonel Sparmiento had given them champagne to drink and perhaps doctored it beforehand, the said colonel took down the hangings and passed them out through the window of his bedroom. The room is on the second floor and looks out on another street, which was not watched, because the lower windows are walled up."

M. Dudouis reflected and then shrugged his shoulders:

"It's preposterous!" he repeated.

"Why?"

"Why? Because, if the colonel had been Arsène Lupin's accomplice, he would not have committed suicide after achieving his success."

"Who says that he committed suicide?"

"Why, he was found dead on the line!"

"I told you, there is no such thing as death with Lupin."

"Still, this was genuine enough. Besides, Mme. Sparmiento identified the body."

"I thought you would say that, chief. The argument worried me too. There was I, all of a sudden, with three people in front of me instead of one: first, Arsène Lupin, cracksman; secondly, Colonel Sparmiento, his accomplice; thirdly, a dead man. Spare us! It was too much of a good thing!"

Ganimard took a bundle of newspapers, untied it and handed one of them to M. Dudouis:

"You remember, chief, last time you were here, I was looking through the papers. . . . I wanted to see if something had not happened, at that period, that might bear upon the case and confirm my supposition. Please read this paragraph."

M. Dudouis took the paper and read aloud:

"Our Lille correspondent informs us that a curious incident has occurred in that town. A corpse has disappeared from the local morgue, the corpse of a man unknown who threw himself under the wheels of a steam tram-car on the day before. No one is able to suggest a reason for this disappearance."

M. Dudouis sat thinking and then asked:

"So . . . you believe . . . ?"

"I have just come from Lille," replied Ganimard, "and my inquiries leave not a doubt in my mind. The corpse was removed on the same night on which Colonel Sparmiento gave his house-warming. It was taken straight to Ville d'Avray by motor-car; and the car remained near the railway-line until the evening."

"Near the tunnel, therefore," said M. Dudouis.

"Next to it, chief."

"So that the body which was found is merely that body, dressed in Colonel Sparmiento's clothes."

"Precisely, chief."

"Then Colonel Sparmiento is not dead?"

"No more dead than you or I, chief."

"But then why all these complications? Why the theft of one tapestry, followed by its recovery, followed by the theft of the twelve? Why that house-warming? Why that disturbance? Why everything? Your story won't hold water, Ganimard."

"Only because you, chief, like myself, have stopped halfway; because, strange as this story already sounds, we must go still farther, very much farther, in the direction of the improbable and the astounding. And why not, after all? Remember that we are dealing with Arsène Lupin. With him, is it not always just the improbable and the astounding that we must look for? Must we not always go straight for the maddest suppositions? And, when I say the maddest, I am using the wrong word. On the contrary, the whole thing is wonderfully logical and so simple that a child could understand it. Confederates only betray you. Why employ confederates, when it is so easy and so natural to act for yourself, by yourself, with your own hands and by the means within your own reach?"

"What are you saying? . . . What are you saying? . . . What are you saying?" cried M. Dudouis, in a sort of sing-song voice and a tone of bewilderment that increased with each separate exclamation.

Ganimard gave a fresh chuckle.

"Takes your breath away, chief, doesn't it? So it did mine, on the day when you came to see me here and when the notion was beginning to grow upon me. I was flabbergasted with astonishment. And yet I've had experience of my customer. I know what he's capable of. . . . But this, no, this was really a bit too stiff!"

"It's impossible! It's impossible!" said M. Dudouis, in a low voice.

"On the contrary, chief, it's quite possible and quite logical and quite normal. It's the threefold incarnation of one and the same individual. A schoolboy would solve the problem in a minute, by a simple process of elimination. Take away the dead man: there remains Sparmiento and Lupin. Take away Sparmiento . . ."

"There remains Lupin," muttered the chief-detective.

"Yes, chief, Lupin simply, Lupin in five letters and two syllables, Lupin taken out of his Brazilian skin, Lupin revived from the dead, Lupin translated, for the past six months, into Colonel Sparmiento, travelling in Brittany, hearing of the discovery of the twelve tapestries, buying them, planning the theft of the best of them, so as to draw attention to himself, Lupin, and divert it from himself, Sparmiento. Next, he brings about, in full view of the gaping public, a noisy contest between Lupin and Sparmiento or Sparmiento and Lupin, plots and gives the house-warming party, terrifies his guests and, when everything is ready, arranges for Lupin to steal Sparmiento's tapestries and for Sparmiento, Lupin's victim, to disappear from sight and die unsuspected, unsuspectable, regretted by his friends, pitied by the public and leaving behind him, to pocket the profits of the swindle. . . ."

Ganimard stopped, looked the chief in the eyes and, in a voice that emphasized the importance of his words, concluded:

"Leaving behind him a disconsolate widow."

"Mme. Sparmiento! You really believe . . . ?"

"Hang it all!" said the chief-inspector. "People don't work up a whole business of this sort, without seeing something ahead of them . . . solid profits."

"But the profits, it seems to me, lie in the sale of the tapestries which Lupin will effect in America or elsewhere."

"First of all, yes. But Colonel Sparmiento could effect that sale just as well. And even better. So there's something more."

"Something more?"

"Come, chief, you're forgetting that Colonel Sparmiento has been the victim of an important robbery and that, though he may be dead, at least his widow remains. So it's his widow who will get the money."

"What money?"

"What money? Why, the money due to her! The insurance-money, of course!"

M. Dudouis was staggered. The whole business suddenly became clear to him, with its real meaning. He muttered:

"That's true! . . . That's true! . . . The colonel had insured his tapestries. . . ."

"Rather! And for no trifle either."

"For how much?"

"Eight hundred thousand francs."

"Eight hundred thousand?"

"Just so. In five different companies."

"And has Mme. Sparmiento had the money?"

"She got a hundred and fifty thousand francs yesterday and two hundred thousand to-day, while I was away. The remaining payments are to be made in the course of this week."

"But this is terrible! You ought to have. . . ."

"What, chief? To begin with, they took advantage of my absence to settle up accounts with the companies. I only heard about it on my return when I ran up against an insurance-manager whom I happen to know and took the opportunity of drawing him out."

The chief-detective was silent for some time, not knowing what to say. Then he mumbled:

"What a fellow, though!"

Ganimard nodded his head:

"Yes, chief, a blackguard, but, I can't help saying, a devil of a clever fellow. For his plan to succeed, he must have managed in such a way that, for four or five weeks, no one could express or even conceive the least suspicion of the part played by Colonel Sparmiento. All the indignation and all the inquiries had to be concentrated upon Lupin alone. In the last resort, people had to find themselves faced simply with a mournful, pitiful, penniless widow, poor Edith Swan-neck, a beautiful and legendary vision, a creature so pathetic that the gentlemen of the insurance-companies were almost glad to place something in her hands to relieve her poverty and her grief. That's what was wanted and that's what happened."

The two men were close together and did not take their eyes from each other's faces.

The chief asked:

"Who is that woman?"

"Sonia Kritchnoff."

"Sonia Kritchnoff?"

"Yes, the Russian girl whom I arrested last year at the time of the theft of the coronet, and whom Lupin helped to escape."[3]

"Are you sure?"

"Absolutely. I was put off the scent, like everybody else, by Lupin's machinations, and had paid no particular attention to her. But, when I knew the part which she was playing, I remembered. She is certainly Sonia, metamorphosed into an Englishwoman; Sonia, the most innocent-looking and the trickiest of actresses; Sonia, who would not hesitate to face death for love of Lupin."

"A good capture, Ganimard," said M. Dudouis, approvingly.

"I've something better still for you, chief!"

"Really? What?"

"Lupin's old foster-mother."

"Victoire?"[4]

"She has been here since Mme. Sparmiento began playing the widow; she's the cook."

"Oho!" said M. Dudouis. "My congratulations, Ganimard!"

"I've something for you, chief, that's even better than that!"

M. Dudouis gave a start. The inspector's hand clutched his and was shaking with excitement.

"What do you mean, Ganimard?"

"Do you think, chief, that I would have brought you here, at this late hour, if I had had nothing more attractive to offer you than Sonia and Victoire? Pah! They'd have kept!"

"You mean to say . . . ?" whispered M. Dudouis, at last, understanding the chief-inspector's agitation.

"You've guessed it, chief!"

"Is he here?"

"He's here."

"In hiding?"

"Not a bit of it. Simply in disguise. He's the man-servant."

This time, M. Dudouis did not utter a word nor make a gesture. Lupin's audacity confounded him.

Ganimard chuckled.

"It's no longer a threefold, but a fourfold incarnation. Edith Swan-neck might have blundered. The master's presence was necessary; and he had the cheek to return. For three weeks, he has been beside me during my inquiry, calmly following the progress made."

"Did you recognize him?"

"One doesn't recognize him. He has a knack of making-up his face and altering the proportions of his body so as to prevent any one from knowing him. Besides, I was miles from suspecting. . . . But, this evening, as I was watching Sonia in the shadow of the stairs, I heard Victoire speak to the man-servant and call him, 'Dearie.' A light flashed in upon me. 'Dearie!' That was what she always used to call him. And I knew where I was."

M. Dudouis seemed flustered, in his turn, by the presence of the enemy, so often pursued and always so intangible:

"We've got him, this time," he said, between his teeth. "We've got him; and he can't escape us."

"No, chief, he can't: neither he nor the two women."

"Where are they?"

"Sonia and Victoire are on the second floor; Lupin is on the third."

M. Dudouis suddenly became anxious:

"Why, it was through the windows of one of those floors that the tapestries were passed when they disappeared!"

"That's so, chief."

"In that case, Lupin can get away too. The windows look out on the Rue Dufresnoy."

"Of course they do, chief; but I have taken my precautions. The moment you arrived, I sent four of our men to keep watch under the windows in the Rue Dufresnoy. They have strict instructions to shoot, if any one appears at the windows and looks like coming down. Blank cartridges for the first shot, ball-cartridges for the next."

"Good, Ganimard! You have thought of everything. We'll wait here; and, immediately after sunrise . . ."

"Wait, chief? Stand on ceremony with that rascal? Bother about rules and regulations, legal hours and all that rot? And suppose he's not quite so polite to us and gives us the slip meanwhile? Suppose he plays us one of his Lupin tricks? No, no, we must have no nonsense! We've got him: let's collar him; and that without delay!"

And Ganimard, all a-quiver with indignant impatience, went out, walked across the garden and presently returned with half-a-dozen men:

"It's all right, chief. I've told them, in the Rue Dufresnoy, to get their revolvers out and aim at the windows. Come along."

These alarums and excursions had not been effected without a certain amount of noise, which was bound to be heard by the inhabitants of the house. M. Dudouis felt that his hand was forced. He made up his mind to act:

"Come on, then," he said.

The thing did not take long. The eight of them, Browning pistols in hand, went up the stairs without overmuch precaution, eager to surprise Lupin before he had time to organize his defences.

"Open the door!" roared Ganimard, rushing at the door of Mme. Sparmiento's bedroom.

A policeman smashed it in with his shoulder.

There was no one in the room; and no one in Victoire's bedroom either.

"They're all upstairs!" shouted Ganimard. "They've gone up to Lupin in his attic. Be careful now!"

All the eight ran up the third flight of stairs. To his great astonishment, Ganimard found the door of the attic open and the attic empty. And the other rooms were empty too.

"Blast them!" he cursed. "What's become of them?"

But the chief called him. M. Dudouis, who had gone down again to the second floor, noticed that one of the windows was not latched, but just pushed to:

"There," he said, to Ganimard, "that's the road they took, the road of the tapestries. I told you as much: the Rue Dufresnoy. . . ."

"But our men would have fired on them," protested Ganimard, grinding his teeth with rage. "The street's guarded."

"They must have gone before the street was guarded."

"They were all three of them in their rooms when I rang you up, chief!"

"They must have gone while you were waiting for me in the garden."

"But why? Why? There was no reason why they should go to-day rather than to-morrow, or the next day, or next week, for that matter, when they had pocketed all the insurance-money!"

Yes, there was a reason; and Ganimard knew it when he saw, on the table, a letter addressed to himself and opened it and read it. The letter was worded in the style of the testimonials which we hand to people in our service who have given satisfaction:

"I, the undersigned, Arsène Lupin, gentleman-burglar, ex-colonel, ex-man-of-all-work, ex-corpse, hereby certify that the person of the name of Ganimard gave proof of the most remarkable qualities during his stay in this house. He was exemplary in his behaviour, thoroughly devoted and attentive; and, unaided by the least clue, he foiled a part of my plans and saved the insurance-companies four hundred and fifty thousand francs. I congratulate him; and I am quite willing to overlook his blunder in not anticipating that the downstair telephone communicates with the telephone in Sonia Kritchnoff's bedroom and that, when telephoning to Mr. Chief-detective, he was at the same time telephoning to me to clear out as fast as I could. It was a pardonable slip, which must not be allowed to dim the glamour of his services nor to detract from the merits of his victory.

"Having said this, I beg him to accept the homage of my admiration and of my sincere friendship.

"ARSÈNE LUPIN"

ON THE TOP OF
THE TOWER [1]

Hortense Daniel pushed her window ajar and whispered:

"Are you there, Rossigny?"

"I am here," replied a voice from the shrubbery at the front of the house.

Leaning forward, she saw a rather fat man looking up at her out of a gross red face with its cheeks and chin set in unpleasantly fair whiskers.

"Well?" he asked.

"Well, I had a great argument with my uncle and aunt last night. They absolutely refuse to sign the document of which my lawyer sent them the draft, or to restore the dowry squandered by my husband."

"But your uncle is responsible by the terms of the marriage-settlement."

"No matter. He refuses."

"Well, what do you propose to do?"

"Are you still determined to run away with me?" she asked, with a laugh.

"More so than ever."

"Your intentions are strictly honourable, remember!"

"Just as you please. You know that I am madly in love with you."

"Unfortunately I am not madly in love with you!"

"Then what made you choose me?"

"Chance. I was bored. I was growing tired of my humdrum existence. So I'm ready to run risks. . . . Here's my luggage: catch!"

She let down from the window a couple of large leather kit-bags. Rossigny caught them in his arms.

"The die is cast," she whispered. "Go and wait for me with your car at the If cross-roads. I shall come on horseback."

"Hang it, I can't run off with your horse!"

"He will go home by himself."

"Capital! . . . Oh, by the way . . ."

"What is it?"

"Who is this Prince Rénine, who's been here the last three days and whom nobody seems to know?"

"I don't know much about him. My uncle met him at a friend's shoot and asked him here to stay."

"You seem to have made a great impression on him. You went for a long ride with him yesterday. He's a man I don't care for."

"In two hours I shall have left the house in your company. The scandal will cool him off . . . Well, we've talked long enough. We have no time to lose."

For a few minutes she stood watching the fat man bending under the weight of her traps as he moved away in the shelter of an empty avenue. Then she closed the window.

Outside, in the park, the huntsmen's horns were sounding the reveille. The hounds burst into frantic baying. It was the opening day of the hunt that morning at the Chateau de la Marèze, where, every year, in the first week in September, the Comte d'Aigleroche, a mighty hunter before the Lord,[2] and his countess were accustomed to invite a few personal friends and the neighbouring land-owners.

Hortense slowly finished dressing, put on a riding-habit, which revealed the lines of her supple figure, and a wide-brimmed felt hat, which encircled her lovely face and auburn hair, and sat down to her writing-desk, at which she wrote to her uncle, M. d'Aigleroche, a farewell letter to be delivered to him that evening. It was a difficult letter to word; and, after beginning it several times, she ended by giving up the idea.

"I will write to him later," she said to herself, "when his anger has cooled down."

And she went downstairs to the dining-room.

Enormous logs were blazing in the hearth of the lofty room. The walls were hung with trophies of rifles and shotguns. The guests were flocking in from every side, shaking hands with the Comte d'Aigleroche, one of those typical country squires, heavily and powerfully built, who lives only for hunting and shooting. He was standing before the fire, with a large glass of old brandy in his hand, drinking the health of each new arrival.

Hortense kissed him absently:

"What, uncle! You who are usually so sober!"

"Pooh!" he said. "A man may surely indulge himself a little once a year! ..."

"Aunt will give you a scolding!"

"Your aunt has one of her sick headaches and is not coming down. Besides," he added, gruffly, "it is not her business ... and still less is it yours, my dear child."

Prince Rénine came up to Hortense. He was a young man, very smartly dressed, with a narrow and rather pale face, whose eyes held by turns the gentlest and the harshest, the most friendly and the most satirical expression. He bowed to her, kissed her hand and said:

"May I remind you of your kind promise, dear madame?"

"My promise?"

"Yes, we agreed that we should repeat our delightful excursion of yesterday and try to go over that old boarded-up place the look of which made us so curious. It seems to be known as the Domaine de Halingre."

She answered a little curtly:

"I'm extremely sorry, monsieur, but it would be rather far and I'm feeling a little done up. I shall go for a canter in the park and come indoors again."

There was a pause. Then Serge Rénine said, smiling, with his eyes fixed on hers and in a voice which she alone could hear:

"I am sure that you'll keep your promise and that you'll let me come with you. It would be better."

"For whom? For you, you mean?"

"For you, too, I assure you."

She coloured slightly, but did not reply, shook hands with a few people around her and left the room.

A groom was holding the horse at the foot of the steps. She mounted and set off towards the woods beyond the park.

It was a cool, still morning. Through the leaves, which barely quivered, the sky showed crystalline blue. Hortense rode at a walk down winding avenues which in half an hour brought her to a country-side of ravines and bluffs intersected by the high-road.

She stopped. There was not a sound. Rossigny must have stopped his engine and concealed the car in the thickets around the If cross-roads.

She was five hundred yards at most from that circular space. After hesitating for a few seconds, she dismounted, tied her horse carelessly, so that he could release himself by the least effort and return to the house, shrouded her face in the long brown veil that hung over her shoulders and walked on.

As she expected, she saw Rossigny directly she reached the first turn in the road. He ran up to her and drew her into the coppice!

"Quick, quick! Oh, I was so afraid that you would be late . . . or even change your mind! And here you are! It seems too good to be true!"

She smiled:

"You appear to be quite happy to do an idiotic thing!"

"I should think I *am* happy! And so will you be. I swear you will! Your life will be one long fairy-tale. You shall have every luxury, and all the money you can wish for."

"I want neither money nor luxuries."

"What then?"

"Happiness."

"You can safely leave your happiness to me."

She replied, jestingly:

"I rather doubt the quality of the happiness which you would give me."

"Wait! You'll see! You'll see!"

They had reached the motor. Rossigny, still stammering expressions of delight, started the engine. Hortense stepped in and wrapped herself in a wide cloak. The car followed the narrow, grassy path which led back to the cross-roads and Rossigny was accelerating the speed, when he was suddenly forced to pull up. A shot had rung out from the neighbouring wood, on the right. The car was swerving from side to side.

"A front tire burst," shouted Rossigny, leaping to the ground.

"Not a bit of it!" cried Hortense. "Somebody fired!"

"Impossible, my dear! Don't be so absurd!"

At that moment, two slight shocks were felt and two more reports were heard, one after the other, some way off and still in the wood.

Rossigny snarled:

"The back tires burst now . . . both of them. . . . But who, in the devil's name, can the ruffian be? . . . Just let me get hold of him, that's all! . . ."

He clambered up the road-side slope. There was no one there. Moreover, the leaves of the coppice blocked the view.

"Damn it! Damn it!" he swore. "You were right: somebody was firing at the car! Oh, this is a bit thick! We shall be held up for hours! Three tires to mend! . . . But what are you doing, dear girl?"

Hortense herself had alighted from the car. She ran to him, greatly excited:

"I'm going."

"But why?"

"I want to know. Some one fired. I want to know who it was."

"Don't let us separate, please!"

"Do you think I'm going to wait here for you for hours?"

"What about your running away? . . . All our plans . . . ?"

"We'll discuss that to-morrow. Go back to the house. Take back my things with you. . . . And good-bye for the present."

She hurried, left him, had the good luck to find her horse and set off at a gallop in a direction leading away from La Marèze.

There was not the least doubt in her mind that the three shots had been fired by Prince Rénine.

"It was he," she muttered, angrily, "it was he. No one else would be capable of such behaviour."

Besides, he had warned her, in his smiling, masterful way, that he would expect her.

She was weeping with rage and humiliation. At that moment, had she found herself face to face with Prince Rénine, she could have struck him with her riding-whip.

Before her was the rugged and picturesque stretch of country which lies between the Orne and the Sarthe, above Alençon, and which is known as Little Switzerland.[3] Steep hills compelled her frequently to moderate her pace, the more so as she had to cover some six miles before reaching her destination. But, though the speed at which she rode became less headlong, though her physical effort gradually slackened, she nevertheless persisted in her indignation against Prince Rénine. She bore him a grudge not only for the unspeakable action of which he had been guilty, but also for his behaviour to her during the last three days, his persistent attentions, his assurance, his air of excessive politeness.

She was nearly there. In the bottom of a valley, an old park-wall, full of cracks and covered with moss and weeds, revealed the ball-turret of a chateau and a few windows with closed shutters. This was the Domaine de Halingre.

She followed the wall and turned a corner. In the middle of the crescent-shaped space before which lay the entrance-gates, Serge Rénine stood waiting beside his horse.

She sprang to the ground, and, as he stepped forward, hat in hand, thanking her for coming, she cried:

"One word, monsieur, to begin with. Something quite inexplicable happened just now. Three shots were fired at a motorcar in which I was sitting. Did you fire those shots?"

"Yes."

She seemed dumbfounded:

"Then you confess it?"

"You have asked a question, madame, and I have answered it."

"But how dared you? What gave you the right?"

"I was not exercising a right, madame; I was performing a duty!"

"Indeed! And what duty, pray?"

"The duty of protecting you against a man who is trying to profit by your troubles."

"I forbid you to speak like that. I am responsible for my own actions, and I decided upon them in perfect liberty."

"Madame, I overheard your conversation with M. Rossigny this morning and it did not appear to me that you were accompanying him with a light heart. I admit the ruthlessness and bad taste of my interference and I apologise for it humbly; but I risked being taken for a ruffian in order to give you a few hours for reflection."

"I have reflected fully, monsieur. When I have once made up my mind to a thing, I do not change it."

"Yes, madame, you do, sometimes. If not, why are you here instead of there?"

Hortense was confused for a moment. All her anger had subsided. She looked at Rénine with the surprise which one experiences when confronted with certain persons who are unlike their fellows, more capable of performing unusual actions, more generous and disinterested. She realised perfectly that he was acting without any ulterior motive or calculation, that he was, as he had said, merely fulfilling his duty as a gentleman to a woman who has taken the wrong turning.

Speaking very gently, he said:

"I know very little about you, madame, but enough to make me wish to be of use to you. You are twenty-six years old and have lost both your parents. Seven years ago, you became the wife of the Comte d'Aigleroche's nephew by marriage, who proved to be of unsound mind, half insane indeed, and had to be confined. This made it impossible for you to obtain a divorce and compelled you, since your dowry had been squandered, to live with your uncle and at his expense. It's a depressing environment. The count and countess do not agree. Years ago, the count was deserted by his first wife, who ran away with the countess' first husband. The abandoned husband and wife decided out of spite to unite their fortunes, but found nothing but disappointment and ill-will in this second marriage. And you suffer the consequences. They lead a monotonous, narrow, lonely life for eleven months or more out of the year. One day, you met M. Rossigny, who fell in love with you and suggested an elopement. You did not care for him. But you were bored, your youth was being wasted, you longed for the unexpected, for adventure . . . in a word, you accepted with the very definite intention of keeping your admirer at arm's length, but also with the rather ingenuous hope that the scandal would force your uncle's hand and make him account for his trusteeship and assure you of an independent existence. That is how you stand. At present you have to choose between placing yourself in M. Rossigny's hands . . . or trusting yourself to me."

She raised her eyes to his. What did he mean? What was the purport of this offer which he made so seriously, like a friend who asks nothing but to prove his devotion?

After a moment's silence, he took the two horses by the bridle and tied them up. Then he examined the heavy gates, each of which was strengthened by two planks nailed cross-wise. An electoral poster, dated twenty years earlier, showed that no one had entered the domain since that time.

Rénine tore up one of the iron posts which supported a railing that ran round the crescent and used it as a lever. The rotten planks gave way. One of them uncovered the lock, which he attacked with a big knife, containing a number of blades and implements. A minute later, the gate opened on a waste of bracken which led up to a long, dilapidated building, with a turret at each corner and a sort of a belvedere, built on a taller tower, in the middle.

The Prince turned to Hortense:

"You are in no hurry," he said. "You will form your decision this evening; and, if M. Rossigny succeeds in persuading you for the second time, I give you my word of honour that I shall not cross your path. Until then, grant me the privilege of your company. We made up our minds yesterday to inspect the chateau. Let us do so. Will you? It is as good a way as any of passing the time and I have a notion that it will not be uninteresting."

He had a way of talking which compelled obedience. He seemed to be commanding and entreating at the same time. Hortense did not even seek to shake off the enervation into which her will was slowly sinking. She followed him to a half-demolished flight of steps at the top of which was a door likewise strengthened by planks nailed in the form of a cross.

Rénine went to work in the same way as before. They entered a spacious hall paved with white and black flagstones, furnished with old sideboards and choir-stalls and adorned with a carved escutcheon which displayed the remains of armorial bearings, representing an eagle standing on a block of stone, all half-hidden behind a veil of cobwebs which hung down over a pair of folding-doors.

"The door of the drawing-room, evidently," said Rénine.

He found this more difficult to open; and it was only by repeatedly charging it with his shoulder that he was able to move one of the doors.

Hortense had not spoken a word. She watched not without surprise this series of forcible entries, which were accomplished with a really masterly skill. He guessed her thoughts and, turning round, said in a serious voice:

"It's child's-play to me. I was a locksmith once."

She seized his arm and whispered:

"Listen!"

"To what?" he asked.

She increased the pressure of her hand, to demand silence. The next moment, he murmured:

"It's really very strange."

"Listen, listen!" Hortense repeated, in bewilderment. "Can it be possible?"

They heard, not far from where they were standing, a sharp sound, the sound of a light tap recurring at regular intervals; and they had only to listen attentively to recognise the ticking of a clock. Yes, it was this and nothing else that broke the profound silence of the dark room; it was indeed the deliberate ticking, rhythmical as the beat of a metronome, produced by a heavy brass pendulum. That was it! And nothing could be more impressive than the measured pulsation of this trivial mechanism, which by some miracle, some inexplicable phenomenon, had continued to live in the heart of the dead chateau.

"And yet," stammered Hortense, without daring to raise her voice, "no one has entered the house?"

"No one."

"And it is quite impossible for that clock to have kept going for twenty years without being wound up?"

"Quite impossible."

"Then . . . ?"

Serge Rénine opened the three windows and threw back the shutters.

He and Hortense were in a drawing-room, as he had thought; and the room showed not the least sign of disorder. The chairs were in their places. Not a piece of furniture was missing. The people who had lived there and who had made it the most individual room in their house had gone away leaving everything just as it was, the books which they used to read, the knick-nacks on the tables and consoles.

Rénine examined the old grandfather's clock, contained in its tall carved case which showed the disk of the pendulum through an oval pane of glass. He opened the door of the clock. The weights hanging from the cords were at their lowest point.

At that moment there was a click. The clock struck eight with a serious note which Hortense was never to forget.

"How extraordinary!" she said.

"Extraordinary indeed," said he, "for the works are exceedingly simple and would hardly keep going for a week."

"And do you see nothing out of the common?"

"No, nothing . . . or, at least . . ."

He stooped and, from the back of the case, drew a metal tube which was concealed by the weights. Holding it up to the light:

"A telescope," he said, thoughtfully. "Why did they hide it? . . . And they left it drawn out to its full length. . . . That's odd. . . . What does it mean?"

The clock, as is sometimes usual, began to strike a second time, sounding eight strokes. Rénine closed the case and continued his inspection without putting his telescope down. A wide arch led from the drawing-room to a smaller apartment, a sort of smoking-room. This also was furnished, but contained a glass case for guns of which the rack was empty. Hanging on a panel near by was a calendar with the date of the 5th of September.

"Oh," cried Hortense, in astonishment, "the same date as to-day! . . . They tore off the leaves until the 5th of September. . . . And this is the anniversary! What an astonishing coincidence!"

"Astonishing," he echoed. "It's the anniversary of their departure . . . twenty years ago to-day."

"You must admit," she said, "that all this is incomprehensible."

"Yes, of course . . . but, all the same . . . perhaps not."

"Have you any idea?"

He waited a few seconds before replying:

"What puzzles me is this telescope hidden, dropped in that corner, at the last moment. I wonder what it was used for. . . . From the ground-floor windows you see nothing but the trees in the garden . . . and the same, I expect, from all the windows. . . . We are in a valley, without the least open horizon. . . . To use the telescope, one would have to go up to the top of the house. . . . Shall we go up?"

She did not hesitate. The mystery surrounding the whole adventure excited her curiosity so keenly that she could think of nothing but accompanying Rénine and assisting him in his investigations.

They went upstairs accordingly, and, on the second floor, came to a landing where they found the spiral staircase leading to the belvedere.

At the top of this was a platform in the open air, but surrounded by a parapet over six feet high.

"There must have been battlements which have been filled in since," observed Prince Rénine. "Look here, there were loopholes at one time. They may have been blocked."

"In any case," she said, "the telescope was of no use up here either and we may as well go down again."

"I don't agree," he said. "Logic tells us that there must have been some gap through which the country could be seen and this was the spot where the telescope was used."

He hoisted himself by his wrists to the top of the parapet and then saw that this point of vantage commanded the whole of the valley, including the park, with its tall trees marking the horizon; and, beyond, a depression in a wood surmounting a hill, at a distance of some seven or eight hundred yards, stood another tower, squat and in ruins, covered with ivy from top to bottom.

Rénine resumed his inspection. He seemed to consider that the key to the problem lay in the use to which the telescope was put and that the problem would be solved if only they could discover this use.

He studied the loop-holes one after the other. One of them, or rather the place which it had occupied, attracted his attention above the rest. In the middle of the layer of plaster, which had served to block it, there was a hollow filled with earth in which plants had grown. He pulled out the plants and removed the earth, thus clearing the mouth of a hole some five inches in diameter, which completely penetrated the wall. On bending forward, Rénine perceived that this deep and narrow opening inevitably carried the eye, above the dense tops of the trees and through the depression in the hill, to the ivy-clad tower.

At the bottom of this channel, in a sort of groove which ran through it like a gutter, the telescope fitted so exactly that it was quite impossible to shift it, however little, either to the right or to the left.

Rénine, after wiping the outside of the lenses, while taking care not to disturb the lie of the instrument by a hair's breadth, put his eye to the small end.

He remained for thirty or forty seconds, gazing attentively and silently. Then he drew himself up and said, in a husky voice:

"It's terrible . . . it's really terrible."

"What is?" she asked, anxiously.

"Look."

She bent down, but the image was not clear to her and the telescope had to be focussed to suit her sight. The next moment she shuddered and said:

"It's two scarecrows, isn't it, both stuck up on the top? But why?"

"Look again," he said. "Look more carefully . . . under the hats . . . the faces . . ."

"Oh!" she cried, turning faint with horror, "how awful!"

The field of the telescope, like the circular picture shown by a magic lantern, presented this spectacle: the platform of a broken tower, the walls of which were higher in the more distant part and formed as it were a back-drop, over which surged waves of ivy. In front, amid a cluster of bushes, were two human beings, a man and a woman, leaning back against a heap of fallen stones.

But the words man and woman could hardly be applied to these two forms, these two sinister puppets, which, it is true, wore clothes and hats—or rather shreds of clothes and remnants of hats—but had lost their eyes, their cheeks, their chins, every particle of flesh, until they were actually and positively nothing more than two skeletons.

"Two skeletons," stammered Hortense. "Two skeletons with clothes on. Who carried them up there?"

"Nobody."

"But still . . ."

"That man and that woman must have died at the top of the tower, years and years ago . . . and their flesh rotted under their clothes and the ravens ate them."

"But it's hideous, hideous!" cried Hortense, pale as death, her face drawn with horror.

Half an hour later, Hortense Daniel and Rénine left the Chateau de Halíngre. Before their departure, they had gone as far as the ivy-grown tower, the remains of an old donjon-keep more than half demolished. The inside was empty. There seemed to have been a way of climbing to the top, at a comparatively recent period, by means of wooden stairs and ladders which now lay broken and scattered over the ground. The tower backed against the wall which marked the end of the park.

A curious fact, which surprised Hortense, was that Prince Rénine had neglected to pursue a more minute enquiry, as though the matter had lost all interest for him. He did not even speak of it any longer; and, in the inn at which they stopped and took a light meal in the nearest village, it was she who asked the landlord about the abandoned chateau. But she learnt nothing from him, for the man was new to the district and could give her no particulars. He did not even know the name of the owner.

They turned their horses' heads towards La Marèze. Again and again Hortense recalled the squalid sight which had met their eyes. But Rénine, who was in a lively mood and full of attentions to his companion, seemed utterly indifferent to those questions.

"But, after all," she exclaimed, impatiently, "we can't leave the matter there! It calls for a solution."

"As you say," he replied, "a solution is called for. M. Rossigny has to know where he stands and you have to decide what to do about him."

She shrugged her shoulders: "He's of no importance for the moment. The thing to-day . . ."

"Is what?"

"Is to know what those two dead bodies are."

"Still, Rossigny . . ."

"Rossigny can wait. But I can't. You have shown me a mystery which is now the only thing that matters. What do you intend to do?"

"To do?"

"Yes. There are two bodies . . . You'll inform the police, I suppose."

"Gracious goodness!" he exclaimed, laughing. "What for?"

"Well, there's a riddle that has to be cleared up at all costs, a terrible tragedy."

"We don't need any one to do that."

"What! Do you mean to say that you understand it?"

"Almost as plainly as though I had read it in a book, told in full detail, with explanatory illustrations. It's all so simple!"

She looked at him askance, wondering if he was making fun of her. But he seemed quite serious.

"Well?" she asked, quivering with curiosity.

The light was beginning to wane. They had trotted at a good pace; and the hunt was returning as they neared La Marèze.

"Well," he said, "we shall get the rest of our information from people living round about . . . from your uncle, for instance; and you will see how logically all the facts fit in. When you hold the first link of a chain, you are bound, whether you like it or not, to reach the last. It's the greatest fun in the world."

Once in the house, they separated. On going to her room, Hortense found her luggage and a furious letter from Rossigny in which he bade her good-bye and announced his departure.

Then Rénine knocked at her door:

"Your uncle is in the library," he said. "Will you go down with me? I've sent word that I am coming."

She went with him. He added:

"One word more. This morning, when I thwarted your plans and begged you to trust me, I naturally undertook an obligation towards you which I mean to fulfill without delay. I want to give you a positive proof of this."

She laughed:

"The only obligation which you took upon yourself was to satisfy my curiosity."

"It shall be satisfied," he assured her, gravely, "and more fully than you can possibly imagine."

M. d'Aigleroche was alone. He was smoking his pipe and drinking sherry. He offered a glass to Rénine, who refused.

"Well, Hortense!" he said, in a rather thick voice. "You know that it's pretty dull here, except in these September days. You must make the most of them. Have you had a pleasant ride with Rénine?"

"That's just what I wanted to talk about, my dear sir," interrupted the prince.

"You must excuse me, but I have to go to the station in ten minutes, to meet a friend of my wife's."

"Oh, ten minutes will be ample!"

"Just the time to smoke a cigarette?"

"No longer."

He took a cigarette from the case which M. d'Aigleroche handed to him, lit it and said:

"I must tell you that our ride happened to take us to an old domain which you are sure to know, the Domaine de Halingre."

"Certainly I know it. But it has been closed, boarded up for twenty-five years or so. You weren't able to get in, I suppose?"

"Yes, we were."

"Really? Was it interesting?"

"Extremely. We discovered the strangest things."

"What things?" asked the count, looking at his watch.

Rénine described what they had seen:

"On a tower some way from the house there were two dead bodies, two skeletons rather . . . a man and a woman still wearing the clothes which they had on when they were murdered."

"Come, come, now! Murdered?"

"Yes: and that is what we have come to trouble you about. The tragedy must date back to some twenty years ago. Was nothing known of it at the time?"

"Certainly not," declared the count. "I never heard of any such crime or disappearance."

"Oh, really!" said Rénine, looking a little disappointed. "I hoped to obtain a few particulars."

"I'm sorry."

"In that case, I apologise."

He consulted Hortense with a glance and moved towards the door. But on second thought:

"Could you not at least, my dear sir, bring me into touch with some persons in the neighbourhood, some members of your family, who might know more about it?"

"Of my family? And why?"

"Because the Domaine de Halingre used to belong and no doubt still belongs to the d'Aigleroches. The arms are an eagle on a heap of stones, on a rock. This at once suggested the connection."

This time the count appeared surprised. He pushed back his decanter and his glass of sherry and said:

"What's this you're telling me? I had no idea that we had any such neighbours."

Rénine shook his head and smiled:

"I should be more inclined to believe, sir, that you were not very eager to admit any relationship between yourself . . . and the unknown owner of the property."

"Then he's not a respectable man?"

"The man, to put it plainly, is a murderer."

"What do you mean?"

The count had risen from his chair. Hortense, greatly excited, said:

"Are you really sure that there has been a murder and that the murder was done by some one belonging to the house?"

"Quite sure."

"But why are you so certain?"

"Because I know who the two victims were and what caused them to be killed."

Prince Rénine was making none but positive statements and his method suggested the belief that he was supported by the strongest proofs.

M. d'Aigleroche strode up and down the room, with his hands behind his back. He ended by saying:

"I always had an instinctive feeling that something had happened, but I never tried to find out. . . . Now, as a matter of fact, twenty years ago, a relation of mine, a distant cousin, used to live at the Domaine de Halingre. I hoped, because of the name I bear, that this story, which, as I say, I never knew but suspected, would remain hidden for ever."

"So this cousin killed somebody?"

"Yes, he was obliged to."

Rénine shook his head:

"I am sorry to have to amend that phrase, my dear sir. The truth, on the contrary, is that your cousin took his victims' lives in cold blood and in a cowardly manner. I never heard of a crime more deliberately and craftily planned."

"What is it that you know?"

The moment had come for Rénine to explain himself, a solemn and anguish-stricken moment, the full gravity of which Hortense understood, though she had not yet divined any part of the tragedy which the prince unfolded step by step.

"It's a very simple story," he said. "There is every reason to believe that M. d'Aigleroche was married and that there was another couple living in the neighbourhoood with whom the owner of the Domaine de Halingre were on friendly terms. What happened one day, which of these four persons first disturbed the relations between the two house-holds, I am unable to say. But a likely version, which at once occurs to the mind, is that your cousin's wife, Madame d'Aigleroche, was in the habit of meeting the other husband in the ivy-covered tower, which had a door opening outside the estate. On discovering the intrigue, your cousin d'Aigleroche resolved to be revenged, but in such a manner that there should be no scandal and that no one even should ever know that the guilty pair had been killed. Now he had ascertained—as I did just now—that there was a part of the house, the belvedere, from which you can see, over the trees and the undulations of the park, the tower standing eight hundred yards away, and that this was the only place that overlooked the top of the tower. He therefore pierced a hole in the parapet, through one of the former loopholes, and from there, by using a telescope which fitted exactly in the grove which he had hollowed out, he watched the meetings of the two lovers. And it was from there, also, that, after carefully taking all his measurements, and calculating all his distances, on a Sunday, the 5th of September, when the house was empty, he killed them with two shots."

The truth was becoming apparent. The light of day was breaking. The count muttered:

"Yes, that's what must have happened. I expect that my cousin d'Aigleroche . . ."

"The murderer," Rénine continued, "stopped up the loophole neatly with a clod of earth. No one would ever know that two dead bodies were decaying on the top of that tower which was never visited and of which he took the precaution to demolish the wooden stairs. Nothing therefore remained for him to do but to explain the disappearance of his wife and his friend. This presented no difficulty. He accused them of having eloped together."

Hortense gave a start. Suddenly, as though the last sentence were a complete and to her an absolutely unexpected revelation, she understood what Rénine was trying to convey:

"What do you mean?" she asked.

"I mean that M. d'Aigleroche accused his wife and his friend of eloping together."

"No, no!" she cried. "I can't allow that! . . . You are speaking of a cousin of my uncle's? Why mix up the two stories?"

"Why mix up this story with another which took place at that time?" said the prince. "But I am not mixing them up, my dear madame; there is only one story and I am telling it as it happened."

Hortense turned to her uncle. He sat silent, with his arms folded; and his head remained in the shadow cast by the lamp-shade. Why had he not protested?

Rénine repeated in a firm tone:

"There is only one story. On the evening of that very day, the 5th of September at eight o'clock, M. d'Aigleroche, doubtless alleging as his reason that he was going in pursuit of the run-away couple, left his house after boarding up the entrance. He went away, leaving all the rooms as they were and removing only the firearms from their glass case. At the last minute, he had a presentiment, which has been justified to-day, that the discovery of the telescope which had played so great a part in the preparation of his crime might serve as a clue to an enquiry; and he threw it into the clock-case, where, as luck would have it, it interrupted the swing of the pendulum. This unreflecting action, one of those which every criminal inevitably commits, was to betray him twenty years later. Just now, the blows which I struck to force the door of the drawing-room released the pen-dulum. The clock was set going, struck eight o'clock . . . and I possessed the clue of thread which was to lead me through the labyrinth."

"Proofs!" stammered Hortense. "Proofs!"

"Proofs?" replied Rénine, in a loud voice. "Why, there are any number of proofs; and you know them as well as I do. Who could have killed at that distance of eight hundred yards, except an expert shot, an ardent sportsman? You agree, M. d'Aigle-roche, do you not? . . . Proofs? Why was nothing removed from the house, nothing except the guns, those guns which an ardent sportsman cannot afford to leave behind—you agree, M. d'Aigleroche—those guns which we find here, hanging in tro-phies on the walls! . . . Proofs? What about that date, the 5th of September, which was the date of the crime and which has left such a horrible memory in the criminal's mind that every year at this time—at this time alone—he surrounds himself with distractions and that every year, on this same 5th of September, he forgets his habits of temperance? Well, to-day, is the 5th of September. . . . Proofs? Why, if there weren't any others, would that not be enough for you?"

And Rénine, flinging out his arm, pointed to the Comte d'Aigleroche, who, terrified by this evocation of the past, had sunk huddled into a chair and was hiding his head in his hands.

Hortense did not attempt to argue with him. She had never liked her uncle, or rather her husband's uncle. She now accepted the accusation laid against him.

Sixty seconds passed. Then M. d'Aigleroche walked up to them and said:

"Whether the story be true or not, you can't call a husband a criminal for avenging his honour and killing his faithless wife."

"No," replied Rénine, "but I have told only the first version of the story. There is another which is infinitely more serious . . . and more probable, one to which a more thorough investigation would be sure to lead."

"What do you mean?"

"I mean this. It may not be a matter of a husband taking the law into his own hands, as I charitably supposed. It may be a matter of a ruined man who covets his friend's money and his friend's wife and who, with this object in view, to secure his freedom, to get rid of his friend and of his own wife, draws them into a trap, suggests to them that they should visit that lonely tower and kills them by shooting them from a distance safely under cover."

"No, no," the count protested. "No, all that is untrue."

"I don't say it isn't. I am basing my accusation on proofs, but also on intuitions and arguments which up to now have been extremely accurate. All the same, I admit that the second version may be incorrect. But, if so, why feel any remorse? One does not feel remorse for punishing guilty people."

"One does for taking life. It is a crushing burden to bear."

"Was it to give himself greater strength to bear this burden that M. d'Aigleroche afterwards married his victim's widow? For that, sir, is the crux of the question. What was the motive of that marriage? Was M. d'Aigleroche penniless? Was the woman he was taking as his second wife rich? Or were they both in love with each other and did M. d'Aigleroche plan with her to kill his first wife and the husband of his second wife? These are problems to which I do not know the answer. They have no interest for the moment; but the police, with all the means at their disposal, would have no great difficulty in elucidating them."

M. d'Aigleroche staggered and had to steady himself against the back of a chair. Livid in the face, he spluttered:

"Are you going to inform the police?"

"No, no," said Rénine. "To begin with, there is the statute of limitations. Then there are twenty years of remorse and dread, a memory which will pursue the criminal to his dying hour, accompanied no doubt by domestic discord, hatred, a daily hell . . . and, in the end, the necessity of returning to the tower and removing the traces of the two murders, the frightful punishment of climbing that tower, of touching those skeletons, of undressing them and burying them. That will be enough. We will not ask for more. We will not give it to the public to batten on and create a scandal which would recoil upon M. d'Aigleroche's niece. No, let us leave this disgraceful business alone."

The count resumed his seat at the table, with his hands clutching his forehead, and asked:

"Then why . . . ?"

"Why do I interfere?" said Rénine. "What you mean is that I must have had some object in speaking. That is so. There must indeed be a penalty, however slight, and our interview must lead to some practical result. But have no fear: M. d'Aigleroche will be let off lightly."

The contest was ended. The count felt that he had only a small formality to fulfil, a sacrifice to accept; and, recovering some of his self-assurance, he said, in an almost sarcastic tone:

"What's your price?"

Rénine burst out laughing:

"Splendid! You see the position. Only, you make a mistake in drawing me into the business. I'm working for the glory of the thing."

"In that case?"

"You will be called upon at most to make restitution."

"Restitution?"

Rénine leant over the table and said:

"In one of those drawers is a deed awaiting your signature. It is a draft agreement between you and your niece Hortense Daniel, relating to her private fortune, which fortune was squandered and for which you are responsible. Sign the deed."

M. d'Aigleroche gave a start:

"Do you know the amount?"

"I don't wish to know it."

"And if I refuse? . . ."

"I shall ask to see the Comtesse d'Aigleroche."

Without further hesitation, the count opened a drawer, produced a document on stamped paper and quickly signed it:

"Here you are," he said, "and I hope . . ."

"You hope, as I do, that you and I may never have any future dealings? I'm convinced of it. I shall leave this evening; your niece, no doubt, to-morrow. Good-bye."

In the drawing-room, which was still empty, while the guests at the house were dressing for dinner, Rénine handed the deed to Hortense. She seemed dazed by all that she had heard; and the thing that bewildered her even more than the relentless light shed upon her uncle's past was the miraculous insight and amazing lucidity displayed by this man: the man who for some hours had controlled events and conjured up before her eyes the actual scenes of a tragedy which no one had beheld.

"Are you satisfied with me?" he asked.

She gave him both her hands:

"You have saved me from Rossigny. You have given me back my freedom and my independence. I thank you from the bottom of my heart."

"Oh, that's not what I am asking you to say!" he answered. "My first and main object was to amuse you. Your life seemed so humdrum and lacking in the unexpected. Has it been so to-day?"

"How can you ask such a question? I have had the strangest and most stirring experiences."

"That is life," he said. "When one knows how to use one's eyes. Adventure exists everywhere, in the meanest hovel, under

the mask of the wisest of men. Everywhere, if you are only willing, you will find an excuse for excitement, for doing good, for
saving a victim, for ending an injustice."

Impressed by his power and authority, she murmured:

"Who are you exactly?"

"An adventurer. Nothing more. A lover of adventures. Life is
not worth living except in moments of adventure, the adventures of others or personal adventures. To-day's has upset you
because it affected the innermost depths of your being. But
those of others are no less stimulating. Would you like to make
the experiment?"

"How?"

"Become the companion of my adventures. If any one calls
on me for help, help him with me. If chance or instinct puts me
on the track of a crime or the trace of a sorrow, let us both set
out together. Do you consent?"

"Yes," she said, "but . . ."

She hesitated, as though trying to guess Rénine's secret intentions.

"But," he said, expressing her thoughts for her, with a smile,
"you are a trifle sceptical. What you are saying to yourself is,
'How far does that lover of adventures want to make me go? It
is quite obvious that I attract him; and sooner or later he would
not be sorry to receive payment for his services.' You are quite
right. We must have a formal contract."

"Very formal," said Hortense, preferring to give a jesting
tone to the conversation. "Let me hear your proposals."

He reflected for a moment and continued:

"Well, we'll say this. The clock at Halingre gave eight strokes
this afternoon, the day of the first adventure. Will you accept its
decree and agree to carry out seven more of these delightful enterprises with me, during a period, for instance, of three months?
And shall we say that, at the eighth, you will be pledged to grant
me . . ."

"What?"

He deferred his answer:

"Observe that you will always be at liberty to leave me on the
road if I do not succeed in interesting you. But, if you accom-

pany me to the end, if you allow me to begin and complete the eighth enterprise with you, in three months, on the 5th of December, at the very moment when the eighth stroke of that clock sounds—and it will sound, you may be sure of that, for the old brass pendulum will not stop swinging again—you will be pledged to grant me . . ."

"What?" she repeated, a little unnerved by waiting.

He was silent. He looked at the beautiful lips which he had meant to claim as his reward. He felt perfectly certain that Hortense had understood and he thought it unnecessary to speak more plainly:

"The mere delight of seeing you will be enough to satisfy me. It is not for me but for you to impose conditions. Name them: what do you demand?"

She was grateful for his respect and said, laughingly:

"What do I demand?"

"Yes."

"Can I demand anything I like, however difficult and impossible?"

"Everything is easy and everything is possible to the man who is bent on winning you."

Then she said:

"I demand that you shall restore to me a small, antique clasp, made of a cornelian set in a silver mount. It came to me from my mother and everyone knew that it used to bring her happiness and me too. Since the day when it vanished from my jewel-case, I have had nothing but unhappiness. Restore it to me, my good genius."

"When was the clasp stolen?"

She answered gaily:

"Seven years ago . . . or eight . . . or nine; I don't know exactly . . . I don't know where . . . I don't know how . . . I know nothing about it. . . ."

"I will find it," Rénine declared, "and you shall be happy."

THÉRÈSE AND GERMAINE

The weather was so mild that autumn that, on the 12th of October, in the morning, several families still lingering in their villas at Étretat[1] had gone down to the beach. The sea, lying between the cliffs and the clouds on the horizon, might have suggested a mountain-lake slumbering in the hollow of the enclosing rocks, were it not for that crispness in the air and those pale, soft and indefinite colours in the sky which give a special charm to certain days in Normandy.

"It's delicious," murmured Hortense. But the next moment she added: "All the same, we did not come here to enjoy the spectacle of nature or to wonder whether that huge stone Needle on our left was really at one time the home of Arsène Lupin."[2]

"We came here," said Prince Rénine, "because of the conversation which I overheard, a fortnight ago, in a dining-car, between a man and a woman."

"A conversation of which I was unable to catch a single word."

"If those two people could have guessed for an instant that it was possible to hear a single word of what they were saying, they would not have spoken, for their conversation was one of extraordinary gravity and importance. But I have very sharp ears; and though I could not follow every sentence, I insist that we may be certain of two things. First, that man and woman, who are brother and sister, have an appointment at a quarter to twelve this morning, the 12th of October, at the spot known as the Trois Mathildes, with a third person, who is married and who wishes at all costs to recover his or her liberty. Secondly, this appointment, at which they will come to a final agreement, is to be followed this evening by a walk along the cliffs, when the third person will bring with him or her the man or woman, I can't definitely say which, whom they want to get rid of. That is the gist of the whole thing. Now, as I know a spot called the Trois Mathildes some way above Étretat and as this is not an everyday name, we came down yesterday to thwart the plan of these objectionable persons."

"What plan?" asked Hortense. "For, after all, it's only your assumption that there's to be a victim and that the victim is to be flung off the top of the cliffs. You yourself told me that you heard no allusion to a possible murder."

"That is so. But I heard some very plain words relating to the marriage of the brother or the sister with the wife or the husband of the third person, which implies the need for a crime."

They were sitting on the terrace of the casino, facing the stairs which run down to the beach. They therefore overlooked the few privately-owned cabins on the shingle, where a party of four men were playing bridge, while a group of ladies sat talking and knitting.

A short distance away and nearer to the sea was another cabin, standing by itself and closed.

Half-a-dozen bare-legged children were paddling in the water.

"No," said Hortense, "all this autumnal sweetness and charm fails to attract me. I have so much faith in all your theories that I can't help thinking, in spite of everything, of this dreadful problem. Which of those people yonder is threatened? Death has already selected its victim. Who is it? Is it that young, fair-haired woman, rocking herself and laughing? Is it that tall man over there, smoking his cigar? And which of them has the thought of murder hidden in his heart? All the people we see are quietly enjoying themselves. Yet death is prowling among them."

"Capital!" said Rénine. "You too are becoming enthusiastic. What did I tell you? The whole of life's an adventure; and nothing but adventure is worthwhile. At the first breath of coming events, there you are, quivering in every nerve. You share in all the tragedies stirring around you; and the feeling of mystery awakens in the depths of your being. See, how closely you are observing that couple who have just arrived. You never can tell: that may be the gentleman who proposes to do away with his wife? Or perhaps the lady contemplates making away with her husband?"

"The d'Ormevals? Never! A perfectly happy couple! Yesterday, at the hotel, I had a long talk with the wife. And you yourself . . ."

"Oh, I played a round of golf with Jacques d'Ormeval, who rather fancies himself as an athlete, and I played at dolls with their two charming little girls!"

The d'Ormevals came up and exchanged a few words with them. Madame d'Ormeval said that her two daughters had gone back to Paris that morning with their governess. Her husband, a great tall fellow with a yellow beard, carrying his blazer over his arm and puffing out his chest under a cellular shirt, complained of the heat:

"Have you the key of the cabin, Thérèse?" he asked his wife, when they had left Rénine and Hortense and stopped at the top of the stairs, a few yards away.

"Here it is," said the wife. "Are you going to read your papers?"

"Yes. Unless we go for a stroll? . . ."

"I had rather wait till the afternoon: do you mind? I have a lot of letters to write this morning."

"Very well. We'll go on the cliff."

Hortense and Rénine exchanged a glance of surprise. Was this suggestion accidental? Or had they before them, contrary to their expectations, the very couple of whom they were in search?

Hortense tried to laugh:

"My heart is thumping," she said. "Nevertheless, I absolutely refuse to believe in anything so improbable. 'My husband and I have never had the slightest quarrel,' she said to me. No, it's quite clear that those two get on admirably."

"We shall see presently, at the Trois Mathildes, if one of them comes to meet the brother and sister."

M. d'Ormeval had gone down the stairs, while his wife stood leaning on the balustrade of the terrace. She had a beautiful, slender, supple figure. Her clear-cut profile was emphasized by a rather too prominent chin when at rest; and, when it was not smiling, the face gave an expression of sadness and suffering.

"Have you lost something, Jacques?" she called out to her husband, who was stooping over the shingle.

"Yes, the key," he said. "It slipped out of my hand."

She went down to him and began to look also. For two or three minutes, as they sheered off to the right and remained close to the bottom of the under-cliff, they were invisible to Hortense and Rénine. Their voices were covered by the noise of a dispute which had arisen among the bridge-players.

They reappeared almost simultaneously. Madame d'Ormeval slowly climbed a few steps of the stairs and then stopped and turned her face towards the sea. Her husband had thrown his blazer over his shoulders and was making for the isolated cabin. As he passed the bridge-players, they asked him for a decision, pointing to their cards spread out upon the table. But, with a wave of the hand, he refused to give an opinion and walked on, covered the thirty yards which divided them from the cabin, opened the door and went in.

Thérèse d'Ormeval came back to the terrace and remained for ten minutes sitting on a bench. Then she came out through the casino. Hortense, on leaning forward, saw her entering one of the chalets annexed to the Hôtel Hauville and, a moment later, caught sight of her again on the balcony.

"Eleven o'clock," said Rénine. "Whoever it is, he or she, or one of the card-players, or one of their wives, it won't be long before some one goes to the appointed place."

Nevertheless, twenty minutes passed and twenty-five; and no one stirred.

"Perhaps Madame d'Ormeval has gone," Hortense suggested, anxiously. "She is no longer on her balcony."

"If she is at the Trois Mathildes," said Rénine, "we will go and catch her there."

He was rising to his feet, when a fresh discussion broke out among the bridge-players and one of them exclaimed:

"Let's put it to d'Ormeval."

"Very well," said his adversary. "I'll accept his decision . . . if he consents to act as umpire. He was rather huffy just now."

They called out:

"D'Ormeval! D'Ormeval!"

They then saw that d'Ormeval must have shut the door behind him, which kept him in the half dark, the cabin being one of the sort that has no window.

"He's asleep," cried one. "Let's wake him up."

All four went to the cabin, began by calling to him and, on receiving no answer, thumped on the door:

"Hi! D'Ormeval! Are you asleep?"

On the terrace Serge Rénine suddenly leapt to his feet with so uneasy an air that Hortense was astonished. He muttered:

"If only it's not too late!"

And, when Hortense asked him what he meant, he tore down the steps and started running to the cabin. He reached it just as the bridge-players were trying to break in the door:

"Stop!" he ordered. "Things must be done in the regular fashion."

"What things?" they asked.

He examined the Venetian shutters at the top of each of the folding-doors and, on finding that one of the upper slats was partly broken, hung on as best he could to the roof of the cabin and cast a glance inside. Then he said to the four men:

"I was right in thinking that, if M. d'Ormeval did not reply, he must have been prevented by some serious cause. There is every reason to believe that M. d'Ormeval is wounded . . . or dead."

"Dead!" they cried. "What do you mean? He has only just left us."

Rénine took out his knife, prized open the lock and pulled back the two doors.

There were shouts of dismay. M. d'Ormeval was lying flat on his face, clutching his jacket and his newspaper in his hands. Blood was flowing from his back and staining his shirt.

"Oh!" said someone. "He has killed himself!"

"How can he have killed himself?" said Rénine. "The wound is right in the middle of the back, at a place which the hand can't reach. And, besides, there's not a knife in the cabin."

The others protested:

"If so, he has been murdered. But that's impossible! There has been nobody here. We should have seen, if there had been. Nobody could have passed us without our seeing . . ."

The other men, all the ladies and the children paddling in the sea had come running up. Rénine allowed no one to enter the cabin, except a doctor who was present. But the doctor could only say that M. d'Ormeval was dead, stabbed with a dagger.

At that moment, the mayor and the policeman arrived, together with some people of the village. After the usual enquiries, they carried away the body.

A few persons went on ahead to break the news to Thérèse d'Ormeval, who was once more to be seen on her balcony.

And so the tragedy had taken place without any clue to explain how a man, protected by a closed door with an uninjured lock, could have been murdered in the space of a few minutes and in front of twenty witnesses, one might almost say, twenty spectators. No one had entered the cabin. No one had come out of it. As for the dagger with which M. d'Ormeval had been stabbed between the shoulders, it could not be traced. And all this would have suggested the idea of a trick of sleight-of-hand performed by a clever conjuror, had it not concerned a terrible murder, committed under the most mysterious conditions.

Hortense was unable to follow, as Rénine would have liked, the small party who were making for Madame d'Ormeval; she was paralysed with excitement and incapable of moving. It was the first time that her adventures with Rénine had taken her into the very heart of the action and that, instead of noting the consequences of a murder, or assisting in the pursuit of the criminals, she found herself confronted with the murder itself.

It left her trembling all over; and she stammered:

"How horrible! . . . The poor fellow! . . . Ah, Rénine, you couldn't save him this time! . . . And that's what upsets me more than anything, that we could and should have saved him, since we knew of the plot. . . ."

Rénine made her sniff at a bottle of salts; and when she had quite recovered her composure, he said, while observing her attentively:

"So you think that there is some connection between the murder and the plot which we were trying to frustrate?"

"Certainly," said she, astonished at the question.

"Then, as that plot was hatched by a husband against his wife or by a wife against her husband, you admit that Madame d'Ormeval . . . ?"

"Oh, no, impossible!" she said. "To begin with, Madame d'Ormeval did not leave her rooms . . . and then I shall never believe that pretty woman capable . . . No, no, of course there was something else. . . ."

"What else?"

"I don't know. . . . You may have misunderstood what the brother and sister were saying to each other. . . . You see, the murder has been committed under quite different conditions . . . at another hour and another place. . . ."

"And therefore," concluded Rénine, "the two cases are not in any way related?"

"Oh," she said, "there's no making it out! It's all so strange!"

Rénine became a little satirical:

"My pupil is doing me no credit to-day," he said. "Why, here is a perfectly simple story, unfolded before your eyes. You have seen it reeled off like a scene in the cinema; and it all remains as obscure to you as though you were hearing of an affair that happened in a cave a hundred miles away!"

Hortense was confounded:

"What are you saying? Do you mean that you have understood it? What clues have you to go by?"

Rénine looked at his watch:

"I have not understood everything," he said. "The murder itself, the mere brutal murder, yes. But the essential thing, that is to say, the psychology of the crime: I've no clue to that. Only, it is twelve o'clock. The brother and sister, seeing no one come to the appointment at the Trois Mathildes, will go down to the beach. Don't you think that we shall learn something then of the accomplice whom I accuse them of having and of the connection between the two cases?"

They reached the esplanade in front of the Hauville chalets, with the capstans by which the fishermen haul up their boats to the beach. A number of inquisitive persons were standing outside the door of one of the chalets. Two coastguards, posted at the door, prevented them from entering.

The mayor shouldered his way eagerly through the crowd. He was back from the post-office, where he had been telephoning to Le Havre, to the office of the procurator-general, and had been told that the public prosecutor and an examining-magistrate would come on to Étretat in the course of the afternoon.

"That leaves us plenty of time for lunch," said Rénine. "The tragedy will not be enacted before two or three o'clock. And I have an idea that it will be sensational."

They hurried nevertheless. Hortense, overwrought by fatigue and her desire to know what was happening, continually questioned Rénine, who replied evasively, with his eyes turned to the esplanade, which they could see through the windows of the coffee-room.

"Are you watching for those two?" asked Hortense.

"Yes, the brother and sister."

"Are you sure that they will venture? . . ."

"Look out! Here they come!"

He went out quickly.

Where the main street opened on the sea-front, a lady and gentleman were advancing with hesitating steps, as though unfamiliar with the place. The brother was a puny little man, with a sallow complexion. He was wearing a motoring-cap. The sister too was short, but rather stout, and was wrapped in a large cloak. She struck them as a woman of a certain age, but still good-looking under the thin veil that covered her face.

They saw the groups of bystanders and drew nearer. Their gait betrayed uneasiness and hesitation.

The sister asked a question of a seaman. At the first words of his answer, which no doubt conveyed the news of d'Ormeval's death, she uttered a cry and tried to force her way through the crowd. The brother, learning in his turn what had happened, made great play with his elbows and shouted to the coast-guards:

"I'm a friend of d'Ormeval's! . . . Here's my card! Frédéric Astaing. . . . My sister, Germaine Astaing, knows Madame d'Ormeval intimately! . . . They were expecting us. . . . We had an appointment! . . ."

They were allowed to pass. Rénine, who had slipped behind

them, followed them in without a word, accompanied by Hortense.

The d'Ormevals had four bedrooms and a sitting-room on the second floor. The sister rushed into one of the rooms and threw herself on her knees beside the bed on which the corpse lay stretched. Thérèse d'Ormeval was in the sitting-room and was sobbing in the midst of a small company of silent persons. The brother sat down beside her, eagerly seized her hands and said, in a trembling voice:

"My poor friend! . . . My poor friend! . . ."

Rénine and Hortense gazed at the pair of them: and Hortense whispered:

"And she's supposed to have killed him for that? Impossible!"

"Nevertheless," observed Rénine, "they are acquaintances; and we know that Astaing and his sister were also acquainted with a third person who was their accomplice. So that . . ."

"It's impossible!" Hortense repeated.

And, in spite of all presumption, she felt so much attracted by Thérèse that, when Frédéric Astaing stood up, she proceeded straightway to sit down beside her and consoled her in a gentle voice. The unhappy woman's tears distressed her profoundly.

Rénine, on the other hand, applied himself from the outset to watching the brother and sister, as though this were the only thing that mattered, and did not take his eyes off Frédéric Astaing, who, with an air of indifference, began to make a minute inspection of the premises, examining the sitting-room, going into all the bedrooms, mingling with the various groups of persons present and asking questions about the manner in which the murder had been committed. Twice his sister came up and spoke to him. Then he went back to Madame d'Ormeval and again sat down beside her, full of earnest sympathy. Lastly, in the lobby, he had a long conversation with his sister, after which they parted, like people who have come to a perfect understanding. Frédéric then left. These manoeuvers had lasted quite thirty or forty minutes.

It was at this moment that the motor-car containing the examining-magistrate and the public prosecutor pulled up outside the chalets. Rénine, who did not expect them until later, said to Hortense:

"We must be quick. On no account leave Madame d'Ormeval."

Word was sent up to the persons whose evidence might be of any service that they were to go to the beach, where the magistrate was beginning a preliminary investigation. He would call on Madame d'Ormeval afterwards. Accordingly, all who were present left the chalet. No one remained behind except the two guards and Germaine Astaing.

Germaine knelt down for the last time beside the dead man and, bending low, with her face in her hands, prayed for a long time. Then she rose and was opening the door on the landing, when Rénine came forward:

"I should like a few words with you, madame."

She seemed surprised and replied:

"What is it, monsieur? I am listening."

"Not here."

"Where then, monsieur?"

"Next door, in the sitting-room."

"No," she said, sharply.

"Why not? Though you did not even shake hands with her, I presume that Madame d'Ormeval is your friend?"

He gave her no time to reflect, drew her into the next room, closed the door and, at once pouncing upon Madame d'Ormeval, who was trying to go out and return to her own room, said:

"No, madame, listen, I implore you. Madame Astaing's presence need not drive you away. We have very serious matters to discuss, without losing a minute."

The two women, standing face to face, were looking at each other with the same expression of implacable hatred, in which might be read the same confusion of spirit and the same restrained anger. Hortense, who believed them to be friends and who might, up to a certain point, have believed them to be accomplices, foresaw with terror the hostile encounter which she felt to be inevitable. She compelled Madame d'Ormeval to resume her seat, while Rénine took up his position in the middle of the room and spoke in resolute tones:

"Chance, which has placed me in possession of part of the truth, will enable me to save you both, if you are willing to assist me with a frank explanation that will give me the particulars which I still need. Each of you knows the danger in which she stands, because each of you is conscious in her heart of the evil for which she is responsible. But you are carried away by hatred; and it is for me to see clearly and to act. The examining-magistrate will be here in half-an-hour. By that time, you must have come to an agreement."

They both started, as though offended by such a word.

"Yes, an agreement," he repeated, in a more imperious tone. "Whether you like it or not, you will come to an agreement. You are not the only ones to be considered. There are your two little daughters, Madame d'Ormeval. Since circumstances have set me in their path, I am intervening in their defence and for their safety. A blunder, a word too much; and they are ruined. That must not happen."

At the mention of her children, Madame d'Ormeval broke down and sobbed. Germaine Astaing shrugged her shoulders and made a movement towards the door. Rénine once more blocked the way:

"Where are you going?"

"I have been summoned by the examining-magistrate."

"No, you have not."

"Yes, I have. Just as all those have been who have any evidence to give."

"You were not on the spot. You know nothing of what happened. Nobody knows anything of the murder."

"I know who committed it."

"That's impossible."

"It was Thérèse d'Ormeval."

The accusation was hurled forth in an outburst of rage and with a fiercely threatening gesture.

"You wretched creature!" exclaimed Madame d'Ormeval, rushing at her. "Go! Leave the room! Oh, what a wretch the woman is!"

Hortense was trying to restrain her, but Rénine whispered:

"Let them be. It's what I wanted . . . to pitch them one against the other and so to let in the daylight."

Madame Astaing had made a convulsive effort to ward off the insult with a jest; and she sniggered:

"A wretched creature? Why? Because I have accused you?"

"Why? For every reason! You're a wretched creature! You hear what I say, Germaine: you're a wretch!"

Thérèse d'Ormeval was repeating the insult as though it afforded her some relief. Her anger was abating. Very likely also she no longer had the strength to keep up the struggle; and it was Madame Astaing who returned to the attack, with her fists clenched and her face distorted and suddenly aged by fully twenty years:

"You! You dare to insult me, you! You after the murder you have committed! You dare to lift up your head when the man whom you killed is lying in there on his death-bed! Ah, if one of us is a wretched creature, it's you, Thérèse, and you know it! You have killed your husband! You have killed your husband!"

She leapt forward, in the excitement of the terrible words which she was uttering; and her finger-nails were almost touching her friend's face.

"Oh, don't tell me you didn't kill him!" she cried. "Don't say that: I won't let you. Don't say it. The dagger is there, in your bag. My brother felt it, while he was talking to you; and his hand came out with stains of blood upon it: your husband's blood, Thérèse. And then, even if I had not discovered anything, do you think that I should not have guessed, in the first few minutes? Why, I knew the truth at once, Thérèse! When a sailor down there answered, 'M. d'Ormeval? He has been murdered,' I said to myself then and there, 'It's she, it's Thérèse, she killed him.' "

Thérèse did not reply. She had abandoned her attitude of protest. Hortense, who was watching her with anguish, thought that she could perceive in her the despondency of those who know themselves to be lost. Her cheeks had fallen in and she wore such an expression of despair that Hortense, moved to compassion, implored her to defend herself:

"Please, please, explain things. When the murder was committed, you were here, on the balcony.... But then the dagger... how did you come to have it...? How do you explain it?..."

"Explanations!" sneered Germaine Astaing. "How could she possibly explain? What do outward appearances matter? What does it matter what any one saw or did not see? The proof is the thing that tells. . . . The dagger is there, in your bag, Thérèse: that's a fact. . . . Yes, yes, it was you who did it! You killed him! You killed him in the end! . . . Ah, how often I've told my brother, 'She will kill him yet!' Frédéric used to try to defend you. He always had a weakness for you. But in his innermost heart he foresaw what would happen. . . . And now the horrible thing has been done. A stab in the back! Coward! Coward! . . . And you would have me say nothing? Why, I didn't hesitate a moment! Nor did Frédéric. We looked for proofs at once. . . . And I've denounced you of my own free will, perfectly well aware of what I was doing. . . . And it's over, Thérèse. You're done for. Nothing can save you now. The dagger is in that bag which you are clutching in your hand. The magistrate is coming; and the dagger will be found, stained with the blood of your husband. So will your pocket-book. They're both there. And they will be found. . . ."

Her rage had incensed her so vehemently that she was unable to continue and stood with her hand outstretched and her chin twitching with nervous tremors.

Rénine gently took hold of Madame d'Ormeval's bag. She clung to it, but he insisted and said:

"Please allow me, madame. Your friend Germaine is right. The examining-magistrate will be here presently; and the fact that the dagger and the pocket-book are in your possession will lead to your immediate arrest. This must not happen. Please allow me."

His insinuating voice diminished Thérèse d'Ormeval's resistance. She released her fingers, one by one. He took the bag, opened it, produced a little dagger with an ebony handle and a grey leather pocket-book and quietly slipped the two into the inside pocket of his jacket.

Germaine Astaing gazed at him in amazement:

"You're mad, monsieur! What right have you . . . ?"

"These things must not be left lying about. I shan't worry now. The magistrate will never look for them in my pocket."

"But I shall denounce you to the police," she exclaimed, indignantly. "They shall be told!"

"No, no," he said, laughing, "you won't say anything! The police have nothing to do with this. The quarrel between you must be settled in private. What an idea, to go dragging the police into every incident of one's life!"

Madame Astaing was choking with fury:

"But you have no right to talk like this, monsieur! Who are you, after all? A friend of that woman's?"

"Since you have been attacking her, yes."

"But I'm only attacking her because she's guilty. For you can't deny it: she has killed her husband."

"I don't deny it," said Rénine, calmly. "We are all agreed on that point. Jacques d'Ormeval was killed by his wife. But, I repeat, the police must not know the truth."

"They shall know it through me, monsieur, I swear they shall. That woman must be punished; she has committed murder."

Rénine went up to her and, touching her on the shoulder:

"You asked me just now by what right I was interfering. And you yourself, madame?"

"I was a friend of Jacques d'Ormeval."

"Only a friend?"

She was a little taken aback, but at once pulled herself together and replied:

"I was his friend and it is my duty to avenge his death."

"Nevertheless, you will remain silent, as he did."

"He did not know, when he died."

"That's where you are wrong. He could have accused his wife, if he had wished. He had ample time to accuse her; and he said nothing."

"Why?"

"Because of his children."

Madame Astaing was not appeased; and her attitude displayed the same longing for revenge and the same detestation. But she was influenced by Rénine in spite of herself. In the small, closed room, where there was such a clash of hatred, he was gradually becoming the master; and Germaine Astaing understood that it was against him that she had to struggle, while Madame d'Ormeval felt all the comfort of that unexpected support which was offering itself on the brink of the abyss:

"Thank you, monsieur," she said. "As you have seen all this so clearly, you also know that it was for my children's sake that I did not give myself up. But for that . . . I am so tired . . . !"

And so the scene was changing and things assuming a different aspect. Thanks to a few words let fall in the midst of the dispute, the culprit was lifting her head and taking heart, whereas her accuser was hesitating and seemed to be uneasy. And it also came about that the accuser dared not say anything further and that the culprit was nearing the moment at which the need is felt of breaking silence and of speaking, quite naturally, words that are at once a confession and a relief.

"The time, I think, has come," said Rénine to Thérèse, with the same unvarying gentleness, "when you can and ought to explain yourself."

She was again weeping, lying huddled in a chair. She too revealed a face aged and ravaged by sorrow; and, in a very low voice, with no display of anger, she spoke, in short, broken sentences:

"She has been his mistress for the last four years. . . . I can't tell you how I suffered . . . She herself told me of it . . . out of sheer wickedness. . . . Her loathing for me was even greater than her love for Jacques . . . and every day I had some fresh injury to bear. . . . She would ring me up to tell me of her appointments with my husband. . . . She hoped to make me suffer so much that I should end by killing myself. . . . I did think of it sometimes, but I held out, for the children's sake. . . . Jacques was weakening. She wanted him to get a divorce . . . and little by little he began to consent . . . dominated by her and by her brother, who is slyer than she is, but quite as dangerous. . . . I felt all this. . . . Jacques was becoming harsh to me. . . . He had not the courage to leave me, but I was the obstacle and he bore me a grudge. . . . Heavens, the tortures I suffered! . . ."

"You should have given him his liberty," cried Germaine Astaing. "A woman doesn't kill her husband for wanting a divorce."

Thérèse a shook her head and answered:

"I did not kill him because he wanted a divorce. If he had really wanted it, he would have left me; and what could I have done? But your plans had changed, Germaine; divorce was not enough for you; and it was something else that you would have obtained from him, another, much more serious thing which you and your brother had insisted on . . . and to which he had consented . . . out of cowardice . . . in spite of himself. . . ."

"What do you mean?" spluttered Germaine. "What other thing?"

"My death."

"You lie!" cried Madame Astaing.

Thérèse did not raise her voice. She made not a movement of aversion or indignation and simply repeated:

"My death, Germaine. I have read your latest letters, six letters from you which he was foolish enough to leave about in his pocket-book and which I read last night, six letters in which the terrible word is not set down, but in which it appears between every line. I trembled as I read it! That Jacques should come to this! . . . Nevertheless the idea of stabbing him did not occur to me for a second. A woman like myself, Germaine, does not readily commit murder. . . . If I lost my head, it was after that . . . and it was your fault. . . ."

She turned her eyes to Rénine as if to ask him if there was no danger in her speaking and revealing the truth.

"Don't be afraid," he said. "I will be answerable for everything."

She drew her hand across her forehead. The horrible scene was being reenacted within her and was torturing her. Germaine Astaing did not move, but stood with folded arms and anxious eyes, while Hortense Daniel sat distractedly awaiting the confession of the crime and the explanation of the unfathomable mystery.

"It was after that and it was through your fault Germaine. . . . I had put back the pocket-book in the drawer where it was hidden; and I said nothing to Jacques this morning. . . . I did not want to tell him what I knew. . . . It was too horrible. . . . All the same, I had to act quickly; your letters announced your secret arrival today. . . . I thought at first of running away, of taking the train. . . . I had mechanically picked up that dagger, to defend myself. . . . But when Jacques and I went down to the beach, I was resigned. . . . Yes, I had accepted death: 'I will die,' I thought, 'and put an end to all this nightmare!' . . . Only, for the children's sake, I was anxious that my death should look like an accident and that

Jacques should have no part in it. That was why your plan of a walk on the cliff suited me. . . . A fall from the top of a cliff seems quite natural. . . . Jacques therefore left me to go to his cabin, from which he was to join you later at the Trois Mathildes. On the way, below the terrace, he dropped the key of the cabin. I went down and began to look for it with him. . . . And it happened then . . . through your fault . . . yes, Germaine, through your fault. . . . Jacques' pocket-book had slipped from his jacket, without his noticing it, and, together with the pocket-book, a photograph which I recognized at once: a photograph, taken this year, of myself and my two children. I picked it up . . . and I saw . . . You know what I saw, Germaine. Instead of my face, the face in the photograph was *yours!* . . . You had put in your likeness, Germaine, and blotted me out! It was your face! One of your arms was round my elder daughter's neck; and the younger was sitting on your knees. . . . It was you, Germaine, the wife of my husband, the future mother of my children, you, who were going to bring them up . . . you, you! . . . Then I lost my head. I had the dagger. . . . Jacques was stooping. . . . I stabbed him. . . ."

Every word of her confession was strictly true. Those who listened to her felt this profoundly; and nothing could have given Hortense and Rénine a keener impression of tragedy.

She had fallen back into her chair, utterly exhausted. Nevertheless, she went on speaking unintelligible words; and it was only gradually by leaning over her, that they were able to make out:

"I thought that there would be an outcry and that I should be arrested. But no. It happened in such a way and under such conditions that no one had seen anything. Further, Jacques had drawn himself up at the same time as myself; and he actually did not fall. No, he did not fall! I had stabbed him; and he remained standing! I saw him from the terrace, to which I had returned. He had hung his jacket over his shoulders, evidently to hide his wound, and he moved away without staggering . . . or staggering so little that I alone was able to perceive it. He even spoke to some friends who were playing cards. Then he went to his cabin and disappeared. . . . In a few moments, I came back indoors. I was persuaded that all of this was only a bad dream . . . that I had not killed him . . . or that at the worst the wound was a slight one. Jacques would come out again. I was certain of it. . . . I watched from my balcony. . . . If I had thought for a moment that he needed assistance, I should have flown to him. . . . But truly I didn't know . . . I didn't guess . . . People speak of presentiments: there are no such things. I was perfectly calm, just as one is after a nightmare of which the memory is fading away. . . . No, I swear to you, I knew nothing . . . until the moment . . ."

She interrupted herself, stifled by sobs.

Rénine finished her sentence for her.

"Until the moment when they came and told you, I suppose?"

Thérèse stammered:

"Yes. It was not till then that I was conscious of what I had done . . . and I felt that I was going mad and that I should cry out to all those people, 'Why, it was I who did it! Don't search! Here is the dagger . . . I am the culprit!' Yes, I was going to say that, when suddenly I caught sight of my poor Jacques. . . . They were carrying him along. . . . His face was very peaceful, very gentle. . . . And, in his presence, I understood my duty, as he had understood his. . . . He had kept silent, for the sake of the children. I would be silent too. We were both guilty of the murder of which he was the victim; and we must both do all we could to prevent the crime from recoiling upon them. . . . He had seen this clearly in his dying agony. He had had the amazing courage to keep his feet, to answer the people who spoke to him and to lock himself up to die. He had done this, wiping out all his faults with a single action, and in so doing had granted me his forgiveness, because he was not accusing me . . . and was ordering me to hold my peace . . . and to defend myself . . . against everybody . . . especially against you, Germaine."

She uttered these last words more firmly. At first wholly overwhelmed by the unconscious act which she had committed in killing her husband, she had recovered her strength a little in thinking of what she had done and in defending herself with such energy. Faced by the intriguing woman whose hatred had driven both of them to death and crime, she clenched her fists, ready for the struggle, all quivering with resolution.

Germaine Astaing did not flinch. She had listened without a word, with a relentless expression which grew harder and harder as Thérèse's confessions became precise. No emotion seemed to soften her and no remorse to penetrate her being. At most, towards the end, her thin lips shaped themselves into a faint smile. She was holding her prey in her clutches.

Slowly, with her eyes raised to a mirror, she adjusted her hat and powdered her face. Then she walked to the door.

Thérèse darted forward:

"Where are you going?"

"Where I choose."

"To see the examining-magistrate?"

"Very likely."

"You shan't pass!"

"As you please. I'll wait for him here."

"And you'll tell him what?"

"Why, all that you've said, of course, all that you've been silly enough to say. How could he doubt the story? You have explained it all to me so fully."

Thérèse took her by the shoulders:

"Yes, but I'll explain other things to him at the same time, Germaine, things that concern you. If I'm ruined, so shall you be."

"You can't touch me."

"I can expose you, show your letters."

"What letters?"

"Those in which my death was decided on."

"Lies, Thérèse! You know that famous plot exists only in your imagination. Neither Jacques nor I wished for your death."

"You did, at any rate. Your letters condemn you."

"Lies! They were the letters of a friend to a friend."

"Letters of a mistress to her paramour."

"Prove it."

"They are there, in Jacques' pocket-book."

"No, they're not."

"What's that you say?"

"I say that those letters belonged to me. I've taken them back, or rather my brother has."

"You've stolen them, you wretch! And you shall give them back again," cried Thérèse, shaking her.

"I haven't them. My brother kept them. He has gone."

Thérèse staggered and stretched out her hands to Rénine with an expression of despair. Rénine said:

"What she says is true. I watched the brother's proceedings while he was feeling in your bag. He took out the pocket-book, looked through it with his sister, came and put it back again and went off with the letters."

Rénine paused and added,

"Or, at least, with five of them."

The two women moved closer to him. What did he intend to convey? If Frédéric Astaing had taken away only five letters, what had become of the sixth?

"I suppose," said Rénine, "that, when the pocket-book fell on the shingle, that sixth letter slipped out at the same time as the photograph and that M. d'Ormeval must have picked it up, for I found it in the pocket of his blazer, which had been hung up near the bed. Here it is. It's signed Germaine Astaing and it is quite enough to prove the writer's intentions and the murderous counsels which she was pressing upon her lover."

Madame Astaing had turned grey in the face and was so much disconcerted that she did not try to defend herself. Rénine continued, addressing his remarks to her:

"To my mind, madame, you are responsible for all that happened. Penniless, no doubt, and at the end of your resources, you tried to profit by the passion with which you inspired M. d'Ormeval in order to make him marry you, in spite of all the obstacles, and to lay your hands upon his fortune. I have proofs of this greed for money and these abominable calculations and can supply them if need be. A few minutes after I had felt in the pocket of that jacket, you did the same. I had removed the sixth letter, but had left a slip of paper which you looked for eagerly and which also must have dropped out of the pocket-book. It was an uncrossed cheque for a hundred thousand francs, drawn by M. d'Ormeval in your brother's name . . . just a little wedding-present . . . what we might call pin-money. Acting on your instructions, your brother dashed off by motor to Le Havre to reach the bank before four o'clock. I may as well tell you that he will not have cashed the cheque, for I had a telephone-message sent to the bank to announce the murder of M. d'Ormeval, which stops all payments. The upshot of all this is that the police, if you persist in your schemes of revenge, will have in their hands all the proofs that are wanted against you and your brother. I might add, as an edifying piece of evidence, the story of the conversation which I overheard between your brother and yourself in a dining-car on the railway between Brest and Paris, a fortnight ago. But I feel sure that you will not drive me to adopt these extreme measures and that we understand each other. Isn't that so?"

Natures like Madame Astaing's, which are violent and head-strong so long as a fight is possible and while a gleam of hope remains, are easily swayed in defeat. Germaine was too intelligent not to grasp the fact that the least attempt at resistance would be shattered by such an adversary as this. She was in his hands. She could but yield.

She therefore did not indulge in any play-acting, nor in any demonstration such as threats, outbursts of fury or hysterics. She bowed:

"We are agreed," she said. "What are your terms?"

"Go away. If ever you are called upon for your evidence, say that you know nothing."

She walked away. At the door, she hesitated and then, between her teeth, said:

"The cheque."

Rénine looked at Madame d'Ormeval, who declared:

"Let her keep it. I would not touch that money."

When Rénine had given Thérèse d'Ormeval precise instructions as to how she was to behave at the enquiry and to answer the questions put to her, he left the chalet, accompanied by Hortense Daniel.

On the beach below, the magistrate and the public prosecutor were continuing their investigations, taking measurements, examining the witnesses and generally laying their heads together.

"When I think," said Hortense, "that you have the dagger and M. d'Ormeval's pocket-book on you!"

"And it strikes you as awfully dangerous, I suppose?" he said, laughing. "It strikes *me* as awfully comic."

"Aren't you afraid?"

"Of what?"

"That they may suspect something?"

"Lord, they won't suspect a thing! We shall tell those good people what we saw and our evidence will only increase their perplexity, for we saw nothing at all. For prudence sake we will stay a day or two, to see which way the wind is blowing. But it's quite settled: they will never be able to make head or tail of the matter."

"Nevertheless, *you* guessed the secret and from the first. Why?"

"Because, instead of seeking difficulties where none exist, as people generally do, I always put the question as it should be put; and the solution comes quite naturally. A man goes to his cabin and locks himself in. Half an hour later, he is found inside, dead. No one has gone in. What has happened? To my mind there is only one answer. There is no need to think about it. As the murder was not committed in the cabin, it must have been committed beforehand and the man was already mortally wounded when he entered his cabin. And forthwith the truth in this particular case appeared to me. Madame d'Ormeval, who was to have been killed this evening, forestalled her murderers and while her husband was stooping to the ground, in a moment of frenzy stabbed him in the back. There was nothing left to do but look for the reasons that prompted her action. When I knew them, I took her part unreservedly. That's the whole story."

The day was beginning to wane. The blue of the sky was becoming darker and the sea even more peaceful than before.

"What are you thinking of?" asked Rénine, after a moment.

"I am thinking," she said, "that if I too were the victim of some machination, I should trust you whatever happened, trust you through and against all. I know, as certainly as I know that I exist, that you would save me, whatever the obstacles might be. There is no limit to the power of your will."

He said, very softly:

"There is no limit to my wish to please you."

AT THE SIGN OF MERCURY

To *Madame Daniel,*
La Roncière,
near Bassicourt.

PARIS 30 NOVEMBER

"MY DEAREST FRIEND,—

"There has been no letter from you for a fortnight; so I don't expect now to receive one for that troublesome date of the 5th of
December, which we fixed as the last day of our partnership.
I rather wish it would come, because you will then be released
from a contract which no longer seems to give you pleasure. To
me the seven battles which we fought and won together were a
time of endless delight and enthusiasm. I was living beside you. I
was conscious of all the good which that more active and stirring existence was doing you. My happiness was so great that I
dared not speak of it to you or let you see anything of my secret
feelings except my desire to please you and my passionate devotion. To-day you have had enough of your brother in arms. Your
will shall be law.

"But, though I bow to your decree, may I remind you what it
was that I always believed our final adventure would be? May I
repeat your words, not one of which I have forgotten?

" 'I demand,' you said, 'that you shall restore to me a small, antique clasp, made of a cornelian set in a filigree mount. It came to
me from my mother; and every one knew that it used to bring her
happiness and me too. Since the day when it vanished from my
jewel-case, I have had nothing but unhappiness. Restore it to me,
my good genius.'

"And, when I asked you when the clasp had disappeared, you answered, with a laugh:

" 'Seven years ago . . . or eight . . . or nine: I don't know exactly. . . . I don't know when . . . I don't know how . . . I know nothing about it. . . .'

"You were challenging me, were you not, and you set me that condition because it was one which I could not fulfil? Nevertheless, I promised and I should like to keep my promise. What I have tried to do, in order to place life before you in a more favourable light, would seem purposeless, if your confidence feels the lack of this talisman to which you attach so great a value. We must not laugh at these little superstitions. They are often the mainspring of our best actions.

"Dear friend, if you had helped me, I should have achieved yet one more victory. Alone and hard pushed by the proximity of the date, I have failed, not however without placing things on such a footing that the undertaking if you care to follow it up, has the greatest chance of success.

"And you will follow it up, won't you? We have entered into a mutual agreement which we are bound to honour. It behooves us, within a fixed time, to inscribe in the book of our common life eight good stories, to which we shall have brought energy, logic, perseverance, some subtlety and occasionally a little heroism. This is the eighth of them. It is for you to act so that it may be written in its proper place on the 5th of December, before the clock strikes eight in the evening.

"And, on that day, you will act as I shall now tell you.

"First of all—and above all, my dear, do not complain that my instructions are fanciful: each of them is an indispensable condition of success—first of all, cut in your cousin's garden three slender lengths of rush. Plait them together and bind up the two ends so as to make a rude switch, like a child's whip-lash.

"When you get to Paris, buy a long necklace of jet beads, cut into facets, and shorten it so that it consists of seventy-five beads, of almost equal size.

"Under your winter cloak, wear a blue woollen gown. On your head, a toque with red leaves on it. Round your neck, a feather boa. No gloves. No rings.

"In the afternoon, take a cab along the left bank of the river to the church of Saint-Étienne-du-Mont. At four o'clock exactly, there will be, near the holy-water basin, just inside the church, an old woman dressed in black, saying her prayers on a silver rosary. She will offer you holy water. Give her your necklace. She will count the beads and hand it back to you. After this, you will walk behind her, you will cross an arm of the Seine and she will lead you, down a lonely street in the Ile Saint-Louis, to a house which you will enter by yourself.

"On the ground-floor of this house, you will find a youngish man; with a very pasty complexion. Take off your cloak and then say to him:

" 'I have come to fetch my clasp.'

"Do not be astonished by his agitation or dismay. Keep calm in his presence. If he questions you, if he wants to know your reason for applying to him or what impels you to make that request, give him no explanation. Your replies must be confined to these brief formulas:

" 'I have come to fetch what belongs to me. I don't know you, I don't know your name; but I am obliged to come to you like this. I must have my clasp returned to me. I must.'

"I honestly believe that, if you have the firmness not to swerve from that attitude, whatever farce the man may play, you will be completely successful. But the contest must be a short one and the issue will depend solely on your confidence in yourself and your certainty of success. It will be a sort of match in which you must defeat your opponent in the first round. If you remain impassive, you will win. If you show hestitation or uneasiness, you can do nothing against him. He will escape you and regain the upper hand after a first moment of distress; and the game will be lost in a few minutes. There is no midway house between victory or . . . defeat.

"In the latter event, you would be obliged—I beg you to pardon me for saying so—again to accept my collaboration. I offer it you in advance, my dear, and without any conditions, while stating quite plainly that all that I have been able to do for you and all that I may yet do gives me no other right than that of thanking you and devoting myself more than ever to the woman who represents my joy, my whole life."

Hortense, after reading the letter, folded it up and put it away at the back of a drawer, saying, in a resolute voice:

"I shan't go."

To begin with, although she had formerly attached some slight importance to this trinket, which she had regarded as a mascot, she felt very little interest in it now that the period of her trials was apparently at an end. She could not forget that figure eight, which was the serial number of the next adventure. To launch herself upon it meant taking up the interrupted chain, going back to Rénine and giving him a pledge which, with his powers of suggestion, he would know how to turn to account.

Two days before the 5th of December, she was still in the same frame of mind. So she was on the morning of the 4th; but suddenly, without even having to contend against preliminary subterfuges, she ran out into the garden, cut three lengths of rush, plaited them as she used to do in her childhood and at twelve o'clock had herself driven to the station. She was uplifted by an eager curiosity. She was unable to resist all the amusing and novel sensations which the adventure, proposed by Rénine, promised her. It was really too tempting. The jet necklace, the toque with the autumn leaves, the old woman with the silver rosary: how could she resist their mysterious appeal and how could she refuse this opportunity of showing Rénine what she was capable of doing?

"And then, after all," she said to herself, laughing, "he's summoning me to Paris. Now eight o'clock is dangerous to me at a spot three hundred miles from Paris, in that old deserted Château de Halingre, but nowhere else. The only clock that can strike the threatening hour is down there, under lock and key, a prisoner!"

She reached Paris that evening. On the morning of the 5th she went out and bought a jet necklace, which she reduced to seventy-five beads, put on a blue gown and a toque with red leaves and, at four o'clock precisely, entered the church of Saint-Étienne-du-Mont.

Her heart was throbbing violently. This time she was alone; and how acutely she now felt the strength of that support which, from unreflecting fear rather than any reasonable motive, she had thrust aside! She looked around her, almost hoping to see him. But there was no one there . . . no one except an old lady in black, standing beside the holy water basin.

Hortense went up to her. The old lady, who held a silver rosary in her hands, offered her holy water and then began to count the beads of the necklace which Hortense gave her.

She whispered:

"Seventy-five. That's right. Come."

Without another word, she toddled along under the light of the street-lamps, crossed the Pont des Tournelles to the Ile Saint-Louis and went down an empty street leading to a cross-roads, where she stopped in front of an old house with wrought-iron balconies:

"Go in," she said.

And the old lady went away.

Hortense now saw a prosperous-looking shop which occupied almost the whole of the ground-floor and whose windows, blazing with electric light, displayed a huddled array of old furniture and antiquities. She stood there for a few seconds, gazing at it absently. A sign-board bore the words "The Mercury," together with the name of the owner of the shop, "Pancaldi." Higher up, on a projecting cornice which ran on a level with the first floor, a small niche sheltered a terra-cotta Mercury[1] poised on one foot, with wings to his sandals and the caduceus in his hand, who, as Hortense noted, was leaning a little too far forward in the ardour of his flight and ought logically to have lost his balance and taken a header into the street.

"Now!" she said, under her breath.

She turned the handle of the door and walked in.

Despite the ringing of the bells actuated by the opening door, no one came to meet her. The shop seemed to be empty. However, at the extreme end there was a room at the back of the shop and after that another, both crammed with furniture and knick-knacks, many of which looked very valuable. Hortense followed a narrow gangway which twisted and turned between two walls built up of cupboards, cabinets and console-tables, went up two steps and found herself in the last room of all.

A man was sitting at a writing-desk and looking through some account-books. Without turning his head, he said:

"I am at your service, madam. . . . Please look round you. . . ."

This room contained nothing but articles of a special character which gave it the appearance of some alchemist's laboratory in the middle ages: stuffed owls, skeletons, skulls, copper alembics, astrolabes and all around, hanging on the walls, amulets of every description, mainly hands of ivory or coral with two fingers pointing to ward off ill-luck.

"Are you wanting anything in particular, madam?" asked M. Pancaldi, closing his desk and rising from his chair.

"It's the man," thought Hortense.

He had in fact an uncommonly pasty complexion. A little forked beard, flecked with grey, lengthened his face, which was surmounted by a bald, pallid forehead, beneath which gleamed a pair of small, prominent, restless, shifty eyes.

Hortense, who had not removed her veil or cloak, replied:

"I want a clasp."

"They're in this show-case," he said, leading the way to the connecting room.

Hortense glanced over the glass case and said:

"No, no, . . . I don't see what I'm looking for. I don't want just any clasp, but a clasp which I lost out of a jewel-case some years ago and which I have come to look for here."

She was astounded to see the commotion displayed on his features. His eyes became haggard.

"Here? . . . I don't think you are in the least likely . . . What sort of clasp is it? . . ."

"A cornelian, mounted in gold filigree . . . of the 1830 period."

"I don't understand," he stammered. "Why do you come to me?"

She now removed her veil and laid aside her cloak.

He stepped back, as though terrified by the sight of her, and whispered:

"The blue gown! . . . The toque! . . . And—can I believe my eyes?—the jet necklace! . . ."

It was perhaps the whip-lash formed of three rushes that excited him most violently. He pointed his finger at it, began to stagger where he stood and ended by beating the air with his arms, like a drowning man, and fainting away in a chair.

Hortense did not move.

"Whatever farce he may play," Rénine had written, "have the courage to remain impassive."

Perhaps he was not playing a farce. Nevertheless she forced herself to be calm and indifferent.

This lasted for a minute or two, after which M. Pancaldi recovered from his swoon, wiped away the perspiration streaming down his forehead and, striving to control himself, resumed, in a trembling voice:

"Why do you apply to me?"

"Because the clasp is in your possession."

"Who told you that?" he said, without denying the accusation. "How do you know?"

"I know because it is so. Nobody has told me anything. I came here positive that I should find my clasp and with the immovable determination to take it away with me."

"But do you know me? Do you know my name?"

"I don't know you. I did not know your name before I read it over your shop. To me you are simply the man who is going to give me back what belongs to me."

He was greatly agitated. He kept on walking to and fro in a small empty space surrounded by a circle of piled-up furniture, at which he hit out idiotically, at the risk of bringing it down.

Hortense felt that she had the whip hand of him; and, profiting by his confusion, she said, suddenly, in a commanding and threatening tone:

"Where is the thing? You must give it back to me. I insist upon it."

Pancaldi gave way to a moment of despair. He folded his hands and mumbled a few words of entreaty. Then, defeated and suddenly resigned, he said, more distinctly:

"You insist? . . ."

"I do. You must give it to me."

"Yes, yes, I must . . . I agree."

"Speak!" she ordered, more harshly still.

"Speak, no, but write: I will write my secret. . . . And that will be the end of me."

He turned to his desk and feverishly wrote a few lines on a sheet of paper, which he put into an envelope and sealed it:

"See," he said, "here's my secret. . . . It was my whole life. . . ."

And, so saying, he suddenly pressed against his temple a revolver which he had produced from under a pile of papers and fired.

With a quick movement, Hortense struck up his arm. The bullet struck the mirror of a cheval-glass. But Pancaldi collapsed and began to groan, as though he were wounded.

Hortense made a great effort not to lose her composure:

"Rénine warned me," she reflected. "The man's a play-actor. He has kept the envelope. He has kept his revolver. I won't be taken in by him."

Nevertheless, she realized that, despite his apparent calmness, the attempt at suicide and the revolver-shot had completely unnerved her. All her energies were dispersed, like the sticks of a bundle whose string has been cut; and she had a painful impression that the man, who was grovelling at her feet, was in reality slowly getting the better of her.

She sat down, exhausted. As Rénine had foretold, the duel had not lasted longer than a few minutes but it was she who had succumbed, thanks to her feminine nerves and at the very moment when she felt entitled to believe that she had won.

The man Pancaldi was fully aware of this; and, without troubling to invent a transition, he ceased his jeremiads, leapt to his feet, cut a sort of agile caper before Hortense's eyes and cried, in a jeering tone:

"Now we are going to have a little chat; but it would be a nuisance to be at the mercy of the first passing customer, wouldn't it?"

He ran to the street-door, opened it and pulled down the iron shutter which closed the shop. Then, still hopping and skipping, he came back to Hortense:

"Oof! I really thought I was done for! One more effort, madam, and you would have pulled it off. But then I'm such a simple chap! It seemed to me that you had come from the back of beyond, as an emissary of Providence, to call me to account; and, like a fool, I was about to give the thing back. . . . Ah, Mlle. Hortense—let me call you so: I used to know you by that name—Mlle. Hortense, what you lack, to use a vulgar expression, is gut."

He sat down beside her and, with a malicious look, said, savagely:

"The time has come to speak out. Who contrived this business? Not you; eh? It's not in your style. Then who? . . . I have always been honest in my life, scrupulously honest . . . except once . . . in the matter of that clasp. And, whereas I thought the story was buried and forgotten, here it is suddenly raked up again. Why? That's what I want to know."

Hortense was no longer even attempting to fight. He was bringing to bear upon her all his virile strength, all his spite, all his fears, all the threats expressed in his furious gestures and on his features, which were both ridiculous and evil:

"Speak, I want to know. If I have a secret foe, let me defend myself against him! Who is he? Who sent you here? Who urged you to take action? Is it a rival incensed by my good luck, who wants in his turn to benefit by the clasp? Speak, can't you, damn it all . . . or, I swear by Heaven, I'll make you! . . ."

She had an idea that he was reaching out for his revolver and stepped back, holding her arms before her, in the hope of escaping.

They thus struggled against each other; and Hortense, who was becoming more and more frightened, not so much of the attack as of her assailant's distorted face, was beginning to scream, when Pancaldi suddenly stood motionless, with his arms before him, his fingers outstretched and his eyes staring above Hortense's head:

"Who's there? How did you get in?" he asked, in a stifled voice.

Hortense did not even need to turn round to feel assured that Rénine was coming to her assistance and that it was his inexplicable appearance that was causing the dealer such dismay. As a matter of fact, a slender figure stole through a heap of easy chairs and sofas: and Rénine came forward with a tranquil step.

"Who are you?" repeated Pancaldi. "Where do you come from?"

"From up there," he said, very amiably, pointing to the ceiling.

"From up there?"

"Yes, from the first floor. I have been the tenant of the floor above this for the past three months. I heard a noise just now. Some one was calling out for help. So I came down."

"But how did you get in here?"

"By the staircase."

"What staircase?"

"The iron staircase at the end of the shop. The man who owned it before you had a flat on my floor and used to go up and down by that hidden staircase. You had the door shut off. I opened it."

"But by what right, sir? It amounts to breaking in."

"Breaking in is allowed, when there's a fellow-creature to be rescued."

"Once more, who are you?"

"Prince Rénine . . . and a friend of this lady's," said Rénine, bending over Hortense and kissing her hand.

Pancaldi seemed to be choking, and mumbled:

"Oh, I understand! . . . You instigated the plot . . . it was you who sent the lady. . . ."

"It was, M. Pancaldi, it was!"

"And what are your intentions?"

"My intentions are irreproachable. No violence. Simply a little interview. When that is over, you will hand over what I in my turn have come to fetch."

"What?"

"The clasp."

"That, never!" shouted the dealer.

"Don't say no. It's a foregone conclusion."

"No power on earth, sir, can compel me to do such a thing!"

"Shall we send for your wife? Madame Pancaldi will perhaps realize the position better than you do."

The idea of no longer being alone with this unexpected adversary seemed to appeal to Pancaldi. There was a bell on the table beside him. He struck it three times.

"Capital!" exclaimed Rénine. "You see, my dear, M. Pancaldi is becoming quite amiable. Not a trace left of the devil broken loose who was going for you just now. No, M. Pancaldi only has to find himself dealing with a man to recover his qualities of courtesy and kindness. A perfect sheep! Which does not mean that things will go quite of themselves. Far from it! There's no more obstinate animal than a sheep. . . ."

Right at the end of the shop, between the dealer's writing-desk and the winding staircase, a curtain was raised, admitting a woman who was holding a door open. She might have been thirty years of age. Very simply dressed, she looked, with the apron on her, more like a cook than like the mistress of a household. But she had an attractive face and a pleasing figure.

Hortense, who had followed Rénine, was surprised to recognize her as a maid whom she had had in her service when a girl:

"What! Is that you, Lucienne? Are you Madame Pancaldi?"

The newcomer looked at her, recognized her also and seemed embarrassed. Rénine said to her:

"Your husband and I need your assistance, Madame Pancaldi, to settle a rather complicated matter . . . a matter in which you played an important part. . . ."

She came forward without a word, obviously ill at ease, asking her husband, who did not take his eyes off her:

"What is it? . . . What do they want with me? . . . What is he referring to?"

"It's about the clasp!" Pancaldi whispered, under his breath.

These few words were enough to make Madame Pancaldi realize to the full the seriousness of her position. And she did not try to keep her countenance or to retort with futile protests. She sank into a chair, sighing:

"Oh, that's it! . . . I understand. . . . Mlle. Hortense has found the track. . . . Oh, it's all up with us!"

There was a moment's respite. The struggle between the

adversaries had hardly begun, before the husband and wife adopted the attitude of defeated persons whose only hope lay in the victor's clemency. Staring motionless before her, Madame Pancaldi began to cry. Rénine bent over her and said:

"Do you mind if we go over the case from the beginning? We shall then see things more clearly; and I am sure that our interview will lead to a perfectly natural solution. . . . This is how things happened: nine years ago, when you were lady's maid to Mlle. Hortense in the country, you made the acquaintance of M. Pancaldi, who soon became your lover. You were both of you Corsicans, in other words, you came from a country where superstitions are very strong and where questions of good and bad luck, the evil eye, and spells and charms exert a profound influence over the lives of one and all. Now it was said that your young mistress' clasp had always brought luck to its owners. That was why, in a weak moment prompted by M. Pancaldi, you stole the clasp. Six months afterwards, you became Madame Pancaldi. . . . That is your whole story, is it not, told in a few sentences? The whole story of two people who would have remained honest members of society, if they had been able to resist that casual temptation? . . . I need not tell you how you both succeeded in life and how, possessing the talisman, believing its powers and trusting in yourselves, you rose to the first rank of antiquarians. To-day, well-off, owning this shop, 'The Mercury,' you attribute the success of your undertakings to that clasp. To lose it would to your eyes spell bankruptcy and poverty. Your whole life has been centred upon it. It is your fetish. It is the little household god who watches over you and guides your steps. It is there, somewhere, hidden in this jungle; and no one of course would ever have suspected anything—for I repeat, you are decent people, but for this one lapse—if an accident had not led me to look into your affairs."

Rénine paused and continued:

"That was two months ago, two months of minute investigations, which presented no difficulty to me, because, having discovered your trail, I hired the flat overhead and was able to use that staircase . . . but, all the same, two months wasted to a certain extent because I have not yet succeeded. And Heaven knows how I have ransacked this shop of yours! There is not a piece of furniture that I have left unsearched, not a plank in the floor that I have not inspected. All to no purpose. Yes, there was one thing, an incidental discovery. In a secret recess in your writing-table, Pancaldi, I turned up a little account-book in which you have set down your remorse, your uneasiness, your fear of punishment and your dread of God's wrath. . . . It was highly imprudent of you, Pancaldi! People don't write such confessions! And, above all, they don't leave them lying about! Be this as it may, I read them and I noted one passage, which struck me as particularly important and was of use to me in preparing my plan of campaign: 'Should she come to me, the woman whom I robbed, should she come to me as I saw her in her garden, while Lucienne was taking the clasp; should she appear to me wearing the blue gown and the toque of red leaves, with the jet necklace and the whip of three plaited rushes which she was carrying that day; should she appear to me thus and say: "I have come to claim my property," then I shall understand that her conduct is inspired from on high and that I must obey the decree of Providence.' That is what is written in your book, Pancaldi, and it explains the conduct of the lady whom you call Mlle. Hortense. Acting on my instructions and in accordance with the setting thought out by yourself, she came to you, from the back of beyond, to use your own expression. A little more self-possession on her part; and you know that she would have won the day. Unfortunately, you are a wonderful actor; your sham suicide put her out; and you understood that this was not a decree of Providence, but simply an offensive on the part of your former victim. I had no choice, therefore, but to intervene. Here I am. . . . And now let's finish the business. Pancaldi, that clasp!"

"No," said the dealer, who seemed to recover all his energy at the very thought of restoring the clasp.

"And you, Madame Pancaldi."

"I don't know where it is," the wife declared.

"Very well. Then let us come to deeds. Madame Pancaldi you have a son of seven whom you love with all your heart. This is Thursday and, as on every Thursday, your little boy is to come home alone from his aunt's. Two of my friends are posted on the road by which he returns and, in the absence of instructions to the contrary, will kidnap him as he passes."

Madame Pancaldi lost her head at once:

"My son! Oh, please, please . . . not that! . . . I swear that I know nothing. My husband would never consent to confide in me."

Rénine continued:

"Next point. This evening, I shall lodge an information with the public prosecutor. Evidence: the confessions in the account-book. Consequences: action by the police, search of the premises and the rest."

Pancaldi was silent. The others had a feeling that all these threats did not affect him and that, protected by his fetish, he believed himself to be invulnerable. But his wife fell on her knees at Rénine's feet and stammered:

"No, no . . . I entreat you! . . . It would mean going to prison and I don't want to go! . . . And then my son! . . . Oh, I entreat you! . . ."

Hortense, seized with compassion, took Rénine to one side:

"Poor woman! Let me intercede for her."

"Set your mind at rest," he said. "Nothing is going to happen to her son."

"But your two friends?"

"Sheer bluff."

"Your application to the public prosecutor?"

"A mere threat."

"Then what are you trying to do?"

"To frighten them out of their wits, in the hope of making them drop a remark, a word, which will tell us what we want to know. We've tried every other means. This is the last; and it is a method which, I find, nearly always succeeds. Remember our adventures."

"But if the word which you expect to hear is not spoken?"

"It must be spoken," said Rénine, in a low voice. "We must finish the matter. The hour is at hand."

His eyes met hers; and she blushed crimson at the thought that the hour to which he was alluding was the eighth and that he had no other object than to finish the matter before that eighth hour struck.

"So you see, on the one hand, what you are risking," he said to the Pancaldi pair. "The disappearance of your child . . . and prison: prison for certain, since there is the book with its confessions. And now, on the other hand, here's my offer: twenty thousand francs if you hand over the clasp immediately, this minute. Remember, it isn't worth three louis."

No reply. Madame Pancaldi was crying.

Rénine resumed, pausing between each proposal:

"I'll double my offer. . . . I'll treble it. . . . Hang it all, Pancaldi, you're unreasonable! . . . I suppose you want me to make it a round sum? All right: a hundred thousand francs."

He held out his hand as if there was no doubt that they would give him the clasp.

Madame Pancaldi was the first to yield and did so with a sudden outburst of rage against her husband:

"Well, confess, can't you? . . . Speak up! . . . Where have you hidden it? . . . Look here, you aren't going to be obstinate, what? If you are, it means ruin . . . and poverty . . . And then there's our boy! . . . Speak out, do!"

Hortense whispered:

"Rénine, this is madness; the clasp has no value. . . ."

"Never fear," said Rénine, "he's not going to accept. . . . But look at him. . . . How excited he is! Exactly what I wanted. . . . Ah, this, you know, is really exciting! . . . To make people lose their heads! To rob them of all control over what they are thinking and saying! . . . And, in the midst of this confusion, in the storm that tosses them to and fro, to catch sight of the tiny spark which will flash forth somewhere or other! . . . Look at him! Look at the fellow! A hundred thousand francs for a valueless pebble . . . if not, prison: it's enough to turn any man's head!"[2]

Pancaldi, in fact, was grey in the face; his lips were trembling and a drop of saliva was trickling from their corners. It was easy to guess the seething turmoil of his whole being, shaken by conflicting emotions, by the clash between greed and fear. Suddenly he burst out; and it was obvious that his words were pouring forth at random, without his knowing in the least what he was saying:

"A hundred thousand francs! Two hundred thousand! Five hundred thousand! A million! A two fig for your millions! What's the use of millions? One loses them. They disappear . . . They go. . . . There's only one thing that counts: luck. It's on your side or else against you. And luck has been on my side these last nine years. It has never betrayed me; and you expect me to betray it? Why? Out of fear? Prison? My son? Bosh! . . . No harm will come to me so long as I compel luck to work on my behalf. It's my servant, it's my friend. It clings to the clasp. How? How can I tell? It's the cornelian, no doubt. . . . There are magic stones, which hold happiness, as others hold fire, or sulphur, or gold. . . ."

Rénine kept his eyes fixed upon him, watching for the least word, the least modulation of the voice. The curiosity-dealer was now laughing, with a nervous laugh, while resuming the self-control of a man who feels sure of himself: and he walked up to Rénine with jerky movements that revealed an increasing resolution:

"Millions? My dear sir, I wouldn't have them as a gift. The little bit of stone which I possess is worth much more than that. And the proof of it lies in all the pains which you are at to take it from me. Aha! Months devoted to looking for it, as you yourself confess! Months in which you turned everything topsy-turvy, while I, who suspected nothing, did not even defend myself! Why should I? The little thing defended itself all alone. . . . It does not want to be discovered and it shan't be. . . . It likes being here. . . . It presides over a good, honest business that satisfies it. . . . Pancaldi's luck! Why, it's known to all the neighbourhood, among all the dealers! I proclaim it from the house-tops: 'I'm a lucky man!' I even made so bold as to take the god of luck, Mercury, as my patron! He too protects me. See, I've got Mercuries all over my shop! Look up there, on that shelf, a whole row of statuettes, like the one over the front-door, proofs signed by a great sculptor who went smash and sold them to me. . . . Would you like one, my dear sir? It will bring you luck too. Take your pick! A present from Pancaldi, to make up to you for your defeat! Does that suit you?"

He put a stool against the wall, under the shelf, took down a statuette and plumped it into Rénine's arms. And, laughing heartily, growing more and more excited as his enemy seemed to yield ground and to fall back before his spirited attack, he explained:

"Well done! He accepts! And the fact that he accepts shows that we are all agreed! Madame Pancaldi don't distress yourself. Your son's coming back and nobody's going to prison! Good-bye, Mlle. Hortense! Good-day, sir! Hope to see you again! If you want to speak to me at any time, just give three thumps on the ceiling. Good-bye . . . don't forget your present . . . and may Mercury be kind to you! Good-bye, my dear Prince! Good-bye, Mlle. Hortense! . . ."

He hustled them to the iron staircase, gripped each of them by the arm in turn and pushed them up to the little door hidden at the top of the stairs.

And the strange thing was that Rénine made no protest. He did not attempt to resist. He allowed himself to be led along like a naughty child that is taken up to bed.

Less than five minutes had elapsed between the moment when he made his offer to Pancaldi and the moment when Pancaldi turned him out of the shop with a statuette in his arms.

The dining-room and drawing-room of the flat which Rénine had taken on the first floor looked out upon the street. The table in the dining-room was laid for two.

"Forgive me, won't you?" said Rénine, as he opened the door of the drawing-room for Hortense. "I thought that, whatever happened, I should most likely see you this evening and that we might as well dine together. Don't refuse me this kindness, which will be the last favour granted in our last adventure."

Hortense did not refuse him. The manner in which the battle had ended was so different from everything that she had seen hitherto that she felt disconcerted. At any rate, why should she refuse, seeing that the terms of the contract had not been fulfilled?

Rénine left the room to give an order to his manservant. Two minutes later, he came back for Hortense. It was then a little past seven.

There were flowers on the table; and the statue of Mercury, Pancaldi's present, stood overtopping them.

"May the god of luck preside over our repast," said Rénine.

He was full of animation and expressed his great delight at having her sitting opposite him:

"Yes," he exclaimed, "I had to resort to powerful means and attract you by the bait of the most fabulous enterprises. You must confess that my letter was jolly smart! The three rushes, the blue gown; simply irresistible! And, when I had thrown in a few puzzles of my own invention, such as the seventy-five beads of the necklace and the old woman with the silver rosary, I knew that you were bound to succumb to the temptation. Don't be angry with me. I wanted to see you and I wanted it to be to-day. You have come and I thank you."

He next told her how he had got on the track of the stolen trinket:

"You hoped, didn't you, in laying down that condition, that I shouldn't be able to fulfill it? You made a mistake, my dear. The test, at least at the beginning, was easy enough, because it was based upon an undoubted fact: the talismanic character attributed to the clasp. I had only to hunt about and see whether among the people around you, among your servants, there was ever any one upon whom that character may have excercised some attraction. Now, on the list of persons which I succeeded in drawing up I at once noticed the name of Mlle. Lucienne, as coming from Corsica. This was my starting-point. The rest was a mere concatenation of events."

Hortense stared at him in amazement. How was it that he was accepting his defeat with such a careless air and even talking in a tone of triumph, whereas really he had been soundly beaten by Pancaldi and even made to look just a trifle ridiculous?

She could not help letting him feel this; and the fashion in which she did so betrayed a certain disappointment, a certain humiliation:

"Everything is a concatenation of events: very well. But the chain is broken, because, when all is said, though you know the thief, you did not succeed in laying hands upon the stolen clasp."

The reproach was obvious. Rénine had not accustomed her to failure. And furthermore she was irritated to see how heedlessly he was accepting a blow which, after all, entailed the ruin of any hopes that he might have entertained.

He did not reply. He had filled their two glasses with champagne and was slowly emptying his own, with his eyes fixed on the statuette of Mercury. He turned it about on its pedestal and examined it with the eye of a delighted connoisseur:

"What a beautiful thing is a harmonious line! Colour does not uplift me so much as outline, proportion, symmetry and all the wonderful properties of form. Look at this little statue. Pancaldi's right: it's the work of a great artist. The legs are both slender and muscular; the whole figure gives an impression of buoyancy and speed. It is very well done. There's only one fault, a very slight one: perhaps you've not noticed it?"

"Yes, I have," said Hortense. "It struck me the moment I saw the sign, outside. You mean, don't you, a certain lack of balance? The god is leaning over too far on the leg that carries him. He looks as though he were going to pitch forward."

"That's very clever of you," said Rénine. "The fault is almost imperceptible and it needs a trained eye to see it. Really, however, as a matter of logic, the weight of the body ought to have its way and, in accordance with natural laws, the little god ought to take a header."

After a pause be continued:

"I noticed that flaw on the first day. How was it that I did not draw an inference at once? I was shocked because the artist had sinned against an æsthetic law, whereas I ought to have been shocked because he had overlooked a physical law. As though art and nature were not blended together! And as though the laws of gravity could be disturbed without some fundamental reason!"

"What do you mean?" asked Hortense, puzzled by these reflections, which seemed so far removed from their secret thoughts. "What do you mean?"

"Oh, nothing!" he said. "I am only surprised that I didn't understand sooner why Mercury did not plump forward, as he should have done."

"And what is the reason?"

"The reason? I imagine that Pancaldi, when pulling the statuette about to make it serve his purpose, must have disturbed its balance, but that this balance was restored by something which holds the little god back and which makes up for his really too dangerous posture."

"Something, you say?"

"Yes, a counterweight."

Hortense gave a start. She too was beginning to see a little light. She murmured:

"A counterweight? . . . Are you thinking that it might be . . . in the pedestal?"

"Why not?"

"Is that possible? But, if so, how did Pancaldi come to give you this statuette?"

"He never gave me *this* one," Rénine declared. "I took this one myself."

"But where? And when?"

"Just now, while you were in the drawing-room. I got out of that window, which is just over the signboard and beside the niche containing the little god. And I exchanged the two, that is to say, I took the statue which was outside and put the one which Pancaldi gave me in its place."

"But doesn't that one lean forward?"

"No, no more than the others do, on the shelf in his shop. But Pancaldi is not an artist. A lack of equilibrium does not impress him; he will see nothing wrong; and he will continue to think himself favoured by luck, which is another way of saying that luck will continue to favour him. Meanwhile, here's the statuette, the one used for the sign. Am I to break the pedestal and take your clasp out of the leaden sheath, soldered to the back of the pedestal, which keeps Mercury steady?"

"No, no, there's no need for that," Hortense hurriedly murmured.

Rénine's intuition, his subtlety, the skill with which he had managed the whole business: to her, for the moment, all these things remained in the background. But she suddenly remembered that the eighth adventure was completed, that Rénine had surmounted every obstacle, that the test had turned to his advantage and that the extreme limit of time fixed for the last of the adventures was not yet reached.

He had the cruelty to call attention to the fact:

"A quarter to eight," he said.

An oppressive silence fell between them. Both felt its discomfort to such a degree that they hesitated to make the least movement. In order to break it, Rénine jested:

"That worthy M. Pancaldi, how good it was of him to tell me what I wished to know! I knew, however, that by exasperating him, I should end by picking up the missing clue in what he said. It was just as though one were to hand some one a flint and steel and suggest to him that he was to use it. In the end, the spark is obtained. In my case, what produced the spark was the unconscious but inevitable comparison which he drew between the cornelian clasp, the element of luck, and Mercury, the god of luck. That was enough. I understood that this association of ideas arose from his having actually associated the two factors of luck by embodying one in the other, or, to speak more plainly, by hiding the trinket in the statuette. And I at once remembered the Mercury outside the door and its defective poise . . ."

Rénine suddenly interrupted himself. It seemed to him that all his remarks were falling on deaf ears. Hortense had put her hand to her forehead and, thus veiling her eyes, sat motionless and remote.

She was indeed not listening. The end of this particular adventure and the manner in which Rénine had acted on this occasion no longer interested her. What she was thinking of was the complex series of adventures amid which she had been living for the past three months and the wonderful behaviour of the man who had offered her his devotion. She saw, as in a magic picture, the fabulous deeds performed by him, all the good that he had done, the lives saved, the sorrows assuaged, the order restored wherever his masterly will had been brought to bear. Nothing was impossible to him. What he undertook to do he did. Every aim that he set before him was attained in advance. And all this without excessive effort, with the calmness of one who knows his own strength and knows that nothing can resist it.

Then what could she do against him? Why should she defend herself and how? If he demanded that she should yield, would he not know how to make her do so and would this last adventure be any more difficult for him than the others? Supposing that she ran away: did the wide world contain a retreat in which she would be safe from his pursuit? From the first moment of their first meeting, the end was certain, since Rénine had decreed that it should be so.

However, she still cast about for weapons, for protection of some sort; and she said to herself that, though he had fulfilled the eight conditions and restored the cornelian clasp to her before the eighth hour had struck, she was nevertheless protected by the fact that this eighth hour was to strike on the clock of the Château de Halingre and not elsewhere. It was a formal compact. Rénine had said that day, gazing on the lips which he longed to kiss:

"The old brass pendulum will start swinging again; and, when, on the fixed date, the clock once more strikes eight, then . . ."

She looked up. He was not moving either, but sat solemnly, patiently waiting.

She was on the point of saying, she was even preparing her words:

"You know, our agreement says it must be the Halingre clock. All the other conditions have been fulfilled . . . but not this one. So I am free, am I not? I am entitled not to keep my promise, which, moreover, I never made, but which in any case falls to the ground? . . . And I am perfectly free . . . released from any scruple of conscience? . . ."

She had not time to speak. At that precise moment, there was a click behind her, like that of a clock about to strike.

A first stroke sounded, then a second, then a third.

Hortense moaned. She had recognized the very sound of the

old clock, the Halingre clock, which three months ago, by breaking in a supernatural manner the silence of the deserted château, had set both of them on the road of the eight adventures.

She counted the strokes. The clock struck eight.

"Ah!" she murmured, half swooning and hiding her face in her hands. "The clock . . . the clock is here . . . the one from over there . . . I recognize its voice. . . ."

She said no more. She felt that Rénine had his eyes fixed upon her and this sapped all her energies. Besides, had she been able to recover them, she would have been no better off nor sought to offer him the least resistance, for the reason that she did not wish to resist. All the adventures were over, but one remained to be undertaken, the anticipation of which wiped out the memory of all the rest. It was the adventure of love, the most delightful, the most bewildering, the most adorable of all adventures. She accepted fate's decree, rejoicing in all that might come, because she was in love. She smiled in spite of herself, as she reflected that happiness was again to enter her life at the very moment when her well-beloved was bringing her the cornelian clasp.

The clock struck the hour for the second time.

Hortense raised her eyes to Rénine. She struggled a few seconds longer. But she was like a charmed bird, incapable of any movement of revolt; and at the eighth stroke she fell upon his breast and offered him her lips. . . .

Notes

Stories from
Arsène Lupin, Gentleman-Burglar

"THE ARREST OF ARSÈNE LUPIN"

For details of this first story's publication, see the introduction.

1. The wireless telegraph was a revolutionary invention that is considered to have begun the modern communications revolution, by freeing it from physical ties to the earth. Advances in understanding electricity and magnetism had led scientists to explore this avenue for decades, and as early as 1832 there was a classroom demonstration of wireless communication. The first well-publicized public demonstration of the new technology had been at St. Louis in 1893. Just as earlier expositions had featured incandescent lighting and the telephone, the St. Louis World's Fair in 1904 widely publicized the wireless telegraph only a year before Leblanc was writing.

2. It is interesting to compare the Lupin resumé in this story with the judge's recitation of his even more outrageous list of jobs in "The Escape of Arsène Lupin."

3. Ganimard will reappear throughout the series, and at least once he will actually outsmart his adversary.

4. "Between Arsène Lupin himself and Arsène Lupin" will be a recurring theme. In a later story in this volume, Lupin enlists the aid of the police to chase another man whom he has identified to them as Lupin; in one of the novels he disguises himself and works his way up through the police ranks until he is assigned to investigate himself.

5. George Eastman, an American bank clerk turned photographic tycoon, had begun producing his Kodak camera in 1888, making

photography available to amateurs. In 1900 Kodak began producing small box cameras and promoting photography as a leisure hobby.

6. This kind of shift in narrator will recur often, taking us into Lupin's point of view for awhile and then away again, but very often we will be misled, no matter who is telling the story.

"ARSÈNE LUPIN IN PRISON"

1. Founded in the seventh century, the Abbaye de Jumièges—the ruins of which have been described as the most romantically beautiful of all Norman abbeys—and the nearby Abbaye de Saint-Wandrille were important medieval religious centers. The consecration of the larger abbey at Jumièges in 1067 was so significant that William the Conqueror attended. They are situated in Normandy, near the Belgian border, where the Seine meanders lazily from Rouen toward the Channel coast at Le Havre; Leblanc was already writing about his home turf and favorite region of France.

2. The Caux region, roughly between Le Havre and Dieppe and Rouen, lies atop a limestone plateau that ends in the steep layered cliffs on the coast. Leblanc's description of the wild geology of this area is accurate; nearby stands the sea-carved cliffs of Falaise d'Aval, one of which famously resembles a rather square-headed elephant dipping his trunk into the sea. The scene is typical of Leblanc's journalistically convincing style, placing his fictional sites amid real ones. Later Georges Simenon would take this method a step further, writing many of his Inspector Maigret novels, as well as other books, on the scene that he was describing.

3. The Prison de la Santé was (and still is) a real facility, notorious for its crowded and dirty conditions and for the brutal treatment of inmates. It was infamously difficult to escape from. As recently as 2000, a former prison doctor caused a furor when she revealed the ongoing abuse of prisoners at the Prison de la Santé.

4. The *Echo de France* was a Parisian newspaper for which Leblanc himself wrote.

5. *Spondulics* was a British slang term for money, thought to have evolved somehow from the Greek *spondylos*, a kind of sea shell once used as money.

"THE ESCAPE OF ARSÈNE LUPIN"

1. Thomas Carlyle's *Heroes and Hero-worship* originated as a lecture in 1840. Besides Lupin's identification with heroic figures, he may also have appreciated Carlyle's denunciation in his other writings of the corruptions and charades of modern European society. Or it may simply have struck Leblanc as an amusing title for Lupin to have around.

2. The Elzivirs were a family of printers from Amsterdam, Leyden, and elsewhere. Beginning in the late sixteenth century, they produced beautiful editions of classic works primarily from Italy and France. An Elzivir book in his cell announces both Lupin's secret wealth and his aesthetic tastes.

3. Epictetus was a first-century Stoic philosopher. His ethic of self-renunciation seems unlikely to appeal to Lupin, but his resignation to unavoidable circumstances might be comforting during imprisonment.

4. The Henry Clay cigar, named for the nineteenth-century American politician, was (and still is) considered to appeal to smokers with a refined taste in tobacco. They still exist, although since the United States' Cuban Trade embargo they are also produced in the Dominican Republic.

5. Bouvier is the magistrate from whom Lupin lifted the watch that he is showing to Ganimard in the final scene of the preceding story.

6. Most of these names will appear in succeeding stories, because Leblanc enjoyed intertwining the adventures. The Château du Malaquis is the home of Baron Cahorn in "Arsene Lupin in Prison."

7. As if it weren't already outrageous enough, Lupin's resumé will actually grow over the years as more species of genius are identified with him.

8. The anthropometrical test was better known, as it is later described in this story, as the "Bertillon system." Alphonse Bertillon was a Parisian police officer who died in 1914, eight years after this adventure appeared. His system of identification comprised a combination of many measurements of facial features and other parts of the body, a complex and faulty system that was soon replaced by fingerprints.

9. *Jiu-jitsu*, now usually spelled *jujitsu*, is a Japanese martial art that emphasizes moral and ethical standards as well as knowledge of

self-defense. Like a forerunner of Batman or some other superhero, Lupin has trained himself mentally and physically for every eventuality.

"THE MYSTERIOUS RAILWAY PASSENGER"

1. Again Leblanc writes about his home region, always setting Lupin's fantasy adventures in the reality of his own everyday life.
2. The Gare Saint-Lazare is Paris's largest and busiest station of the Metro trains. It was opened in 1834 and by Leblanc's time was a bustling and essential terminal. Monet famously painted a train belching a cloud of smoke under its cathedral-like arches.
3. *En-tout-cas*: an elegant parasol for fashionable women. The French phrase means literally "in any event."
4. Lupin's thirty-five-horsepower Moreau-Lepton would be a priceless antique if it weren't imaginary. There was no such automobile.

"THE QUEEN'S NECKLACE"

1. In these opening paragraphs Leblanc is playing his favorite game of interweaving reality and fantasy. *L'affaire du Collier*, as it has been called ever since, took place as Leblanc describes—up to a point. The second paragraph is factual, the third sliding offhandedly into fiction. As far as anyone knows, the necklace was not reconstructed later. This saga of intrigue and deception had already fascinated historians and scandal fans for more than a century when Leblanc was writing, and it is still doing so today, having inspired a dreadful movie as recently as 2001.
2. Now that the story is over, it isn't unfair to mention that occasionally in his later aliases Lupin uses his actual given name, Raoul, without identifying it as such.

"SHERLOCK HOLMES ARRIVES TOO LATE"

This story heralded an entire series of feeble parodies, gathered together in *Arsène Lupin contre Herlock Sholmes*, published in 1907. In the opinion of the present editor, this one is by far the best.

1. *Fais ce que veulx* is a motto from Rabelais' *Gargantua*, published in 1534—or rather it is the modern French version of the

Renaissance Latin, *Faictz ce que voudras*. It means "Do what you wish."

2. Benedictine: a brandy liqueur originally made by Benedictine monks in France.

3. "The ax whirls in the air that shudders, but the wing opens and one goes all the way to God."

4. Translator Alexander Teixeira de Mattos added a footnote here in his English edition: "It can hardly be necessary to explain to modern English readers that, in French, the letter H is pronounced *hache*, an axe; R, *air*, the air; and L, *aile*, a wing."

Stories from
The Confessions of Arsène Lupin

"FLASHES OF SUNLIGHT"

1. The story that Leblanc does indeed title "The Sign of the Shadow" has been omitted from the present collection.

2. "Shadowed by Death" has been omitted.

3. A reference to *The Hollow Needle*, published in 1909.

4. A reference to *813*, published in 1910.

5. *Fiat lux*: Latin, "Let there be light."

6. Another of Lupin's Sherlockian axioms. The more of a detective he became, the more he spoke like one.

7. The French poet and dramatist Alfred de Musset died in 1857, and these oft-quoted lines from one of his poems are still familiar to anyone who passes his tomb in the famous Père Lachaise Cemetery in Paris.

"THE WEDDING-RING"

1. Velmont's address is at his club. The Cercle (the usual French name for a social club) de la Rue Royale offered impressive social status and luxurious surroundings in which barons of finance could discuss business deals and politics. It would have been the perfect place for Lupin to stay aware of which people in Paris had money and how they were spending it.

2. See "The Escape of Arsène Lupin."

3. See "Sherlock Holmes Arrives Too Late."

"THE RED SILK SCARF"

1. The "Dugrival business" takes place in the story "The Infernal Trap," which precedes "The Red Silk Scarf" in the original *Confessions of Arsène Lupin*, but which has been omitted from the present volume.
2. Leblanc always has so much French history on tap in his brain that it spills over. The Pont-Neuf (New Bridge) arches across the Seine to connect the Paris of the Right and Left Banks. Along with draining swamps and encouraging education and building roads and commanding other improvements, King Henry IV commissioned the Pont-Neuf. Today a visitor can't cross it without seeing a statue of Henry's bearded figure astride a bronze horse that is rather more handsome than His Majesty.
3. With these convincing deductions, so much more reasonable than most of his antics, Lupin bests Sherlock Holmes at his own game without Holmes having to appear.
4. *36, Quai des Orfèvres,* as readers will have come to expect, was indeed the address of the Paris police. Today it is still the headquarters of the Police Judiciare (criminal police). The address has become shorthand (as in "10 Downing Street" or "1600 Pennsylvania Avenue") for the Direction Centrale de la Police Judiciare (Central Directorate of Judicial Police). In 2004 the French director Olivier Marchal used the address alone as the title of a thriller.

"EDITH SWAN-NECK"

1. *Verbum sap.* is short for *verbum sapiente* ("a word to the wise"), sometimes shortened even more to *verb. sap.*
2. Again Leblanc saturates a story with historical tidbits. Only months after his coronation and his marriage to Edith Swan-neck in 1066, the young Saxon king fell to the Norman invader, William the Conqueror, at the Battle of Hastings.
3. A reference to the play *Arsène Lupin* (mentioned in the introduction), which Leblanc along with the English writer Edgar Jepson had turned into a novel in 1909.
4. Victoire appeared first in the Lupin novel *813*.

Stories from
The Eight Strokes of the Clock

Leblanc prefaced these eight stories with the following note:

These adventures were told to me in the old days by Arsène Lupin, as though they had happened to a friend of his, named Prince Rénine. As for me, considering the way in which they were conducted, the actions, the behaviour and the very character of the hero, I find it very difficult not to identify the two friends as one and the same person. Arsène Lupin is quite capable of attributing to himself adventures which are not his at all and of disowning those which are really his. The reader will judge for himself.

M. L.

"ON THE TOP OF THE TOWER"

1. This, the first story in the series, sets up the relationship between Lupin and Hortense Daniel that will provide the framework for the volume *The Eight Strokes of the Clock*. Like his infatuation with Nellie Underdown in "The Arrest of Arsène Lupin" and "Sherlock Holmes Arrives Too Late," his unsolicited attachment to Hortense Daniel seems nowadays considerably less romantic than Leblanc imagined at the time. Naturally when Lupin decides to help people, he does so in his usual domineering way.
2. "A mighty hunter before the Lord" is a phrase from the King James version of Genesis 10:9, referring to Nimrod but apparently employing an already familiar phrase.
3. The Suisse Normande, Little Switzerland, is also in Normandy, southwest of Leblanc's summer home near Honfleur. See the Introduction for more information on the author's affectionate relationship to Normandy, especially the coast near his birthplace in Rouen.

"THÉRÈSE AND GERMAINE"

1. Étretat on the Norman coast is famous for its towering cliffs and the dramatic formations that the ocean has carved from them. Victor

Hugo called these natural formations "the grandest architecture that ever existed."
2. The Needle is a geological formation that features prominently in the adventurous Lupin novel *The Hollow Needle*, which had proven enormously popular when published a decade before this story collection. To this day, various sites on the Norman coast still advertise their relationship with Maurice Leblanc, including the Arsène Lupin Museum in Étretat.

"AT THE SIGN OF MERCURY"

1. The Roman god Mercury, usually identified with the Greek Hermes, was the patron deity of travellers, but especially of merchants and travelling merchants, as his frequent portrayal with a money pouch indicates. He had winged sandals because he was the messenger of the gods.
2. As he does in "On the Top of the Tower," Lupin reveals a great deal of the troubled psychology behind his criminal career, and fully explains why he has made the transition to detective. It may also suggest why he sees romance as a contest of wills.

Acknowledgments

My heartfelt thanks to three scholars of crime fiction who critiqued my introduction to this volume: Otto Penzler, editor of the *Best American Mystery* series and founder of Mysterious Books in New York City; Roger Johnson, BSI, editor of *The Sherlock Holmes Journal* in England; and Douglas G. Greene, professor of history at Old Dominion University, biographer, and anthologist. I welcome this opportunity to thank my wife, Laura Sloan Patterson, who encouraged this project and critiqued the introduction; my mother, Ruby Sims, who provided an endless parade of mystery novels to entertain my teenage imagination; the fine staff of the Greensburg and Hempfield Area Library in Greensburg, Pennsylvania, especially director Cesare Muccari and reference librarian Jim Vikartosky; the Carnegie Public Library in Pittsburgh and the Hillman Library at the University of Pittsburgh; and the many libraries participating in the AccessPennsylvania system of interlibrary loans. I particularly want to thank the meticulous and affable crew at Penguin Classics, especially former executive editor Michael Millman, assistant editor Carolyn Horst, production editor Jennifer Tait, and cover designer Jasmine Lee—the people who do all the taken-for-granted work behind the scenes.